Blue Star Highway

Blue Star Highway

A 14-year-old boy's Report from the
Ocean County Juvenile Detention Center
October-November, 1963

A Tale of Redemption from North Florida
by
Ed Ray Smith

MILE MARKER 12 PUBLISHING

Blue Star Highway
Copyright © 1998 by Ed Ray Smith

Printed and bound in the United States of America by:
Columbus Bookbinders and Printers • Columbus, Georgia

First Edition
Library of Congress Cataloging Number 97-93757
ISBN   0-9659054-0-3

Published by Mile Marker 12 Publishing • Atlanta, Georgia

For additional copies of Blue Star Highway
please visit your local Bookseller or call
Toll-Free: **1-888-868-6612**

Attention Schools and Libraries: Quantity discounts are available on bulk purchases of this book. Please call Toll-Free number listed above for more information regarding this offer or write to:

Mile Marker 12 Publishing
3870 North Peachtree Road
Atlanta, GA 30341

Excerpt from THE SECOND COMING by Walker Percy. Copyright © 1980 by Walker Percy. Reprinted by permission of Farrar, Straus & Giroux, Inc.
New York, New York

Jacket Design: Jorge Brunet
Photo Retouching: Tim Blackstone

• Acknowledgements •

Thanks to the following
for their assistance and encouragement
in putting together this book:

Berkey Newman, Neil Rashba, Bob Rast,
Carlton Higginbotham, Jerome Joseph, Douglas Tappin,
Sol Hirsch, Rev. Tim Thomas, Tom Pittman, Bruce Kachel, Jim Gonia

---

Thank you, Rubye Goodlett, for supplying much needed doses of
patience when I was fresh out.

A very special thanks to Jorge Brunet, *artiste extraordinare,* for the
great cover... and more than a little understanding.

Last... but not least... thanks to my family for letting Marty and
a host of other characters come live at our house, off and on, for the
last several years.
Thanks, guys.

*   *   *

We Remember Always:
Sonya Koreen Smith
"River Angel"
1973-1981

Dedicated to ...
Doris,
Ian,
and Elliot Smith

•

Living proof, all three, that you
don't always get what you deserve ...
sometimes there's lots more!

*You don't ever really learn anything
you didn't know when you were thirteen.*

– Walker Percy
The Second Coming

Chapters

In Medias Res

In the beginning it was wonderful to see Pawpaw again. Not having seen him for nearly two years it was like Halloween, Thanksgiving and Christmas all together, all at one time, when he got there in person. That is a long, fair amount of time if you stop and think about it when you are twelve yrs. old.

It just so happens that I'd done some thinking about it... time... and I thought I could see why people, especially older folks, were always saying how it can slip up on you. It is slippery by it's very nature. When you are twelve years old two years is nearly twenty percent of your entire lifetime up to that point, but if you are, say... fifty, it is only four percent... a lot less. The thing I can't figure out is if that means it goes by any quicker; I mean if it *really* does and not just seems to. You'd think that four percent of something would go by... happen... lots quicker than twenty percent. That would make sense. If this is true then the older you get the faster time would go by. Could be. I do know there were some days when I was little that seemed to go on and on, forever like. Especially some summer days I can still remember; days when my father was still alive.

Anyway, if it hadn't been for Derek comin' out after us like he did our goose's would'a really been cooked out there on the river, out by the sign. *Melinda* was doing okay; to this day I still don't think she woulda' let us down, but the water was slapping at her bow so strongly by then that the Evinrude was about to be swamped out, I do believe. Once that had'a happened we'da been sittin' ducks... no ifs, ands or buts about it, and at the total mercy of the tide and the waves and whatever else the river was fixin' to throw at us that afternoon.

What he did was come out in that new boat of his and let me tell you was he ever a sight for sore eyes. His was an aluminum boat also, but with two differences from *Melinda*. The first difference was the color, for instead of an olive-drab green Derek's boat was gray, what you'd call a Navy gray which makes sense seeing as where it was from originally, and the next by far more important difference was the size of his boat. It was a sixteen footer, plus, just as important, she must have been an easy five feet across at her beam or mid-section. Compared to *Melinda's* insides this boat Derek was in felt and looked like an ocean-liner. There was another difference too, one I hadn't counted on at first and that was the fact that he did not have any motor to run his boat with. She was all self-propelled, meaning she was powered by Derek hisself, meaning, of course, oars.

The two oars Derek had on that barge have got to be the largest I've ever seen, hands down. As much as oars, they looked when I first spied them, like a coupla' telephone poles cut down a tad for use as oars. I couldn't believe it when I first saw him heading through the water like he was with just those two oars either. Not that I saw him coming for any length of time.

By now there was something of a fog coming on, also. It came on so quickly, just about the time I started having trouble steering *Melinda*, that I guess I didn't take that much notice at first. With all the confusion of the old man having his setback right out there on the way over and the waves lapping in over *Melinda's* stern it's not that surprising, I reckon, to think that I had not noticed something else was going on, also. Fog has got a tradition of coming on rapidly, before you even know it, around here. Leah told me about one time before I was born when she and dad were coming home from somewhere(probably the dog track), one night and they all of a sudden got caught up in a thick fog only half a mile or so from the house. It was so thick that before they knew it they couldn't even see the road or the huge live oaks that lined it on either side with Spanish moss hangin' down almost to the car top in some places, but luckily my father had a hurricane lamp and some kerosene in the trunk of the Ford. What they ended up doin' was he sat on the hood, feet on the front fender, and held the lantern out as far forward as he could on the end of a golf club while she drove. That's how they got home that night.

It wasn't that thick out on the river but you could tell it was a fog and not just some mist coming up off the water. Looking back on it I guess it was the right thing... for there to be such a fog out there... because the place we were headin' to was certainly like no other place I'd ever been before, that's for dang sure. That fog being like it was kinda' gave us a preview, or a warning, of that very fact.

Yeh, lookin' back on it that's exactly what it did.

Preface

Trying to explain just how I could end up in a mess like this (not to mention how I wound up in here), is one big job, believe me, but I will attempt to do so, anyways. I reckon what I oughta' do is begin not at the beginning, but nearer the end.

The Justice of the Peace (he wasn't even a real judge), said to me: "It's like drivin' son... it's a privilege, not a right."

I'm not so sure I agreed with that, but there's basically how I ended up writing and putting all this together. To give you an idea of what it is like inside a juvenile hall, let's put it this way. Since Hell already has used:

-Abandon Hope, All Ye Who Enter Here -

then I reckon the next best greeting for this place would be:

No Easier Place To Get An Ass-Whippin'... And For No Good Reason.

Anyways, what the JP was referring to was the fact that we were out on the water, we being myself, the old man (my grandfather), and a friend of ours, Big George (a colored man), headin' back from this island stuck out in the middle of the river in its broadest part. I believe he got me on a technicality, the fact that my boat didn't have a sticker or even any numbers on it. Dang, but everyone around here has a boat like that. I mean on a bigger craft you are gonna' have a registration, but on the kinda' skiff I was operating– barely bigger than a bathtub –nobody goes to all that trouble (not to mention the expense, it turning out they want $ 5.50 payable every other year). It is ridiculous, and if you ask me borders on the criminal. But back to how this all came about.

What you are reading now is just talk, basically. What I mean by that is it is the written-down version of what I have spoken into a tape-recorder. It's a cheap (is there any other kind?), Japanese version of a tape-recorder (SONY?). It get's the job done, though. I reckon what these are are reports more than stories (even though that's what I call them), seeing as it's what really happened and I haven't even bothered changing any of the names of anyone. To paraphrase Mrs. Johns, my English teacher:

"When you make stuff up is when you have a real story."

There's a room off the library here that you can go into if you want, but no one ever does so it's quiet and that's where I have done my recording. My intention is to put the written-down spoken version together with some of the stories I have written over the last year and a half to give them some cohesion (the JP's word); sort of an explanation, I guess would be the best way of describing it, of what each story is about and all. They need something. That's not necessarily my opinion, but is more in line with what the Justice of the Peace said for me to do. I think he was stalling, really. I mean by that I think he was surprised to see that I could put together so much information and in such a short time. What I failed to tell him was they were stories I had already written, for the most part. How they came about I will explain a little later, but basically what I did was round 'em all up (along with some additions), and put 'em all in a notebook hoping that everything together would be good enough to get me out of here in record time. It'd been less that two weeks after he (the JP), had handed down my sentence of writing everything out (the story of how we all came to be heading back from the island together), and I should have known that was too short a time; that he was not expecting to see me again anywhere near that soon, and that it would not satisfy him.

Well, that's when he said I needed to write a preface (his term), to some of the stories giving a little background to help him keep better track of what was going on. He was a teacher himself years ago right at the very same high school I go to now– Oceanside High School –so he knew what he was talking about, he said. He even taught English some of that time and he was curious as to how I was able to write so much, so quickly. What he wanted to see, I know, was if I could write some more stuff that was up to the same level as the stories (or reports). He never came right out and said it, but I knew what he was thinking. I'd gotten used to it by then.

I wasn't always good with words, but eversince the accident I reckon is when you could say I have been. I even heard a teacher once say it borders on the uncanny. It sounds sorta' strange, but I know it has something to do with the time I fell out of a lemon tree when we were downstate visiting the old man. I was seven, and Leah, along with Maxine (the old man's second wife and the best person I've ever known before she died of cancer), and I were at the train station waiting for the Silver Meteor coming in with my dad and I started climbing this tree. Before I knew it I fell out of it and cracked my head a good one. They even took me to a hospital where I got a tetanus shot (what for I have no idea. I don't remember bleeding), and eversince then I could spell any word just like I could see it in my mind plain as day first. I've always thought something was stuck up there and that fall unstuck it. Sadly, nothing similar can be said about my math scores. Well, I guess it's true– you can't have it all. But even if the JP doesn't believe it, I have written every one of these stories myself.

The other thing is I can remember whatever I have read right on *the page I read it, no matter how long ago it was. There's the two good things. Now, for the not so good.*

It's not serious (usually), but sometimes I get in the habit of counting and can't stop. I don't mean I start counting and keep going, but I count to say a number like seven... one, two, three, four, five, six, seven ... and I have to keep repeating it over and over again, in my mind. What is bothersome about this is you don't have any choice in the matter. You have to do it. It's like when you're walking thru a doorway and you have to take so many steps before you enter and if you don't do it just right then you have to go back and start all over again, if that makes any sense. Well, it doesn't. I know. That's the problem. After a while it stops, goes away, so I keep trying my best to ignore it.

What I said earlier about getting caught on a technicality is the truth, at least the way I see it. The problem is that JP didn't wanta' say what it was he was really gettin' me for. It wouldn't sound right. The fact that we had all headed out there in my little skiff trying to rescue an innocent man from a growingly bad situation and ahead of the Sheriff was bad enough. The fact that it was a colored man we were trying to help made it doubly worse, if you ask me. (I don't know if it is a compliment to him or to me, but the one we were looking for, to help out... well... I didn't even think of him as being colored.)

The funny (not funny ha, ha, but funny peculiar), thing about my being in here is I have always felt bad for my brother (even though I would never say so to him) whenever he is put into Hope House, the crippled children's home in Riverville, and now here I am in a place that is probably not much better, and in some ways worse. What matters most I reckon is neither one of them is the kind of place you would choose to be in, nor can you leave when you want. Out of everything, that is the worst feature of both places; the fact that you are there until someone you don't even know (so you know they don't know you), has got the power over your life to tell you when you can leave. It is disheartening, that fact all by itself.

Anyways, what you have got here is over a dozen stories (or reports), some with a preface, some not. For the ending I have changed the format* some and switched back to the stuff I recorded off the top of my head. It just seemed like the right thing to do, the way to end up, for whatever reason. I've done some thinking about this and have come to the conclusion that it would not be going too far out on a limb to say what I have written (and recorded), these stories... well... maybe it has all just been an attempt to keep my sanity going.

Two more things: Originally, I had a good many swear words in these stories (mostly, thanks to things my brother said), but decided that wouldn't go over so well with the J.P.. I went ahead, though, and left a handful– five or six –in for one good reason— to see if he really read it. If he did I knew I'd hear about it. The other thing is the J.P. mailed me a list of 50 words a coupla' days later which he said I was to use or "work-in" to my stories and for me to put an asterisk by each one so it would be easy to identify. Also, I needed to add at least another 50 I didn't think he knew and put an asterik by them, too. His rule was the word had to be "appropriate"– not seemed forced into the story. My guess is he thought it'd just be something to keep me in here longer.

It's been nearly eight weeks now and I am supposed to hand everything in to the JP this Friday afternoon, the 22nd, at his house; the front part of which is where he has his chambers, I reckon you would call it. It's dark paneling in there, with a brick fireplace and he sits at this big dark wooden desk with stacks of legal looking papers on it. Hopefully, with the prefaces I've added and the ending describing how the three of us came to be heading back from the island together in Melinda, I will be permitted to leave here... freed. Believe me, it's time.

P.S. *– There's an old saying that you could lock up a room full of monkeys and give 'em each a typewriter and before the end of time they would come up with either all of Shakespeare or the Bible, I forget which, but the point I am trying to make here is that, number one, I don't have that much time and, number two, there is only one of me so the odds are unfair to begin with. That is a long-winded way of saying that I may have bit off a little more than I can chew here and though my intentions are good hopefully you will excuse any errors in grammar, syntax and the like. Remember, most of this stuff happened when I was 12 and 13 and now that I'm 14 (almost 15), some of it seems sorta' immature, even to me.*

Also, about Leah. She's not really my (or Grayson's) mother (just what she is is hard to explain... so I'll save it for later), but she serves the purpose of one, pretty much. I even call her that when I'm feeling good or think she needs to hear it. I'm not sure if she knows I know. We've never really talked about it.

M.W. Crane
O. C. Juvenile Detention Ctr.
November 19, 1963

Melinda

... and Oceanside was North Florida– full of saw-palmettos, scrub oaks and marshgrass islands –and just what was that?

IN 1962 WE WERE STILL LIVING AT THE BEACH. If you weren't accustomed with the area, and that term– *The Beach*, it mighta' sounded like we were living in one of those houses up on stilts above the dunes– the modern-looking kind like they've got out in California. That's what I thought five years before when Leah first told us we were moving. I remember her telling us, my brother and I, right there at the River Oaks Cemetery that we were moving across the river, all the way to the Beach(I reckon she figured a change of scenery would do us all some good). What we moved into instead was a two-bedroom cinderblock job more than a mile back from the ocean– another Florida tract-house not much different than the one we'd just left in town and closer to the intracoastal waterway than the beach. The driveway to this house like the road it led out to were both hardtack paths of crushed oystershells. Trying to look on the bright side I figured maybe this was meant to lend a beachiness to the place; to make up for the fact of having to live so far back. Chances were those shells were the residue* of some Indian feast hundreds of years ago as it was they, the Indians, who populated this area back then (oysters being a well-known mainstay of their diet).

Not long after the move, before I had a chance to make any friends in this place, I woke up one morning to the discovery you could smell the ocean from back here. And at night laying in bed listening at it through the dark you could hear the surf in the distance, rolling up the shore all through the night like some long deep secret. After that I felt better about the move. After that I figured we were close enough.

Out of the blue (as usual), and totally unannounced, our globe-trotting grandfather (Leah's father), drove up from his orange grove downstate one day and started putting up a little pine-paneled room at the back of the house so there'd be a guest room for him when he visited. With it's freshly stained and varnished knotty-wood walls this add-on the old man built was my favorite room in the house. Not having seen him in nearly three years (ever since our father's funeral), to Grayson and I it was a dream come true to have the old man back again. Before he even came inside the house, while he was still out on the carport, I caught a whiff of his pipe and I knew right then he was back. That was the same trip he built that contraption for Grayson's wheelchair– that little table-top that sat on his arm-rests to do his homework on back when he could still write.

For heat there's an oil drip-heater sitting squatdab in the front of the dark hallway. First winter there we found out this squarish contraption was okay as long as it didn't get too cold. On the rare day when it got down below forty there was nothing to do but stand in the hallway getting as close to the boxy heater as you could stand if you wanted to shake off the cold. First summer in the new place all the windows were cranked open and you prayed for a breeze, learning to listen for the rustle of the palm fronds in the front yard. That summer (and every one since), Grayson and I spent a lot of time outside under the shade of the concrete-floored carport.

The term *The Beach* is nothing more than a catchall word people around Oceanside use when they're talking about the thin sliver of Ocean County up here in the northeast corner of Florida— bordered on the east by the Great Atlantic Ocean and on the west by the Intracoastal Waterway. Whenever I see a map of the state it always puts me in mind of a long-handled pistol, and if you think about it like that then Ocean County is right where the hammer of the gun is. Half-a-dozen small towns go to make up this area, but the one folks are talking about mostly when they say *The Beach* is Oceanside. Seventeen miles to the west, beyond the thick green hammock of live oaks, wild palms and turpentine pines, and all the way on the other side of the river, sits the much bigger city of Riverville.

Riverville is what's called a booming Southern metropolis, grown up snug by a wide shallow spot on the big river, a place in the old days where it was easy to ford livestock, which is why early on folks called it Shallowford. (The reason I know so much about all this is we studied the history of Riverville some last year in Mr. Warren's Civics class.) Maybe it wasn't a very exciting name for a growing town, but it sure beat the old one– Cowford. Don't get me wrong. Riverville has it's fair share (and then some), of mansion-like dwellings, most of them lined up right there along the river on a street even called *Riverside*.

Like a lot of cities near a large body of water Riverville grew up into a port town and cargo ships and tankers from all over the world started coming in and adding to her a worldliness otherwise out of character with her real location. Despite a little big-city charm Riverville still was less than an hour's drive south of the border separating Florida from Georgia. Once, it'd been the biggest city in the state, until this railroad-baron-turned-developer by the name of Henry Flagler, hellbent on heading south, finally came to the end of the line; the place where land ran out at the bottom of the state; the place where he became determined to invent the city of Miami. Over the years Riverville residents (*Townies* to Beach folks), have come to consider the Beach their own unofficially annexed parcel– treating it that way, too, meaning they largely ignore the place until they're ready to go lie out on the sand or bathe in the ocean waters during the long hot days of July and August. Then come Monday mornings and the sun, the same fiery orb that is now bearing down high above Northern Africa, begins rising up from the Atlantic across the rosy-hued horizon, its first rays of daybreak on the beach revealing the fresh trash townies have left behind for prisoners of Oceanside's tiny jail to pick up. For the colored inmates I reckon it's the only time any of them can recall ever being allowed on the beach.

• The sand on the beach at Oceanside is the kind that when you kick it it squeaks. If you're out on a certain kind of windy day and these fine grains are sailing down the beach you can hear it sing.

• If he never learns a thing else during his school career, an Ocean County student knows the body of water flowing through Riverville is the second largest in the northern hemisphere that streams north. First is the more famous one in Egypt; the one Cleopatra floated down in her barge– The Nile. Both of these rivers, strangely enough, are situated on the very same latitude.

• Sometimes it's seems this river, though, that splits Ocean County from top to bottom is so much a part of who these students are– each and everyone –that they don't even know it.

THE THING I LIKE BEST about Oceanside is its openness. Of course, you'd expect a place right on the coast to be open; after all, you've got the ocean right there. But even inland among the myriad* marshgrass islands and pine prairies there is this feeling of vast openness— a seeingness to all that flat land and domed sky that can't help but give you a feeling of freedom. There's even something about the dark moss-draped forests here that prompts hope, because there can't be anymore glorious sight in this world than when you're heading down a tree-lined dirt road that all of a sudden opens up and gives way to a body of water; that moment of exhilaration when you see the first patch of blue, not certain if what you are witnessing is sky or water!

*   *   *

In the winter before I turned twelve I acquired a boat. Truth is I inherited it, sort of. An old aluminum boat, faded chalky green with a flat bottom and squared-off bow, abandoned by the family that used to live near the creek in one of those little houses behind Johnson's Fish Camp. They up and left one day in late February after their father lost his job at the papermill for what some of the neighbors suspected was drinking on the job. Before they left the father said I could have the boat if I wanted, they sure as hell weren't gonna' haul it back with them. It had plenty of dents and was pretty much worn out, several small leaks. They were heading up north back to Massachusetts, a place they should have had more sense than to leave in the first place.

"Least folks up thata'way got the good sense to mind their own business... not hold it against a hardworkin' man for takin' a drink now and again", the father said as he pulled tight a rope-end holding a carton on top of their boxy and already tired-looking Rambler. One car with two adults up front and a teenage girl and two boys in back and all their worldly goods in a small overloaded homemade trailer packed and going at five o'clock in the wintery lead-sky afternoon, leaving behind the small rented two-story block house. I had a good idea of their route: across the Main Street Bridge into downtown; then up through Callahan towards Hwy. 17; then over to Brunswick and on north towards Savannah (the place my father used to call the *pearl of the South*), and after that I could not imagine as that was as far north as I'd been back then– at least in a car. The three kids waved from the backseat when their father jerked the piled-up car into gear and pulled off. I always thought the girl was pretty, in a tomboy sort of way, but I never did work up the nerve to talk to her. Watching them leave, I knew I'd miss the two boys, especially the older one.

Before long I decided the left-behind boat needed a name, so after an inaugural* excursion* down San Pablo Creek I came up with *Melinda*. I'm still not sure where it came from, it just popped into my head looking at her, but it seemed to suit her. I patched her with radiator sealant and sanded that down to the point where she no longer let in water and I got good at moving her around the skinny waters of the creek with only the pair of bleached wooden oars Pawpaw brought up on one of his visits from downstate. Before that I'd navigated her with a long skiff-pole made from a piece of bamboo I rescued one day floating down the creek. I got pretty good with that pole, but the oars were better on open water. Besides the oars and pole, I had a cushion life preserver which doubled as a seat most of the time, a Ted Williams rod and reel spinning outfit (Pawpaw had given me that for Christmas), and a four-foot casting net for capturing minnows (or shiners, as everyone I know calls them), shrimp and other baitfish.

Everytime I've ever caught a shellcracker, (or red-eared sunfish, and I've caught a mess of them in the last few years), I'm always amazed at the beauty of him. Myriads* of iridescent hues– reds, of course, but if you look closer also some blues, and if you look closer still and the light is right even luminescent* green and orange become evident. These creatures have got a life too, and ever since I can remember, fishing– as exciting as it is –has always been tinged to some degree with a certain amount of regret. It felt better when Pawpaw, sensing once these stirrings of sorrow, told me that several of the apostles were fishermen too, and if that was good enough for Jesus... well then who could argue with that? It's not that I'm overly religious or anything (or the old man either for that matter, believe me), but after hearing about this somehow it made it okay; like even someone as perfect as Jesus knew there is a way to the world, sad as it is.

*   *   *

The Maxwell House coffee plant nestled up close to the big river (right where it takes a sharp turn just east of downtown on the last leg of it's long procession* to the Atlantic Ocean), spews out large billowing clouds of dirty white smoke much like the papermills all around Ocean County, but unlike a papermill the coffeeplant's spewing is something to be savored and is mostly regarded by Ocean Countians as more a blessing than a nuisance, I reckon. Being one of Riverville's top employers, there are lots of jobs inside that building. Once, when I was riding into town with my uncle Rad, and we drove over the bridge that passes over the coffee plant, Rad stuck his nose up into the air, closed his eyes and declared, like the Kingfisher of Amos & Andy:

"Aahhh... 'dat do smell like money."

Leah insists I'm too young to drink coffee on a regular basis, but I've had a taste on numerous occasions ever since I can remember, always in cold weather during fishing trips with the old man when he will pour the steaming fragrant brew from the dinged-up ancient quart thermos he carries religiously on cold weather excursions– be it fishing, rabbit or turkey hunts.

"For thermo-medicinal purposes only, my boy" the old man will sing out in his W.C. Fields voice offering up a enameled cup with three fingers of blond sweetened coffee in its bottom. If it's cold I like the feel of the warm tinnish cup in both my hands. If it's really frigid (to the point where your nose and ears sting from the air), I hold it close to my body, hugging the heat of the cup for all it's worth. There've been mornings with the old man when it was so cold my fingers liked to have gone on strike and the simple task of tying a lure onto my line was an arduous* undertaking requiring all the dexterity* I could muster from my clumsy fingers. These are times I look forward to my grandfather laying aside his rod and am grateful at the sight of the old man hoisting in his weathered hands the battered thermos he'd prepared in the early-morning hours before.

'Now you just tell me if that's too sweet for you, boy.'
The old man sings straight-faced sometimes when he offers me a cup. Other than when we are actually catching fish this is my favorite time on the water, with *Melinda* hedged up against some tall marshgrass to cut the November wind and Pawpaw and I huddled together in the small boat sipping coffee and eating cheese crackers. Unless one of us says something there is no other sound out here but the occasional spooked rail or marsh hen screeching out from the tall grass, and when that passes and all is hushed again there is only the hollow rhythmic lapping of the creek's purling gray wavelets pushing steadily against *Melinda's* dusky sides. Even if it's cold and the sun is muted, hiding behind some clouds, I remember occasions like this as being warm times.

"They may be empty calories, but they're calories just the same," the old man will continue, *"... and in weather like this you need fuel boy... Lord, you need fuel."*. Then he clinches his fists and holds his arms in close to his body, showing in a language stronger than words that yes it's cold but we can take it, and not only can we take it, we can relish and even delight in the cold if we want. All we need is the right attitude... and a little coffee.

*   *   *

I've noticed a difference in my grandfather when we're out on the water together. On land– back at our house and even down at the grove –the old man is lots more reserved since the death of his second wife from cancer three years ago. There's not any doubt in my mind that this has had a deep and lingering effect on him. He still cuts-up like he always has, but he's not as quick with the jokes as he once was. But out here his mood sometimes lifts, and the grandfather I've known, the one that looks like a cross between Robert Mitchum (like in *The Longest Day*), and Clark Gable with the wide ears and thin mustache (like in *The Misfits* with Marilyn Monroe. When he wears that Stetson he sure enough looks like Gable), returns. Funny, how I think of the old man in terms of movie stars. Maybe it's because he seems larger than life, at least to me.

He's in his sixties now, but he still has his strength. Even so, there's the one thing that always gives away his age– his hands, and the fact he gets awful bouts of arthritis when his knuckles swell up the size of marbles under his skin sometimes; when removing a fish from a hook can become a grimace-inducing task. Even so, even then, he keeps on. (I can always tell when it really gets to hurting him; he starts in on the Bufferin.)

Out here Pawpaw still comes alive lecturing on subjects like *"the caloric benefits of sugar-laden coffee in cold weather"*. He's a lot more apt* to kid me about things like how skinny I am out here, too, calling me a tall drink of water and saying things like I've gotta' run around in the shower to get wet and if I turned sideways and stuck out my tongue I'd look like a zipper. For the most part I try and take this kidding in the same good-natured spirit it's delivered in. Things like being permitted to drink a clandestine* cup of coffee with the old man just make it better.

Whatever else I gotta' worry about, I know my coffee drinking habit, at least out here on the water, won't ever get back to Leah.

*   *   *

A coupla' years before I got *Melinda*, I got my very first taste of what all can go wrong out on the water, even on a day you think is gonna' be clear and trouble-free.

I'd gone along one afternoon three years before with Pawpaw and a friend of his, Old Dr. Cordray, and the three of us got caught up in an afternoon storm that arose out of nowhere late one spring day when some pretty rough waters began kicking up on the long straight and narrow intracoastal lake that stretches from just below Ponte Vedra nearly down to St. Augustine. Neither Pawpaw nor I could coax the small outboard attached to the doctor's boat to kick over and the old doctor commenced to cussing and yelling at the two of us and his outboard motor and the approaching storm, and the rough waters, in between frequent and numerous nips at the silver pint flask he kept inside his fishing coat (for just such trials, I reckoned).

Abandoning all hopes of ever starting the motor, we both grabbed an oar and began rowing, moving the small wooden vessel hopefully back towards the ramp just off AIA by Palm Valley, where we'd put in. Pulling desperately to outrace the ominous* looking dark clouds and streaks of lightning headed straight towards us, we were all three drenched by the time we got the boat to shore; as much from the downpour as from the lapping white-capped waters of Lake Guana that had poured steadily over the gunnels of the small craft all the way back.

Later, the event would always bring to my mind a short story we read in Mrs. John's class called *The Open Boat*; particularly the part where the newspaperman muses*, or thinks, to himself:

> *"If I am going to be drowned– if I am going to be drowned– if I am going to be drowned, why, in the name of the seven mad gods who rule the sea, was I allowed to come thus far and contemplate sand and trees?"*

Drunk as he was, the old doctor managed to start bailing out the bottom of the boat with a rusty coffee can he kept on board while Pawpaw and I rowed for all we were worth. It was the closest I've ever come to being lost at sea, and it was an experience that still gives me the heebie-jeebies whenever I think of it. That damn kicker Old Dr. Cordray had on the back of his boat had nearly done us in. Later that evening, after dinner, Pawpaw passed on a little bit of wisdom I knew I'd remember always.

Gently rocking in the old aluminum and redwood rocker on the carport, looking out across the backyard and the open field beyond, the old man began the hourly ritual of slowly and methodically packing and then lighting his pipe. As he drew on the stem clenched in one corner of his mouth he spoke from the other corner. It was a feat I always marveled at.

"Remember boy, there are few things in this life as dependable as a good dog, skillet cornbread and a well-maintained Evinrude outboard motor. That piece a' junk of ol' Cordray's hadn't been tuned in years I'll bet, and I'm as much to blame as he is for the hellacious predicament we got ourselves into today. We dodged one hell of a bullet this day, boy. You remember that."

Summer Bass

"It's so dang hot I don't think we'll do any good... 'less maybe we wait a while and go around sundown."

The old man spoke from one corner of his mouth as large beads of sweat dripped from his brow. Not his usual pipe, but a collection of eight penny nails stuck out from the other corner. All this was as a result of laboring over the doghouse we were building for Jim, the Moore's old Chow. While we labored, Leah was driving Grayson to Riverville for his appointment at Bremen's Brace, to be fitted for a new one. Though his arms and legs did not seem to be gaining any the same could not be said for his gut and it was getting more difficult to get my brother into the old worn corset brace and then to get it strapped on. As usual, when it came to spending money Leah had held out till the bitter end and it was only because of Grayson's constant complaining about the brace's tight fit and the fact that the top strap had finally torn at the spot where it was stitched onto the brace's side that she was finally doing something about it. Just because Grayson was getting a new brace, though, didn't mean things would suddenly be hunky-dory. I knew my brother would find something wrong with this new one, also. It would pinch him somewhere or the straps would be too loose and he'd moan and groan about the way it fit till it was finally broken in.

Two years before, Grayson had moaned and groaned then also as the now worn-out one was put on for the first time. Mr. Bremen himself had come into the little room where Grayson lay upon the table like at a doctor's office and in a bellowing voice urged him to be patient.

"Think of it like you would a new pair of shoes, son," Mr. Bremen had said. "It takes a while to break in... to conform to your body." Mr. B. smiled as he placed a big hand on top of the brace and made like he was adjusting, fine-tuning, it.

"Sure, I'll do that." Grayson spoke laying on his back, strapped into the new metal and cotton canvas contraption. His voice was shaky from being jostled, pulled and pushed by Mr. Bremen's adjusting. "Only a new pair of shoes don't dig down into your pecker, or pinch you under the arms like this damn thing."

Leah gasped, lowering her head. I remember laughing.

*   *   *

"Hope that dang critter appreciates his new abode."

"He'll love it Pawpaw, 'specially when it gets cold. He's gettin' old, but next winter he's gonna' be lots warmer."

"Well, one thing's for certain- it sure as hell's keeping me warm right now. It must be close to a hundred out here."

Pawpaw shouted above the high-pitched whining of a spinning circular saw he was using to cut out a section of doghouse roof from a fresh sheet of plywood. The cut wood smelled of deep, rich resin almost as good as turpentine, I thought– though not as sharp. I loved that smell. It was right up there with the smell of gasoline being pumped into Leah's Ford and the smell of my father's leather belt (I could still recall it), the one he always wore on the train. Sometimes, when I helped the old man with a carpentry project, I would even go so far as to pick up a handful of the powdery sawdust that lay scattered on the ground underfoot and hold it up to my nose to inhale the pungent* aroma.

"Porch thermometer says ninety-three, Pawpaw."

"That's funny. Didn't know it could talk," the old man replied and I looked puzzled for a moment. Then there was a grin on the old man and it suddenly hit me what I had said.

"Porch thermometer *indicates* ninety-three," I said, still grinning.

"Well, I tell you what though... that thing's in the shade. Out here it's hotter... a helluva' sight hotter, I guarantee." The old man stopped leaning over the twin sawhorses before him and stood straight up now, grabbing a large thermos full of ice water at his feet on the way and raising it to his mouth. He guzzled a long drink from the sweaty thermos– the sound of rattling ice cubes jostling around inside the metal vessel. Finishing, he held it out towards me and spoke:

"Why don't we take this stuff up on the carport and work? If I had the good sense God gave a grasshopper we'da started up there to begin with. I just didn't think it'd take as long as it has to finish this thing. If you got a little book where you write down truisms, I'll give you a new one right now, free of charge:

'*All construction projects... no matter how small... take at least half again as long as you first figure to complete.*'

"That being said, I'll move the car and you start bringing the tools and stuff up there. It'll be a helluva' sight cooler."

"Yes sir," I replied, and began rounding up the tools– the power saw, a straight saw, the framing square and the box of nails with oriental looking hieroglyphics of some type on it's side –and moved everything onto the carport as instructed.

"Think they'll be biting later, Pawpaw?" I asked.

The old man was heading back onto the carport from the side-yard where he'd moved his car. He squinted into the shade (a hand above his eyes like a hat brim), to where I stood, looking to see just where I was speaking from.

"I don't know, to be honest with you. Hell, I've seen bass have lockjaw all day on a day as hot as this and then in the evening when the sun gets level go crazy hitting anything you'd throw at 'em. Could be this is one of those times. Can't ever be sure about bass. But I'll tell you one thing I do know."

"What's that ?"

"We'll never know for sure unless we go find out for ourselves. Let's get this canine box done with so we can do just that."

*   *   *

It was later in the evening. The temperature had gone down some meaning it was not quite as unbearable as it had been earlier when we'd been in the midst of constructing Jim's new home. Still, it was hot.

But we were out on the creek now in *Melinda* and that meant the water was there for us– all around us –just a scant eight inches or so beneath the boat's gunnels and rowing to that spot in the creek where it took a wide bend and flattened out and opened up into the area of a good-sized lake, a gentle breeze miraculously began to pick up, blowing across the broad waterway. I could see evidence of this breeze coming our way- ripples across the water's glassy dark surface that gave away the motion and direction of the force before it arrived, much like the pair of glasses he forgot to remove gave away the movements and whereabouts of the Invisible Man. When the ripples finally found their way to us it was a welcome relief- the first stirring of air either of us had experienced all day.

"Let's head across to the far bank over there, bubba. That'll be our best bet, right now."

"I thought you said we were gonna' try the hole down from Johnson's. It's been so hot they're all probably down in that deep hole trying to cool off," I answered. I'd had some luck there the last time I was out and was beginning to think of myself as something of an expert now because of it.

"Could be, but with this good breeze we oughta' try the bank over there before we go to the hole," the old man answered right back.

"What's so great about that side, Pawpaw? I've never caught a thing over there," I said, careful not to sound too insistent, but perplexed* anyway by the old man's strategy.

"Maybe so, but when you get a wind like this in the summertime it'll blow a lot of small bugs in the direction of the wind, and the little fish'll follow those bugs, and the little bigger fish'll follow the little fish and so on. Could be a lunker sitting back over by those stumps waiting to pick off a fat minnow just like this one." As he spoke, the old man was busy tying on a four-inch broken back Rebel lure. The floating variety.

I knew then he was serious, for that Rebel was one of the oldest tempters in his tackle box and when it came to top water lures for bass it was without a doubt the old man's favorite.

"If there's one over there this'll get him... plum guaranteed."

"Okay. I'll row us over; you tell me when to stop."

"Head for that grouping of stumps, boy, till I instruct you otherwise."

I rowed Melinda towards the far bank till Pawpaw, seated up front and without turning around, signaled back with a wave of his hand to slow down. Then he made a short, quick motion with his open hand which I correctly interpreted as stop. I did so, and the old man pulled back his rod and whipped it swiftly in the direction of the stumps. Just as he flung out the greenish lure the wind suddenly picked up and the cast, which without any assistance would have been perfect, instead flew well past the old logs— at least five feet onto the raised shore.

"Hell's Bell's. What did I have to go and do that for?" the old man whispered to himself, though in the utter quietness of the lake I could hear it also.

"Couldn't be helped, Pawpaw. Woulda' been perfect if that wind hadn't a' gushed in on us like it did."

"Yeah, maybe so. But I still gotta' get it outa' there."

"I'll row us up a little closer."

"Nah... don't do that. I know there's a bass hanging out by that big stump. I can feel it. Let's see if I can't get turned loose here."

The old man pulled hard and swift on the flexible rod, snapping it back from a position level with the water to straight up twelve o'clock just in front of his face all in one instant. Though he seemed to be pulling hard he wasn't– just quickly –and after two or three quick snaps the lure suddenly let loose from it's hold on the thick crabgrass of the bluff above and came flying back towards the boat, hitting the water twenty feet in front of Melinda's dusky bow. It danced across the water for a couple of feet and the old man began reeling in the thin gossamer-like line making sure as he went that it was not fouled or knotted. When he'd completely reeled in he picked a tuft of grass off from the dangling lure's rear treble hook. Then he pulled the rod back again using only a smooth motion with his wrist and flipped the lure in the direction of the stump once more.

This time there was no unwelcome assistance and the cast was perfect– dead on, about two feet past the large stump and positioned to the left of it in such a way that when he reeled in it would almost surely bump up against the log. But first he let the lure rest motionless for a few long seconds, the time it took for the expanding concentric ripple rings it's landing had created to completely dissipate*, and only then did he begin slowly reeling in the old lure, twitching and jigging it ever so slightly as he did, actually stopping it a time or two, trying as best he knew how to create the same wiggling action as a large minnow in distress. Soon the lure was equal with the stump and here the old man twitched it a good one and let it rest for a suspenseful moment, certain that there was going to be an explosion any second. Nothing. He twitched again, and waited. Again, nothing.

Then he began reeling in, increasing the speed of the lure across the water's top as though he'd given up and was anxious now to retrieve the lure and cast again, and he was halfway back to the boat with the lure when it happened...

BAM!

Up till then I had never heard a freshwater fish hit a top water lure so loudly, so violently in my life and the unexpected commotion caught me so off guard that I actually gave a little jump in my seat and I felt the first involuntary rush of my bladder loosening for just the slightest part of a second. But I tightened up quickly and regained control of that part of my anatomy as rapidly as I had nearly lost it.

"Woo-eee!" the old man shouted.

Looking out over Pawpaw's right shoulder I could hardly believe the glorious sight I now beheld. In what seemed like slow motion, a very large fish leapt from the water's surface a good two feet, arching it's body sideways and shaking it's huge head to and fro in a manic effort to spit out the lure. It was a sight of pure delight to see such a fish and to see my grandfather come alive now and to know that this gorgeous green and black and white creature, this largemouth bass, was connected to Pawpaw by the very sheerest of mediums– six pound test monofilament fishing line –and the fish continued to fight and to jump; twice now, and three times, and four, and once more, that made five, and the old man let the fish have his head and kept the line taunt and his rod bent just enough to keep the creature under his control. Too much slack, I knew, and the fish would be able to pick up steam and make a run (probably back towards the stumps), and would be gone before your knew it. Too much pressure on the line and the fish would easily snap it and the whole exercise would have been for naught and great disappointment would be upon us both. Especially the old man.

(I knew he would never keep such a fish, it was too big to eat– best size for eating-bass was between one and a half to two pounds, the old man always said; he would just want to land him to bring him into the boat with us for a few moments and feel the heft of him and admire his scaly creatureliness, and to look into his sad fish eyes for a few moments and wonder at his large mouth and to see him spread open his fan-like gills and then gently release him and let him swim off for another day... and in doing all this feel good about it.)

The old man was playing the fish perfectly and I thought to myself that I knew I was watching a master. I had never seen my grandfather horse a fish in his life and truth be known I only wished I could say the same for myself. It was so hard a thing not to do– especially with a big fish –not to play him too hard. That urgency of wanting to net him and get him into the boat or on shore and to hold onto him for one brief eternal moment was just too much to resist sometimes, especially if you hadn't caught a good size fish for a long while. Every fisherman knows this feeling. But the old man had this fish which must have weighed at least eight pounds, maybe more, and he was bringing him in slowly but surely. He was coaxing this big creature who was in his element– the water, and who did not want to be brought in, but my grandfather was doing just that, while still being careful not to rush the fish which had now finally stopped jumping but was making perhaps his final strong surge several feet under the water. I could see that the old man's rod was bent over more severely than I had ever seen it bend before and just when I began to think that the old rod could not stand the strain any longer or that the line would snap, the beautiful creature jumped once more, only this time it was more of a leap and I could swear that it was in slow motion again and I could swear also that the fish was twice as large this close up as I'd first thought and I was looking at the velvety white beneath his neck and underbelly when it happened... **Ping!**... the line snapped.

It was so loud you could hear it, and the fine line which had done such a good job of staying taunt and strong was all of a sudden slack and falling to the creek like an injured strand of spider's web, and instead of being straight was loose in the air now with curves and ripples as it died, floating lazily back down to the creek's shiny black surface.

The worst part– the insult to this injury –was the fact that the fish had the lure. I held my breath and stared at my grandfather's backside, expecting any second now to witness some evidence of his regret and dashed expectation, but instead the old man turned around and announced with a wry smile:

"Well, I was wondering when I'd get shed of that old lure. Damn thing's been cluttering up my tackle box for thirty years."

Was that all he had to say? After losing what he'd kept no secret was his favorite top water lure?

"Pawpaw, that was your best lure. You aren't mad?"

"Let me put it to you this way, boy. Every once in a while you gotta' laugh to keep from crying, and right now is one of those times. Let's head on over to Johnson's like we said to begin with. There's plenty of good fishin' light left in this day."

And for a little while we both fell as silent as the creek.

*   *   *

At first, I thought it was a silence of reverence as though if neither of us said anything for a while the loss would somehow be easier to take. But it wasn't this as much as the fact that neither of us knew what to say. Hell, there was nothing to say. So we both were trying to come to terms with the loss of the fish and the lure, neither knowing what to say to make it better, when the last thing either of us expected to happen, happened:

WHOOSH!!!

Exploding not ten feet from *Melinda's* left bow was the very same fish which had taken the old man's lure a full minute before and the reason I knew it was the same fish was because it still had the same lure stuck in it's huge cartilaginous* mouth. And just as the creature (which appeared almost black now), reached the apex of it stupendous leap it shook it's head violently back and forth twice, and the lure, which rattled in the air above him but was still connected to the fish, suddenly came flying out of the giant creature's mouth and landed on top of the water while the defiant fish– like every physical object in the history of the world before it –succumbed finally to the earth's gravity and once again entered into the black backwaters of San Pablo Creek.

Unbelievable! That fish had spit out the lure.

Without a word I rowed in the direction of the floating Rebel lure and when we were right on top of it the old man leaned over *Melinda's* shallow side and scooped up his lure, examining it for any damage that might have occurred during this last battle. Flipping the newly beat up but intact piece of tackle back into the top drawer of his open box the old man looked back at me for the first time since we'd entered the creek and spoke:

"Looks like I spoke too soon. You might get that rattletrap yet, someday. Let's go on over by Johnson's and hunt us up some bream, boy. I got a hankerin' for a fish dinner tonight."

I rowed.

Blue Star Highway
"We deal in lead, friend"
– Steve McQueen, *The Magnificent Seven*

LA GRAN PELEA! That's how I'd a' said it if I'd been in Mrs. Hernandez's class, where you can only speak Spanish.

The Big Argument. That's what Grayson and I called it. It was the altercation* that kept the old man away for over a month and set Leah to drinking more than she had at any other time since right after our father had died.

It was a bad time for everyone, the six weeks the old man stayed gone. Leah could barely get to work. Three times during the two weeks right after the big argument she was late though, and only by staying past her usual quitting time, was she able to placate* Mr. Davis and keep her job. Twice I had to roust her from her bed, lead her to the shower, and get the coffee going and both those times she'd been so late Grayson's bus had already gotten there to take him into town to the Crip School (his term). It was during this last mess-up that I tried to question her about whatever reasons she had for arguing so vehemently* with her father:

"That doesn't happen to come under the head of your business, bub."

It was her standard response to my questioning, that is when she even responded at all. Sometimes she was just too sick.

If what she meant when she said it was not my business was the fact that she and her father were on the outs, well, maybe she was right. If she meant the argument itself she was lying. I knew; I overheard part of their discussion, before it erupted into the full-blown melee. I remember the old man's voice rising and him saying something like:

"Why, 'cause I take him fishing... I spend time with him?"

And then her answering:

"That's part of it, yes."

And then the old man continuing: "A boy his age needs to be around men. You don't want him turning out funny, do you."

"Oh, Dad. Shut up!"

"What? What did you say to me? You better put a cork in that bottle little lady and leave it there. If you weren't all grown up I'd put you over my knee right now and tan your behind. Oughta' anyway... the way you're acting. Sure ain't grown-up like."

After that the true yelling and gnashing of teeth had commenced and that's when they really went after each other making wild statements and uttering the sorta' cruel and cutting accusals only blood-kin seem wont* to deliver. Then Pawpaw left. Or rather he was invited to leave.

By then he was so mad he walked right past Grayson and I, right there in the carport, paint-stained khaki's and all without so much as a wink or a nod. All afternoon I reckoned he'd come rolling back in, but when the old man backed his mammoth Imperial out of the rutted parking spot on the sideyard, crunching two paths across the oystershell driveway in the process, Grayson murmured:

"Won't see him again for a while."

Either it was a lucky guess or Grayson was someway more tuned in with how these things played out, but there was no denying later on that he'd delivered a much more accurate appraisal* of the situation than me.

"He'll be back. He's just going down to the Seven Seas or Palm Valley for a beer. When he cools down he'll be back," I said.

"Don't count on it," Grayson replied.

"You'll see."

"Wanta' bet?"

"Wanta' bet, wanta' bet! Shut up, dipstick. Why does everything have to be a bet with you?" I was pretty upset by now. Even so, I rarely swear— that's more in Grayson's department.

"Bite me. I might be a dipstick, but you're a *dipshit* if you think he's coming back any time soon." See what I mean.

True to form, our argument got down to it's usual low level, meaning Grayson continued taunting me to the point that I got so mad it took all of my powers of self-control not to put my hand over his mouth until his face turned red. Not that it's anything to be proud of, but more than once it has come to that.

*   *   *

After a coupla' days, I resolved myself to the fact that the old man really wasn't coming back anytime soon. That's when I figured I needed to begin *The Search*.

As usual, The Search produced not a bottle, but bottles.

Three to be exact. One active pint about two thirds gone and two empties– both quarts. *Vodka...the choice of discriminating drunks*, I murmured to myself. It was something the old man would say. Maybe I'd even heard him say it once and just now recalled it. Regardless of it's origins, it was the truth. It was pitiful how she thought if she stuck to drinking vodka no one would detect it on her breath. What good did that do her passed out? She might as well drink straight whiskey for all it mattered.

On the way out of the house I stopped at the kitchen to pour the pint's remaining contents down the sink and along with it throw out the two empties. Right when I was about to throw all three bottles into the brown paperbag beneath the sink, I stopped.

I had a better idea. Back in her room, I lined all three clear bottles in a neat row on top of her dresser, centered between the two photographs I recalled as having always existed: The one of our father and the old man together on the lake down at Pawpaw's and the one taken in front of the house in town with Leah standing at the front door holding a newborn Grayson the day they'd returned from the hospital. Before going, I opened her purse. I rifled through it's contents until I found the keys to the Ford, then hid them in the back of her bottom dresser drawer.

Finally, out of the house and on my way to school I felt I could breathe again and through a light sprinkling I headed towards Davey's. Some mornings when our timing was right the four of us– Davey, Mick, Will and I met at Davey's to shoot the bull and walk the mile or so to school together. This was one morning I felt I could use the company.

Crossing Penner Road, I was careful to look both ways, especially left— the dangerous direction. Running across, I thought of what lay at the south end of Penner, the road it dead ended into– US 90. Around Oceanside it was known as Beach Road and I'd crossed it hundreds of times on my bike the three years I'd been in Little League, on my way to practice. Across the rest of the country it was known as the Blue Star Memorial Highway. I didn't have a clue where it had gotten that name. That's just what it had always been called. Maybe something to do with it's southerly route? *Sunny blue skies?*

There was a large bronze plaque that looked like an historical marker down on First Street next to the Red Cross Lifeguard Station where the highway officially started. Or ended, I mused. Of course, that would depend on which way you were headed– coming or going. For me it would be the beginning.

Right at the Atlantic Ocean.

As far east as you could get, heading west.

THE FIRST LANDMARK would be the largest building in Oceanside– the bowling alley; then Nino's Pizza in that great irridescent-green squat-block building that looked like a small fortress– then the oak-laden and Spanish moss-draped cemetery across the highway from Nino's– then up the little hump of a bridge that crossed over the intracoastal from where you could witness the long alley of a waterway meandering through the attendant marshes and palm isles for a mile or so both north and south– then miles of nothing other than prairie-looking fields of saw palmettos and the rising scrub-pine on either side of the road– then a scattering of forlorn looking cinderblock houses– then rows of single-story buildings that housed small businesses on both sides of the now wider highway– then eventually the long bridge into Riverville that crossed over the big broad river which flowed the wrong way (north), just like the Nile– then all the way across the northern part of the state straight through Tallahassee, the state capital– then through Alabama, Mississippi, Louisiana, Texas, New Mexico, Arizona, and finally... *California!* All the way into Los Angeles (which was Spanish, Mrs. Hernandez our Cuban-refugee Spanish teacher had told us, for the the *City of Angels*). Through this city finally, to some street or highway there that ended at the Pacific Ocean. I always wondered if there was a marker out there at that end of the highway, too– this highway that ran all the way to the end of the line... *all the way out to the land of Movies.*

I knew it sounded strange (I'd never told anyone about it); maybe I'd gotten my wires crossed somewhere along the way, but over the last coupla' years I'd come to connect a Sunday word– *Sanctuary*, with a Saturday place– the *Movies*. Much of what I knew about life and the world was born, nurtured and took shape in the seated blackness and flickering images inside a free-standing block building right up on First Street– the Beach Cinema.

Places and times like the Old West from *Gunfight at O.K.Corral* and *The Man Who Shot Liberty Valance*, New England Whaling from *Moby Dick*, and World War II from movies like *Mister Roberts*, *Pork Chop Hill*, *The Great Escape*, and *The Longest Day*.

One Saturday the summer before I joined together with Mick, Davey and Will to go see *Bridge On The River Kwai*, and the four of us became so enthralled* with this film that all the way home (through a light afternoon sun-shower), we strode in step and whistled the spirited theme song, the tune dying out from time to time but always picked up again by one of us and quickly joined in by the others as we trod steadfastly through the small puddles and balmy air of the late summer's afternoon... escaping from the evil Japanese and their POW camp... returning back to the safety of our neighborhood and homes. Collectively, we appropriated this tune as our unofficial theme song that summer and for the next several weeks whenever we saw each other it was a safe bet one of us would break out into the "*Bridge*" whistle.

*   *   *

I felt something for the smallest part of a second that seemed eternal in some way; like looking up at the stars on a clear night (a really clear one, the kind that only come in winter), wondering how many years it took for the twinkling they emitted to reach your eyes and you almost had it and your thoughts were not only in your head, but out there with the stars at the same time, where the light traveled. (Once, I couldn't remember just when—it was a coupla' years ago anyway, but once, the old man had told me something that seemed to go along with this: *The only thing faster than light is a thought,* he'd said.) And I thought for a second of how many times I'd crossed the Blue Star Highway, and because it connected Oceanside all the way to California did that mean in some way it connected me to there, too? It seemed that close— and that far away.

Just as I crossed Penner I felt The Blue Sky Highway was close. Not as close as I would like (of course), but close.

Before things get too far out of hand I will go ahead and admit (on the record), to the fact that I don't mind going to church, that much. I mean, it's not like I am chompin' at the bit to get there, but once I am there it really isn't all that bad.

Of course, the major drag is having to get up early again just like on a school day and of course that means getting Grayson up, too. And what that means is except for Saturday, Sunday's no different than any other day of the week. At least on school days once I have loaded him onto the bus it is over for awhile. After that I am on my own. On Sundays, though, even after I have loaded him into the Harnishs' car and stowed his chair away into the trunk we are still together. Where we are going, we are going together.

Once we are there, though, I do get a respite. Grayson wheels off to his Sunday School class and I to mine, so for an hour or so things are all right.

Back at the time of this story is when I first began noticing Patti. Truth be known, I must admit back then I didn't consider it all that harmful spending an hour or so staring at her back. Like I say in the story, because of Grayson's chair we always sat in the rear–last row, corner. That worked out good in two ways. One, it was less evident whenever Grayson made any of his snide (not-so-under his breath), remarks about whoever it was he'd decided to make fun of that morning and two, it gave me a clear shot and a great chance to check Patti out.

Where you are up to here will give you an idea of what it was like back then going to church with Grayson, and how complicated it could get if I tried making conversation with someone I liked.

You'd think somebody who lived at the Beach would be familiar with the ocean at various times of the year; you know, what it's like at different months, but the truth is I have not seen it all that much during the winter. Even though school is only three blocks back, still that is three blocks in the wrong direction if you are headed home and no reason to meander up that way. Especially on a chilly day.

The walk along the beach Grayson and I took on our way to the bakery put me in mind of a famous short story written by someone who knew far better than I how to describe the ocean on a winter's day. "The Open Boat" by Stephen Crane is the one I'm referring to. Mrs. Johns calls it the greatest American short story of all time. I don't recall if that was her own opinion or the critics', but you could tell she really liked it just by the way she taught it. It was enough to get me started, making it one story I paid a lot of attention to.

For some reason her liking it so much and making it a point of bringing it to everyone's attention made me proud, in a funny sort of way; like I was getting something, some recognition, but it didn't cost me anything. Usually, you gotta' do something, some sort of work, to feel the way I felt, but all I'd done was have the same last name as the author– Crane!

The walk along the beach and our trip up to the bakery happened pretty much like recorded here, too. I have thrown in some other things (mostly remembrances of our father), but the truth be known, some of this could be made up.

One thing is certain. The part about the Coke and peanuts is real. I will never forget the time he showed us that. Or how to make a double-decker peanut butter and jelly sandwich using three pieces of bread instead of two.

Funny, what ends up sticking with you.

P.S. – *Two guys escaped from this place last night, meaning there's lots of excitement here now. How they were able to pull it off I have no earthly idea since there is a good-size fence... lots taller than the one surrounding the football field at school... plus it has barbed wire on top to boot, and that stuff is serious looking, believe me. I had no idea they were going, but some hearsay alludes* it was common knowledge. I knew one of the boys; the same one that talks about his old man beating him up. So, I guess it is safe to say he probably won't be heading in the direction of home.*

Palms Methodist

"Far away the noise of strife upon my ear is falling.
Then I know the sins of earth beset on every hand.
Doubt and Fear and things of earth in vain to me are calling,
None of these shall move me from Beulah land."

As the hymn closed Mr. Bobo (the choir director who, during the rest of the week, ran Bobo's Used Auto's on the corner of Beach Road and Ocean Blvd) sat down with the chorus and Rev. Timmons, a tall and almost handsome man, approached the pulpit to address the assembled:

"Please join me in the reading of the Word. Turn now in your Bibles, if you would, to the New Testament... Paul's letter to the Romans. Chapter eight... verse twenty-six:

"The Spirit also helpeth our infirmities: for we know not what we should pray for as we ought: but the spirit itself maketh intercession for us with groanings which cannot be uttered."

Grayson and I were in our usual spot– last row, corner. Reverend Timmons often joked about his congregation's reluctance to fill the first few rows, even suggesting from the pulpit one Sunday morning during announcements to... *"Come early and get a good seat in the back"*.

The way I had it figured, though, locating back here made perfect sense. Grayson could never sit up in one of the slick metal folding chairs here, so he had to stay in his wheelchair and even when I removed that last corner chair in the row (for rolling my brother's chair into it's place), his left wheel stuck out some in the aisle. Even so, back here we managed to stay pretty much out of the way.

When we first moved to the Beach Leah got us going to the other Methodist Church up towards Seminole where they had real cushioned pews, and Grayson was able to sit up easily there. But even though they had that great seating up there neither one of us felt comfortable because it was where Ocean County *old money* spent Sunday mornings for the most part– at least that's the way Pawpaw described it. So Leah began another search, looking around for some other church in the area that her two sons might find more accommodating*.

After much investigating Leah finally narrowed her choices down to three: another Methodist church (Palms) about a mile south of Beach Road, an Episcopal church up on Third Street and a little Unitárian congregation across the Beach Road Bridge, nestled in a thick pine grove overlooking the intracoastal waterway. When the old man got wind of her searchings he remarked that finally, here was an easy decision. From the carport I overheard their conversation that Saturday afternoon:

"Damnation, daughter... Episcopalians ain't nothin' but rich folks hedging their bets and Unitarians are just atheists who can't break the church habit. For once, seems like an easy call to me."

That settled it. Normally hesitant to agree with her father, this time Leah sensed the old man's reasoning (though strangely convoluted*), was basically sound. And that's how the next morning Grayson and I found ourselves attending Palms Methodist Church for the first time.

It was a good move despite the lousier seating arrangements. I recognized a couple of guys from school here and because of this I didn't feel like a total stranger. Reverend Timmons was sorta' athletic looking and the first Sunday we were there we found out he had a sense of humor, too. From the pulpit he told a story on himself of how he had once inadvertently* played a joke on himself:

"Before I came here to Palms, I was downstate at a small Methodist church down in Micanopy where I was something of a one man band. Even had to type and print up the church bulletin sometimes if we didn't have enough volunteers. One week I created the masterpiece of all typographical errors. Announcing activities we were planning after Wednesday Night Supper I typed that immediately following the meal there would be a 'glorious time of group sinning'. Mimeographed two hundred of those bulletins... never discovered the error until I read the announcement Sunday morning. Well, of course, what I'd meant to say was group singing, but I must admit, we had the best turn-out of the year that Wednesday Night. The Lord does work in mysterious ways." I made up my mind right then and there that I liked this new guy.

*   *   *

It was curious how I was always so hungry in church. Of course, I was always hungry– but never like here. This place seemed to put an edge on my appetite, and my hunger was so relentless this morning that I was glad it was Communion

Sunday and looked forward to relieving my pangs with the thimbleful of grape juice and half-inch bread square I would receive, even if it meant a service that ran longer than usual. I was that hungry.

I steeled myself from thinking of food for a moment and soon found I had no difficulty turning my thoughts elsewhere. Specifically to a girl seated five chairs in front of us, towards the middle of the row. Patti Prentiss was her name and as she rose with her mother and sister to go forward with the others in her row to take communion, I found myself transfixed by that special curve made by the back of her coral wool skirt.

Patti and I were in the same grade but she ate lunch during the period right before me. Several weeks before I found that if I got to the cafeteria early I could see her there talking with some of her girlfriends. I wasn't sure when I first thought it, but lately I'd begun to think her attractive in a vague* sorta' way. Usually I saw her when she was just leaving the lunchroom, but once I bumped into her in my rush to get into the growing lunch-line, which got me real close and I caught a whiff of her and it seemed that ever since then I saw her more and more in the cafeteria. Truth be known, we were both shy about exchanging glances and when one of us caught the other staring we usually broke off. Once though, while I was in line and searching for her through the clamor and confusion of the large loud room, I caught her staring at me from the corner, all the way across the cafeteria above about a hundred heads. I looked back and kept looking this time and after awhile I found out I couldn't turn away and when the bell rang and Patti turned and walked away to her next class I felt my first pangs of love.

Soul-Stare. That's what Mick called it when I depicted the incident to my friend. God, it was unreal how beautiful she was. Her eyes were like large dark pools that I could get lost in and she was the most beautiful creature I had ever seen in my life, this girl that only several weeks ago I had never even taken notice of before, even though we had gone to the same school for nearly two years (*what had happened to her? what strange magic had wrought this change?*), and it was driving me crazy being this close to her without being able to get closer. All through the hour long service, through the Affirmation of Faith, and the Invocation, and the Lord's Prayer, and the Sermon I thought only about this girl and how she smelled so fresh (*I'd never smelled anything like her in my life*), and how she was somehow so sophisticated (though she was no older than me), and I wondered if I might be in love with her, if that was what this was all about. When I thought more about it in a more placid* state of mind it hit me that I hadn't ever spoke to her. Hell, we'd never even been formally introduced.

Somehow in church she was even more beautiful than in school (if this was possible), and I sensed that here might be the right place to engage her in conversation for the first time. None of my friends would happen upon us here and if I blew it, if I said something really stupid and scared her off, I could just suffer the rejection silently without having to worry about it getting around. I only needed to work up a little more courage and this could be the day. No, I told myself– this *would* be the day!

Maybe.

* * *

After communion Rev. Timmons stood in front of the altar, and raising his right hand above the congregation, closed with a benediction:

"*The peace of God, which passeth all understanding, keep your hearts and minds in the knowledge and love of God, and of his Son Jesus Christ our Lord; and the blessing of God Almighty, the Father, the Son, and the Holy Spirit, be among you, and remain with you always. ... Amen.*"

Now was the time. I knew that I had to make my move and make it soon. Patti and her sister were coming down the aisle behind us and would be upon us in a matter of seconds. I turned my brother's chair around and stood next to it in the little fellowship area (between the last row of seats and the kitchen at the back of the building), wracking my brain for an opening line, hopefully something funny, but nothing came. I was blank. There the two girls were now, right in front of Grayson's chair and I knew this was it– the moment of truth. Patti turned her head and looked at me. It was now or never. My mouth opened. Words came out.

"Good morning," I said, looking at the beautiful girl.

"Good morning, Marty," she said, smiling. God, what a smile it was, too. A moment of silence. It was my turn.

"Hope nobody gets drunk on that grape juice."

Oh, man! What did I say? Where did that come from? How lame. No one said anything. I should have shut up while I was still ahead with just the greeting.

"Great thing to say in a church."

Who'd said that? I heard a voice speaking, but who said it? It wasn't Patti answering. Was it Grayson? Yes, it was! Of course, it must be! Once again, my brother was jumping into the act, trying to get me fouled up.

"I don't know. I think it was rather cute.... witty," Patti said. She did. She said it was *cute*– and better yet, *witty*.

"Sarcastic's more like it. Stick around if you like sarcasm. He's full of it... among other things." Again Grayson spoke. I nudged–actually kicked –the wheel of my brother's chair.

"Really? I enjoy good sarcasm. It shows a sharp mind," Patti said.

"I wouldn't go that far," Grayson chuckled.

"Hush,Grayson. Nobody pulled your string. Get back in your cage," I said. Patti and her sister both laughed, trying half-heartedly to hold it back. Then Patti's older sister spoke:

"Don't be so mean to him. He can't defend himself," She said, still laughing a little.

"Bull! Don't worry about me. I can take care of myself."

"But he's in a wheelchair. Mother says we should always go out of our way to be kind to those less fortunate," Patti's sister said, speaking, it seemed, to Patti and me only, as though Grayson were not even present.

"Tell your mother to go out of her way somewhere else. I don't need her help." I could tell my brother was getting worked up and taking an instant dislike to this girl's condescending* tone.

During a moment of awkward silence a kindergarten-aged boy walked by, pulled along by his mother's hand. Slowing as he passed Grayson's chair, the boy stopped dead in his tracks and just stared. He never even turned around, but craned his neck backwards instead to maintain his view of my brother and this strange contraption which contained him. Finally, staring straight down at the small boy, Grayson spoke:

"Take a picture ya' little twerp, it lasts longer."

The boy, when he saw whatever this thing was could talk, turned around and got alongside his mother again, fast.

"Little brat. Nothing better to do than stare at those *less for-tu-nate*." Grayson spoke these last two words slowly and deliberately, drawing each of the syllables out for all they were worth.

"That wasn't nice," Patti's sister said. He didn't mean anything by it. He was just being curious." She truly looked upset.

"That's okay. No problem. Grayson was just kidding... just playing with the boy," I said.

"Well, it sounded mean to me. He hurt that little boy's feelings. He scared him is what he did," Patti's sister continued.

"Bull honkey. Whatever happened to *those less fortunate*?"

"I don't think it counts when they're mean," the girl replied.

I couldn't believe it. All I was trying to do was strike up a conversation with Patti and now this, my brother was engaged in a full-blown argument with her sister. Unbelievable!

"How'd you like someone staring up your dress? Not much?"

"Shut up, Grayson... enough," I said, getting upset now myself.

"That's different. That's aberrant behavior," Patti's sister shot back. She was fast getting into this argument now just as much as Grayson– giving him tit for tat.

"Not really. Staring is staring... it doesn't matter. It's bad manners no matter who does it or what they're staring at. Nobody appreciates being stared at, for any reason." Grayson was close to preaching now, I thought, and that gave me an idea.

"Okay brother... enough. We've already heard one sermon this morning." I was trying to keep my voice down. Several congregants were still standing nearby and I had the feeling our discussion was beginning to attract some attention.

"That's funny. You really are very funny," Patti said.

Once more, I couldn't believe it. This girl whom I thought so marvelous was telling me all sorts of great things; complimenting me left and right. It was almost an embarrassment of riches.

"Let's go Patti. Mom's outside waiting, and it's cold. Nice meeting you two." Patti's older sister gave Grayson and I both a scant nod, then turned and began walking away.

"Don't go away mad... just go away," Grayson said in a low, barely audible* voice aimed at the departing girl.

"It was nice talking to you, Marty. You too... Grayson, is it?"

The words were poetry coming from her mouth. She had done it; had said my name again, a name I thought of as plain, as ordinary, but she had spoken it and turned it into something else, something wonderful and now I wasn't sure if I wanted to hear anyone else use it. I'd *never, never* heard it sound this way, this good, before.

"Catch you later, Patti." She smiled when I spoke her name too, flashing perfect white teeth.

"Yeh, see you at lunch." She raised her eyebrows up towards her straight-cut bangs and kept smiling, even when she spoke.

God, how could anyone be so beautiful and talk and keep smiling so wonderfully. And all at the same time?

And then she was gone.

*   *   *

I watched as Patti turned and followed her sister out the double doors to the walkway that led to the shell road in front of the small church. Through the glass doors I could see their mother waiting for them in the driver's seat of the running car.

"Let's get a move–on, Marty. We're supposed to meet the Harnish's out in the parking lot... remember? Grayson said.

"Let's walk home," I replied, still watching through the doors as Patti got into the front seat of the tail–finned green Dodge alongside her sister and mother and closed the car's door. What motion, what *beauty of form* as she entered that car and glided her legs (knees bent splendidly, always together), so gracefully in after her.

"What! That's three miles. You're nuts," Grayson answered.

"At least up to Arnett's. That's only a mile. Aunt Bertie'll sneak us some donuts." I watched as the car drove off. "I just feel like walking. We can walk up to the beach. The tide'll be out," I said.

The car started down the road as I spoke. Not until it was completely out of sight did I direct my full attention back to my brother.

"Why not, can't dance," Grayson said.

"I'll go out and tell Mr. Harnish. You wait over by the door. I'll be right back," I said.

And I was gone.

*   *   *

By the time we got down to the beach we were both working on second thoughts as to whether this trek to the bakery was such a great idea. What might be just a chilly day a few blocks back could be downright frigid up here next to the surf. When the sun went behind the low gray clouds and settled there as it did this day there was no way of telling if it was just noon. Or afternoon. Or how much after noon.

The sky and ocean looked the same. Dull lead in color and rumpled and angry in nature. The occasional splotches of shifting white in the sky mirrored themselves in the corresponding whitecaps which popped up often and randomly from the sea below.

Here was an ocean that I did not want to be upon in any vessel, no matter how large or sea-worthy. But we were here and it was dead low-tide (as far out as I'd ever seen). The sand, after being beaten upon by this mighty tide, was packed hard, which was good because it meant easy rolling for Grayson's chair. Grayson didn't get this close to the ocean very often and given his total fear (not to mention defenselessness), against even the most sedate body of water he was reluctant to get very close to the breakers. Especially on a day like today.

In all directions it was desolate and forlorn looking. No houses were evident here. It was still a stretch of coastline that despite the best efforts of developers and builders hell-bent on dotting every square foot′ of beachfront property in the state with housing, somehow remained pristine and dwelling-free. As far (or rather, as little), as we could see there was only vast ocean to our right and long broad beach and then sand dunes to our left and we rolled and walked together down this imaginary dividing line separating the twain for half a mile or so in quiet reflection without so much as a wisecrack or an insult as though perhaps not still waters but rough ones were what was necessary to quieten both our spirits. Today we had the beach all to ourselves. Pieces of driftwood, broken-up shells and bottles, seaweed and seagrapes– flotsam and jetsam the ocean was continually spewing forth and offering up at the feet of passersby –were the only entities offering any witness to our pilgrimage.

Rolling along the hard-packed beach, moving closer to the water's edge (our courage built up now by the realization that as awesome as it sounded and looked nothing was likely to jump out of this tumultuous* sea and grab us), we both spied the faint hazy outline of the long fishing pier in the distance, jutting out a hundred yards to stab right into the very heart of this angry sea. We now had a sense of where we were for the first time since we'd come onto the beach. We had a landmark of sorts in this pier, and knew that once we got that far it was only a few short blocks more to the access road which would lead us up off the beach and across First Street. Then, just a short jaunt on to the bakery.

As we moved steadily along, the matchstick-looking telephone pole supports of the pier grew larger and became more spaced apart and as we finally passed under the gigantic construction we stopped for a second directly underneath it to look down the full length of the pier. We were both surprised by how much abuse the old structure was taking at the hands of this tumultuous sea. All the way down the line the pier was noticeably swaying. Before long we decided to move on.

The cold was starting to get to us both and I could feel my stomach beginning to grumble. I still had the acrid stale taste of grape juice in my mouth (I'd forgotten to get a drink at the cooler before we left), but the thought of hot chocolate and a fresh eclair drove me on, through the heavy mist and chill.

*   *   *

The day before had been a Saturday and even in this inclement weather *townies* drove out to the beach to cruise along the three-mile stretch between Coast Boulevard and Beach Road. These were the two spots where it was easiest to enter and exit the beach and though the boardwalk was closed for the season many folks from town still came at this time of year to view the ocean from the warmth and comfort of their cars.

It reminded me of the time five or six years before when my father was alive and we had all come out here on a stormy winter's day much like this one to cruise the three-mile stretch and eat the tiny square hamburgers we'd picked up at the Krystal on Beach Road on the ride out. It was the best I'd ever felt, being with my mother and father and brother inside the cocoon of that two-tone Ford slowly cruising down the winter beach, the wind blowing so hard that it rocked the sturdy car and witnessing the turbulent sea whose breakers, though ill-formed, were enormous and so loud you could hear them crashing even with the windows rolled up tight. Like today, the tide then had been way low and we were able to get close to the sea and a coupla' times along the stretch our father had to stop the car and go outside to wipe the film of salt spray from the windshield with his handkerchief. Once, the mist had been so thick that he'd had to jog down by the water's edge and wet the square piece of cloth to cut the film, and when he got back into the car he was covered with sea. His black hair (brushed back and flecked with gray), and even his rumpled sweatshirt all had a coating of sea spray as though he'd been running or exercising in some way and the mist which covered him was his sweat transforming him and making him seem even more handsome and healthy than I already knew him to be.

I would never forget that trip, that adventure, for that's what it had been, an adventure. Something sublimely outside of our normal everyday lives, that Saturday trip years ago (another lifetime ago, really), to the winter beach.

We went home that day the long way. through Mayport, and though Leah had protested, Grayson and I became excited at our father's suggestion that we take the ferry across the mouth of the river, and we both ranted and raved until she relented. But only after convincing our father to stop at the little store a block before the ferry to go inside and get her some seasick pills. I could still picture how peaceful and safe that neat little woodframe store looked with its lights on in defiance of the late afternoon's blustery dark grayness. How our father went into the store for just a few moments and joked with the old man behind the counter (I still remembered seeing them both laughing through the panes of the front door), and then my father emerging from the store with the pills for Leah, but also bottles of coke for everyone and a bag of salted peanuts that he showed us for the first time how to pour into our cokes and how wonderful it was the first time I tasted this treat our father had imparted to us. Who would have thought that the combination of these two things could be so great? Only someone like him, like my father.

When we boarded the ferry the passing was so rough the captain came on the loudspeaker warning the passengers to stay in their cars, please, and Grayson and I were disappointed some by this, but still it was a great ride. We could feel the massive boat rolling and pitching with the river's every rise and fall and we all loved every minute of it, all except Leah. Midway through the ride our father opened his door (to our amazement and Leah's dismay), and stood up by the car with the door still open to better see the water, he said. Right away Grayson and I began clamoring to get out also, and over the protestations of Leah were permitted to do so by our father. It was incredible how much you could see from the top of the car, I remembered thinking as I sat on the salt-dusty roof of the Ford. With Grayson beside me (he could still sit up on his own back then), I felt on top of the world perched on the Ford's roof. The two of us rode that cartop like some wild ride at the boardwalk, the motions of the rollicking rolling river accentuated, coming up through the ferry and the Ford, and a coupla' times I had to steady myself with both hands up there and I noticed my father had to really hold on to Grayson, and once we rocked so violently– the whole ship pitched so steeply forward all of a sudden –our father had to reach out and grab me by the arm also, and for an instant I felt both the quick adrenal gush fear of falling and then the power of my father's sure grip and I knew I would be okay– that no matter what our sleepy strong father would never let any harm come to me or my brother. That day my father was a match for the river.

Later, when we were safely back in the car, and Leah's scolding had subsided and I lay down in the backseat with my brother (already fallen asleep), and I looked up through the car's back windows at the passing telephone poles, and the building tops and the billboards searching the sky for some familiar landmark that would give our location away without sitting up to look, I licked the palm of each of my hands tasting the saltiness they'd collected from the Ford's roof and I knew somehow that once this taste was inside me that I, and this day, would be complete and somehow I would be more like my father.

*   *   *

Pulling with all my might I was able, at last, to get my brother up the ramp to First Street. Here we stopped, at Grayson's insistence, to straighten him in his chair before proceeding on to the bakery. The walk had been exhilarating, but I was nearly out of breath now from the last hundred yards of dragging my brother and his wheelchair through the mounds of sand that had collected on the ramp.

"Looking kinda' tired there, boy. You sure you haven't been smoking?" Grayson asked.

"Not really. Just good exercise," I puffed.

"Yeah, that was quite a workout. Whew, I feel much better now," Grayson laughed as he spoke.

"Getting chilly," I said as I sat down on the curb beside Grayson's chair, removing both of my loafers and pouring the sand each had collected into a little pile directly in front of me. It felt good to rest here for a second before the last push on.

"Chilly, hell," Grayson said. " It's colder than a witch's tit in a brass bra. Let's get going."

Coach Heisman, Thanksgiving & a Prayer

"Tell me that story about Coach Heisman again Pawpaw... please."

I spoke in hushed tones to my grandfather as we sat out in *Melinda*, waiting for the tide to turn on a cold and clear November day– in quest, finally, of gator trout.

"Which one, boy? Reckon I don't know but about fifty of 'em."

The old man had a wealth of stories about the fabled coach, all gained firsthand as he'd been a player on Heisman's famous 1917 championship Georgia Tech Football Team some 45 years previous.

"The one that sounds sorta' technical... like a geometry teacher talkin', or something like that."

"Oh, yeah... I know the one you mean. Well, on the first day of practice he always held up a football high above his head not saying a word. After a little while everything would get quiet... which is what he was waitin' for... and only then, certain all eyes were upon him, would he begin his speech. Same thing every year."

-- "A prolate spheroid -that is, an elongated sphere- in which the outer leather casing is drawn tightly over a somewhat smaller rubber tubing... Better to have died a small boy than to fumble this."

"Yeah, that's the one. I love how that sounds."

"Ol' Heisman... what a character. Shakespearean actor, also. Very dramatic man. He could be a pretty tough taskmaster though, that's for damn sure. Wouldn't let any of us use soap. Claimed it made our skin soft. Football was as much an art as a science to him. He had some great teams back then... went undefeated three years in a row... but that '17 team was the best. Greatest backfield ever: Everett Strupper, Judy Harlan, Albert Hill, and that Indian boy– Joe Guyon."

"Boy, I'll say... National Champs," I spoke boastfully for my grandfather.

"I'd love to lie to you boy and tell you how great I was back then but it just weren't so. Never played much until my last year, and we had so many injuries early in the season that year anyone who could still walk and chew gum at the same time by then was playing a lot of football– both offense and defense. Heisman's Forward Pass– that's what we called it. Yahoos watch television today assumin' it was always a part of the game, but he was the one chiefly responsible for it."

"What'd he do... just kinda' think it up to throw the ball forward?"

"Nah. Claimed he actually saw his first pass at a game back in 1890 somethin' between North Carolina and Georgia. The fullback for Carolina was back to punt, but those Georgia boys come in on him in such a hurry he was forced to scramble around. And then in desperation he just flung the thing downfield. One of his teammates looked up just in time to see the ball... it was more the size and shape of a small basketball back then... sailing towards him, whereupon he had the good sense to catch it and run across the goal line. Pop Warner... he was the Georgia coach... well, he started screaming bloody murder saying it was an *illegal play!... illegal play!* The ref was bewildered, but he allowed it saying he never saw a pass, just a Carolina player with the ball crossing the goal line. Heisman was intrigued, but for a few years after that didn't do nothing about it. Eventually, he began toying with the idea of puttin' it into the game, though... saw the potential there to open the game up and turn it into something other than scrummage."

"So he started his teams passing then?" I asked.

"Hell no! First nobody wanted any part of it. Finally, though, he managed to get some converts... Amos Alonzo Stagg and ol' Pop. That really opened up the game. Made it a lot less bloodier too. Hell, boys used to get killed back then playing the type of roughneck ball they was used to. Yeh, looking back on it, Coach Heisman changed the game quite a bit. Quite a bit."

Once more, I thought, Pawpaw was becoming more like his old self out here on the water talking about his early football days. I hadn't heard him discuss any of this in a good long while.

"If we don't get into somethin' in the next coupla' minutes I'm gonna' pull anchor and move us down to the next creek mouth. Tide's just about to change and they should be hitting by now if they're goin' to." As he spoke, the old man slowly reeled the tiny shrimp-like green Mirrorlure attached to the end of his line in towards the boat, lightly jigging and popping the floating lure every second or third revolution of the reel. Suddenly, right at about twelve feet out the lure disappeared and his six foot, light-action Penn rod arched violently into the glassy gray water of the silent stream.

"All right, here we go. What'd I tell you, boy. They're here. Throw out towards that oyster bar by the big grass clump." The old man spoke excitedly as he struggled with the fish.

"Dang, what you got there? Must be a redfish, or one heck of a big spec ," I said. Standing up in the boat and leaning over towards my grandfather, I had the wooden-handled landing net at the ready.

"Naw, it's a trout all right, but a big one... no doubt about that. Get the net ready for action, boy. I only got six-pound line on this reel. Man, he's a fighter, I'll tell you what."

As my grandfather played the fish closer to the boat being careful not to horse him in too quickly, I gingerly leaned over and stretched the net's open mouth towards the spot where the old man's line entered the water. Just as I had the net as close to the line as I dared, the silver–speckled fish broke from the water's surface and emerged mouth–first.

"Get 'dat net under him, boy, this line's as taunt as can be. There ya' go. Glory-be, damn that's a nice fish," the old man spoke proudly.

"She's a beaut, Pawpaw. Best one I've seen all year. Dang, must be a seven, eight pounder ," I cried.

The old man lifted the two foot long fish from the black criss–crossed strings of the landing net and admired it for a brief moment. Turning the fish, he exposed it's iridescent* colors and markings on both sides to the day's full sun. Then he gently hefted the plump trout back out over the edge of the boat down towards the waterline and released it.

"At least six, son. At least six."

"It's as big as the one Hank caught a coupla' weeks ago down at St. Augustine and it was seven pounds somethin'. Boy, I didn't know they could fight so well. He didn't wanta' cooperate at all," I said excitedly, placing the net back against *Melinda's* inside wall.

"Let me tell you something about speckled seatrout son. Everyone says they don't put up all that much of a fight and that's partially true; but if you hook one on a topwater lure it's a totally different ball game, I'll tell you right now. They may not jump, but they'll fight like hell... no if, ands, or buts about it. Now let's go catch some puny two or three pounders. They're the best eating size. The big ones are fun to catch, but the smaller ones taste better... least I think so."

*   *   *

In the next forty minutes we caught twenty-two fish, the division of labor perfectly even: eleven fish each. When we decided we'd had enough, (and the interval between strikes had lengthened considerably), my grandfather broke out the rumpled dinged thermos, pouring us each half a cup of blond sweetened coffee. Then the old man reached into the breast pocket of his heavy flannel shirt and pulled out a pack of cheese and peanut butter crackers. Savoring these provisions, neither of us said another word and the day fell softly quiet as the outgoing tide began picking up strength and with this strength numerous swirling eddies and vortexes* manifested themselves alongside *Melinda.*

I dazed off into the stillness of the afternoon for a little while. Only when my grandfather finished his coffee and quietly leaned back on his bench seat to tap me on the knee to start the Evinrude did there come the first noise to break the silence.

That noise was nothing more that the sudden loudness of the last few trout we'd caught thrashing in the icy confines of the now much heavier Coleman cooler.

Thanksgiving Day started off gray and blustery but by late morning whatever foul weather had blown in swept through the area, leaving by noon a sky of blue and a temperature in the mid-50's. Leah had gotten up early to stuff the 17 lb. bird Paw-paw shot over near Yulee and delivered the week before, and already she was looking to yours truly for some help on this day when everyone would be coming over to our house for dinner.

First, there was the cantankerous table to wrestle with. I had to painstakingly pull it apart, working on either side a little at a time to insert the leaf for it's annual holiday debut. Next, I was called upon to peel potatoes (a task not too awful for here was something I could do in the living room and still watch the Macy's Thanksgiving Day Parade), the potatoes in a brown paper bag on the left side of my chair, another paper bag on the floor in front to receive the peels, and a large glass bowl for the freshly skinned tubers on the right. In truth, I did not find the televised parade all that interesting, but thought of it more as kind of a traditional prelude* to the day's real event– the annual Thanksgiving Day matchup between the Detroit Lions and the Chicago Bears. Now there was something to be savored alongside the turkey and stuffing and gravy and sweet potatoes and cranberries and whatever else anyone brought along.

Part of what made this game so wonderful each year was the fact that no matter in which city these two teams played– Chicago or Detroit –you could always count on it being played in the snow. A couple of years ago the game had been played in Chicago in a blizzard so severe that all afternoon the only thing you could see on the television screen was white snow. With just the faintest ghostlike outline of the players evident, it looked as though the channel selector was a click off its proper setting. Grayson and Leah had both railed at me that day for watching what looked like terrible reception, and even though I tried to educate them to the fact that no, I was not watching static, but one of the greatest and most time-honored football rivalries in the history of the National Football League, but of course, it was all to no avail. They just didn't get it. To the two of them the name of George Halas (the revered and crusty old coach of the Bears), evoked nothing special and was a name which may as well have belonged to the assistant conductor of the Chicago Symphony.

"What time are Aunt Bertie and Uncle Rad coming over?" I called out from the living room to Leah, still in the kitchen, constructing yet another pie."

"She said they'd be over about one, Marty. Why?"

"Is Porter coming?" I asked about Rad's brother, a thin balding bachelor around thirty who was nothing like Rad. Porter had a way of getting on my nerves bad.

"I imagine so. He's invited and he usually does."

"Did she say anything about a mincemeat pie?" I asked.

"No, but I'm sure she'll bring one. She always does."

"Why don't you ever make one?"

"Because I can't stand them, Marty. And neither can anyone else in their right mind."

"Aunt Bertie likes them."

"No she doesn't, not really. She just bakes them because you and your grandfather like them. She might take one spoonful, but that'll be it, I assure you."

"Well, Pawpaw and I like 'em. Glad somebody cares about that."

"Quick, let me get my violin out. Poor boy might not have enough to eat," Leah spoke in mock-pitiful tones. "I haven't noticed anyone going hungry around here lately."

"Okay, okay. I hope they get here soon, though. I love the smell of that pie. It just doesn't seem like Thanksgiving until I smell one of Aunt Bertie pies." Actually, sweet potato was my favorite in the pie department, but for some reason(probably because my grandfather liked the old-fashioned pie), I looked forward to my Aunt's pungent-sweet mincemeat. When that wafted through the house then I would feel like it was Thanksgiving– not until.

"What time did Pawpaw say he'd be here?"

"About the same time, Marty. Listen, do you need something else to do?" She walked into the living room now blocking my view of the parade and wiping her hands on the hem of her apron as she spoke. "Why don't you go get Grayson up, he's been sleeping nearly twelve hours, now. It's time for him to get up. Go get him up, right now!"

"Oh jeez, do I have to? I'm almost through with these potatoes. Give me another min......"

"No sir, right now! Do as you're told."

"Yes 'mam."

I did as Leah said.

*   *   *

"This is just the best turkey, Leah... really moist. You've outdone yourself, per usual." Porter declared the first obligatory* compliment on the meal shortly after grace was offered and we'd all loaded our plates. All at the big table seconded Porter's appraisal*.

"Well, certainly Dad deserves some of the credit. He supplied it,

I just cooked it."

"Good Bird, Colonel," Porter said, calling my grandfather by his military rank. It usually excited me when I heard someone address my grandfather with this title, but there was something about the way Porter mouthed it that conjured up shades of trying to butter the old man up. It just didn't sit right.

"Yeh, good bird, Pawpaw," I chimed in, taking some delight in parroting Porter's reference to the main course.

"Beats road-kill, I reckon," the old man spoke with a mouth full of dressing. A slight chuckle emitted nonetheless.

"You put that so wonderfully, Dad," Leah said.

"You know what I mean, daughter. You done a fine job of fixin' him. Not many folks know how to cook a real walkin' around gobbler as opposed to one of them frozen store-bought items. You done good, hon. Real good"

"Well, thank you... I think."

"Don't mention it sweetheart," Pawpaw spoke while chewing, his fork in mid-air and beaming at his daughter who, it looked to me anyway, was making a point of not beaming back.

Whether everyone remained silent as a gesture of politeness or because we didn't know what else to say the effect was the same– a long awkward silence that only accentuated* the sounds at the table: silverware on plates, tinkling of ice in glasses, and worst of all– the sounds of group mastication* as we struggled with our silence. Finally, to the delight of all (which was rarely the case), Porter spoke up. Instantly the room that only seconds before had been caught in a sort of suspended animation, came mercifully to life again and once more it was okay to breathe.

"We sure showed that Mr. Kruschev a thing or two. Don't you think, Colonel."

"Sure did, Porter. That fat Russian S.O.B. thought he could bluff us. Kennedy stared him down though, thank heaven. Let's see him pound his shoe now, heh... after we put it where the sun don't shine, heh, heh."

"Dad, please, it's Thanksgiving," Leah pleaded.

"I know, hon. I just get excited when I think of that fat old goat and what he put us through trying to sneak them missiles into Cuba. I wouldn't pee on him if he were on fire and standing right in front of me."

"Dad!"

"Boy, ain't it the truth!" Rad said. "That was about as close as I ever care to come to nuclear annihilation. Scary couple of days there. Pass the sweet potatoes, honey." Rad spoke to Bertie. "I hope ya'll left some marshmallow topping... oh good, there's a little left."

"Well, I tell you folks what. You may think Kennedy is the greatest thing since giblet gravy, but if Nixon had'a been in it never would'a gotten that far in the first place," Porter said.

"How the hell do 'ya know that, Porter? Hell, he ain't worth the powder it'd take to blow him to hell and back."

"If I remember right, Colonel, this President didn't exactly shine at the Bay of Pigs," Porter said.

"Oh hell, Porter... I didn't say he was God. He messed up good there and it was a tragedy, no two ways about it... but he came away learning something and he pulled our fat out of the fire this time, and by *our* I do mean the whole world. Nixon's such a nincompoop, why we'd all be blown to smithereens by now, more than likely."

"Well, heck fire, Edward, you don't know that for sure, either," Porter offered somewhat lamely, aware of the old man's arguing abilities and not wanting to get him too riled up. There was some significance to the fact that Porter dropped the military nomenclature* now too, I figured.

"I got sense enough to figure it out, though."

"Well, think like you like, but he isn't getting my vote next time."

"He'll survive." The old man half-chuckled as he spoke.

"Maybe, but I'm going for Goldwater next time. Little more age; lot more sense."

Easter Sunday (the last time we were all together), Porter and the old man had gotten into a heated political debate and Pawpaw had called Porter a *mugwump*. After the feast I went straight to my room for my dictionary where I was disappointed to find the strange sounding word pertained* to politics. By it's sound (plus the way the old man had said it), I'd suspected something a lot juicier. The old man had been correct, of course. Porter was, if nothing else, a true mugwump and the only adult I knew so far who had announced his intention to vote for Goldwater. And now, at perhaps the zenith* of President

Kennedy's popularity so soon after the successful resolution of the missile crisis.

"Yeah, AuH2O, he's for me. Got a bumper sticker last week says just that. That's as good as 'I Like Ike'. AuH2O in Sixty-Four. Pretty clever, don't you think?" Porter said.

"What in the world are you talking about, Porter?" Bertie asked, trying to make sense of her brother-in-law.

"Think about it Bertie. AU...H2O... you know, A...U as in the symbol for gold and H2O as in..."

"Oh, I get it now. How clever," Bertie broke in.

"Glad you get a kick out of that Porter, 'cause I got news for you... it's probably gonna' be the high-water mark of his campaign. That old Arizona buzzard might be a good aviator, but I wouldn't give you a plug nickel for his presidential aspirations."

"We'll see, Colonel." Jeez, there he went– switching back again.

"Gentlemen, please. Can we maybe change the discussion." Leah gently tapped the side of her glass with her salad fork as she spoke, knowing this would get her father's attention. Once again there was a moment of awkward silence at the table but this one was short-lived as my grandfather spoke up, his tone noticeably softer now.

"You're right sweetheart. We shouldn't be arguing today, given the special occasion and all. I think we're all just a little excited and a lot happy to be shed of that mess down south," the old man said.

"Well, maybe you should have said so when you offered up the prayer, Dad," Leah said.

"You're right, hon." The old man reflected for a moment, smiled slightly, and spoke again:

"Everyone... stop eating. Please... come on, put down that gorgeous flatware and I'll offer up a little auxiliary prayer of real thanksgiving." At first none of us were sure how to take this given my grandfather's penchant* for practical jokes and he found he had to coax us a little more.

"I'm serious. Porter, Rad, Bertie. Let's pray.....Good, okay." The old man bowed his head and began his prayer:

"Dear Lord... please forgive us here today in our haste to partake in these bountiful provisions for forgetting something most important. And that is the act of thanking you in all the humbleness we can muster for bringing us out of the terrible mess our country was in last month. Thank you most especially for directing our young President and imbuing* him with the courage and steadfastness to see that awful incident to it's peaceful conclusion." Here Pawpaw paused a second and cracked an eye towards Porter, looking to see if this last bit had illicited any response. As hoped, Porter's lower lip drooped pronouncedly. The reason I know all this is because I was peeking at the same time. The old man continued:

"And if it is you will, dear Father, we humbly beseech you to smite down that fat, bald-headed, Russian sonova...ow...uh, Premier Kruschev, that is...uh...of course, if it is in thy will. We pray in Jesus' name. Amen."

"Amen." We all repeated.

At the proverbial* wobbly, folding-leg cardtable which I'd set up earlier in the living room, Grayson and I, along with our cousins (Bertie's daughters– Wendy and Allison), stopped eating long enough to make prayer hands and listen to the old man offer up this second blessing; after which we broke out into a spontaneous applause. Across the room I even caught Leah smiling, for the first time all day.

Meanwhile, I noticed my grandfather was leaned over the sidearm of his chair wearing an uncharacteristicly bewildered, almost grimaced, expression. At first I thought the old man had dropped something or maybe his arthritis was kicking up on him, but the longer I looked the more I realized that wasn't the case at all. What the Colonel was actually doing was rubbing the shin of his right leg.

The one closest to his daughter.

Hurricane

" Show me a man who can't get excited about a hurricane and I'll show you someone who might as well go on ahead and cash in their chips. "
– Coach Sutter, as quoted in *Rebel Yell*

I had heard about it and its after effects all my life, eversince I could remember, and even if it was a rare occurrence I heard it talked about so many times by so many folks that I felt like it was a part of my life. At least the hearing about it. But even at thirteen, though I felt like I knew alot about this natural phenomenon, I still had not experienced it firsthand.

It, was Hurricane.

There is an ironic* softness to this word. In the first syllable you have the *hur* which sounds like *her* (they're always named after women). And the way it flows; the fact that it is a triple syllable word that seems to go up and down and back towards up again evoking* some sorta' undulating* wave or tidal force that, when conditions are right, grow from a storm to a tropical depression to a gale and finally— to Hurricane.

There'd been a bunch of times in the last few years since we moved at the Beach that I thought I'd finally get to experience a hurricane firsthand, but as luck would have it each of these had either fizzled out over the water or taken some other course away from our part of the state. All Oceanside had received from these duds was bad weather. A coupla'-three days of rain and a little wind, but nothing truly bad. Just enough weather to make it too wet to play football or take to the woods to wage war with BB guns. If my friends and I were going to be robbed of some playing days we ought to at least be rewarded once with a real blow. That was the prevailing attitude among my friends and I.

Hurricane season starts June 1st and runs through October. Two years ago a gale had come towards us late in the season, around Halloween, and was picking up steam real good about a hundred miles southeast in the Atlantic. It looked on a Friday afternoon after school like finally we were in for it. But that one fizzled, too. Mick and Davey and I snook down to the beach that Saturday morning to witness a pretty mean looking ocean– the roughest by far I'd ever seen. Tremendous waves crashed on the huge granite boulders that had been placed snug-up to the seawall to shore up its weak spots earlier that summer. The waves meeting those rocks sent huge flumes of seawater into the air twenty and thirty feet over our heads like geysers cascading over the bulwarks and onto the top of the seawall where the three of us stood. We all three got drenched and we all had some explaining to do when we got home, and for what? A look at an angry sea? Okay, so the giant waves themselves might have been worth the trip down to the beach, and, truth be known at any other time we would have regarded this as a major event. But we'd wanted more. We wanted the real thing.

All we talked about on the way home was scenes each of us had seen on television of roofs being blown off of houses and trees (thick trunked palms), bent way over by the force of the tremendous winds a hurricane had spawned until they were nearly parallel with the ground.

Mick told us about seeing a man once on the news trying to walk down a dark street in the middle of a hurricane. There was the man, dressed in shorts and a windbreaker leaning into the fierce wind and rain and not going anywhere, like something out of a silent movie. Not only was he not making any headway, he was being blown backwards by the force of the winds! Right at the end of the news clip the man was knocked down by the wind, and the camera's last scan saw this poor fellow on his hands and knees struggling to get back up; reaching for a street sign pole which itself was being wobbled to hell and back by the fierce wind. Mick's parents were watching, too, and they both remarked at how utterly stupid this fellow was. Here was the difference between parents and kids, Davey said. There wasn't much any red-blooded American boy worth his salt wouldn't do for the chance to walk around in a hurricane; just to see if he could do it first, and so he could brag about it later to his friends and classmates. But parents had no appreciation for this sort of thing, no sense of adventure. Maybe they had at one time, but not now. Yeh, Mick said, N.G.N.G.–No guts, No glory

So it was that there were to be several false starts before I was to experience my first full-blown hurricane.

* * *

Doreen. That was her name. Although technically not an island, the Beach was a bulwark to Riverville seventeen miles to the west and was separated from the river city by the intracoastal waterway. Something about bad weather brought out in Oceansiders a true sense of being islanders, though, and finally, thank goodness, here was some bad weather.

Reports from the Hurricane Center in Miami said that Doreen

had reached hurricane strength in the early morning hours and she was getting stronger, heading north-northwest at around twelve miles an hour. Twenty-four hours earlier Doreen had been responsible for seventeen deaths in Haiti, and later three more in Cuba. Now it was only Monday and there'd been school, but if Doreen kept on coming like she was that would soon change.

I pushed Grayson down the short curved road that connected Mick's house with our own. Leah had called right after I got home from school to let us know she would be late. Because of the storm, Evan's was inundated* with orders for kerosene and dry ice but she'd be home as soon as she could. Meanwhile, stick close to the house. The old man was out of town visiting friends and had planned on staying overnight. Instead, he'd called her an hour earlier to say he was heading back.

All day in school the only thing anyone had talked about was the approaching storm. Some kids had even brought in transistor radios (in blatant violation of school policy), and a loose network of news was formed by the student body, it's dissemination* effected mostly between classes in the hall. All day long Doreen was being tracked by hundreds of eager amateur meteorologists. Coach Sutter had brought in a shortwave radio for our 8th grade Science class, keeping it tuned low to the local National Weather Service station. Besides the one week in October, during the World Series, it was the only other time I could recall transistor radios being tolerated inside this building.

The question of the hour was could the Oceanside Pier withstand the fury of a hurricane? Right after it was first built, Coach Sutter said, it had withstood some pretty rough winds when a big blow had come in just north of St. Augustine, thirty miles south. But that was twenty-five years ago and if anything the pier had surely weakened some since then. Especially susceptible would be the ramshackle building that served as a dance hall and restaurant at the very end of the pier.

"Be a real shame if the bandshell got obliterated. Most of you hot dogs haven't even had a chance to get out there and cut a rug yet." Coach Sutter spoke of the cement stage and seating pavilion that sat front and center on First Street– directly across from the bakery. The bandshell had played weekend host to local bands for years and was a popular gathering spot for Oceanside teens. This news concerned me. It was not so much the welfare of the bandshell I was worried about but the fact that Arnett's was so close by. I raised my hand.

"Crane.," Coach Sutter, seated on a stool at the front of the classroom, pointed at me.

"How old is the bakery, sir."

"It's been there for forty forever's, Crane. Why?"

"Do you think it could withstand a hurricane, sir?"

"No telling. Just to be on the safe side, if you've got a wedding cake on order there I wouldn't waste any time picking it up." The entire class (with the exception of yours truly), laughed. Coach Sutter, sensing my apprehension, tried to soothe it over.

"Really, there's no telling, Crane. It's an old building, but it's all cement block so I guess it'll have as good a chance as any that close up to the beach. Time will tell."

The last report our class heard was that Doreen was now traveling at twelve miles per hour and was expected to make landfall early the next morning somewhere between St. Augustine, Florida and Brunswick, Georgia. If you drew a line on the map between these two spots and then bisected that line at it's midpoint there would be Oceanside, Florida. This was sizing up to be all that I had ever hoped for, and then some.

The bell rang and our 8th grade science class dissolved into a mass of boys and girls anxious to hit the halls, to trade information and share in the excitement of the coming storm.

*   *   *

I rolled the sooty barbecue (containing the ashes from a chicken grilled the night before), across the carport and into the utility room. There wasn't much room left and I still had to get the redwood rocker, my grandfather's favorite chair, into the room. The double-seater would have to stay out in the carport. Maybe I could cut off some of the Venetian blind cord Leah kept in the washroom and secure the piece of furniture to the house in some way. I decided to leave it for now. The old man would know what to do. Hopefully, he'd be back in time to check after me on things like this.

With one ear I listened through the screen-door to the transistor radio on the dinner table as Alvin and the Chipmunks squeaked on in anticipation of Christmas. The disc jockey (who normally restricted his banter to talk of records), came on as the song faded and I stopped what I was doing to listen.

"...and although Doreen seems to be weakening some, persons residing immediately on the shoreline are still advised to evacuate their homes. Those persons residing between the coast and the intracoastal waterway are strongly urged to do the same. In the last hour the National Weather Service reports Doreen has turned north. Her present course has her headed towards landfall sometime in the early morning hours áround Brunswick, Georgia. In other news..."

"Hear that Marty?" Grayson yelled from inside where he was stationed in front of the television.

"Yeah, I heard. But we're more than a mile back." I replied.

"Yeah, but we're still this side of the intracoastal." Grayson said. "Think Pawpaw'll move us out?" he added.

"No way." I yelled. "We'll stick it out. You watch."

"I wouldn't bet the farm." Grayson yelled back.

Just one thought occupied my mind now. *Would we stay?*

*   *   *

My grandfather was back and I was still filling the tub, wondering what the next twenty-four hours might bring when I heard the crackly-crunching sound of the Ford driving onto the shell driveway, followed by the slam of the car's door.

"Hello, everyone. Hey dad ," Leah shouted as she came through the front door.

"Hello, daughter. Looks like they kept ya'll a little late. I tried calling, but all the lines were busy."

"Oh brother, tell me. You wouldn't believe it... that place was a zoo. Hello Grayson ," she said, dropping her purse on top of the television set and jostling the rabbit ears (and the set's reception), in the process.

"Hi, mom."

"They're still going at it but I lied and told Mr. Evans I had to get home... the boys were here alone. How was your trip?" Leah asked.

"Just fine. Avery's as honery as ever. Celestine say's to give you her love ," the old man answered.

"I miss them both. Best neighbors we ever had," Leah said quietly, as though she were thinking back, I imagined.

"Good folks, all right ," Pawpaw replied.

"So what's going on here?"

"I've got Marty filling up the bathtub with clean water in case we need it later. Grayson and I were going over some provisions I bought in Palatka on the way up."

"What for? You're not thinking of staying, are you?"

"Sure. No reason not to. This thing's headed north."

"Well, with all due respect dad, have you lost your ever-loving mind? What if it turns back? They're so unpredictable. You don't know what this thing will do."

"You're right, I don't. But I got sense enough not to high tail it every time the wind picks up a little. Now don't get over-excited. We've been through worse than this."

"It's just I remember the one we went through when I was growing up and..." Leah's voice was gaining both volume and agitation.

"That was a different thing altogether, hon. We didn't have no warning then and it'd already been raining a week, to boot. This one sounds like it's taming down some, although I'll grant you you never know for sure about these damn things."

"We could go into town. What's wrong with that?"

"Where? To Porter's? No thanks, I'd rather have teeth pulled out with pliers, first. I've had it done before, too, and it wasn't any fun."

"Red Cross is opening shelters in town," Leah replied.

"Jesus Christ, daughter, do you actually want to go stay in some high school gymnasium with three or four hundred other folks packed in like cattle for a couple of days? Think about it."

"They're urging people on the radio..."

"I know. I've been listening, too. All day long." For a moment my grandfather stopped talking and during that moment I thought the old man might be whispering. Even after I turned the water down, then all the way off, I could hear no voices. Just the drip of the faucet. Then the old man resumed:

"Earlier... this afternoon... I'd just about made up my mind to evacuate all of us but it looks now like this thing is winding down. We'll just get a bunch of rain and it'll blow like hell for a few hours. This house is old but, it's in good shape. It can take it. Plus they're saying now it'll probably come in closer to around Brunswick. Grayson and I just heard it on the radio before you drove up. We'll be all right." Again, there was a long silence in the conversation. Then:

"Well, if we're staying somebody's going up to Murphy's and get me a gallon of milk, *please*," Leah said, stretching out the last word. From back in the bathroom it sounded a lot like sarcasm.

"It would be my *pleasure*." The old man stretched out his last word also. Ditto on how it sounded.

*　　*　　*

Standing with my grandfather in the check-out line at Murphy's, I got my first inkling of what it felt like when folks said they could taste the excitement. The quaint atmosphere of the old Beach store with it's dark wooden floor, high ceiling and ceiling fans enhanced the feel of impending* danger tightening it's grip on the small Beach community. But there was this feeling like sanctuary, too, in this old store and I felt a specialness here– like I was a member of an exclusive club; *The Stayers.* Even if everyone was in a hurry to get back to their house each and every person in the store (even those in the long check-out line), was going out of their way to be polite and neighborly. Suddenly thrown together into danger, those who elected to stay were coming together, and there wasn't a better place in the little Beachtown to do it than right here. Huddled together here at Murphy's you could witness the others who had elected to ride it out also, and it was this witnessing which went a long way in making valid* each person's decision to stay. Misery loves company. So do fear and apprehension, I thought.

"Ed. Ed Bartram!" A voice called out from behind us. My grandfather and I turned at the same time to look towards the spot where the voice came from– the end of the line. It took him a second, and he had to squint some, but my grandfather soon recognized the caller.

"Ben, how you doing?" My grandfather said to a man who looked to be his age, maybe a little younger, near the end of the line.

"Can't complain. Leastwise, not yet. How about yourself, Colonel?"

"Same here. I won't ask what brings you out on such a glorious evening," Pawpaw said, walking back towards the other man and then shaking hands with him.

"Ain't it the truth," the other man replied, laughing. "Just pickin' up some candles, just in case."

Not sure if I should follow my grandfather I elected to stay put; to keep our place in line if nothing else.

"How're the boys?" my grandfather asked the man.

"Doin' fine. Tobias is still in French Indochina... Vietnam they callin' it these days... trying to help 'em get shed of them Reds and Matthew is finally fixin' to graduate from Tech."

"That's right, Matt did go to Georgia Tech, didn't he. Always said there was a smart boy."

"Naw, he had to. Couldn't get into M.I.T."

"I know you're lying, now."

"Ha, ha. Same ol' Ed. Think we're gonna' get a little bit of a blow here?"

"I don't know what to think about this durn thing. First it was headed right at us. Now it's heading north." My grandfather moved his hands when he spoke of the hurricane's change in direction as though he were tracking it with the motions. "I've never seen one this late in the season do much harm, though."

"Fine with me. I had my fill back in the thirties and forties."

"Ain't that the truth. Have you met my grandson.... Marty?" The old man turned to find me, looking surprised some when he discovered I wasn't right there at his elbow.

"Don't believe I have. Hello, Marty," the other man said, looking up the line and waving at me.

"Marty, this is Mr. Emerson." The old man motioned me back as he spoke.

"Hello, Mr. Emerson." I said, walking to the rear of the line and joining my grandfather and shaking the other man's offered hand.

"What do you think of all this hoopla, son?" Mr. Emerson asked. I wasn't sure how honest I could be with the man and I looked up at my grandfather for a second, but the old man gave me no indication. I was on my own.

"I hope it blows right through here, sir." More than a few folks turned to see who was speaking this brand of nonsense.

"Spoken like a true teenage boy, son," Mr. Emerson said as he laughed.

"Yeah, and spoken like someone who's never been through one before, too," the old man said. For a while neither man said anything, but I could tell my grandfather and the other man were not done yet. Then Mr. Emerson spoke, quieter and more seriously:

"I tell ya', Ed. There's some buildings around here that just can't stand too much of a blow. City Hall and the old Library come to mind, right away. They're both just old, wood-frame houses that've seen better days, when you get right down to it."

"I know what'cha mean, Ben," my grandfather replied in a like tone. There was a look in the old man's eye, the kind he got out on the water sometimes, like he was thinking about something that might have happened long ago, and after a moment he spoke again. "How's the pier? I haven't been out there in ages."

I was anxious to interject* when I heard my grandfather mention the pier, for here was a subject I could bring some light to, thanks to Coach Sutter.

"It's doing all right, but I'd sure hate to be on it if this thing turns and heads in head first."

As the two men talked the line continued to shuffle slowly forward. When I turned to look I was surprised to find we (at least the spot we'd formerly occupied), were only three patrons away from being checked out. For once in my life here was a time when I was not in any special hurry to be at the front of the line. Murphy's was the place to be this evening and I would be sad to leave. Here was where the older crowd (the hold-outs, my grandfather called them), still shopped. There was no arguing that point as I looked around and guessed the average age of the store full of shoppers to be at least sixty-five.

The two double doors at the front of the store were both open. Two senior high boys I didn't know but had seen around school were busy bringing in stuff– things that'd spent the day outside on the sidewalk –back into the store. They were placing them wherever they could find room near the front so it would be a short trip back out when Doreen's threat was over, I figured. Wheelbarrows, racks of garden supplies and tools, and rolled-up rabbit wire all joined the more animated inhabitants of the store inside. Though I reckoned this was a nightly ritual– this bringing in of items that graced the sidewalk during the day in hopes of luring customers inside –it occurred to me that tonight it was especially appropriate to be bringing this stuff in. Anything you cared about and wanted to see again needed to be brought in or else tied down real good, I thought. And then I remembered the two-seater back at the house. A second later I thought of *Melinda* and the thought gave me a start.

"Looks like we're fixin' to get out of here, after all. Not a second too soon, the way this boy's jumping," My grandfather said. "Good to see ya', Ben."

"Same here, Ed. Call me sometime. We'll go up to the pier for old times sake. If she's still there."

"I'll do that."

"The boy fish?"

"He's learning," my grandfather said, grabbing me by the shoulder with one hand like he was fixing to give me a playful pinch.

"He ain't bad."

"Good. Bring him with you. Maybe he'll bring us some luck." Mr. Emerson said.

"Or get lucky hisself, and put us to shame," my grandfather added, jokingly, as he shook his friend's hand and then moved back up the line, yours truly following right behind.

Both men laughed the kind of comfortable laugh that can never be forced or even imitated well. It was the sorta' laugh that only old friends are capable of, I reckon.

Hurricane II

The wind was blowing now.

My grandfather pulled the Imperial into the side yard and neither of us wasted any time getting back into the house. It was pitch black outside, blowing in gusts I guessed to be around forty miles an hour, plus it was starting to rain. It didn't seem like a lot but it was hard to tell the way the wind was pushing the drops. Rain was supposed to fall from the sky straight down, but this stuff was being pushed and shoved all around– one moment it was coming sideways from the east the next moment from the north. Then from two or three or seemingly all directions at once. Sometimes it even seemed like it had stopped, but that was just the wind halting it for a few seconds, gathering it up, only to push it forcefully in a giant burst when released. Funny thing was it seemed like there should be lightning in this sky, but I couldn't see any. Just the same charge in the atmosphere I'd felt earlier pushing Grayson.

All the way back from Murphy's we listened in the dark to the radio station my grandfather always tuned to which had abandoned it's usual evening schedule of Dixieland and Big Band music. Instead, it was reporting now on weather conditions throughout our corner of the state, and frequent updates on Doreen's location. The last report we'd heard placed her about ninety-five miles east of St. Augustine, headed north-northwest at ten miles an hour with winds at her center between ninety-five and one hundred and five miles per hour. It looked like she was picking up steam again. The NWS was holding to it's prediction Doreen would make landfall somewhere near Brunswick in the early morning hours. I wondered if I would still be awake then. Though I had tried, and tried hard, on several occasions, I'd never been able to stay up all night. As we entered the house Leah met us at the door.

"Did you remember the milk?"

"Right here, daughter." My grandfather held up the half-gallon carton of milk. "Little on the wet side, I'm afraid."

"That's okay... thanks," she said, taking the carton and heading for the kitchen.

"Getting a little on the blustery side out there," the old man said gazing out the front window into the maw of the darkening, rainy storm.

"Boy, I'll say," Grayson said. "I was watching those palm trees across the road in the Andrews' front yard while ya'll were at the store. Boy, they were swaying like crazy!"

"Wait a while. We're likely to get some good gusts outa' this thing yet, even if it does head on up to Jor-gee," my grandfather said. It was the way he always said Georgia– 'Jor-gee'.

"Serves 'em right if it does, all the mean cusses that state's produced."

"What are you talking about Pawpaw? What mean cusses?" I asked. I pretty much knew he was trying to pique my interest, that he was baiting me so to speak, but even so I couldn't resist.

"Ty Cobb and Doc Holliday, to name a couple," the old man answered. This caught me off guard. I knew about Ty Cobb being from Georgia, after all he was nicknamed *The Georgia Peach*, but Doc Holliday? The same Doc Holliday of OK Corral fame? I'd never heard of him being from the Peach State. If I knew anything about my grandfather though it was that while he was seldom wrong on almost any subject, when it came to historical personalities he was *never* wrong.

"Valdosta," the old man said, looking straight at me.

"Huh?" I asked, bewilderingly.

"That's where Doc Holliday was born... Valdosta," my grandfather replied. "I could tell you were thinking about it. Now do me a favor and go out and see if we got a paper. We'll call it payment for passing on that little bit of biographical information."

"Sounds fair to me," I replied. Though the front door was closer I headed for the back, by the kitchen, grabbing my hooded parka on my way back out into the night.

It was even gustier now than it had been just the short time ago we'd come back from the old store and it took me a minute to find the evening paper in the dark. On fair days it was easy to locate, even at night, for the white bundle with its green rubber band stood out plainly against the fescue and crabgrass, but on days when it rained and the paper was tucked inside a waxed brown paper bag I had to look harder to pick it up against the dark ground. Finally, I spied it (nearer the road than usual), and as I gathered up the bundle I could not resist slipping out it's contents to take a peek at the headline.

There it was, in bold print across the top:

DOREEN HEADS FOR COAST

I refolded the paper and slid it back into the brown sleeve of a bag, knowing even though my grandfather would likely say nothing about it, the old man liked being the first one to open the newspaper. Turning to go back into the house, I don't know if it was just because I'd suddenly turned towards the east or if the wind had just coincidentally picked that very moment to gust, but the effect was the same, and a new one for me. I was thrown off balance by the force of the gust and for a fraction of a second I thought I might be blown down completely by the gale. But I caught myself and leaned into it, my awkward posture reminding me of that poor soul Mick had talked about seeing on television once. Just before I entered the house I scolded myself for doubting Doreen's fury. And she wasn't even here yet.

"Here's the paper, Pawpaw," I said, handing my grandfather the brown bundle.

"Thanks, bubba.," the old man said, removing the newspaper from it's crinkly cocoon. "Let's see what it says here about this storm....yeh here it is... 'Doreen Heads For Coast'. Boy that headline man down there's got a wonderful grasp of the obvious, wouldn't you say?"

"Yes sir. That says it all," I answered.

"Yeh, says it all,"my grandfather said lowly, puffing on his pipe.

The old man sat down in his chair and I took a seat on the sofa against the wall. In the center of the room Grayson sat in his chair watching television. Leah was still in the kitchen. I intentionally waited several minutes, giving my grandfather some time to digest the front page before I asked my question.

"Dont'cha think I oughta' go check on *Melinda*... maybe bring 'er up on shore a little farther. Maybe tie 'er to a tree or something?" I asked my grandfather in a low voice.

"Good thinking, bubba," 'the old man said lighting a match and taking exaggerated puffs on his pipe in an effort to get it lit. "Only problem is you shoulda' thought of it earlier," the old man said looking at me over the top of his reading glasses and shaking the match out.

"Yes sir, I know. It's just that I've had so much to do and then we went to Murph..."

"Don't hand me that. You didn't have to come up there with me. You shoulda' gone and tied that boat up, instead. Now it's getting dark, and..."

Leah, an apron at her waist now, walked back into the living room and spoke, interrupting her father:

"That's right, young man. It's pitch black out there and you are not leaving the house now with this wind picking up like it is."

"Well I've gotta' do something about it. I can't just leave her out in this. What if she gets blown out into the creek?"

"You should'a thought about that earlier, Marty. You really think I'd let you go out in this now?"

Silence. I thought furiously about how I might persuade my mother to let me go, but no valid argument came to mind. Even if I could persuade my grandfather into taking me in his car to the end of the road there was still almost a half-mile stretch of road before you reached the loose sand path that would have to be traveled on by foot. Even if I cut through the forest of live oaks and scrub pines it was still a good long ways to go. Especially in the dark.

"Don't ask again, Marty. You can check on that boat tomorrow, after this has all blown over."

"Yeah, if she's still there," I answered back in a soft whisper, just audible enough for my mother to know I had said something without letting her know what it was I had said. It was a way to get the last word, even if I was not going to get my way.

"How does breakfast... ham and eggs sound to everyone?"

"Sounds great, dear," the old man said

"How many eggs do you want."

"Two's fine, thank you."

"Two, too," Grayson answered, without looking away from the television. Lassie, was on. Along with the collie there was an increasing amount of snow on the screen now, too.

"Same here, I reckon," I said.

"All right, and I'll put a pot of coffee on for us Dad," Leah said.

"That'd be great, hon," the old man replied, lowering his paper and glancing over its top for a second to look at his daughter.

*   *   *

Leah returned to the kitchen and Grayson went back to watching the television which no one else was paying any attention to except the every fifteen or twenty minutes when the local station broke in to give an update on Doreen– her whereabouts and her likely path over the next several hours. Then the screen would flash a listing of area schools up and operating as emergency shelters. I watched, looking for Oceanside, but it wasn't on the list. Three blocks from the ocean didn't exactly qualify as a place to seek shelter, I reckoned. As I sat on the couch watching my brother watch television and my grandfather read the paper, it began to dawn on me that after the initial hoopla and excitement, and after getting as prepared as you could get, waiting on a hurricane was boring business. Several minutes went by and I sat there still brooding over the prospects of losing *Melinda* when my grandfather, lowering his newspaper again, leaned over and addressed me in a hushed tone.

"Why don't you call Johnson's and see if someone... maybe Fred, will go down and tie the boat up for you? I bet he might."

"That's a great idea, Pawpaw. Why didn't I think of it?"

"'Cause you got too discombobulated, that's why. Rule Number One: Always keep your cool."

"Yes sir," I said sheepishly. I stood up and headed down the dark narrow hallway towards the phone.

*   *   *

He sounded friendly enough on the phone, but I could tell right away Mr. Johnson was not gonna' be receptive towards performing any task that entailed* going outside.

"I don't know, Marty. I'd like to help you out, but I just sent Fred home about twenty minutes ago. We've been tying up boats and anything else that'd blow away all day and he was beat... plumb tuckered out. It's gettin' nasty out there. If it weren't for this cane I'd go down there myself. Wish you'da called earlier... when it was still light out."

"Thanks anyway, Mr. Johnson," I said.

"Try not to worry, son. It'll probably be all right; but if she's missing you come see me and we'll find her."

"Thanks," I said

"No problem. Ya'll sticking around?"

"Yes sir."

"Your grandfather in town?"

"Yes sir."

"Good. Tell your mother and the old codger I said hello."

After I hung up the phone I went back into the living room where the old man now stood in front of the television set. On the other side of Grayson stood Leah, also watching the boxy set intently.

".... our latest report from the National Hurricane Center indicates Hurricane Doreen is once again gaining strength. The big news though is this storm has shifted it's path westerly and forecasters at the National Hurricane Center in Miami are calling for Doreen to make landfall just north of Fernindina Beach near the Florida-Georgia border in the early hours tomorrow morning. Stay tuned to WRTV for additional reports on Doreen on the quarter hour. We now return to our regular broadcast."

"I knew we should have gone." Grayson spoke lowly.

"Oh, Lord's sake, boy. Don't you ever get tired of being right all the time?" the old man said. I couldn't tell at first if my grandfather was kidding, but soon I saw the corners of his mouth rise and I knew then he was putting Grayson on.

"Somebody around here needs to have some sense." Grayson said back to my grandfather, all the while looking over at me.

Leah finished cooking just in the nick, for by the time we all got to the table– before my grandfather could even offer up grace –the lights went out.

Suddenly, the Crane's of Oceanside, along with one grand-father, were seated in darkness.

*　　　*　　　*

With no lights and television it seemed the wind was blowing harder than just a second ago. I knew this probably wasn't the case, but while we were all seated around the hushed table with the television off the only sound to be heard was the wind. This was the first time I'd clearly heard the howling low whistle made by the gusts blowing through the front door's weather-stripping– a thin strip of brass flashing tacked to the inside doorjamb designed to keep blowing rain and wind from seeping through the slender space still left when the door was closed. I had never heard it protest so loudly before, and in the dark the effect was down-right eerie. Not a continuous sound, still it was grating as it took turns getting louder, then quieter, depending on the direction and velocity of the blasts. While the television was on the whining had been relegated to being nothing more than background noise and as such was bearable. But against a backdrop of silence the sound was soon maddening. Something would have to be done about this, I thought.

*　　　*　　　*

Doreen kept coming at us. In fact, with each pronouncement from the National Weather Service it seemed more like she had her eye directly on Oceanside and was curving her path to end up right there. She was moving slower now- around nine miles per hour -but her winds had picked up to about 125 mph. That fast was hard to imagine. I'd ridden with Rad once when my uncle had gotten the Mercury up to about 95 back on the old St. Augustine road and that was fast. I knew because I'd stuck my hand out the open window and had tried to hold my palm flat-out against the wind, but as hard as I tried I couldn't do it; couldn't hold it steady at 95 and that was still thirty miles an hour less than this hurricane! It made sense now, what Coach

Sutter had told our class. About how they removed all the coconuts from the trees down in Miami during hurricane season. If a baseball at 90 miles an hour could hurt you, just think what sorta' havoc a coconut doing 125 could wreak.

When the old man had loaded new batteries into the radio and turned it on the first thing we heard was a report of conditions at American Beach. That was just a scant twenty miles to the North, but it was the latest pin-pointed location of predicted landfall. Already, winds there had been clocked at sixty-five miles an hour and Doreen was still a good eighty-five miles off the coast. I did some quick math and decided at her present rate it would take her nearly nine hours before she hit land. That would put her arrival at 6:00 A.M.– the same time I was normally getting Grayson dressed and in his chair, ready for the bus.

It was like a holiday in itself, looking forward to not having to perform that little task in the morning. But there was still one thing nagging at me and which kept me from taking the full measure of delight in this reprieve. I was still worried about *Melinda*.

*　　*　　*

Though I gave it a good try, by 10:30 I knew there was no way I would be able to stay up all night. I really thought it would be more exciting than this. I helped Grayson go to bed around 10:00 and Leah had gone to her room shortly after, leaving only my grandfather and I to fill up the night.

We sat at the table, whose surface (along with the close-by walls), was dimly lit by the kerosene lantern the old man had set up just after the lights went out. To preserve the batteries my grandfather had said we shouldn't listen to the radio steadily; instead, we'd turn it on every twenty minutes or so to catch updates. The wind was howling with about the same intensity it had for the past several hours. Maybe it had picked up a little, but any increase had been so incremental* and the blowing had been so constant for so long neither I nor my grandfather were alarmed now by the howl. Funny what you can get used to, I thought staring at the flickering tongue of light inside the lantern's clear chimney. Any excitement I felt came more from the change in routine, the fact that our usual schedule was broken. For that we could certainly thank Doreen. Earlier, Leah had stuffed some old towels into the spaces between the front door and it's jamb and that had done the trick, silencing the shrill whistle of the weatherstripping. Of course, the towels were all sopping wet now, but no one was figuring on opening the door anytime soon and so we let it be. There would be plenty of time later to straighten things out.

When the radio wasn't on I found himself getting tired. All this time I had thought a hurricane was the most exciting thing that could ever happen and here I was with my grandfather sitting at the dinner table, eating a bowl of Wheaties, listening to intermittent reports on Doreen (stalled now about forty miles off the coast), and trying hard to stay awake.

"Why don't you get some shut-eye, bubba? She must have hit the doldrums out there. Anything exciting happens, I'll get you up."

"Sounds like a good idea, Pawpaw. I don't know why, but I'm tired," I said, yawning and stretching both my arms over my head.

"Can you find your way back to the room, or do you need the flashlight?" my grandfather asked.

"I can make it," I answered, rising from my chair and heading towards the kitchen sink with my empty bowl and spoon. "What time is it, anyway?"

"Let's see," the old man said sticking his left arm out towards the lantern and turning his wristwatch into the light. "Eleven fifty-five. Go get some sleep. You're not gonna' miss anything. She'll just blow like this for the next few hours. Probably won't get started up good 'til around daybreak," the old man said.

"See ya' a little later," I said, as I headed out from the broad halo of light and into the darkness of the living room and hall towards my room.

*   *   *

All that night and into the next morning the wind howled like a wild banshee. Just what a wild banshee was and exactly what it sounded like I wasn't sure, but I thought it had something to do with a female ghost or spirit, and later, after looking the word up in my Funk & Wagnalls, it seemed the most apt* description for the ferocity of the winds that howled throughout the night and into the morning.

What I did that night could not be called sleep even though I layed in my bed, the top bunk, and closed my eyes. A couple of times I thought I'd finally fallen to sleep, but there would come a loud howl or whistle and suddenly I was awake again. Once, I'd almost fallen off, but the fronds on the big palm in the front yard right in front of my window began rustling so loudly that I was quickly brought back to wakefulness. It was so loud I wondered if there would be anything left of the tree besides a straight trunk when daylight next came. Then I worried some about Jim. Surely, his owner had let him inside. Last but not least, I thought about Dosha Fay, the colored maid Leah sometimes used when the ironing piled up, and her boys. Surely, they had sought refuge.

Despite the persistent loud howling throughout the night at no time did I feel that our house (or any other house in the neighborhood), was truly in jeopardy. In between fits and starts of sleep I wondered about other things, too. Like the shacks and shantys on the other side of Beach Road that made up a good portion of colored town. It would be a miracle if half of these survived.

With all this worrying and wondering the longest I'd been able to sleep was a few minutes, a little before first light, and when I came too this time I knew I'd been in the middle of a dream about *Melinda*. With this knowledge I became anxious, even more than the evening before in Murphy's when I first remembered she wasn't shored up well.

As if her only reason for existing was to heighten my worrying, Doreen blew even harder as I lay in my top bunk worrying about my boat, and when it got to going so hard I didn't think it possible for it to blow any harder, it blew some more. And it kept blowing. Long gusty sheets of wind, one right after another blew through and for the first time I understood about that poor soul Mick had told Davey and I about. Unbelievably, Grayson slept right through this fury. Once or twice during the night he'd moaned like he was having a bad dream, but he never once awakened. I leaned over and peeked through two of the wooden slats of the window's blinds next to my bunk letting in some of the scant little light there was. Gray- that's all I could see. That was all there was to see. I couldn't even see well enough to tell if there was any damage. For all I knew ours could be the only house left standing (I knew that wasn't so), for the wind was blowing the rain so hard and flat against the window that all you could make out was a scene of diffused wet grayness, like I figured it would look if you drove through a rainstorm in a car with no windshield wipers. Becoming somewhat used to the wind and the rain I found myself mesmerized* by the torrent* of water against the panes of glass. After a while it began to slow.

And then it stopped. Just like that.

Just like jet engines suddenly being shut off, the wind and the rain both stopped and it was quiet, quieter than I could ever remember. (*Was it always this quiet or was this some special quiet that only occurred around hurricanes? Could it be I'd finally fallen asleep and was dreaming?)* So strange for it to stop like that. A minute ago it sounded like it would blow forever. I climbed down the bunk's four steps to the floor below and left the room to a sleeping Grayson.

Padding softly down the dark hall to the living room I found my grandfather asleep on the couch, snoring. A thin hooked shawl lay over him. He could not have been that way long, for the kerosene lantern still softly illuminated the kitchen table and there wasn't much of a wick. My guess was my grandfather had only been like this for less than an hour. I thought I might find Leah in the kitchen, but she wasn't up yet, either. I half expected to catch her there in the midst of making coffee, but she wasn't and I knew she must still be in her room. I wasn't about to go back down the hall to see. If she was awake she would soon be in, and if she wasn't I didn't fell any great need to wake her.

Making my way quietly to the kitchen, I picked up the transistor radio, pressing it up against my ear. Pushing up the round serrated knob, I felt a single click and suddenly there was the faint white noise of static. That was strange. I checked the tuner. It was still set at the exact same station we'd been listening to– the same station I'd listened to last night with my grandfather before going to bed. But there was no station there! Just grainy atmospheric noise that sounded like the day looked.

I moved the tuner slowly in one direction and could pick up nothing all the way to the end of the tuner's rotation except once when I thought I'd heard a voice but it was so faint it would not stay in. Then I began back the other way, thumbing the tuner ever so incrementally slowly and again all I could hear was static. Had every radio tower in the state been blown over? Then, when I was almost to the other end where the numbers got higher, at about 1500 KhZ I could suddenly make out a station plainly and my heart gave a quick start. But it was Spanish, spoken so quickly I could barely make out one single word per sentence. Frustrated now, I rapidly tuned all the way back down to the lowest setting and slowly pulled back up again. There! There was something! At about 590 KhZ it was. I heard the faint but definite roar of a lion, or more correctly a tiger, and I knew then I was picking up *The Big Cat,* the best rock n' roll station in Riverville. It was nowhere near it's usual clear signal, but it was all I could get. The longer I listened the more attuned* my ear became and the more I could make out......

"... at four-fifteen this morning. Presently, the eye of Hurricane Doreen is situated directly over Oceanside, Florida on a northwesterly course and is expected to remain heading inland on that course for the next one to two hours. Those residents of Riverville as well as greater Ocean, Nassau and Coastal Counties who have elected not to go to a shelter are strongly urged to stay indoors. Doreen is a Level 4 hurricane with sustained winds clocked as high as 135 miles per hour. Her winds have subsided considerably since reaching land but were clocked at 5:30 A.M.. at the Red Cross Tower at Oceanside at 117 miles per hour. Oceanside police station...er...ah, that is... the police at Oceanside are reporting extensive damage to the boardwalk and pier there and also to businesses and buildings along the First Street area. Stay tuned to 590 for more information on this ......"

So that was it. We were in the eye No wonder. Hell, I should have guessed. It made sense. Coach Sutter had said that it would die down like this, but I'd never guessed he'd meant this quickly.

If we were in the eye that meant I would have time. Only about twenty minutes or so, but if I hurried I could make it. If I hurried I could see *Melinda,* I thought.

I hurried.

*   *   *

Nothing could have prepared me for this. Not even the phrase *extensive damage.* Words on the radio were not nearly descriptive enough for what I now saw as I rode my bike down the road through the dripping wet gray, swerving left and right, dodging the half-a-dozen or so fallen trees I came upon, just on our end of the road!

Like I'd surmised* all the day before, anything that wasn't tied down had indeed been blown to hell and back by Doreen. Lawn chairs, pieces of wood, old tires, a beat-up tricycle, abandoned toys and on and on. Things no one any longer cared for and things folks had hidden away in their yards somewhere and forgotten about were now everywhere. It looked like a scene from some war movie, only it had not been war (unless you considered it a battle between nature and man), and it was not a movie.

Swerving to miss a humongous live oak torn up at the roots, I saw my first downed power line and I got off my bike and left the road, making a wide arc around it all the way over into the Dinsmore's front yard. Only a coupla'–three blocks more now and I would be at the dirt road, and then about a quarter–mile walk down it to the creek.

At first, from the road, the woods looked the same. It was such a tangled, jungly mess in there normally it would be difficult to discern much damage, but after I parked my bike and walked along the sandy wet way for a few minutes it became obvious this place too had been affected. It was different in here now. For one thing it was eerily quiet; so still the rattling rasp of the saw palmettos when I brushed up against some seemed deafening.

Always, when you entered this canopied forest it got dark fast, but even if it was much less sunnier than usual this morning I could see the forest was letting in more light than normal. That could only mean one thing– fewer trees.

About halfway through the woods I came to the spot in the road where it forked. To get to *Melinda* I would need to bear right, but I took the left fork instead which I followed for twenty yards or so. I had to take a moment to see if The Tree was still there.

The Tree was an incredibly straight, incredibly tall, oak which kids had been climbing and congregating around for generations. Evidence of this was incised in its massive trunk. Names and initials of other kids (those known and those long for- gotten), could be found carved in The Tree. Some of the names were worn and barely discernible while others looked newer. I had never carved my initials, or anything else, in The Tree. It didn't seem right. Despite it's size, to me the giant still seemed defenseless. utterly at the mercy of any idiot with a knife.

Through the years there had been many attempts to build forts or landings in The Tree as evidenced by an occasional two by four and the likes scattered up among it's dark thick branches, but only one, about thirty feet up, was still operational. It was the one Davey, Mick and I had built over several winter weekends two years before, in the very depths of our war affliction. It was a great spot to occupy during a BB gun war and was considered prime real estate during such skirmishes. Reticent* to take a knife to The Tree, I felt no such qualms against building a retreat in it; somehow, that was fair.

I continued on down the path crawling once over another large tree whose dark thick limbs reached high into the air (another Doreen victim, I thought), and finally coming to the spot where The Tree should be, it was not. It had disappeared–vanished. But how could it? Something as big as The Tree did not just vanish. I kept looking. Why couldn't I see it? There was just no sign of it at all. And then it hit me. I had just climbed over it! *The Tree was down.*

The tallest tree in the woods– the very same one Duane Dinsmore had climbed to the very top of only last summer where he swore to God he could see the Atlantic Coastline Building in Riverville some seventeen miles to the west –was no longer. Unbelievable! I had a great and sudden urge to tell someone (Mick and Davey, of course), this awful news, that The Tree had fallen. But it would have to wait. First I had to run check on *Melinda.* There was something about The Tree's demise that lent my trip more urgency.

Before I'd seen this I had great faith and hope *Melinda* would be safely on shore, but now I knew anything was possible.

I retraced my steps back to the fork and taking the other path this time ran as fast as I could. It was only about a quarter of a mile further and as I ran I prayed; prayed to God and Jesus and Jesus's mother that I would find *Melinda,* find her safe where I had left her last, and I had to slow down twice to climb across two good-sized pine trees that Doreen fell also and which lay together now across the path, and after I scaled the second tree I saw something I had not been ready to see. Not yet. *The creek.*

It couldn't be. I was certain, absolutely positive, I had another fifty or sixty yards to go before the shore. There was the big clump of saw palmettos on my right, the same clump I had dodged for years– of this there was no doubt. The creek was supposed to be another half a football field down the path from this clump, not right up here next to it!

I looked. I looked along the water's edge down to the left and back down to the right, but *Melinda* wasn't on shore. Shore... *what* shore? *Hell, there was no shore!*

Johnson's Fish Camp was still perched down there on the right. Good... that was reassuring... there was still some order left in this world. But a second, harder look revealed the creek had not missed claiming the camp by much. The deck of Mr. Johnson's screen porch, where the docks began, was under a good three feet of black creekwater. Seeing this sight, I knew.

I was seldom certain about anything, but of this bad news there was no doubt.

Melinda was gone.

Aftermath

Of course, I wasn't the only soul at Oceanside to suffer loss from Doreen. To some extent Aunt Bertie, and to a larger degree the Arnett's, were both greatly affected by the hurricane. Bertie had lost a job, but the Arnett's had lost Arnett's.

The bakery– built to withstand the type of weather expected in an area known to host frequent fierce northeasters as well as the occasional hurricane –was no match this time for the prolonged gusts of high winds and tremendous surge of water which broke over the beach and seawall scattering the heavy sharp–edged boulders of angular granite placed to fortify the sagging wall. Not only the bakery but the bandshell directly across the street was felled, too, by Doreen.

It would be a long while before any Oceansider danced under the stars within the sound of the surf or partook of fresh baked-goods anywhere near First Street.

The bakery was down, and the bandshell was down, but also the bus station, as well as the pharmacy where Leah had her many and frequent prescriptions filled. Plus the little alley-wide Mexican Chili Parlor, and the Surf Maiden Restaurant, "*Home of the Rebel Burger*". Dozens of other small businesses up along First Street were either totally obliterated or injured beyond repair.

Aunt Bertie, being Aunt Bertie, took her newly acquired loss of employment with a great deal of grace.

"Oh, hell.," she said. "I was getting tired of toting donuts and coffee to those old coots, anyhow. Besides, the only one's tipped worth a damn were *The Men of Corinth* and it won't be long before they'll all be fixin' to croak. Good time to move on."

There was much speculation the first coupla' days after Doreen's departure that maybe Mrs. Arnett would rebuild; either right there at the same spot or a little farther back, and perhaps the old lady had considered such a move, but if she had she never let on to anyone who was any good at spreading the rumor. No; as difficult as it would be to let go it was a good time to call it quits, she told her former employees. Besides, she had no sons. There were three daughters, all graduated from Oceanside High School and living in other cities now (either finishing up college or working), and none of them had expressed the slightest interest in rebuilding and then running a bakery. Hence, so was fostered the regrettable demise of what most everyone at Oceanside considered not only a landmark in their very midst, but also the best dang source of salt-rising bread ever put on God's green earth... or at least Northeast Florida.

While I wouldn't regret losing my occasional job of cleaning the bakery's sea-fogged windows, I thought, there was no doubt that the donuts, eclairs, and other baked delights that Arnett's had produced here for five decades would be sorely missed. Not just by Grayson and me but by hundreds of others as well; all the other customers who had ever been attracted for nearly fifty years to the double doors right on the corner of First Street and Beach Road. Why, sometimes just the smell wafting out of that building in the early morning hours was enough to sustain a soul, giving him that little extra incentive to face another day.

As you went further back from the beach and First Street Doreen's effects became less evident. That didn't mean there was no damage back here, but only that it was not injury caused directly by the Ocean. Starting several blocks back from Third Street the damage and havoc was wreaked by Doreen herself– by her persistent and mighty winds. Roofs were blown off of houses and the contents therein left exposed all the way up to the sky. Trees were uprooted, trash and debris– anything that had not been tied down securely –was blown and scattered any and everywhere. Power lines and poles as well as telephone lines and their poles were down all over Oceanside and though Florida Power and Light (with the help of crews from neighboring Georgia Power), had most electrical service back up within days, it would prove weeks before the telephone company straightened out the multiple messes they confronted.

*   *   *

During the weeks following Doreen's visit you never knew when you picked up the phone what you might hear. Sometimes there was a dial-tone, but more often than not there would be voices. And lots of them. Several conversations could often be going on at once and they would fade in and out over the course of a few minutes while you held the receiver, trying to get through. During that time it was like all of Oceanside was one big party-line. Rumors flew even more wildly than usual, some the product of legitimate gossip, but others the result of combinations of conversations; little bits and pieces of information picked up from different discussions and mixed all together. It was a recipe for social disaster caused by a natural disaster and it would be months (in some cases years), before some of the rumors and misunderstandings spawned by Doreen were straightened out. It was as though these many rumors and bits of misinformation were the last lingering vestiges* of the hurricane. A little something she'd left in her wake for the good citizens of Oceanside. Verbal and emotional tornadoes, they were spawned and sent hurtling willy-nilly throughout the community, the unseen remnants left by the long departed storm. Ultimately, it meant that long after the physical reconstruction was complete there was still much psychic* reconstruction to attend to.

The one man-made structure around Oceanside that more than any other piece of construction represented the Beach way of life fell victim to Doreen, also. The pier had finally been swept away by Doreen leaving only a scattering of telephone poles sticking out from the water, and I pondered this, too. For weeks– up and down the beach –there was more than ample driftwood along the beach.

I never really cared for pier fishing. It was the only sorta' fishing I couldn't get excited about. Some of my friends, Glenn Allen in particular and also Hank Wooley along with his father (when sober), loved it though, and they went up there from time to time (always when something like a pompano or bluefish run was on), but it didn't interest me any. I just couldn't catch fire about the pier. I thought about my grandfather's friend, Mr. Emerson's, invitation to the old man and I to come up there with him sometime and wet a line. That was now officially one invite I didn't need to worry about, I thought, when I first saw what was left of the rambling, old, wooden structure– the same edifice* Grayson and I had stood directly under just a few weeks before. Before Doreen.

That few weeks seemed like a real long time ago, now. We watched the pier sway back and forth back then for a good coupla' minutes as it was getting pummeled by an angry winter ocean and I recalled how at the time I wondered what it would take to bring the whole thing down. Now I knew.

Just a little old gal by the name of Doreen passing on through.

If it can be said that I am on shaky ground anywhere the story coming up would be at about that spot, I reckon. Writing stories about my brother and even my friends I have no trouble with, but when it comes to writing about a whole other segment of the population who seem to live and run their lives in a whole other town (if not whole other planet), well then, suddenly things are lots different.

Who I am talking about, of course, is the colored, or, as some folks say, negro population of Oceanside. For the most part I'd never had much contact with these folks, other than to see Dosha from time to time. She's the girl, or woman rather, who does our ironing sometimes– when it starts piling up on Leah and she gets behind. One afternoon in Dosha's presence and you will be caught up quick, believe me. Not only on the ironing, but on all you'd ever want to know about colored town. She has got to be queen of the gossip world there, of that there is no doubt. Of course, there is also Big George of whom you will hear more about later.

Still, there is this problem of not being around these folks much, but trying anyways to write about them. This is not altogether true. I reckon I see a fair bit of them. They are all over the southside of the Beach, down below the pier, (or where it used to be), but what I reckon I mean is at the time I wrote this story, I (as well as most other white folks at Oceanside), usually don't come into contact with them much. That's more like it.

Also, there is the problem of what you think about them which involves trying to figure out what they think about you. Like most boys my age I grew up hearing colored folks referred to as niggers so often you begin to not think about it all that much. I've always known it is no term of endearment•, it doesn't take an Einstein to figure that much out, but it is so common after hearing it time and again it sorta' loses it's punch. Anyways, after a while it didn't seem all that awful. That's how I felt about it until that summer afternoon Gerald Rickenbacher called me one– a nigger, and I gotta' say it stung. It wasn't only the word but the venomness he used saying it (spitting like he did), that made it such an ugly affair. Everytime I hear someone say it now I reckon I feel a little different about it.

To her credit, Leah will not stand for it. She detests the word. I remember one night we were eating supper and talking and the old man said that word, or something that sounded awfully close to it, and she had a fit. It was like it'd hurt her ears the strong reaction she had. It was one of only two or three times I have ever heard her jump the old man. He came right back at her though, saying:

"That's not what I said. What I said was nigra'!"

"That's hardly different, Dad."

"It's lots different daughter... lots. And don't be telling me what I can or cannot say ......"

"I will when it's being said in my house!"

Well, like always, they went on. Finally, the old man let in a little and apologized some, as much as he'd ever apologize, which entailed telling her she just misunderstood him and about that he was truly sorry.

The little bit in here about Cecil is true, true, true. I have only changed his name because to tell you the truth I forgot it. Although that could very well be it– or something close. I will never forget him, though.

Funny, how even at the age we were back then, which was around eight, you can tell just what a person is like and what they will continue to be like from then on. There was a peacefulness and a kind of honor to him that I had never experienced before in anyone my own age, much less an adult. Obviously, it has got to be something you are created with... a direct gift from God.

P.S. – Leah came by today, it being Sunday (or Family Day... ha, ha), and I wished she hadn't. If you read the story titled Blue Star Highway you can guess what I'm talking about. As plastered as she was no one else acted like they noticed. Maybe what they were all doing was pretending not to notice. Which is fine with me. I really don't care anymore. I just hope she got back home in one piece.

Colored Town

Everyone, even a first time visitor to the Beach, could always tell where the white part of Oceanside ended and the black part began. It was easy. All you needed to do was drive south of the demarcation* line, Beach Road, where the paved roads ended and the dirt roads began. That's how you knew you were entering Colored Town.

That's how everyone (i.e. white people), usually referred to it: Colored Town. Occasionally some folks called it Little Africa (or used other, uglier terms), but generally it was spoken of as just colored town as though those not white were so segregated from the rest– the main part of the little Beachtown –that they were not even figured part of the same community. Colored town reflected this by consigning* to the non-whites their own little name for that part of the Beach in which they stayed.

Those who changed tires in the service stations...washed and ironed clothes in countless white homes... cleaned the bathrooms and mowed the grass of the motels along the beachfront... cleaned fish... shucked oysters... cooked in the kitchens of the handful of restaurants scattered around and picked up the garbage all over were definitely relegated* to a defined and isolated part of the Beach. It was like the row of shops and buildings along the southside of Beach Road were really just a Hollywood prop, built to disguise the ugliness and deprivation* of the community situated directly behind them.

Behind the tall bowling alley, behind the new Winn-Dixie, behind the row of service stations– that's where colored town was. Not that there weren't some nice homes back here, because some of the area's folks still managed to keep up a nice yard and a neatly painted house. A coupla' colored town's dirt streets had even been covered over with oyster shells.

There were parts of colored town that almost looked quaint. When you got away from the streets of dark sandy dirt (which so readily turned to mud when mixed with even the lightest rain), and drove on one of the few crunchy streets with it's oystershell covering, and passed by a couple of those brightly painted houses (some even with a smattering of gingerbread decoration on their front porches), why, it was almost like you were in some other country. Some festive and tropical place like Bermuda or

Jamaica. Of course, you weren't going to see any colored folks actually on the beach. That is, besides the prisoners on Monday mornings picking up trash.

About the only reason for any of the white residents of Oceanside to go into colored town (besides the police who were always there), was to either pick up a yard man or, more commonly, one of the black ladies who worked as a domestic. Hardly anyone ever used the term domestic, though, for it implied a permanent full-time position. Except for the real nice homes (like down below Ponte Vedra and around Seminole), which were able to afford full-time help, for the most part the men and women of colored town had to pick up any work they could sorta' catch as catch can. A day of ironing here, another day of cleaning house there. Maybe another day during the weekend cooking for some big party at one of the large houses right on the beach in Ponte Vedra. This established a loose network of hirers and hirees which meant that eventually everyone, on both sides of Beach Road, came to know everyone else.

Every once in a while I went with Leah into colored town to pick up the woman who did our ironing– Dosha Fay. Dosha was in her mid to late twenties; maybe a little younger or a little older, it was hard to say. It was especially hard for me to tell, for to me she wore that nearly featureless expression much of the time that you noticed on the faces of many of the colored people you came into contact with.

I had thought about this a lot and concluded that here was the final and ultimate barrier that some of colored town's inhabitants used to resist being taken over completely by the white society and it's strictures* they were unrelentlessly forced to obey and comply with. It was a way for them to keep something of themselves to themselves, since it seemed that white people were always there to use them– and the only thing they had of any negotiable value –their labor, to full advantage. It was like if you didn't show too much by way of expression then you would not have to fear the white people attempting to take that away from you, too. *If you didn't show too much, they wouldn't know too much.*

It was like only by becoming expressionless was there a way for the colored residents of Oceanside to literally save face. That was the real tragedy of this situation; the fact that some of the people of colored town thought they could safely hide behind an expressionless facade*, for even though it worked at some very basic level, the asking price was always way too high.

*   *   *

I stood with Leah at the door on the side of the little wooden house barely much more than a shack, and as we waited there outside in the freezing rain I couldn't help but notice the tired-looking structure before us seemed to be leaning. Several panes of glass in the window by the door were missing and had been replaced with pieces of makeshift cardboard to keep out the cold. Clearly, this was not one of colored town's quainter houses. Even a coat of bright paint wouldn't do much for this place, I thought. In fact, the house looked so old and run down that the weight of a coat of paint might be the proverbial straw that broke the camel's back. It was funny how a word you'd just learned so often sprang up right after you had learned it, conveniently ready to be used. Standing under the shack's narrow eaves with my mother in a futile* effort to keep from getting any wetter, I thought of a new word I'd learned just last week in Mrs. Johns class– dilapidated.

Leah knocked on the door again and after a few seconds a little boy, clad only in baggy underwear and a tight knit shirt that barely covered the bulge of his fat tummy, opened the door slowly. At first it was too dark inside to see well, but after a few moments (our eyes having a chance to adjust to the dim surroundings), I could better see the messy interior of the precarious* structure. The only light came from a heater in the middle of the room and the air in the small shack was tinged with the odor of kerosene. Dosha was scurrying about trying to get ready, scolding the three boys all the while, warning them to be good and not to mess up the house while she was gone. I found this warning perplexing. No matter what the three of them did to the inside of this place what difference would it make? The most they could possibly do was move the mess from one part of the crude little cabin to another. Unless Dosha knew exactly where everything was among this disarray how was she ever going to be able to tell if they had 'messed the place up'?

When the three of us– Leah, Dosha and I–gathered at the door to leave, the two smallest boys began wailing while their older brother, who looked to be about eight, stood behind them with a dark hand on each of their shoulders. Dosha turned and gave them all a quick look that left no room for disobeyance, and for one brief moment her sphinx–like facade* dissolved as she reprimanded her children.

'Ya'll young'uns hush, now. You gram-mah' be 'long directly.'

To my amazement the boys did just that. As Leah started the Ford and we drove off the smallest boy (the one who had answered the door earlier), peered out the window through one of the remaining panes of glass. He was searching the departing car, I knew, for his mother's face. Dosha, in a faded, worn, blue raincoat with her standard red kerchief covering her head, sat in the backseat of the car and looked straight ahead, her expression returned to a blank stare. Once again, I felt like I didn't have a clue of what she was thinking about as Dosha's face took on an impenetrable* glare.

By the time we reached Penner, passed the Pak n'Sak, and arrived back at our neighborhood the rain had begun to lighten up some and I noticed that I looked at the houses on our street, especially my own, in a different light. True, the sun was beginning to break through the clouds so you'd expect things to look a little rosier now, but it was more than that. P.O.V., or Point of View as Mick would say. That's what it all boiled down to. If we had just come back from Ponte Vedra or Seminole I would probably be looking at this neighborhood with my usual gaze of disinterest, but right now things around here looked pretty darn good. Maybe some of the houses could stand a coat of paint, but none of them were in any danger of falling down, and everyone around here had grass and a curb. The things you took for granted sometimes.

The thing I noticed most (and here was the thing, ironically, that I most often cursed during the long hot summers at the Beach), was the fact that other than Sunset most of the neighborhood's streets were paved. I couldn't imagine what it would be like to have to push my brother's chair through a neighborhood of dirt roads like the ones in colored town. Boy, the things you took for granted sometimes.

*   *   *

"I sure is glad you 'izzen no police boy no mo'. 'Dem pants an' 'dat shirt sho'nuf wuz sumpin to rassil wid'."

Dosha referred to the 100% cotton khaki shirt and pants I'd worn every day of the school year during the sixth grade and my stint in the schoolboy patrol. She had discovered back then– the first time she called me a police boy –that it elicited a howl of delight from Grayson and I both, and eversince then she had tried to throw the phrase in at least once whenever she was over to iron. Of course, Grayson had found a way to capitalize on Dosha's inadvertent guffaw and during that entire school year whenever the two of us were bickering or fighting over something he always held the ace card in the name-calling department and would play it at just the right moment by calling me a *'police boy'*. Somehow, Grayson had a way of uttering this that evoked an image directly at odds with the one I imagined for myself. But two years had passed so it seemed like ancient history to us now. Accordingly, Dosha was not able to get much of a reaction from either of us with the police boy reference these days.

"I had the durnest time 'wid 'dem pants. Dey 'wuz like cardboard. 'Sho 'nuf glad you ain't no *police boy* no 'mo."

Neither of us said anything.

Dosha was ironing and had gotten down to the pile of sheets and pillow-cases which were easy as a very light pressing was all that was necessary to make them relax.

"Grayson, how you liking school 'dis year?"

"Huh? What's that Dosha?" Grayson's concentration was devoted to Saturday morning cartoons and he had failed to hear all of Dosha's question.

"I said how you like 'de schoolhouse you goin' to. Pay 'tenshun boy." This mock reprimand managed to elicit a response and Grayson and I both laughed at Dosha's command as she stared straight at Grayson with one hand on her hip while the other still held the iron.

"It's okay, I guess," Grayson chuckled, though still largely glued to the television set.

"I put a brand on you butt if you don' quit 'norin me, boy. What so funny 'bout 'dat cat chasin 'dat mouse anyhow? 'Dat ain't funny. Come to my house an I sho' you 'da real thing. Ain't no laffin' den. I don' like no mices. No way, no how."

"You don't like Tom and Jerry, Dosha? Everybody likes Tom and Jerry," Grayson said.

"Not if dey gotta' live wid' the real Tom an de' real Gary, whatever dat mice one's name is, dey don't. Uh, uh, no way. I hate's dem' mices, I dun' told you dat."

"Yeah, but this is just a cartoon," Grayson said.

"I don' care. He still a mouse, cartoon or no cartoon. Dey ain't good for 'nuttin, 'cept puttin' a hole in a flour bag, maybe. Uh-uh. Don' let me see no cartoon mice in my house. I gotta' broom dat'll whomp de' daylights right outta' him. Sho 'nuff."

"Oh, you wouldn't hurt a poor little mouse, Dosha. You're just saying that. Look at how cute he is." I pointed to the television screen and it's frantic goings–on.

"Oh yes I wud', mister Motty. Truss me. I put him down jus' like I duz wid' da' rest of 'em."

"We oughta' call the S.P.C.A. on you Dosha. You hurtin' dem' poor little mices," I said.

"You do dat'. 'Dey say da' same thing I is. Ain't nobody like dem' mices."

"Who don't like 'dem mices?" The old man emerged from the back room and was now entering the living room area where Grayson, Dosha and I were.

"Why hallo 'dere mista' Ed! How you doin'?"

"Just fine Dosha, just fine. How ya'll gettin' along?"

"We's gettin along jus' fine too, mista' Ed... jus' fine."

"How's ol' Redfish?" my grandfather asked.

"Still 'onery like always. We don't see him much, but he's a workin' man so I can't talk too bad 'bout him."

"He always was a good working man. Wear out two mules and an axe-handle before noon when he gets going, that's for sure. It's sure good to see you, Dosha. Tell Redfish hello for me when you see him"

"I will, mista' Ed. I'll do that very thing."

"Marty, turn off that idiot box when them dad-blamed cartoons are over and ya'll can go up to Murphy's with me... if you want."

"Yeh, Pawpaw!" we both exclaimed.

"Shoot, I'll turn it off now," I added.

"Ya'll need anything from the store Dosha?" the old man asked.

"I sho' would like it if you could bring me back a cold co-cola mista' Ed. It sho' nuff hot standing over dis' here iron."

"You keep drinkin' them sody pops, it's gonna rot your teeth out," the old man said.

"Shoot, mista' Ed, I ain't never had one little cavity all my live-long days. Dey's good for ya'... 'de pause 'dat re-freshes'. Dey gets my blood goin'." Dosha turned from the ironing board and leaned over to pick up her large purse from beside the chair I'd been sitting in.

"No problem... I gotcha' covered," the old man told Dosha.

"Thank you kindly, mista' Ed. Thank ya kindly." Dosha's broad black face flattened even more and she showed a mouthful of perfectly white teeth (save for one large gold tooth up front), as she smiled at the old man.

"You sure them pearly whites are all yours."

"Every single one. I wuz born wid every tooth you lookin' at."

"That's funny. I ain't ever known anyone that was born with a gold tooth before." the old man said, smiling.

"Ha, ha!" Dosha let out a big round laugh. "You get outa' here mista' Ed. You sumpin' else... you know that? You sumpin' else."

*   *   *

I loaded Grayson into the front seat of my grandfather's car and instead of putting his folded up wheelchair in the trunk, I fit it into the spacious leg area behind the front seat. Then I walked all the way around to the other side of the mammoth vehicle and got in the back, directly behind my grandfather. As always, the inside of the car smelled like the old man's pipe. I liked the smell, always had and always would, I knew.

As we turned onto Fifteenth Avenue and headed east towards First Street and Murphy's, I looked in the rearview mirror at my face. I liked this mirror. I had seen my face reflected here many times before, and was always glad with the way I looked in it. Something about the glass (it was smoked or something), that made you look tan no matter what time of year it was, not like the mirror in our bathroom which did nothing of the sort to hide the numerous pimples and blemishes I was sporting more and more lately. I looked away for a second, not wanting to get caught by my grandfather looking at myself too long. Stealing one more look, it was one look too many, for the old man locked eyes with me in the mirror the second I focused in.

"Don't worry boy, you're looking pretty. Ha, ha." It was a good natured laugh the old man let out. "What's up, got a hot date tonight?" the old man asked still looking, by way of the mirror, to the backseat.

"Not tonight, Pawpaw," I answered back, laughing a little also, in spite of myself.

"Not any night in this lifetime," Grayson said from his side of the front seat.

"No comments from the peanut gallery," I answered, kicking the back of Grayson's seat.

"Truth hurts, huh?" Grayson said. I could tell from the tone in his voice he was beginning to get a little riled up.

"All right, that's enough. No bickering in the car." The old man spoke, turning serious all of a sudden. All three of us were silent for the next minute or so. Then I asked:

"Who's Redfish, Pawpaw?"

"Who?" the old man asked back.

"Redfish. You told Dosha to tell him hello."

"Oh, Redfish... yeh. I never did know what his real name is, but he sure came by that nickname honest enough. He's got the reputation of catching the biggest red drum out of the river anyone'd ever seen around here when he was just a boy. Folks said it weighed over forty pounds. Can you imagine?"

"What! Are you kiddin'?" I asked.

"I swear it. That ain't the best part. They say he caught it on a cane pole." the old man said.

"Oh, come on now!" I said incredulously*.

"No, I swear it. I don't make this stuff up. I'm just reporting the story the way I heard it. Everybody knows about Redfish. He helped me dig some postholes over near Live Oak once years ago when I was running some fence for some folks. Strong fella'. Do the work of two men. While the rest of us were all struggling with eighty pound bags of concrete he was totin' two on his shoulder all day long like they was nothin'."

"Well, how does Dosha know him?" I asked.

"He's ... uh... Dosha's husband... sorta'."

"Sorta'?"

"Well, he's the children's father, put it that way. I don't think they're rightly married, though. Colored are like that sometimes."

"Oh," I said, recalling the little boy who'd looked at us from the broken window earlier that very morning. The boy searching for his mother.

*   *   *

The rain had picked up again and as my grandfather pulled into Murphy's parking lot on the side of the old store I wondered for a moment if it was as bad having a father and never seeing him as it was having no father at all. The only way I would ever know the answer to that question would be to talk to Dosha's sons about it and I could not, in my wildest dreams, ever imagine doing that. It just wasn't done. Whites and coloreds did not socialize, at least on that personal kind of level (except for rare occurrences), and I thought about this for a while and tried to think when the reality of it became apparent to me.

Mixed messages. That phrase best described– summed up –how I felt about coloreds and whites together. Back in the sixth grade (when I was in schoolboy patrol), one morning one of my best friends had started reciting a little ditty:

> "Two, four, six, eight -We don't wanta in-te-grate.
> Eight, six, four, two- We don't want no jig-a-boos."

As he walked down the hall carrying the folded American flag my friend sang the song and I had joined in. Thinking back on it, I doubted either of us had even really known what the word *integrate* meant. It was just a funny little rhyme– a funny little song. A *Song of the South*.

I'd never been in a classroom of any sort with colored boys and girls before, but I could remember a time years ago when I thought that maybe somewhere this did happen. In town, at the little sunday school Grayson and I used to attend when our father was still living, I could remember this picture (a drawing really), of black and white children playing together. It seemed so strange to me at the time sitting in that sunday school room listening to Bible stories and seeing on the wall such a scene. Maybe this was a picture of what it was like in heaven, I thought. Or maybe it was the artist's idea of what would happen if everyone believed and took to heart Jesus' teachings. The one thing that really stayed with me about that picture, though, was the back of the head of the little colored boy in the foreground-the boy nearest the viewer. His head looked like it was covered with ants! I knew it sounded dumb, but there was no other way to describe it. The more I studied that picture the more it looked like the boy's head was covered with ants. If that was supposed to be hair it sure as hell had me fooled. Maybe someone had instructed the artist (against his wishes?), to paint such a picture of black and white children playing together and this was his subconscious way of rebelling at the request. Or maybe this was a true effort, the only way the artist knew of depicting a colored person's hair. Who knew? All I knew was the only colored friend I ever had, a little black boy who was the son of Pawpaw's cook down at the grove, well... his hair sure didn't look anything like the boy's in this picture.

I only got together with this boy a coupla' times when visiting my grandfather's house downstate. Cecil... that was his name. Cecil and I enjoyed each others company right from the start, partly because there weren't any other kids around maybe, but I truly believe we liked each other, anyway. The old man lived on about sixty acres of mostly grapefruit and orange trees and as far as I could tell there weren't any other kids anywhere near the place so I was always glad when Cecil was there.

Truth of it was, I'da never had the chance to play with Cecil under normal circumstances, but I didn't even think about such things back then. All I knew was that Cecil was there and he was fun and we really liked each other. Besides, just by his wardrobe I could tell Cecil was not all that different from me, or any other boy in Florida during the summertime, for that matter. He wore a pair of shorts, no shirt and, of course, he was barefoot.

The first smattering that something was amiss with this kinship was one especially hot afternoon when Cecil and I had been running from one adventure to another, climbing the thick dark limbs of the large citrus trees behind Pawpaw's house and playing with my grandfather's kind old boxer, Susie. During those summer visits it was customary for Leah and Maxine, (technically my grandmother since she was Pawpaw's second wife but due to her relative youth and vitality there was nothing grandmotherly about her (unless it counted that she was the kindest person I had ever met), so I just called her Maxine), and I to go for an afternoon swim in the lake behind Pawpaw's house. So it made perfect sense to invite Cecil.

"Hey Cecil, wanna' go swimming with us after lunch?"

"Sure. That'd be great!"

"Marty! Marty, come in here for a minute, will you." I had known instantly by the sound of Leah's voice that something was wrong. My first guess was that it was something Cecil and I had done that morning; what else could it be? We'd had a lot of fun so naturally we must have done something wrong during the course of such a splendid time together. What was truly the matter perplexed me no end though as I stood before my inquisitor, who tried hard to explain.

"I don't think it would be a good idea for Cecil to go swimming with us this afternoon, Marty," Leah said.

"How come?"

"I just don't think it would be such a good idea, that's all. You need to go back outside and tell him. He'll understand."

"Well, why not? I like Cecil. We're having fun together. There's nothing wrong with him, we haven't gotten into trouble once all morning."

"I didn't say there was anything wrong with him, Marty. He's a good boy, but you just do as I say. We"ll talk about it later."

"What? Tell me now. I'll understand, now."

But I never did catch on that day. Eventually, I went back outside and did as she told me. But I made up a little lie also, saying I was being forced to take a nap after lunch and I wasn't exactly sure when we would go swimming– or even if we would that day. Maybe some other time would be better. One thing Leah was right about, though. Cecil did understand. And even though he seemed to take it well, was almost nonchalant about the missed opportunity, still there was just a scant second when I thought I could detect a look of regret on the boy's dusky face. But no tears. Not Cecil, no way.

After that things seemed different. Something had changed. Even though our paths were to cross several more times, it was never the same as it had been before the time I had to dis–invite my one and only colored friend to go swimming.

*   *   *

Lifting Grayson from my grandfather's Imperial, I placed my brother into his chair and then put his board on. Releasing the chair's brakes we were free to roll now and we followed our grandfather along the sidewalk towards the front of the old store.

It was the first time I'd been up here since Doreen's visit and the moment we turned the corner and faced the front of the store I could see the hurricane had left its mark here, too. One of the store's large plate-glass windows had been destroyed, I could tell, for even though there were Christmas decorations around the edge of the window the new glass sported no lettering like the old one had indicating that here was Murphy's. Evidently, no one had called in the sign painter yet.

Not nearly as large as Arnett's windows, still the sheets of glass that graced the front of this store were big. And with no lettering on the new piece you could really tell (even from back here, two blocks from the ocean), how much salt and grime found its way to this place.

Someone would have to clean that new window before the sign painters came in, I thought as I pushed down on the chair's handlebars, lifting it's small front wheels, and my brother, over the threshold and up onto the worn, wooden floor of the dark and musty old store.

Carport Talk

Unlike other polio kids his age my brother did not seem to be getting any better. In fact, if anything his strength was seeming to diminish some the past year. For months Leah was expressing her concern about this to me and Aunt Bertie, out of earshot of Grayson. Finally, in January, after the hoopla of the holidays was over she made arrangements through Dr. Cordray (younger), to take Grayson to University Hospital in Gainesville for a muscle biopsy.

Leah tried to make it sound like a grand adventure but whatever else I could say about him, Grayson had sense enough not to be excited by the upcoming trip.

I tried on a coupla' occasions to bait my brother, but he wasn't buying. The eve of their departure, after the Dick Van Dyke show he asked me to roll him back to our room. Since I had big doings planned also for the next day Leah proclaimed it was bedtime for the both of us. I think Grayson was nervous about the next day, which was understandable.

Laying in the top bunk with my brother already asleep below, I fell asleep wondering about the procedure he was fixing to undergo. What might be learned from it? I knew Grayson was apprehensive* about being cut on, but would never admit this to anyone, especially me. Just before I fell asleep, two words were rattling around my brain that would more than likely comprise Grayson's reply if the subject were even brought up: Bull Honkey!

The next day Grayson and Leah drove off through a foggy Friday morning just before sunrise for the three hour trip south. Grayson's operation was scheduled for two o'clock that afternoon. Supposedly, it was a routine procedure and the yellow confirmation letter that came in the mail and instructed Leah where to go when arriving at the hospital also informed her that it would be necessary for Grayson to stay over one night– for a follow-up examination the next morning. The yellow notice had stayed pinned up next to the calendar for nearly a month.

*   *   *

Pawpaw was there for the weekend to stay with yours truly and the two of us sat out on the carport after supper, the old man in his usual rocker and I sitting across in the matching two-seater. I could tell something was on the old man's mind; that I was in for a speech or story of some kind. And after the long deliberate ritual of packing his pipe and tamping the loose tobacco down into the dark wooden bowl like he liked it, the old man reached down and pulled a strike-anywhere match across the concrete floor of the carport. The wooden stick suddenly erupted into a mini-torch he used to suck fire into the pipe's bowl.

Puffing for several seconds until he was content the mixture was lit, the old man leaned back in the redwood and aluminum rocking chair and spoke:

"Let's talk about bein' stupid for awhile, boy. It's a good night for story swappin' anyhow."

"Okay." Oh boy, I thought, here we go.

"All through your twenties stupid don't matter much 'cause all you're aiming at anyhow is having a good time, and you can do that and still be stupid at the same time; in fact, it helps sometimes. But by your early thirties that's kind of run out and you gotta' start getting serious to some degree. By around forty or so it starts lettin' up some and say mid-forties to fifty it gets even better 'cause by then no matter how stupid you are, even if you're the stupidest person you know, you've learned some things. Maybe the hard way, which if the truth be known is really the only way to learn a thing, anyway. With any luck, one of those things you learn is not to be so hard on yourself. It gets easier, thank goodness, it does get easier."

"I'm not sure I follow you, Pawpaw."

"Reckon you wouldn't right now, boy. Some day you will, though. Hell, you're about at the age where you're sure you're as smart as you'll ever get anyway, so it'll take a while. But later you'll see. Maybe you'll even remember I told you a little about it. Just try and go easy on yourself when the going get's rough, that's all you need to remember. It ain't ever as bad as you think. We humans got a way of complicatin' the hell out of everything and there'll come a time when you think things are so bad there's no way out. That's when you need to quit pushin' and take it easy. Even when things are lookin' bad, even real bad, you never know what the next day might bring."

Jeez, where'd this all come from? Something certainly had gotten into him– the old man –I thought.

"Had two friends who lost everything during the Crash of '29, back when the stock market went to hell in a handbasket. One,

Preston Tucker, lived in Atlanta. Took a real bath, he did. Lost a fortune. Jumped from the tallest building he could find. Seventeen floors high, dead as a doornail, right away. The other fellow, Hector Gomez... we played football together... well ol' Hector was luckier. He had the good fortune to be living in Valdosta at the time and the tallest building over there back then was three stories. So, off ol' Hector goes, drunk as a coot flying through the south Georgia night... leastwise he was tryin' to. Turns out it was a hotel roof he'd jumped from and he landed on top of a big ol' canvas awning, right smack dab over the front door of the place. Luck was with ol' Hector that night, though, 'cause he still managed to break a leg, and... "

"You call that lucky... ?" I said.

"Hush your yap a second, boy, and you'll see. Compound fracture. Nasty break. On crutches six months. He managed to get around okay on those crutches, but they kept sliding out from under him. Had these little tin tips on the ends back then so the wood wouldn't wear away and they could be kind of slippery if you weren't careful. Well, ol' Hector took about all of that slippin' he could stand and finally one day he thought of putting something that wouldn't slip so easy on the end of those crutches and to make a long story short he started playing with the idea and before too long he invented a molded rubber tip for those crutches. Got a patent even and started making the darn things– crutches with rubber tips. Coupla' years later he had twice as much from that invention as he'd lost earlier, and he was doing real work, too... making something. You never know... some life."

"What I'm gettin' at here is sometimes you gotta' step back and take it easy. Go fishin'. And if you can't do that just think about going. Sometime's that's enough."

"No sweat there, I'm always ready to go fishing. You know that."

"Yeah, boy, I do know that. But there's fishing and then there's fishing, and that's something else you'll catch on to some day."

The old man continued puffing on his pipe, removing it only to take a long pull from the tall glass of bourbon and iced tea he'd concocted right after supper.

"Another good thing about getting older, too, is you can't stay mad at anybody for any length of time because your own cumulative sins and errors of omission catch up with you and in moments of self-honesty you realize you really ain't a lick better than anyone else anyway, pure and simple. You may walk around thinking so, but every once in a while it hits you.

Sometimes it hits you real hard. Guess what it boils down to is unless you're ready to cast the first stone, you best lay off the other fella'."

"That sorta' makes sense," I said.

"Well, that's sorta' Bible talk, I reckon, and somehow it always does make sense. It can be some high falutin' preacher telling it or the village idiot, don't matter. The gist of the scriptures has a way of comin' through, regardless. Nothin' to fret about. Just somethin' else to ponder on a quiet evening after supper."

Pawpaw continued to rock and puff, and for a long while the only sound on the carport was that of the metal rockers carrying the old man's weight rolling to and fro over the cool concrete floor.

After a while, the old man spoke:

"Somethin' on your mind. Sumpin' you wanta' talk about?"

"Well, I don't know if you can answer this one."

"Never know unless you ask."

"Okay. I got a question for you." I sure didn't how to phrase it, though.

"Ask away. I'll do my best."

"It's about Leah... I mean Mom. What gets into her to make her act like she does sometimes?"

"You mean what makes her drink, don't you? I wanna' be sure we're talking about the same thing here."

"Yes sir, I reckon that's what I mean."

"You're right, that is a good one. If I knew the answer to that one I'd be ready for the *"64 Thousand Dollar Question"*, but I can probably shed a little light on what's eating at her. For starters, she's always been mad at me for quitting the Law. She never come right out and said as much, but I could sense it when she got to be a teenager– about your age. I think she had this notion that if I'da kept at it we'd have been rich or something, and she could have grown up in a fancy house instead of out in the grove."

"What's wrong with the grove. It's great out there."

"Well to a boy it might be, but girls' got a little different idea of what's great, sometimes. I think she felt isolated out there and felt like if she could have grown up in town, nearer her friends, she'd have had more of a social life. You gotta' remember, back then twenty-five years or so ago, we were out in the sticks. The store wasn't out there then and the nearest neighbors were over a mile away. They were great friends, we'd visit a lot, but their kids were grown and gone. Your mother felt isolated out there, and she let me and her mother know it, too. Also, I think she's always held it against me that her mother died, though Lord knows what I coulda' done about it. She got sick bad, and it wouldn't a' made a bit of difference if we'da lived at the Sheraton Biltmore in downtown Atlanta. She still woulda' died. Leah was just a teenage girl, though, and she needed to be mad at somebody. Guess it didn't take a whole lot of imagination on her part for that somebody to be me."

Because it was getting late and we'd intentionally left the overhead light off, I had trouble telling if there were tears in the old man's eyes, but it sort of looked that way and then I saw my grandfather put a finger up to his cheek and slide it back behind his glasses, wiping quickly.

"Dang gnats. Can't come outside for five minutes without 'em gettin' at you."

Before thinking, I spoke:

"It's February, Pawpaw. No gnats out this time of year."

"Well, he must be a scout, 'cause I sure felt him." The old man removed his glasses and pulled a handkerchief from his back pocket, rubbing his eyes for several seconds. Moving the handkerchief around in his hand for a moment, he raised it to his nose and blew several times hard. Wadding the handkerchief back up he put it into the rear pocket of his khaki's and took another drink from his special concoction.

From behind my grandfather, Jim, the neighbor's dog, came lumbering up slowly onto the carport, heading straight to me. He nuzzled his nose under my right hand in a signal both of greeting and in an effort, I knew, to get me to pet him. After I rubbed his head for a moment, paying particular attention to his ears and all the while telling him what a good dog he was, Jim lay down on the cool concrete floor at my feet. He looked like he was settling in for the evening.

"The Moore's must be fighting again. That's the only time he comes up here at night; when they're yelling at each other." I said. "It scares him." I reached down to scratch the dog again behind his ears. "But he's a good boy, he sure is, yes he is." The old man said nothing– only looked at me and the dog as he still held his pipe in the corner of his mouth and continued to rock slowly. After a minute or so he continued:

"Don't know about you boy, but I'm about ready to turn in. Whadda' ya' say? We gotta' get up early tomorrow morning and start on that kitchen like your mother asked." He referred to the fact he had promised his daughter we would paint the cabinets and walls of our small kitchen while she and Grayson were away the next day.

"I'm gonna' sit out here for a little while longer, Pawpaw. I'll be in in'a minute."

"All right... but don't fall asleep out here, you hear?"

"I won't." I laughed. "Do you think I'm still a kid?"

"Naw, you're all grown up. You my fishin' buddy?" my grandfather asked.

"Yes sir."

"Good. That's what I wanta' hear. Get to bed shortly."

"Yes sir." The old man picked up his glass and pipe and headed for the screen door which lead into the kitchen. Just before he grabbed the door he turned around and looked at me.

"Hey, bubba?"

"Yes sir?"

"You worried... thinkin' about Grayson?"

"Naw, not really," I lied.

"He's gonna' be all right, you know," the old man said.

"Yeh, I know." I lied, again.

"Goodnight," my grandfather said.

"Sleep tight," I answered.

"Don't let the bed-bugs bite," the old man finished.

*   *   *

The evening, cool and clear, reminded me of one years ago— nearly five years ago, now. Boy, but time really seems to fly when you get older, I thought. Just after my father died when we still lived in town— on the other side of the river –I developed this problem. I couldn't sleep. Well, that wasn't exactly it– I couldn't sleep inside, was more like it. So, I took to just laying there in my bed unable to sleep and unable to cry (I'd done all of that I could at one big wallop two weeks before), waiting. Waiting for both my brother and Leah to drift off so I could go. There was no way she would permit me to go and there was no way I could explain it to her anyway, so there was nothing to do but just go.

Padding softly to my closet grabbing up the musty green Army down mummy-bag of my father's (which I'd discovered the week before going through his things in the house's cavernous attic), then padding softly down the narrow hall to the stairway my father had built (careful not to step too heavily upon any of its treads lest there come a squeak), I made my way downstairs. From here it was out the backdoor, the door at the very rear of the living room where I would have to step carefully down into the backyard. It was something my father had never gotten around to doing (and never would now, I thought), building some steps for this backdoor down into the backyard. Then I was out. Out where I could sleep, or at least spend the night.

It was several nights spent outdoors like this before I thought of bringing along the flashlight. I didn't really need it. I could find my way around the house both inside and out without it, but for some reason I'd grabbed it up from the kitchen drawer one afternoon and taken it into my room, putting it under my mattress for later.

Lying in the warm sleeping bag (too warm really, for mid-May), that first night with the flashlight, I clutched it close to my chest like it was some stuffed animal I had decided to take, to be with and comfort me. But after a while I sat up, my legs still crossed inside the bag and began to play around with the flashlight; shining it up into the tall pines in the backyard between our house and the nearest neighbors. The light's strong beacon did an ample job of making visible even the darkest spots on the tall pines, the places where the tree's top branches joined its trunk. The places where a raccoon would seek solace if treed by a dog. Boring of this after a short while I shone it under my chin like my father used to do and made what I thought was a scary face baring as much teeth as I could. Then I cupped my hand over the light extinguishing its rays almost all the way until I slid it under my fingers. Placed like this my hand took on a fiery glow and it looked like I'd made an X-ray of my hand, for it was easy to see the darker areas that I knew were the bones of my fingers. After a while I began to bore of this game also, and it was just about the time that I decided to lay back down in the sleeping bag and try to get some sleep (school in the morning, after all), that I sent out the first signal.

That's what you'd call it, after all, wasn't it– a signal? Three short flashes, followed directly by three long bursts. Then again, three more quick flashes: . . . – – – . . . . If I was right that was the correct signal, the right combination of dots and dashes; the universal code for SOS.

The first one I sent was to the tallest tree in our backyard– to the very top of it, and I was able to see the flashes right as they were produced. Maybe they weren't as bright as I'd thought they should be, but still you could make it out without too much imagination. Then I sent my first real signal, out towards the star Alpha Centauri knowing which star it was thanks to a little rhyme I made up in grade school to help me remember its name:
Alpha Centauri— Brightest Starry.

After that I began sending the signals out regularly to other stars, towards whole constellations– Orion, Leo, The Twins, even The Ram and the more signals I sent out the more I came to believe that something might just come of it. After all, it was 1957. IGY or International Geophysical Year was here and many people thought anything was possible in this new time, this new age of Space. The Russians had surprised everyone and put up a satellite– Sputnik. It was up there now in fact. So who was to say there couldn't be others up there also, from other planets, other worlds? UFO's (unidentified flying objects), could be circling all over the globe right this minute. Maybe one of them would see my signal. Who knows, maybe even God himself would take notice. But how would I know? How could I ever be certain either of them had seen my signal? And then, which one: UFO's or God himself? Maybe that's the way God worked in situations like this– through a UFO. And what about the simple, old-fashioned notion of a lucky star?

Within a month two good things happened and with their mutual occurrence I would have what I felt was my answer.

First, we moved from the house my father had built, a house that I thought I would live in always and would miss terribly, but a house that I was finding more and more impossible to stay inside, to live in now, it evoked my father so much.

Second, Aunt Bertie (my father's sister and only sibling), came back from California out of a clear blue sky. There was her car one day, a brand new orange and white two-tone Mercury parked in front of our new house (new to us, anyway), at the Beach, bringing along with her two new cousins (both girls). For reasons they still weren't even sure of Rad had all of a sudden been transferred from Long Beach Naval Yard to Mayport and with their transfer, coming all the way back across the conti-nent, bringing with them something for me; some leverage of sorts. This aunt whom I could only vaguely remember from years ago when I was not much more than five, but who at the same time I felt immediately close to (she had such a fantastic sense of humor), brought with her return a much–needed resource* for me, for us.

Newness. That's what the signals had brought. New relatives, new house, new little town, new friends. And last, but not least, a new life. Among all this newness, though, was at least one thing that was old, and it was the one thing old I would always hold onto. My old life, I guess you'd call it, or the better part of it.

The part I'd spent with my father.

You would be amazed at the amount of stuff people in a small town know about each other. Of course, that's assuming you are not already living in one, for then you would know. It's downright scary when you think it over that lots of folks know more about you than you'd ever imagine. It's always a result of the fact that most folks just cannot keep a secret. But, then, somebody my age doesn't have a sufficent history to matter much when it comes to rumors. Still, it can make you see why a lot of kids are chomping at the bit and can't wait to escape by the time they've finished high school. Even some of the ones who act like they're happy all the time.

The story that follows is about someone I hardly know, at least in the way folks mean when they say they know someone. The thing is, in some ways I feel like I know Derek better than I know a lot of people I have spent a good amount of time around. Whether that is something that can be said on my account, or his (or both), I'm not sure. My guess is it has something to do with both.

Basically, what you have here is stuff I have been able to pull together from whispers, rumors and not-so-common knowledge. A good portion of it comes from Dosha Fay who truly has got a knack for telling stories about everyone she knows. Come to think of it, she wouldn't let the fact she wasn't acquainted with someone stop her from talking about them. When she is ironing and really gets going it's incredible how much information about all sorts of people, colored and white, comes out. Not knowing many of the folks she is talking about, there is no way of knowing exactly what is fact and what is pushing the limit.

For the most part, though, I would say this story is pretty much just like I have written. You'll have to take my word for it, though it may make you feel better to know it is the only one I ever turned into Mrs. Johns and got an A+ on. No corrections, either.

I know that doesn't mean it's true; but it doesn't hurt, either.

Derek

Derek was Redfish's brother. At least his half-brother, because even though everyone knew they shared a mother, the same could not be said with any certainty in regards to a paternal lineage*. Derek was lots lighter than both his brother and mother, and there was some suspicion his father might have been a white man. But only one person had ever been callous enough to confront Derek with this directly. That confrontation, while Derek was still in high school, had resulted in a bloody broken nose for the inquirer. After that everyone kept their suspicions to themselves.

Growing up, the two brothers exhibited similar physical traits and both became famous around Oceanside for their athletic prowess. Besides being a mythic angler, Redfish excelled at football and track setting new records at both sports at the negro high school in town. Meanwhile, younger brother Derek proved more than able at baseball. The past two seasons he'd played semi-pro ball for the Double A team over in Mobile. The same team Hammerin' Hank Aaron had played with before being called up to the majors. In 1960 he'd come in third in the league for Rookie of the Year honors, and last season he'd batted .327, hit 24 home runs and come in second in balloting for League MVP. If he could put together another good year like that he was certain he'd get his shot at the majors. He could taste it.

Sadly, a freak accident during the off season threatened to cut short Derek's baseball career. It happened one cold morning in late January while working on a high-tension wire as a lineman for Florida Power & Light. Crossing two wires that should never have been crossed gained him an instant ticket off a thirty foot pole and onto the dusty hard winter's ground below.

Nearly any other mortal would have given up the ghost after such a strong jolt, but Derek– stunned for a moment –got back up and was able to walk under his own strength. For about two steps, whereupon he again hit the ground. This time he stayed there. An ambulance was summoned to cart him off to Waters Clinic (Riverville's negro hospital), west of town.

After an examination it turned out his body had weathered the shock extremely well. It was the fall he was suffering from and which he could thank now for not only a badly separated shoulder but also a lower back injury. X-rays showed several fractured vertebrae. The emergency room doctor (a retired-naval doctor who had seen it all), was able to force the shoulder (where a large bump the size of a softball jutted out in front), back into it's socket. Having performed this procedure on a number of occasions the physician was flabbergasted at Derek's composure.

With little anesthesia Derek barely grimaced in a situation that, as a rule, provoked screams of agony. It seemed that the muscle and tissue surrounding the joint was so dense that no type of retaining device, even a sling, was necessary to keep the torn socket mended.

The veteran doctor had questioned Derek: "Good Lord, young man, doesn't that hurt?" he'd asked, mashing the skin lightly around the affected area.

"It did a little, 'fore you popped it back in. Now it feel's good; lots more natural this way," Derek answered, rotating the shoulder as if working out a cramp.

"I've popped my share of those things back in, but I've never seen one that looked so bad go in so well. There doesn't seem to be any tissue or muscle tear at all. It's just like new," the doctor said, looking at X-rays of the injured shoulder.

"Thanks, doc."

The injured vertebrae were another matter.

"You're going to need to take it easy with that back though, son. No more pole climbing, I'm afraid. You've got a slight hair-line fracture on two of these lower vertebrae," the doctor told him, pointing with a pen to the two spots on the X-rays.

"Tell you the truth sir, I'm kind of glad you said that. I was gettin' tired of messin' wid' them wires. 'Bout time for me to start playin' ball again, anyway," Derek said, taking a deep breath.

"You play a little baseball?" the doctor asked.

"Yes sir. Over in Mobile for the last two seasons."

"Hey, that's Double A! You mean you play professional ball?" the doctor exclaimed. "Well, I'm sorry son, but I'm afraid that's out of the question, too... at least until these vertebrae mend."

"What!" Derek had exclaimed. It was the most animated* he'd gotten since entering the clinic.

"You're not to be running around with your back in that condition for at least six months... probably more like a year."

"Can't do that, sir. I gotta' play ball. They're counting on me. What else can I do?" Derek asked pleadingly, standing up from the examining table and opening both palms to the room.

"I don't know, son, but I do know you can't play baseball this season. One bad turn, something like sliding into second base wrong and you might never walk again, much less hit a baseball... I don't care how strong you are. Give it some time to heal. At your age, and in your physical condition, it oughta' mend just fine. Just have to give it a little time, that's all. In the meantime, go on disability. The power company can afford it."

Derek was devastated. He could withstand the trauma of being blown off a power pole. Even the excruciating pain of having his shoulder popped back into socket. But the blow of having to sit out a whole season of baseball was too much to take and left him stunned for a good long while. There was no way he was going to go on any disability. He had too much pride. Not only in himself, but for his whole family. It was simply not an option. Until he could play ball again he would just have to find another job.

That's how Derek ended up on a golf course.

*   *   *

The course he ended up on was the only one at the Beach. The one that lay just south of Beach Road, named, aptly enough, Oceanside Municipal Golf Course.

Thursday was colored day at the course which meant black golfers who cared to could play the eighteen holes that sat like a demilitarized zone between the two separate worlds of white and black Oceanside. This accommodation afforded the caddies and groundskeepers who worked the rest of the week serving the clientele and maintaining the facilities of the municipal course some playing time. Among this black population were some of the best golfers in the area.

It was the only day of the week the colored golfers could play the course, and play it they did. It was not unusual for many of these golfers to play twenty-seven or even thirty-six holes on Thursday. All week long they had witnessed other golfers– white golfers –on this course who were free to play as many holes as they wished. There were some businessmen (lawyers and doctors mostly, it seemed), who were out here two and three times a week. When all you got was one day a week if you loved the game like most of the caddies and groundskeepers out here did you took all you could get. Great big chunks of golf at one whack, all the while knowing that the rest of the week would be spent carrying someone else's bag or mowing fairways.

*   *   *

In mid-February, instead of going to spring training Derek headed for the golf course. He'd heard the assistant pro was looking for another laborer to fill out his groundskeeping corps. Turned out he was a day late, though. The pro had filled the position only twenty-four hours before. But he could still use some help out on the driving range which sat at the back of the parking lot. Shagboy was what it was called. While most of the big courses in Riverville had vacumn-buggies to pick up the hundreds of balls that sat out on the driving range at any one time, the limited budget of the Oceanside course did not permit such a luxury. Hence, they must rely on physical labor to gather up the multitude of little white dimpled spheres to be put in a long cotton-pickin'-looking bag the shagboy wore over his shoulder to be dragged back up to the front of the range and into the pro shop; whereupon they were segregated into buckets (small ones going for fifty cents– larger ones seventy-five), once again to be whacked back out to the awaiting range.

Lacking any other prospects of gainful employment Derek said he would be glad to gather golf balls. It was outdoors and it was temporary, he told himself. He was going to play baseball again and soon, he thought. Sooner than that doctor in town had said. Why, he might even be able to get over to Alabama before this season was over and help his team win the pennant. That is if they could stay close long enough without him.

*   *   *

His tailbone hurt sometimes, mostly in the early morning when he first got out of bed. He'd hobble around the little house he still shared with his mother (and sometimes Redfish), like an old man and it would take a little while– after he'd had a cup of coffee –before it would begin to feel better. Then he could straighten up and walk like someone his age should. Walking around the driving range all day would be good for his back, Derek told himself. He would look upon it as getting payed (albeit, precious little), for exercising. That way he could still help his mother out some with the rent, the fuel-oil bill, and groceries. It wasn't anywhere near as much as he'd made as a lineman, but it was better than going on disability. Besides, he wasn't disabled. He was gonna' play ball again. In just a few short months, too. He would show that doctor. He could feel it.

Meanwhile there were golf balls to shag. Lots of them. Everyday– day in and day out.

Derek shagged balls all through February and March, arising early each morning to leave the house in time to pick up a

Florida Times-Herald at the gas station on the corner of Beach and 4th on his way into work. The first section he turned to was Sports. He was able to keep up this way with what was happening in the Grapefruit League down in the central and southern part of the state and with his team over in Alabama. Reading the scores kept him close to the game and kept his spirits up. He discovered that by tracking the events of organized baseball he was better able to tolerate his present conditions (meaning not only his physical struggle, but his struggle on the employment front as well).

The actual work was okay. A little monotonous maybe, but it was outdoors and on the range he was mostly by himself. There was no one looking over his shoulder and telling him what to do out here and that was the single positive aspect of the job. Folks in the clubhouse and pro shop were tolerable, for the most part. He had not (nor did he expect to), made any lifelong friends here, but again, he was just passing through. He was more than able to handle the occasional whispered remark and slight laughter he had heard as far back as he could remember when around white people. That's just the way things were, and always had been.

For the most part everyone in the clubhouse steered clear of talk about racial matters. At least around him. But on occassion there would be in the news something about a negro boycott of white stores in North Carolina or a civil rights march in Atlanta, and sure enough either the course pro (who spent much of his time giving lessons), or the assistant pro (who operated the cash register and assigned tee times), would make some snide remark about "them damn trouble-makers" or "them ungrateful nigras" and every time he heard something like this Derek had to bite his tongue and stuff down the anger welling up inside him. As a lineman he'd worked right alongside whites, but when you worked with someone as an equal, particularly in a dangerous endeavor, well, there just didn't seem to be any room for all that other stuff to seep in. As a lineman, he and those he worked with were always too busy to engage in discussions of what was going on anywhere else. They had all they could say grace over just traveling from one part of town to the other making sure the power stayed up, come hell or high-water. Thinking about this, Derek decided perhaps that was the problem here at the municipal course. These fellas' just had too much time on their hands. Worse, they used it pontificating on who had the right to do what, when and where and with whom.

So, Derek decided to let them have their little court where they decided how things should be as long as they left him alone at his job. Give and take– that was the secret; and in this area he was expert. Particularly at the take part. He didn't know anyone from his part of town that wasn't, come to think of it. At least anyone who had managed to live some semblance* of a life.

Things went along pretty well until April Fool's day.

As usual, Derek had gotten up early. Leaving his mother's small neat house, he walked down to the gas station on the corner for a paper. The Yankees were tearing up the Grapefruit League and his team over in Mobile was only a game behind Richmond in Double-A. It was a balmy morning after a good rain the night before. The sun was just coming up at his back as he walked along Beach Road on his way to the course.

Deeply inhaling the tropical April air, he could feel a gorgeous spring day was in the making. The kind of weather he'd discovered from his travels with the team only occurred in this special little part of the world. The combination of a perfectly clear-as-a-robin's-egg blue sky after last night's shower, and the eternal effusiveness* of the ocean a scant four blocks away was creating a brand newness to the day that eluded* description. It was the sort of day everyone you met made some remark, right off the bat, about how glorious a day it was. The only thing that could possibly make it any better was if it was Friday, and it was. Payday!

The day before he'd played a round of golf with Andrew– the best player by far among the crew of men who worked at the course. Derek was a natural, Andrew had said. Though he'd only been playing for a month and a half he'd shot an 82. Andrew, in his early fifties and a natty dresser when away from the job, managed a 69. Hell, the way he was going sooner or later he'd have a good shot at matching, maybe even breaking, the course record, a 67 held by Kingsley Cormack. King, as he was known to his friends, was a big beefy fellow in his early thirties whose father owned the cement mill. The same plant Derek passed in front of twice daily just a half a mile or so down the long dirt road that dead-ended into the course parking lot.

Kingsley worked in the office at the cement factory, nominally, but just as often could be found out on the course. Though he was a big blondish fellow who was a little on the loud side after a few beers, when he held a golf club in his hands he was the picture of perfect decorum*. He had a beautiful, almost delicate swing and he possessed the uncanny ability to put a golf ball just about anywhere he wanted. A few years back he'd even flirted with the idea of trying out for the professional golf tour but his daddy had scuttled that idea in a hurry. If Kingsley was off playing golf for a living who would be there to look after and run the cement plant when he retired?

In the end the old man had gotten his way, as usual, but ever since Kingsley had wondered in the back of his mind what it would have been like, how he would have done, traveling the country and playing golf for a living.

*   *   *

When Derek got to the course that Friday morning at seven-thirty (right on time), Kingsley, and a couple of his buddies were already there hitting balls on the driving range before heading to work. As Derek passed the group on his way to the clubhouse he nodded to Kingsley and his friends, and said good morning. The three men nodded back to Derek in a mumbling style, none of them speaking directly to him.

A few minutes later Derek emerged from the clubhouse carrying the ball satchel and a paper cup full of coffee he'd gotten from the vending machine inside. As he blew across the top of the coffee he watched Kingsley drive a ball straight down the range from a grassy lie, without benefit of a tee. It had looked like he barely hit it and the sound was a sharp and very distinct *click*. The same sound a new golf ball made when dropped on a hard surface– like a sidewalk or a terrazzo floor. As happened more times than not, Kingsley had hit the ball with the sweet spot of the driver. It's trajectory had as much written all over it as the ball sailed out in a line-drive past the 250 yard marker, straight down the range. There was no doubt about it. This man was superior to Andrew off the tee. The difference had to be in Andrew's adeptness on his approach shots and on the greens. One of Kingsley's buddies spoke up:

"Nice one, King. Keep that up and old Andrew'll never catch you." All of the men, including Derek, laughed. Kingsley, though, did not laugh as heartily as his friends, but instead shot Derek something of a wry look. Derek took this as his cue to head out to work and did so, walking along the sandy path that bordered the entire length of the range on the right.

Kingsley's other buddy spoke now:

"Wilson said Andrew shot a 69 yesterday, King. Better watch him." Again, Derek could hear chuckling from the group and again, even from twenty yards away, he could detect from the laughter only two of the men were truly getting a kick out of the banter. When he was nearly halfway down the range one of the men called out to Derek's back:

"Hey, boy."

Derek stopped, and turned slowly. As he'd suspected (knew), it was Kingsley.

"Do me a favor boy, and shag them balls for me, hear. They're not the course's, I brought my own. I play a Titlest, and they got a red KM stamped on 'em. And run 'em through the ball washer, too. I can't stand playing golf with dirty balls. Give ya' a little extra if you hustle. We'll be over to the putting green." Again, all three men laughed, pretending to keep their mirth in their own midst. But even from where he stood Derek could tell that this time Kingsley was as earnest in his laughter as his friends.

It wasn't the request itself so much as the tone in which it was illicited* that sent a shiver up Derek's back and made the hair on the back of his neck stand up. It was a split-second decision and in that small timeframe Derek was able to control both his mouth and his body. Able to contain his fury. He would take this abuse. Hell, he'd taken lots worse than this before; when he was younger, just a skinny teenager– before he'd filled out. But he would shoulder it for a variety of reasons. Good reasons they had to be, and good reasons they were. Like his mother, his grandmother and his brother. And baseball. Besides, it was Friday, payday; and he wasn't about to let something some cracker said mess that up for him.

Turning towards Kingsley and looking him straight in the eye, Derek spoke across the driving range:

"'Sho 'nuf, sir. Be my pleasure." Derek stood still after he spoke and continued looking at Kingsley who, moving somewhat self-consciously now, walked over to his big bag and shoved his three wood down forcefully into it. Then he grabbed his driver. Derek turned and continued walking along the path, heading for the back of the driving range.

Kingsley Cormack emptied the entire contents of a large basket of golf balls on the ground at his feet and with his polished driver began separating the balls from each other, shuffling a few golf balls towards the front of the group. Then, picking out one ball and bringing it a little closer, he addressed it quickly and swung, sailing it out well past the 200 yard marker. Meanwhile, Derek had come to the end of the path where it died out, returning to wild fescue and dandelions, and it was at this spot that he turned left and walked onto the driving range. He was almost at the 250 yard marker where he would start gathering the balls the three men had spent the early morning hitting.

As he began collecting the balls he soon noticed that all of them back here (all the balls which had been hit the farthest), had Kingsley's initials KM on them. The other two men were hitting around 150, sometimes 200 yards, but neither of them had put one out here near the 250 marker.

Suddenly, Derek heard a shrill call, and as he raised his head in the direction of the voice he could see Kingsley with a hand cupped up towards his mouth and he understood, through the combination of sight and sound, that the golfer was yelling:

"FORE!"

In an instant a ball sailed past his left shoulder not more that ten feet away; dropping with a dull thump on the ground at his back; then bouncing another thirty yards. Derek raised his hand and waved his arm to acknowledge that he had heard the warning and was not hit. He was okay. Turning around to retrieve the ball, he'd taken just a few steps when again he heard the same shrill yell:

"FORE!"

and again a golf ball sailed past him– this one barely missing his head. He heard the ball whistle as it went by, an auditory sensation that was both immediate and nasty sounding.

Again, Derek was just about to raise his hand to signal he was okay when he saw that the group of men seemed to be laughing. It was not what he could hear so much as what he could see. The three men's body language spoke great laughter– guffawing, even. Now he understood. Now he knew what was going on. They, or rather Kingsley, was playing with him.

And it was not a good-natured game.

*   *   *

His first inclination was to get off the range. He wouldn't run, he would casually saunter off, but he knew that getting off was the smart thing to do. The sound that last ball made blazing past his ear was not a pleasant one and he'd had to fight the urge to hustle off the range. But fight it he did. He was not going to let these three rednecks run him off from anywhere, much less run him off from his job.

For a brief second Derek debated which way to go. It seemed like golf balls were flying by every couple of seconds now and because he was right in the center of the range he couldn't decide if it would be better to go left or right. Kingsley was hitting golf balls like some kind of machine and they were coming out regularly and fast. They weren't high lofty shots either. They were screaming line drives which seemed to cut him short whenever he started to exit either way from the course and Derek, knowing he was on the verge of panic, began to back up.

There was still some room at the back of the range– just past the 300 yard marker –before it died out and gave way to a sharp bank of briars, which in turn led down to a smelly and dank algae-covered pond. Derek began walking quickly to the back of the range sensing he was about to leave harm's way. And none too soon, for there were only a few precious yards of level ground left before it gave way to the gnarly bank.

With three feet remaining between him and the fall-off, Derek turned to look back at the golfers, certain now that he was beyond Kingsley's range and the instant he turned he knew it was a mistake that even his quick reflexes could not save him from.

The last thing his left eye saw was a flash of white which instantly changed to a big confusing blur as he fell down the bank tumbling into the briars and coming to rest finally in the shallow green pond.

Even through the immense pain, the horrible pressure that seared deep through his head like a scalding hot poker, Derek maintained enough control to make a decision.

He would get up from this swamp and he would go get the man called Kingsley Cormack.

March Day

It was the sorta' March day at the beach abundant in false hope. One moment it was sunny and still and you were shot forward into a glorious spring day in May, eager to sniff the budding gardenia. Fifteen minutes later the sun was behind the clouds, the sky was gray, and the wind had picked up. Suddenly there you were, plopped back down smack dab in the middle of February.

The old man heard they were having luck surfcasting for pompano at Southbeach just above Mickler's Pier so we decided to get out of the house on this Sunday afternoon and try our luck. Leah and Grayson were visiting the Towner's for the afternoon (Mr. Towner would help with Grayson, getting him in and out of the car), so no one was home to make us feel guilty for going fishing for a change. We knew we'd best take advantage of this opportunity. Fortunately (for me), my grandfather had demanded that I bring along a jacket. At first I balked saying-why? it felt like summer outside. But the old man was persistent:

"Listen, boy; if I don't succeed at teaching you anything else, I am gonna' teach you this. When you are in or near the water... I don't care what time of year it is... even in the middle of summer, you make sure you take along some extra clothing. Especially an extra pair of socks and a cap. That's where you lose most of your heat- your head and your feet. I've seen a grown man get so cold in the middle of July in the Gulf Stream after a surprise afternoon hailstorm that came out of nowhere that he couldn't stop shaking. All he'd needed was a sweatshirt or thin parka and he'd 'a been all right. There's no such thing as bad weather, boy... just bad gear. You listening?"

"Yes sir," I said, grabbing the thinnest parka I owned from a wooden peg on the wall-mounted coat-rack by the back door. Then I was out and on my way to the utility room where the old man and I both stored our rods and tackle boxes.

My grandfather was right behind me as I emerged from the cluttered room with our gear and because my hands were full with fishing gear my grandfather placed on my head a cap; the one I'd worn during my last year in Little League. Even if the back band was elastic and still fit, I was still embarrassed to wear this green and white cap. After all, I'd been finished with

Little League for over a year. It seemed a demotion somehow to still be wearing this cap with the big D (Dodgers), emblazoned on it's front. Wearing this cap placed me back in that time again. It was as good as admitting that this was as far as I would ever go in organized athletics and for this reason I felt horribly uncomfortable at the thought of putting it on. I'd only kept it on the rack as a memento, not as something to wear. Sensing the old man was already in a lecturing mood I thought twice about removing the cap and after stowing our tackle boxes in the trunk and rods in the back seat of the spacious Imperial I sat up in the front, my head still bearing this relic from my past.

On our way to the beach we made a quick stop at Albright's, a combination curb market and bait shop at the far south end of Oceanside. I followed my grandfather inside, first surreptitiously* removing my cap. The old man walked straight down one of the dark narrow rows of canned goods to the back corner of the store; the section where the bait was kept. Here he bought a dozen live shrimp for a dollar and a pound of frozen shrimp wrapped in pinkish butcher-paper for fifty cents. An ancient and dark negro man, Mister Lincoln, was the attendant back here (had been for over thirty years). I had seen this man before and studied him like I always did as he slowly but deftly* captured the shrimp from the boxy livewell in the dark dank backroom of the store. Here was the only colored man I knew of whom everyone, colored and white, addressed as Mister. It was like finally, in his extreme old age this man had been granted some special dispensation*, transcending* and outranking the usual customs of our region. Or was it just because folks felt funny calling him by his first name, the one he was given in celebration of his timely arrival on this planet– Freedom. Rumor had it that the old black man was born in the very last year of the Civil War– on Emancipation Day! If that was true then he had been born free instead of a slave and some quick mathematical calculations (an exercise I repeated whenever I saw this man), placed the man's age at 97! So what if he had no birth certificate; for my part I believed– longed to believe –the story. You could just look at him and tell he was that old, at least. There was an air of antiquity, mixed with an ancient, almost primitive dignity to this old, old man and compared to him my grandfather looked... well... almost young. Well, at least middle-aged.

As we were leaving, Mr. Albright called out to my grandfather: "Good luck, Ed."

"Thanks Joe, but luck ain't got nothing to do with it."

"That so?"

"Been my experience."

"Well, look at it this way. If ya'll don't catch nothing I'll be here late tonight, so you just stop back by and get you some more of them shrimp and some cocktail sauce. I'll even throw in a box of Saltines.... that oughta' do it. Ha, ha." Old man Albright reared back his head and laughed showing off a mouthful of crooked yellow teeth.

"Don't keep the place open late waiting for us, Joe."

"I won't Edward, I won't. Ha, ha"

*　　*　　*

Back in the car and driving south down Ocean Street I quizzed my grandfather:

"Do you like Mr. Albright?"

"Oh, he's all right, I guess. Why?"

"I don't know. He just seems kinda' strange to me. Reminds me of an old lady, sometimes."

"Kind of a busybody, you mean?"

"Yeah, that's it. Sort of a busybody."

"Probably 'cause he's a holy-roller. He and his wife go to that holiness church down in Palm Valley. Most of them folks got a bad habit of wanting to know what you're up to and who you're up to it with... especially curious to know if you've been saved."

"What's a holy-roller."

"It's sorta' what the Bible calls a zealot."

"Yeh, I've heard of that before. What exactly is it?"

"A zealot? Well, I guess the best definition would be a screwball. Nah, forget I said that boy; it ain't fair to Albright and the other screwballs that go out there. Better let me think about that one for a while."

We both fell silent and the old man and I spoke not another word until we were on the beach.

*　　*　　*

When we finally made our way onto the beach I glanced north along the shoreline where I could see half a dozen fishermen scattered along a line a coupla' hundred yards long. To the south, down towards the pier, were more– maybe a dozen or so. This beckoned well for our chances, I thought. We just might get lucky. Even if the old man didn't put stock in that sorta' thing.

"Must be something going on, Pawpaw. Good crowd," I said as I struggled to open the top of the dented bait pail we'd put the live shrimp in.

"Don't mean nothin'. Could be they're all just bored like we were. If there was a football game on probably half of 'em would be back home with their fat butts parked in front of the idiot box."

I struggled some with the pail, finally managing to remove it's top. Looking down into the container I saw the shrimp, all gray and grouped together along one side of the can.

"Careful doing that," the old man said, squinting as he tied on a new hook. "Those are Keys shrimp... got mean horns."

"I know," I replied.

Reaching into the pail, I was careful as I lifted out one of the big shrimp for my grandfather. I'd been stabbed before by the small briny horns these little animals bore like wicked crowns on the tops of their heads, and I didn't need to be told twice to watch it.

Rigging his line with a one-ounce pyramid sinker the old man slipped the sharp steel hook through the shrimp's body, just below it's head. Then he drew back his battered eight-foot rod and threw the afternoon's first cast.

A hundred and fifty feet of green and white Dacron cord spun out in a blur from the black and chrome Penn Squidder casting reel the old man had attached to the rod with two stainless steel screw clamps, and the sinker and shrimp plopped down into the gentle gray waveless sea before us, creating a small, almost noiseless splash. The sinker, attached to the line about eighteen inches above the shrimp, hit the water first and sank quickly, dragging the shrimp down with it. Ideally, the sinker stayed on the ocean floor while the tethered shrimp swam above. Before he threw out his line the old man had pinched off the shrimp's tail and the crustacean now exuded enough *essence of shrimp* to alert any fish in the vicinity.

Pawpaw set the drag on the right side of his reel and pulled out line with his left hand to test it, all the while watching me with one eye. I knew he was studying my form as I sailed my shrimp out also; just shy of his own mark and about twenty yards to the left. Then the old man picked up on our earlier discussion:

"The screwy thing about being a zealot boy is if you're even just a little bit off, well that's all she wrote, you might as well hang it up. You've gotta' be dead-on to be right. Too damn narrow-minded, far as I'm concerned."

"Well, didn't Jesus say something about narrow is the way?" It had just come to me, from where I had no idea, but I was proud of my question.

"Yeah, but somehow I don't think he was referring to this particular notion. Where was I... oh yeah... let's say you're starting off in the desert on a trip and you're just fifty miles from your destination. Assuming you even got a compass, you better dang sure know the exact degree to head out 'cause from just that far out if you're off even one degree, just one degree, you're not gonna' make it. You'll miss your spot by miles. Do you get my analogy, boy?"

"Yeh, I think so. But what difference does it make? I mean, it sounds to me like you're saying it's so hard to try and reach heaven anyway then why even try. Who's good enough to make it?"

"Exactly! And the answer is nobody. Nobody is *good enough* to make it, so thank goodness that's not the criteria... to have to be good enough."

"Huh?"

"Show me where it's written you have to be good enough."

"Well, I thought that's what the Bible was all about. Like it was supposed to tell you how to be good enough."

"No, no, no... forget all that. That's bull. It's not there to tell you how to be good enough. If anything, it's there to tell you how to deal with things when you're not good enough. When you've finally become convinced in your own heart and mind you don't measure up, and never will on your own. You're not gonna' learn a thing from it until you become convinced of that. No matter what you believe."

"What do you believe, Pawpaw?" I'd been thinking of posing this very question for a long time. Now that I had it, I wasn't about to let the chance slip away.

"Me? I don't know... some folks say I'm atheistic. Not so sure they're wrong, either." The old man reeled in line as he spoke.

"What? Come on Pawpaw, you're pullin' my leg now. I know you're no atheist. You believe..."

"Never said I didn't boy. A body can doubt... can be atheist even, and still believe in God."

"What? What's the difference, then... whadda' you mean?"

"Syntax, boy... syntax. Power of words. Think on it."

As we stood on the beach neither of us said anything more for a while. There was only the sound of squawking gulls floating in the air just above us, as though suspended by invisible wires. While the grey and white birds wavered above I thought on this riddle of my grandfather's. How could he believe in God and claim atheism at the same time? Pondering this I made an effort (to my embarrassment), to look like I was thinking, just in case the old man glanced over at me. After an amount of time I deemed as sufficient to this goal, I queried my grandfather again:

"I still don't get it."

"Listen... if I say I'm atheist all it means is I'm not a Theist. And if I'm not a Theist... well... then I must be an a-Theist."

"All right then, what's a *Theist*?"

"Now you're cookin'. Can't do all your work for you, though. Go look it up in your Funk and Wagnalls."

I wasn't sure if the old man was trying to be smart now or what, but that's exactly where I would look it up. In one of the little green-bound Funk and Wagnalls volumes with the gold lettering Leah had been bringing home from the Winn-Dixie for the last six months. Every few weeks a different set of books was made available at the store and it was in this manner she was able to afford an encyclopedia for Grayson and I. I couldn't remember for sure now if I had this one yet. Seems like I recalled just getting P-R which meant the next volume would be S-T. Soon as we got home I would have to go to my room and check on this. Meanwhile, little was happening with either of our lines. Not even a nibble.

*　　　*　　　*

After about forty-five minutes of non-activity the old man layed his rod on the sandy shore and began filling his pipe with sweet pungent cherry tobacco. Turning his back to the gentle sea-breeze, he lit the mixture. I had noticed a little earlier about half of the fishermen both north and south of us had given up and as the afternoon wore on their numbers on the beach dwindled further to the point where only a few men in either direction (besides me and my grandfather), were still out. And so it was that those remaining would reap in the rich reward which was to strike just as the late afternoon sun began to sink behind the giant white grass-frocked dunes at our backs.

*　　　*　　　*

The first sign our luck was about to change came soon after my grandfather put a new shrimp on and changed sinkers. He'd decided to go to a half-ounce weight partly because the ocean was so gentle now late in the day. Also, he said he thought it might not be a bad idea to let this fresh shrimp have a little more leeway. The shrimp were large enough to actually pull this smaller weight across the ocean floor. The old man thought this increased activity might do a better job of attracting any pompano that might wander into the area; that is, if there were any pompano. Maybe they'd all moved out of the area. A stiff cold wind had picked up earlier blowing clear what little wispy cloud cover there'd been. As I zipped up my parka I recalled my earlier debate with my grandfather concerning even bringing the light jacket along.

All doubts were relieved in due course, for no sooner had the old man sailed his line out and tripped the reel's bail than he felt the quick sure tug of a fish. Pulling the surf-rod up hard, Pawpaw let out a whoop and began backing up onto the beach, reeling in as quickly as he could. The sudden action caught me daydreaming, off guard, and it took me a moment to realize what was happening. My grandfather had a fish!

"Whoa, Pawpaw! You got one!"

"Of course, what do you think we came out here for? To work on our tans?"

"Boy, he must be a good one," I yelled.

"He's pulling like he is. Put a fresh shrimp on and change to a half-ounce. If this is a big pompano like I think it is there'll be lots more around."

I did as my grandfather instructed as quickly as I could. In fact, I had to fight the urge to go too fast. Whenever someone else has a fish on I suffer this urge to take shortcuts when rigging up. Like making four instead of six wraparounds with my line when tying on a new lure like the old man taught me and I had to fight it now, telling myself to slow down. If the fish were here like my grandfather suspected there would be plenty of time. Just take my time and go around three times, four times, five times, then one more made six and go through the loop the line made at the top of the hook and back through the larger loop you just made and pull up slowly to cinch the six knots in. Completing this task, I pulled back my rod and flew out the new shrimp tethered to ten-pound monofilament line.

Barely had my shrimp had a chance to get wet when I also felt a distinct thump...thump, and set my hook. Whoa! I was truly stunned at the resistance I felt at the end of my line. My grandfather was just pulling in his fish and true to his suspicions I could tell as the old man pulled his catch in through the small lapping waves and white foam at the shore's edge, it was indeed a pompano. No surprise there maybe, but the size of him was definitely a surprise! Struggling with my own fish, I couldn't resist a glance back at the one my grandfather had brought in. A real beauty; a good four pounds if he was an ounce. As the old man hefted the writhing round-shaped creature by it's scissortail and walked towards me, I quickly turned my attention back to my own struggle. For that's all you could call what was going on here– a struggle. Never in my life had I felt such a sharp pull from a fish this close to shore. No two ways about it. Bringing in this fish was not going to be an easy task.

"Back up with him, boy. Don't try to reel him all the way in. You'll wear yourself out. Let your legs do the work."

I took the old man's advice and began backing up towards the tall dunes festooned* with sea oats which looked all the world like a shimmering golden wheatfield behind us. Backing up, I stole a quick glance towards the remaining fishermen just north about a hundred yards– three men, all with fish on their lines. I took another quick look south towards the pier and there also were several men– all, it looked, either engaged in battle with, or just having conquered a large fish. Boy, this was something else, I though to myself. What are we into here? All the while I kept backing and reeling, backing and reeling, and finally– long past the time I thought my line should be all the way in –I saw the end of my line and attached to it the creature which had made it so difficult for me to reel. Almost as big as the old man's, who was leaning over the bait pail now in search of another live shrimp. Dragging the struggling, large pompano onto the shore, I continued reeling and walking towards the flapping fish, not able to take my eyes off the bulk of it's blunt-nosed, flat, silver and white body.

"Everybody's catching 'em Pawpaw. How many are out there?"

"Good question. I won't say for sure, but there must be a bunch 'cause those fellas down south and those up that 'a way are all looking pretty busy now, too. Must be a big school. A big school like I haven't seen in a long while." The old man spoke as he impaled one of the few remaining live shrimp with the silver steel Mustad hook. "Not but a coupla' live shrimp left, but I don't think it'll matter much. Seem so hungry they'd hit spit."

"We've still got that bunch of frozen shrimp in the cooler. Should I break them out, Pawpaw?" I asked as I continued the struggle with my fish, now trying to remove the hook from it's briny and uncooperative mouth.

"Yeah, pull 'em out and put 'em in the pail. They'll thaw out quicker that way," the old man answered.

I took out the paper bag from the cooler, removing the green rubber band which held it together, and unraveled the parcel, searching for the clump of frozen shrimp in it's middle. I found the clustered mass and dumped it into the pail disturbing the remaining two live shrimp enough to make them suddenly active again. I reached in to grab one, excited over the prospect of parlaying it into a big catch, wondering if maybe this was all just a good dream– the kind of great dream you didn't want to wake up from. Maybe this was the kind of dream where you resisted waking so much that when you did you even tried to trick yourself back to sleep by lying perfectly still, but all for naught, because... **Ouch!** This was no dream, I knew as I dropped the shrimp back into the pail. The damn thing had stung me, and stung me good.

"Get'cha, boy?" my grandfather asked.

"Sure did," I replied, shaking my hand.

"They'll do that," the old man chuckled.

Pawpaw was in such a good mood there wasn't even going to be a lecture I thought as I rubbed the palm of my hand with a clump of gritty moist sand. I reached back in to grab one of the shrimp– hoping I was getting the offender so I could take some delight in sailing him out to his doom. I was being careful, too, not to suffer a second stab.

It was just as I almost grabbed one of the shrimp that I heard the old man's first moan:

"Oh, hell! Not those sons-of-bitches."

Instantly, I abandoned my quest for bait and stood up. I'd never heard my grandfather use this term before and I knew then something was happening, or fixing to. Something bad, too.

*　　　*　　　*

"Those sons-of-bitches." the old man said. "I can't believe it."

"What? What's going on, Pawpaw?" I asked. I could see my grandfather looking out to sea towards the north, but I couldn't see what he saw because I couldn't see anything. Just the ocean, still as a lake.

And then I saw it. A big wooden skiff with an outboard motor and two men it looked, about a hundred yards offshore and heading south, slowly. Big deal. What was so wrong with that? If they were fishing that was okay, I thought. There was enough fish out here now to make everybody happy. Plenty to go around, I thought.

"Those sorry S.O.B.'s" my grandfather said. "I can't believe it."

"What? Why are you so upset?" I said, still in the dark over my grandfather's sudden ill disposition.

"There! Look there, and there!" My grandfather pointed to the small craft and a little farther north at another larger vessel I hadn't noticed before. The way my grandfather pointed at the boats made me know they were somehow connected in whatever it was he was upset about.

"What are they doing?" I asked.

"It's not just what they're doing. It's what they are." the old man answered.

"What? What are they?" I still didn't get it.

"They're netters... illegal netters!" my grandfather answered. "The lowest form of life on the planet. Look at the size of that net! If that's not an obscene sight, I don't know what in the hell is."

"Didn't the apostles fish with nets?" Again, the biblical reference just came to me. I didn't know how, or why, and its sudden emergence from my thinking surprised even me.

"Yeh, *casting* nets. That thing out there's a totally different creature, though. A net that big shouldn't be used for anything but shrimpin'."

I could see now how the smaller outboard was indeed stretching a net from the larger boat. The two craft were about a hundred yards apart and as the skiff continued southward, slowly unraveling the net, the larger boat (which looked like some sort of homemade tugboat), was stationary. I could make out a large humped mass at the back of it. Then it hit me– this hump was the remainder of the net!

"Good gosh, Pawpaw. How big is that net?" I asked.

"It's big, boy," the old man replied. "It's real big."

As the old man and I stood there on the beach watching, the skiff kept on southward down the beach towing the net, which continued to spill out from the rear of the larger craft.

When the smaller boat was about a quarter of a mile from the tug it suddenly turned towards the beach and began heading straight to the spot where we stood. As it came closer I got a better look at the two men now. The unflattering moniker* my grandfather had used earlier wasn't far off the mark, I thought, for here were two of the roughest looking characters I'd ever layed eyes on. The fact that they were coming right towards us didn't thrill me, either.

"Why are they coming this way?" I asked my grandfather.

"They're making the loop," the old man answered, watching the skiff. "Somehow they got wind the pompano are running through here and they're chasing 'em. The little boat takes one end of the net and tries to encircle the whole school with it.

Then the big boat pulls in the net and there goes all the fishing for the afternoon... if not longer."

"Isn't there something we can do? They can't come in here and take these fish. They're ours! They're for us and those other men," I cried, as I motioned both up and down the beach in the direction of the other fishermen on shore. By now the men in both directions had stopped also, busy watching the unsporting travesty they had suddenly become witness to.

The skiff kept on coming and was no more than thirty yards from the beach when it suddenly turned north, veering back in the direction of the tug. As he whipped the boat around, the ill-shaven man in the rear (operating the tiller), stared at my grandfather and me, abruptly breaking out in a big Jack-O-Lantern grin. Then he removed his cap, tipping it in our direction.

That did it. This insult to injury proved too much for the old man to bear. It was like pouring salt into the wound to take our fish like this in the first place, but then to mock us by tipping his hat in thanks was too much. First, the old man just looked straight at the helmsman and smiled back for a long couple of seconds. Then, suddenly, he lifted his right fist high up into the air while grabbing the crook of his elbow with his left hand and, so positioned, duly executed what's known in certain circles as the *Italian Salute*. It was something, he told me later, he had seen demonstrated firsthand numerous times during WW II in Italy some twenty years before. Even so, he said, it was the first time he had executed the salute personally.

While signaling his disgust, he yelled out:

"LOUSY POACHERS!!!"

I'd never seen my grandfather so angry. Usually the old man did a pretty fair job of reigning in his temper (I knew this better than anyone, I thought, for I could always tell when the old man was mad), and it was rare that he let himself lose control. You really got the feeling he prided himself on this fact. But on this occasion my grandfather made no attempt whatsoever to contain himself. He was fuming worse than I had ever seen. True, when he drank sometimes he was known to let loose with an expletive or two, but that was more in the colorful language or old character vein. We'd been together all day and I was certain my grandfather had not taken a drink during that time. No, this was pure old man. Madder than a hornet, too.

To my horror the small skiff (after finishing its loop, rendez-vousing* with the larger craft and delivering it's end of the net), was now coming back towards us again. I looked up at my grandfather's face for a second to catch his expression. Somehow, I was none too surprised when the old man said:

"Good. I was hoping that'd bring 'em back."

The small outboard came in as shallow as it could and the instigator* of the old man's anger shut off the motor. For a few seconds the small skiff bobbed up and down in its own wake and I could tell the one in the back of the boat was about to speak. I braced myself for whatever was coming.

"What'd you call me, old man?" There wasn't more than fifty feet between us and the skiff now, and over the water it wasn't difficult to hear the man, the one I'd nick-named Pumpkinhead, speak.

"I said you're a lousy poacher. You know what that is, dont'cha?" the old man shot back.

"Yeh, but we ain't poachin'. We got a license to fish." the man said. "Good and proper."

"You call that fishing? Maybe for someone too damn lazy or too damn stupid to catch fish in any honest way. You know, someone who has to rely on a big ol' net to do his work for him."

"Hell, mister. You don't think this is work, you come out here and try it for a day. Put your dick in the dirt in less time than that, I bet."

"Nah, afraid I can't do that. Unlike some folks, I still got a little pride left."

"Well, you keep your pride, old man. We'll take the fish... that's all we want." At this, the unkempt character in front let go a snickering snort of a laugh and looked back at his friend.

"Hell, Buddy, let's go. Leave the old coot alone. He's just pissed off 'cause we got his fish." Again, the one up front emitted a little half-snickering laugh.

"You ain't got 'em, yet," my grandfather said.

"What's that mean, old man?" Pumpkinhead asked.

"You heard me. You boy's are netting illegal here. Florida State law says you gotta' stay back four hundred yards offshore with a net that large this time of year, and I'm calling you on it."

"Well, that's just fine and dandy old man, but who says we ain't that 'fer off the shore. Seems to me we was further than that. How 'bout you, Tate? How 'fer you reckon we're fishin' off the shoreline here?" The snaggle-toothed netter spoke to his accomplice up front.

"At least that far, Buddy. Maybe even farther," he laughed.

"See. We got two of us and just one of you. Unless ya' gonna' count Pee-Wee there," Pumpkinhead laughed. Being referred to at all by either of these two was no great honor, but my ears were especially stung by this belittling epitaph, especially seeing as who it was coming from.

"Oh, I wouldn't be too sure about that, cowboys. Maybe we got more witnesses on this beach than you're giving us credit for," the old man shouted back at the two.

"Oh, yeh? Where?" the one in the bow of the little skiff asked, laughing. Of the two, he appeared to be the most belligerent. It was his snickering half-laugh that betrayed him so.

"There... and there." The old man pointed to the two groups of men at either end of the beach, both of whom were now hastily approaching my grandfather and I.

"Who'da hell are they?" the one up front asked, a look of quizzical consternation growing on his face.

"They're sportsmen, just like us, out for a little Sunday afternoon recreation 'til ya'll spoiled the sport," my grandfather replied.

"Well listen, old-timer, they ain't nothing I can do about it now, even if I wanted to, ya' see. It ain't my rig. Belongs to the man out there." The man up front pointed towards the tug. "We're just hired help."

"Well, I suggest ya'll scoot on back to the man out there then and tell him what I just said, ya' hear. And while you're at it you can tell him there's a member of the Florida Marine Commission on the beach here and if he don't cut that net in the next five minutes I'm calling the District Supervisor up in Fernandina and my witnesses and I are gonna' swear out a warrant for his arrest. It's a thousand dollar fine and three months in jail... an' I'll guarantee you sure as hell he'll get both... ya'll, too. I already took down his registration number... and yours... so ya'll better hustle and go, quick. Clock's a runnin'."

As he lectured the men, the old man reached into his back pocket for his wallet, flipped it open in front of him, and flashed an official-looking blue card with a bold silver star displayed prominently on it's front. Pumpkinhead suddenly appeared visibly shaken by this bit of evidence and turning to his friend up front who seemed to be calling the shots, waited for some sign as to what they should do. After a long coupla' seconds in which the man in the skiff's bow looked back to the tug and then again at my grandfather (all the while wearing a growing look of consternation*), he spoke:

"Shit! Guess we oughta' 'least tell Herb what the old man said.

Start her up, Buddy. Let's scat."

At this command Pumpkinhead turned around on his small bench seat and grabbing the starter rope, gave it a series of hard pulls. After the eighth or ninth tug the motor came to life, coughing and spewing smoke fiercely. I ain't sayin' what sorta' motor it was, but I can assure you it was not an Evinrude. I watched their flared wake as the outboard headed back towards the tug. Then I turned to my grandfather. There was something I didn't understand and the only way I knew how to get an answer was to ask the old man.

"How could you make out the registration number on that tug, Pawpaw? I've got 20/20 eyesight, and it was a blur to me."

"Me too boy... though I'd bet a dollar to a doughnut your blur was clearer than mine. I bluffed em'... pure and simple. Now we just gotta' wait and see if they fall for it."

I, along with the two groups of men who had congregated near us (and who also had overheard my grandfather's challenge to the two netters), all laughed nervously while looking out to the sea towards the small tug.

As the skiff approached the larger vessel it shut off it's motor and I could make out the two men in the smaller boat talking to the larger man in the tug who was operating the winch, slowly and laboriously* pulling in the abundantly loaded net. While the men in the skiff talked they motioned back, pointing in the direction of the beach towards all of us congregated there.

Suddenly, the large man became animated and for the first time I could hear a voice booming out across the long stretch of water.

The scene was almost comedic*. Sight being faster than sound and the man being far enough away for this discrepancy* to matter added up to the fact that the man's motions did not quite fit his gestures– or vice-versa. It was like a film whose picture and audio were skewed, just a little off, but it didn't take a great leap of the imagination to guess this man was angry. As his voice became louder and his motions more animated Pawpaw began to laugh and the sparkle I had come to know and appreciate, that look in the old man's eyes that more than anything else in the world told me everything was gonna' be all right, returned to the old man's face for a brief moment. I sensed for the first time during this incident that it was possible everything was going to turn out favorably for my grandfather and I and the rest of the men on the beach.

I became certain of this in the next few seconds. Watching across the water I saw the winch that had been pulling in the giant net stop. Then, the man on the back of the tug wielded what looked to be a giant machete and with two quick whacks across the stretched net (right at the spot where it fed into the winch), the remainder of the net plopped down unceremoniously into the sea. Still wielding the broad-bladed knife the big man raised it above his head, shaking it as he shouted ugly and incomprehensible curses towards the beach, the indignities skipping across the water like obscene flying fish.

As if on cue, Pawpaw and I, along with the group of surf-casters, erupted into a cheer and began slapping each other on the back as both the tug and the skiff began moving off over the water, heading north.

"I never knew you were a member of the Florida Fishing Commission... or whatever you called it." I said above the well–wishing shouting.

"Oh." the old man laughed. "It's the Florida Marine Commission, boy... but I kinda' got carried away there. Took a little liberty with the truth, you might say."

"But what about that card? It looked like the Real McCoy to me."

"Fooled you too, huh? The old man replied, grinning. Then he pulled out his wallet once again, flipping it open for me and the group of men who had collected near us to see. "That's my membership card to the PX down at McDill."

Once more, we all laughed, this time being a lot more relaxed.

*   *   *

Despite our victory, I was still troubled by the turn of events and felt compelled once more to question my grandfather:

"What good is this gonna' do us though? Seems like such a waste. The fishing is still ruined, plus those pompano'll just rot out there."

"That's one less net that'll be working these waters boy, and as far as I'm concerned that's doing plenty 'a good. Besides, I'm not so sure those fish will rot." The old man turned and addressed the half-dozen men nearby. "I'll bet we could bring that thing in if we got started before it settles down real good. Whatta' you men say? Ya'll game in helping me bring in that net?"

After some brief murmuring all of the men answered back in hardy affirmative tones, each of them laying their rods and tackle boxes upon the beach. Then they each followed the old man as he marched into the water.

I layed down my rod, which in all the excitement I hadn't even noticed I was still holding, and followed after them, entering also the gentle sea.

*　　　*　　　*

An hour later, my grandfather and I, along with our six accomplices, stood on the beach as the last pompano was pulled from the monofilament net we'd struggled so heartily to rescue from the ocean floor. When we finished dividing up our bounty it came to nearly sixty pounds of fish for each man. Just as the sun's last rays slipped beneath the duned horizon the gladdened and weary group (after exchanging what seemed like almost reverent farewells), broke up– heading for their cars and home. As always, the old man produced twenty feet or so of loose Venetian blind cord from his tackle box and from this strand he fashioned two long stringers. One for each of us.

Because I'd just been to Mr. Torello's the afternoon before for a fresh burr–cut I could feel the cool night air stirring around my ears more intimately now than I could just a coupla' days ago and I pulled up the hood of my thin parka to cover my head, glad now that I'd brought the light windbreaker along despite my earlier protestations*.

As we began threading the cords through the fish, I had one more question for my grandfather:

"What about faith? That's a whole lotta' what you hear Reverend Timmons preaching about these days."

The old man thought about this for a moment, then spoke:

"Faith? Why, faith ain't nothin' more than a by-product of doubt, boy. If you don't remember anything else, you remember that. Without doubt, there ain't no faith." Beginning our trek across the dusky quiet beach, I thought that once again here was one of my grandfather's pronouncements* that I was just gonna' have to save to mull over later. Not wishing to give away any of my uncertainty in regards to the old man's statement, I decided it would just be safest to change the subject.

"What we gonna' do with all this fish ?" I asked, stopping for a moment to re-hike the heaving stringer up over my shoulder.

"Hmmm... good question. Don't know 'bout you boy, but I know precisely what I'm doing with mine... 'least a fair portion of it," the old man answered, stopping to perform the same shifting task himself while grimacing from what I reckoned was the arthritis. Then he took turns resting each hand for a second, opening and closing each one slowly like he was trying to make sure they still operated okay, and to work out the ache.

"What's that?" I asked.

"Taking it back to Albright's, of course. He oughta' be paying least a buck a pound for pretty pompano like this. Even if he isn't, I just wanta' see the look on that old buzzard's face when he sees all this fish. How 'bout it? Hell, he'll probably take all we got."

"Boy, that'd be a pretty penny!" I said, doing some quick calculating. "I'd like to keep some, too, though. I kinda' thought I'd surprise Dosha. She's always saying how much she likes seafood but can't ever get up to the fish market."

"Now there's some good thinking. That'll surprise her no end, boy. In fact, I predict she'll love it."

For the first time in a long while I saw the old man's face dissolve into a full smile as we walked back up the dark beach together, happy and content, each of us bent forward some from hefting a long, full stringer of pompano.

The tail ends of both stringers dragging through the sand left twin parallel lines across the beach as we headed for the old Imperial and home.

Steinhatchee Dreaming

"Steinhatchee's where we need to be, I do believe."

The old man spoke from the front swivel seat of the 14 ft. fiberglass skiff Mr. Johnson lent us in lieu* of *Melinda*'s absence.

"I don't know what's got into these fish around here. Hatten' noticed we're out in a brand new boat, I reckon. No respect for a coupla' old hands."

"Is it good there?" I asked.

"Good where?"

"Steinhatchee."

"Oh. Almost always."

"Almost?"

"Don't matter. A bad day there is a great one anywhere else."

"When's the last time you were there?"

"About six years ago. Keep meaning to get back. Had a good friend retired there... Charlie Frost. Had cancer real bad last time I went... eat up with it, but there wasn't a whine in him, even at the very painful end. We took out one day that trip and got into 'em real serious. Out on the flats, at the mouth, and all the way back into the river, about as far back as you could get. Big trout, twenty–four inch and up. Largemouth bass, too. Never been somewhere you could catch freshwater bass that close to saltwater. Got to where we started calling them bass trash-fish we were so set after the trout and reds. Ol' Charlie was hurtin' too. He didn't like to let on, but I could tell. He just kept on smoking them cigarettes though like there was no tomorrow. Guess that's how he had it figured by then. Skinny as a rail. Used to be a big man... over six foot... went about two–twenty when we played football. Bet he barely weighed a hundred and twenty by then. But he could still fish. Musta' caught a hundred trout that day. Wouldn't keep 'em if they weren't two foot."

"Whoo-ee! That's a bunch. I'd settle for one that size right now," I said.

"Ain't it the truth," the old man agreed.

For a while neither of us said anything else. The sun was an hour past noon, high in the sky, and in search of some shade I rowed the new boat towards a massive oak whose broad, bifurcated*, limbs laden thick with Spanish moss hung reaching out over the wide creek. I got the boat into the shadows and quit rowing. The old man spoke again:

"You haven't said what you think about the boat."

"Oh, it's all right. Kinda' slippery, though."

"Sure rows easier, don't it?"

"Maybe... a little bit."

"Little bit, my foot. This thing cuts a path, boy. Jon boat's okay if you got a motor but for rowing all you're doing is pushing water."

"I never thought it was all that hard. Plus, it's a good work–out. Builds muscles, rowin'."

"Yeh, I hear ya'," the old man said, rolling his eyes heavenward.

"It does. I was in lots better shape after I got *Melinda*."

"If you say so. I'm giving up on this spinner. You bring any crickets?"

"A handful."

"Smart move. Don't ever go fishing without crickets if you can help it. No matter what else is, or isn't biting, it's a cold day in Hades when you can't scare something up with a cricket."

The old man reeled in his spinner, lopped it off with a finger-nail clipper he pulled from his pocket (and to which he'd attached a long loop of pink masonry string), and in only a few seconds tied on a No. 2 brass hook with one hand. Three inches above the hook he nestled onto the line a single splitshot not much bigger than a BB and holding the lead shot up to his mouth crimped it down on the line with his front teeth.

"Hand me that small silver box right in front of you, boy. I got some quill floats in there... and find me a cricket, one that's got some kick left in him... there you go. Let's see what we can scare up here." The old man slid the sharp hook into the hinge just behind the insect's head and a tiny glob of milky white fluid emerged from the wound as the cricket began a writhing spasm, extending all of it's legs out sharply. Then he cocked his wrist and nonchalantly whipped the supple rod towards the bank near a collection of cypress knees sticking up a foot or so above the creek's surface. The quill bobber fell into the liquid blackness and floated on its side and as the cricket sank down the quill began to tilt. Before long it stood erect among the knobby wooden knees worn smooth from the erodic* effect of decades of wind and water.

"Now get on down there and introduce yourself to somebody quick, Mister Cricket."

"I think you got a good idea there. I'm switching to crickets, too. Tired of throwing this good-for-nothin' plug."

"Get ya' one of them quills. They're just right for back in here."

"That's all right. I got some bobbers."

"Suit yourself... whoa... lookout... got a little tug here." the old man nodded his head towards the quill which was bobbing up and down on the creek's surface now, creating a ripple of rings among the polished knobby knees.

"Here we go. Here we go!" The quill sank straight down beneath the creek's surface and the old man whipped his rod right up hard creating an arch which pointed straight toward the spot where the quill had disappeared. "Throw around those knees. There's a mess of specs or bream one down there."

I threw my cricket towards the cypress knees and watched my bobber sail five feet past the grouping. I reeled in some, finally placing the red and white balsa float next to one of the innermost rounded lumps. Watching my grandfather from the corner of one eye do battle with whatever it was he was fighting I expected a hit on my own line any second. The old man patiently played the bantam fish who refused to surface, and reeling him all the way up to the boat leaned over to retrieve him from the creek. Doing so, he hefted up a good-sized bream that looked to be at least a half, maybe even three-quarters of a pound.

"Nice one, Pawpaw." Darn, I'd let slip. Just when I was doing so well, too.

"It ain't no gator-trout but it'll do. You having any luck?" The old man asked, gently working the small hook from inside the fish's tiny paper-mache-like mouth.

"Not yet, but any second now."

"All right, get ready to move over. I'm coming back in."

"Come on, there's plenty of room."

Delicately impaling another cricket the old man threw his line out again in exactly the same spot and this time before the quill had a chance to stand up straight it was sucked back down below the water's surface even more forcefully than the first time.

"That's what I wanted to see. Hot dang, this one's a biggun!" the old man said as his rod quivered, then bent acutely from the pull of the struggling fish.

"Darn, you got another one. Leave some for the rest of us," I said half joking.

"I'll try, but there's no guarantees. You getting any nibbles?"

"Not a one. I got a feisty cricket on, too."

"Not to be telling ya' how to fish, but that's a pretty stout float ya' got there," the old man said, struggling some to reel in.

"I don't think so, really. I mean it oughta' move some if a fish would just bump it a little," I replied. For a while we were both quiet as the old man coaxed the splashing panfish towards the boat. My grandfather broke our silence first.

"My theory is by this time of the year they've seen a whole bunch of bobbers. They may not be smart enough to figure it all out, but believe it or not I think they got sense enough after a while to be leery of certain colors... like red and white. Too many of their friends got a habit of disappearing when those hues show up on the scene." The old man spoke leaning over the side of the new boat and pulling up another bream– this one a pound and then some.

"Maybe you got something there. Hard to believe a fish can tell colors, though."

"Hell, who knows? I sure can't say for sure. Least a quill's a natural color. It's something you'd see in nature, so a fish ain't likely to be too spooked by it. Those bobber's are a different story, though. Red means danger to most critters. Prob'ly fish, too. It's just painted that color 'cause it's easier for the fisherman to see."

"Gosh, that's true. I never thought of it that way. No wonder it won't catch anything next to your quill," I said as though I was genuinely surprised by this sudden revelation.

"Oh, the red ones catch all right."

"You just said they... "

"They catch the fisherman." The old man said popping open the cooler lid and dropping the big bream into the chest alongside the first fish.

"Huh?"

"You bought it, didn't you?" he said, smiling as he reached down to the boat's bottom and retrieved the cylinder of a wire basket containing the crickets.

"Yeh."

"Well, there you go... it worked. It caught you. Hee–hee." The old man laughed lightly, like he was tickled with himself and his change of luck. Still smiling, I shook out another cricket from the round basket and put the cork back into its small spout.

"I'll take one of those quills now, please."

"Sure thing. Be my guest," my grandfather replied as he tossed the metal box to the back of the boat towards me. "There's a slot at each end. Just tuck your line into those slots whatever depth you wanna' fish and have at it."

"Thanks."

"No problem. Glad to be of service."

"Probably won't help."

"Why you say that?"

"'Cause, even though I agree with your bobber theory I got a feelin' that's not my main problem."

"And that would be?"

"I got bad luck."

"Since when?"

"Ever since I lost *Melinda* ."

"That's just plain superstition."

"Well, that's how I feel."

"If that's how you feel then you're right... you got bad luck. But it ain't 'cause your boats missing. It's because you think it's 'cause your boat's missing. Just as bad, if not worse. Means you feel guilty about losing her. If you're meant to find her you will. Takes some..."

"*THERE SHE IS!!! THERE SHE IS!!!* Holy Moly, I can't believe it!"

"What? Where... what!?"

"Right there. Down the creek. Look!" I pointed down the middle of the creek out to a spot on the intracoastal about 200 yards north where, on the water's horizon you could see the full profile of a small boat with a single figure standing up in its front. The figure looked to be poling the boat.

"How in the world do you think that's your boat, boy? They ain't but twenty dozen jonboats on this creek."

"That's her! I know it. That is *Melinda*."

"You're letting yourself get carried away, son. You're guessing. That could be anyone of a ..."

"I'm not guessing, Paw... sir. I know it certain as we're sitting on this creek. I can tell by the back. *Melinda's* the only aluminum boat I've ever seen with a stern that slopes back like that."

"Well... could be... I reckon. But we're still too far off. Row us on over if you're so dadblamed certain. Be interesting to see what this fella' thinks about it."

Before my grandfather had finished his sentence I was rowing out of the creek and into the intracoastal waterway.

* * *

I pulled on the two oars with every ounce of strength I could muster and in a short time we were less than a hundred yards from the other boat, closing in quickly. As we approached the boat I turned my head around once to confirm my suspicion. I was still certain. It was still *Melinda* we were pursuing, and in her bow I could readily make out the lone tall figure of a light–complexioned negro man.

"That's her Pawpaw! That's *Melinda*. *We found her*! I can't believe it, but there she is right there, right down the way. *What good luck!*"

"Slow down, boy. We don't wanta' come up on this fella' too fast. He ain't goin' nowhere." I obeyed my grandfather and reduced my rate of stroking. I hated to admit it- even to myself -but this new boat *was* lots easier to row. Or maybe it was because I was so excited it just seemed like the rowing was easier. *Melinda* plowed through the water, just like my grandfather said, but this new boat cut through. Still, I'd never trade, even straight up.

"That's good. Let's hang back here for a second." the old man said softly. "See what kinda' mood this fella's in 'fore we come right up on him. You let me do the talkin'... I don't care what. You hear?"

"Yessir."

I did as my grandfather said and rested the two oars upon the new boat's gunnels.

"Afternoon," the old man called out to the negro.

"Afternoon, sir," the man called back to my grandfather and nodded at me. I nodded back to the man and then noticed a wooden-handled machete laying at the negro's barefeet, across *Melinda's* bow. Miscellaneous chicken parts lay scattered atop a clump of newspaper next to the large knife. The heap attracted the usual circle of buzzing flies.

"Any luck?"

"Not much, sir. How's ya'll doin'?"

"Coupla' bream's all."

"Jes' trying to get me sum crabs, but dey got the lockjaw, too, it seem like." The large man smiled and I couldn't tell if there was something wrong with the negro's left eye or if he was just squinting from the reflection of the sun off the water.

"There's some big ones out here."

"Yessir, I know it. I come up with some big ones yestiddy. This the bes' spot on both coasts of Florida for blue crabs. But dey jest ain't livin' up to they reputation today."

"Hold on, now. You ever been down to Hobe Sound? Some nice crabbing down that way."

"No sir. I jes' been 'round here and 'round Mobile and Pensacola. Everybody swear 'dis here good as it gets, though."

"Well, could be. Nice boat you got there."

"Thank you, sir. I like that one ya'lls in too. Pretty one, sho 'nuff. Look bran' new."

"Yeh, she's a loaner." The old man looked off north towards Mayport and was silent for a long moment before speaking again. At first the dark man on the skiff looked at the old man, studying his face, then he looked up the waterway towards Mayport, also.

"Well, good luck," the old man finally said.

"Same to you, sir." The negro tipped his head towards the old man.

My grandfather signaled for me to begin rowing again and as I straightened the two oars out perpendicular* to the skiff's sides I couldn't resist stealing a glance back, just to make sure I was certain. There was no doubt about it. It was *Melinda* all right.

There was no doubt now also that the man's squint was the result of something other than the glare off the water, for just before he turned his head back to begin rowing, the negro let down his guard and for a split second I saw into the ugly dark gash in the vacant socket that had formerly housed an eye.

*   *   *

"That was her, I know it. I'd swear on a stack of bibles. Couldn't you tell?" I spoke only after we were far enough away from the negro not to be overheard.

"Shhhh! Let it be. Sound carries somethin' fierce over this water." My grandfather replied under his breath, without turning around. The old man's reprimand was barely audible, but there was no mistaking it's cautionary and resolute* tone.

When we were far enough away and I was sure we could no longer be overheard, I spoke up once more:

"What are we doing? We can't let him be. That was *Melinda*! *I'm certain of it!*"

"Are you absolutely and unmistakably certain, boy?"

"Ninety–nine point nine, nine, nine percent, at least."

"Which means you're not positive."

"No... I mean yes, I'm positive... bu–but...I ma–mean... darn it, that's my..."

"Slow down. It don't help nothin' gettin' riled up."

I quit trying to talk and took a couple of deep breaths before I resumed.

"Okay. That's my boat he's in unless there's an exact twin out here in existence. All the markings look the same. Remember that long scrape along the side? It was there!"

"Hell, boy, all boats like that got scrapes. Did'ya see anything distinguishing; anything unique besides the shape of the back and the scrape?"

"If we'da gotten to see the other side there's another place right up front. It's another scrape that looks just like a tornado slanted to one side. If we'd a seen that, then I'd be one-hundred-percent–no-two-ways-about-it–definitely sure. Definitely!"

"Never know, boy. If it was real peculiar he might have sense enough to paint over it or remove it somehow."

I thought for a second about what my grandfather said as though there must be something else, something I knew was there, only I couldn't put my hands on it. Like a forgotten word on the tip of the tongue. And then I had it.

"There's another mark."

"Where?"

"Under the back bench. I put my initials, MWC under there, plus eight... four... forty–nine. My birthday."

"Good thinking."

"Well, what are we leaving for? Let's tell him about *Melinda* missing and all. Maybe he just found her somewhere on the creek after the storm. He'll understand, 'specially since I can identify the marks under the seat. There's no way he looked under there. You'd need a flashlight to see, even in the daytime.

"Ain't that simple."

"Why? It seems real simple to me. He seemed nice... and reasonable."

"It ain't the boat, boy."

"Whadda' ya' mean?"

"I'm saying, it ain't about the boat."

Up until this point in our conversation the old man had not bothered to turn all the way around to face me directly. Instead, he'd remained at about the halfway mark, his back to the starboard side of the new boat. Now he deliberately turned the swivel seat to look right at me.

"Remember back a coupla' months ago that trouble surrounding Kingsley Cormack?"

"Sure. Everybody's heard about that. His daddy owns the cement plant over by the golf course."

"You remember how it was some colored fella' worked at the golf course that attacked him?"

"Yes sir. I mean I didn't know he worked at the course, but I remember it was a colored man."

"I got a sneaking suspicion we may have just seen him. The man we just spoke to."

"What!? They say that man nearly killed Kingsley. That fellow we just saw didn't look mean."

"He's described as being light–complexioned, almost mulatto. Just like this fella'. That ain't all that uncommon, but there's something else that is, and this man fits the bill there... to a tee"

"What's that?"

"Kingsley got in a good lick too, they said. This colored man's supposed to have a bad hurt eye."

"Really? Darn, how hurt?"

"Last time anyone saw him said it looked like he'd been shot in the eye. That fella' we just saw's either missing an eye or it's so hurt it's not doing him any good. Either way, I'll bet a dollar to a donut that's him. I just got a feeling about it."

"Just my luck. The one person that finds my boat is the only one in Oceanside that's running from the police."

"Let's get back to Johnson's, boy. We can call Chief Franklins from there. He needs to hear about this."

"I'm not lookin' to get anyone in any trouble. All I want is my boat back," I said. But the old man either wasn't listening or didn't think the remark required a reply.

I rowed the sleek new boat across the intracoastal back towards the blackwater creek and Johnson's Fish Camp, thinking only of two things: The muscular and light–skinned colored man with one eye we were leaving behind, and the dusky green boat he was poling.

I reckon getting older it is pretty much natural to start to get a little more smart-aleck as well, and it may seem like this next story sees me getting just that way, but I don't really think so. Maybe a little, but believe me when I say you cannot get very smart-aleck with the old man and get away with it. Somehow or other there would be a price to pay. He may be old, but he is certainly not feeble.

Sometimes you have got to do a thing you know may get you in trouble, but you have got to do it, anyway. That's what it was like that late afternoon (evening almost), in Davey's front yard when I washed the butch wax out of my hair.

I'd just come from Mr. Torello's barbershop where I had asked him to let the front stay longer than usual. Sitting in the chair there I didn't have the courage to tell him what I was thinking about doing. He knows the old man too well and would have given me a hard time about it– I was sure. I just said I was thinking about pushing the front up a little higher, in a wave or something.

By the time I rode down Penner to Davey's, though, I had worked my nerve back up and decided it was time. The only person to witness this act was Davey himself who was in the front yard. I told him what I was planning on doing and he thought it was a cool idea, too, although he was not considering it himself, he said. Davey has got black, almost jet-black, hair and it would not look too good... a surfer-cut with black hair. Not that I am bragging, but the color of my own hair– brown, is about perfect for it. See, besides growing out the front bangs the next step is to comb hydrogen peroxide through this grown-out front and then you go stand outside in the sun for a half-hour or so. Some guys have done it with lemon juice, but I don't think that works quite as well.

Anyways, after keeping the butch wax out the next day was Sunday and that's when I combed in the peroxide. After Grayson and I got back from Church. It looked pretty good. The only problem was the front was still a little short. Instead of laying down on my forehead like bangs are supposed to that front part just sorta' shot straight out. I reckon the combination of it being a little short still and the fact that I had been pushing it up for the last several years all came together, working to keep it from going down.

But you could tell what I had done, though, and boy did Leah get p.o.'d. She yelled, but there wasn't much else she could do. A coupla' years ago I reckon she could have taken me back down to Mr. Torello's and demanded that he cut it out, but I am too big for that now and she knows it, even though she threatened to anyway.

I didn't say anything when she made the threat, but I swear I almost cut a smile. Boy, but that would have really sent her through the roof (not that that was ever my intention).

So, having got by with her just yelling some the only other obstacle was the old man. By far, he was the more serious. Of that there was absolutely no doubt. Looking back, I am wondering if the fact that he wasn't feeling so well had anything to do with the fact that he wasn't any harder on me about it. Not that he would get mean, like mean mean, but more like he was upset. The thing about the old man is you never can be quite sure exactly how he will take to something like this. With Leah it is easy. You know right when she will get upset about something so you can sorta' brace yourself accordingly, but with the old man there is no telling from which direction he will come after you. The only time I can think that he really yells is if there is sort sort of emergency going on, like when a fish is about to get off the hook. Otherwise, he plays it pretty cool. Believe me, sometimes when he is doing something like reading the paper and you don't think he is thinking about whatever it is you hope he is not thinking about and then all of a sudden he puts the paper down and looks up over the top of his glasses at you with that pipe in his mouth. Well, you are just about fixing to have a situation on your hands, then.

Again, it is not a mean look as much as a serious one and that is exactly what I was hoping not to get into when the old man caught a whiff of what was going on with the top of my head.

If you want to know exactly what all happened then you will just have to read on. It pretty much happened exactly like I have written it this time, too.

P.S. – *I read 'The Open Boat' again last night just before going to bed and am beginning to see why Mrs. Johns claims it's the best American short story of all time. Who would have thought that a story about this neck of the woods would be so good? But it is full of excitement– the kind that stays with you long after you are through reading it. How he does it, I don't know. I mean, you can look at all the words– none of them big or impressive sounding –but he's got this talent for putting regular words together in such a way to keep you hooked to the very end and caring about what happens to those men in that little boat– if they will make it or not. The story is alive and it makes me proud to have the same last name as the author.*

I think about this every time I read it and it puts goose bumps on me.

Surfer Cut

"Goodgawdamighty, boy. Now, just what in the hell is that?"

My grandfather peered across the rim of his coffee mug at my head, staring at its top like there was something alive perched there. It was late (and dark), the night before when he'd gotten in and obviously he'd not noticed the new cut then. At the breakfast table it was harder to conceal.

*　　　*　　　*

I probably oughta' fill you in a little on what exactly was going on with me now; about my hair and the new way I was wearing it. Seems like overnight I was noticing lots of girls around Oceanside with longer and straighter hairdos. I didn't know it had to be ironed to get it that straight. I heard the rumors and thought it was all a joke until Will convinced me it was true. He'd seen it with his own two eyes just the day before when his sister Kelly had wet and combed out her previously permed hair. Then she shielded it with wax paper, flattened it against the ironing board, set their Sunbeam iron on polyester and proceeded (with a girlfriend's assistance), to iron her hair. Weird. She didn't even look like the same girl now, Will said. What was previously a head full of curls was now draped all down and around her head, hanging straight down. Long, coal-black hair as straight as could be. Jeez... the lengths girls would go to in the name of fashion.

One thing I was certain of– and Mick, Davey and Will would all agree with this –that come hell or highwater no self-respecting boy from our neck of the woods was about to grow his hair out and peroxide it blond like they were said to be doing out in California, where the top band now, The Beach Boys, hailed from. No matter how much we dug their music. Surfer cut... *crazy!*

I was sure that I could dig the Beach Boy's music without feeling the least little bit compelled* to adopt their look. And I was certain, also, that long hair would never catch on in the South. No matter how trendsetting California might be, some things were meant to stay out there and not infect the rest of the population. Everyone (Californians, as well as the rest of the country), would be better off that way. No two ways about it, *'bushy bushy blond hairdo'*, wasn't ever gonna' fly down South.

Two weeks later I was combing down the small amount of front bangs I'd instructed Mr. Torello to leave this time, claiming I was thinking about going to a flat top. On my way home from the barbershop I stopped at Davey's where I stuck my head under the spigot at the front of the Mercano house and washed out the Butch wax Mr. Torello had applied to the front of my new coif*.

When I got home I went straight to the bathroom, combing this front part down, wetting it with hydrogen peroxide. It was the first time in my life I'd taken any notice of my hair. Looking in the mirror at the wet bangs (which were just long enough to stick straight out despite my vigorous combing), I imagined how I might look on the beach with a bleached blond surfer cut and a new surfboard. Surely, Patti would be impressed. She would have to be. This, at least, was my ardent* wish and most fervent* hope.

*   *   *

Instinctively, I reached up to touch the top of my head. Satisfied there was no foreign object there I reconciled myself to the fact that what had so alarmed the old man was indeed my new haircut. It'd had several weeks to grow since my grandfather had last been around and instead of sticking straight out like it did in the beginning, the front bangs were tamed some now and long enough to lie down on their own. They now stopped about midway down my forehead, an inch or so above my eyebrows.

I noticed a few days earlier whenever I moved my head the bangs shimmied across my forehead like the fringe on a buckskin jacket. A week or so after I'd started the new cut I found it was necessary to comb hydrogen peroxide through the bangs every few days if you wanted to maintain the *maximum effect*. It was something I'd failed to anticipate when I started, this maintenance deal.

Contrast was the key for maximum effect. While most of my head appeared as though it still sported an All-American burr-cut the bangs were longer and blond– bleach blond. The burr portion did not receive the peroxide treatment and so remained my natural color of brownish. It was by benefit of this color difference that a lot of the desired effect was obtained.

"You been out in public like that?" my grandfather spoke between sips of steaming coffee.

"It's called a surfer cut, Pawpaw," I said, between slurps of cereal. "Lotsa' guys are wearing 'em."

"Funny, I hadn't seen one but your's so far."

"Well, you wouldn't see 'em downstate... least not yet. They're just popular on the coast. You know, the surfing spots."

"Surfing spots, huh? Oceanside's turning into a big surfing spot, now? the old man said deadpan, lifting the mug to his lips.

"Well, it's about to. It's all anyone talks about at school."

"That so?"

"Yeah. I'm fixin' to get a board." I said, finishing the last of my cereal and lifting the bowl up to my mouth to pour the remaining milk in.

"A board?" the old man grimaced slightly at my table manners.

"A surfboard. It's what it's all about. It's what you stand on... balance on... to surf the waves," I said, jumping up from my chair and standing next to it, imitating the classic surfer stance: knees bent a little, my left foot in front of my right, and arms out to either side, waving as if to gain and maintain balance.

"Oh. How much are they?"

"Around ninety or a hundred bucks," I answered, continuing to mock–surf.

"Lotta' money. Where you gonna' get your hands on that much dough?"

"Lawns."

"Lawns?"

"Yeah, mowing lawns," I said, stopping surfing long enough to take the empty cereal bowl to the sink.

"Right. That's a lotta' lawns."

"Yeah, but it'll be worth it. I figure in about six weeks I oughta' have enough to get a board. If not, I'm thinking also about selling Grit."

"Grits? Why would anyone buy grits from a ..."

"Not grits, Pawpaw... Grit. It's a newspaper. I saw an ad in the back of a comic about it. You gotta' send away and all, though... somewhere in Tennessee... Nashville, I think. Guys make big money selling it around their neighborhoods."

"What guys? Anybody you know?"

"No, but it says so in the ad."

"Why don't you just get a paper route? Support local industry."

"I've already tried. You gotta' be fourteen," I said sitting back down now at the table.

"You've only got a few months to go. It won't be long."

"Yeah, but I'm ready to get going now. I need a board before the end of summer."

"Where they sell these boards?"

"California's the big place, but Eric Benefield told me the other day there's a new factory that makes 'em just opened in Cocoa or Cocoa Beach."

"Great fishin' down there. Banana River country. Caught the biggest red drum you'd ever wanna' see on that river about ten years ago on a flyrod. Your daddy was with me and when... "

"Yeah, I remember... I saw the photo. Mom's got it in the scrapbook." I said. "You know how to cut a circle out of plywood?"

"A circle? Sure. You need a bandsaw, though. What do you want to cut a circle out of plywood for?"

"To make a skimboard."

"Skimboard? I thought you were after a surfboard."

"Well, until I get a surfboard. See, you take a piece of plywood and cut it into a circle, about three feet across, and then you sand it down real good and put a bunch of coats of varnish on it, and then you can skim with it."

"Skim with it?" the old man said pushing back his chair, rising from the table, and heading for the kitchen and the coffee pot.

"It's sorta' like training for surfing."

"Sounds cheaper," my grandfather said, pouring himself one more cup of coffee from the percolator atop the stove.

"You throw it down on the beach right at the water's edge, or in a slough... anywhere there's a coupla' inches of water, and then you run real fast and jump on it and it carries you skimming down the beach."

"Fascinating," was all the old man said as he returned to the table. Sitting down, he spooned up two generous measures of sugar from the bowl.

"It's fun as heck. I tried it on Eric's board last Saturday."

"Well, if you had a skimboard, why would you want a surfboard?"

"They're different, Pawpaw. Skimboarding's good for learning on, but what you really want to do is get out there and ride the waves."

"Girls probably like that more, huh... surfing?"

"Girls? Girls don't have anything to do with it."

"Oh. I just thought surfing might look more dangerous, being way out there where the big waves are, and all. Seems natural girls would find that more appealing... not that it matters any."

I could usually tell when my grandfather was trying not to laugh, at least not to smile, but he wasn't doing a very good job of it. Knowing him like I did, he probably was just *pretending* not to be doing a very good job. Anyway, the result was the same. A hint of a grin was forming on the old man's face, and to help conceal it he put his coffee cup up to his lips and peered at me now over the rim of the mug. His eyes betrayed him, still.

"You think I'm just getting into surfing for girls? I can't believe you'd think that." I said, mustering all the indignation I could.

"I didn't say that, although I can't think of a better reason, personally."

"I'm not, you know. In fact, that's the last reason I'd do it. It's fun. It's more than fun... it's fantastic!"

"I'm sure it is."

"It is. It's great! All that room out there and nothing but you and your surfboard and the waves," I said, spreading my arms expansively*.

"Too bad."

"What's too bad?"

"With all that room, seems like there'd be somewhere to fit in a gal."

"Oh, come on, Pawpaw. You don't need girls to surf."

"Good thing. That haircut'd probably scare 'em off, anyways."

"I don't think so. Girls love it, for your information."

"What kinda' girls?"

"Good-lookin' ones. Eric just got written up in the school paper for having the coolest hair at Oceanside, and his cut's lots longer than mine."

"I'm having some difficulty believing any self-respecting girl is gonna' find that appealing– a boy with hair like a girl's."

"It's not like a girl's. It's totally different. You just don't get it, Pawpaw."

"I get it, all right. Don't think ya'll got dibs on the first fad to hit the world. That's all this is bubba– a fad. Someday, and soon I hope, you'll look back and think how ridiculous you looked." the old man said, waving his fingers above his own forehead; sign language– my grandfather's style –for my new cut.

"I know. Let me get you some pink ribbons. I'll pick 'em out when I go up to Murphy's, later. I'd invite you to come with me to pick 'em out yourself but I gotta' admit I'd be a bit embarrassed to be seen with you in public wearing that thing." The old man nodded with both his head and his coffee mug at the top of my head and did the sign-language bit again, as though inferring* it were a separate living entity that this house, if not the entire world, would be a much better place without.

"Well, I'm sorry you don't like it, but it's only because you don't understand what's going on now."

"What you're saying is I'm gettin old!" the old man shouted.

"I didn't say that, Pawpaw. I just said you don't understand. That's all."

"Oh, well thanks... that's better. I just ain't got any sense now."

"No. I didn't say... "

"Well, I got sense enough to know when I'm looking at a sissy, and with that haircut, boy, that's exactly what I'm lookin' at. Here's a dollar. Get a haircut today... a real one. Otherwise, I'll bring back those ribbons and you can do it up right." The old man grabbed for his wallet, picked out a single bill and flung it at the table towards me. Instead, it fluttered over the table's surface like a green and white moth, falling lazily to the floor; coming to rest finally underneath my chair. I reached under my chair, retrieved the errant dollar and placed it back on top of the table, sliding it across the table's top over towards my grandfather.

"Here's your money, Pawpaw. I don't need a haircut. Not yet, anyways."

"Keep the dollar, son. You can use it for lipstick or makeup." the old man said, pushing the bill back towards me and rising from the table.

"I'm heading up to Murphy's. Get Grayson up before I get back."

"Yes sir," I said.

*   *   *

After the old man left, exiting through the kitchen door, I guessed the last thing he'd said was meant to be a peace-offering of sorts. An attempt to smooth things over some. There wasn't any need for my grandfather to tell me to get Grayson up. He'd never said anything like that before. Why now? I knew what was going on, that he was just trying to end our discussion on some neutral subject. It was a way for my grandfather to save face, too. He'd given me a command I was sure to follow.

The old man was treating me like a kid and I was getting tired of it. Part of the trouble was that I still talked like one. I was getting too old to call my grandfather *Pawpaw*, and I was determined now to quit it. Only trouble was I'd have to think of some other name, some other word, to address the old man. The old standards– *'grandfather, grandad and grandpa'* –just didn't cut it, didn't sound right. I'd have to think some more about this. It wasn't all that easy to quit calling somebody something you'd spent your whole life (so far, at least), calling them.

Later, when Leah got home, I was looking forward to getting out of the house and meeting Eric on the beach up by his house at the end of Sea View Road where the two of us would spend the afternoon skimming in the sloughs up and down the beach and talk about surfing.

I arose from the table and headed back to the bedroom to get Grayson up.

*   *   *

Part of me wished *Melinda* was still around and that the old man and I were headed out on the creek today like we used to. I couldn't recall ever having had an argument with my grandfather (not a real one anyway, where we stayed mad with each other for a whole day), when we were out on the water together in *Melinda*. I wondered for a second if this was because of the boat or because of the water, settling finally on the observation that probably it was a little of both. Who could stay mad for very long when out on the creek in such a craft?

Thinking of the afternoon I was looking forward to with Eric made me glad. Thinking of the afternoons that used to be, out in *Melinda* by myself, but especially with the old man, didn't.

Oh, Happy Day

"Crane residence."

"How soon can you get over here, Marty?" Right off the bat I recognized the voice of Mister Johnson.

"Why's that, Mister Johnson?"

"Hadn't anybody ever told you it ain't polite to answer a question with another question, son."

"I didn't mean to be impolite, sir. I thought ..."

"Just kiddin' wid'ya, boy. But I think we got somethin' over here you been looking for."

"Somethin' I've been lookin' for? I don't know what... whoa! What? Is my boat there?"

"Come on over and take a look for yourself. Durndest thing I seen in a long time."

"How could it be?"

"Quit asking so many questions and get on over here, boy"

"Yes sir. I'm on my way."

Struggling with the phone's cord and missing the cradle the first two times, I finally hung up the black receiver and made a dash down the hall for the front door, certain I broke all records for getting outta' the house, onto my bike and down the road.

Out of the blue!

Now I understood that phrase.

Now I realized what it truly meant.

The last several weeks I'd begun to reconcile* myself to the fact that I might never see my boat again, but I'd kept up a strong front, telling my grandfather and Grayson (and anyone else who would listen), that I would find her. Or rather, that she would find, return, to me. And now, unless Mister Johnson was playing the cruelest trick he could think of playing, I was about to be reunited with her. Someway, somehow, I always knew deep down this day would come. That *Melinda* would return.

*   *   *

"Fred saw her first. Over there... side 'dem cattails."

I stood out on the dock with Mister Johnson and Fred, the colored dockman who'd been working at Johnson's Fish Camp since day one.

I had biked, and then run so fast that I was out of breath. Bending over– hands on knees –I gasped for air as the two men told the story of the boat's sudden and unexpected appearance.

"Yessur. Dats' sho' nuff, right. She was tucked in 'dere real good, like someone wuz being real careful, wantin' her to stay put." Fred said through a mouth with as many teeth absent as were still present.

"Where is she?" I asked, scouring the docks and the water for the boat.

"At the end of the first dock there. Behind that new boat I let you and your grandpa' borrow." Mr. Johnson stretched out his arm that wasn't holding the cane and pointed a half-smoked cigarette over a passel of various boats– towards the end of the wooden slat dock.

I turned from the two men and headed down the dock.

"Don't worry, boy. She ain't going nowhere. Fred tied her up good for you."

"Sho' did. I knew that boy don't wanna' be missin' 'dat boat agin'," Fred laughed. "She's jes like I found her too... note 'n all."

Just as Mister Johnson had said, there she was. As pretty a sight as I'd ever seen, her open dusky greenness floating upon the black-as-ebony creek. And like Fred had said, there was a note taped down to the back bench with two pieces of weathered duct tape– one at the top and another at the bottom. The note was handwritten on a piece of lined notebook paper which had been torn from a spiral notebook as evidenced by the frazzled edge of the paper which ran the length of it's left side. I stepped down from the dock into *Melinda's* stern lightly (as though to safeguard myself if it turned out this was just a dream), my sneakered foot landing right behind her back bench. After a few seconds spent standing in the stern I came to realize, to accept, that it was truly her. Looking down at the bench I reached for the note and slowly pulled it up, careful not to tear any of it. Even allowing for the great amount of humidity present in the July air the tape lifted from the bench's surface with ease. The tape had obviously been used for some other purpose before being employed to hold down this note.

Holding it in both of my hands my first impression was of the penmanship. It looked as though it had been written by a fourth grader; one who'd had some trouble with penmanship and spelling, both.

I read the note:

> ## To: M. W. C.
>
> I saw you out on the creak the other day with the old man & I knew thin this waz yer boat. It was not stollin but wuz fond by me in some tallgrass ovur by Cryin Childe
> islund on Easterday.
>   I figurued it wuz blewn up their bye the hericane
> and set their by hersself til I fond her. I new it wuzn
> abandoned or let go intenshunly by any one as it looks pretty well take-in careof. I always thot that if I new who owed her I wuld give her back to them.
>
>
>
> thank you
> &
> you are welcumed
> -D
>
>
>
> ps- you're inishulls(?) wer undure the seat.
>   thats how I new she waz youre's.

I folded the note carefully and slid it into my back pocket.

*   *   *

One mystery was solved, but in it's place two more had cropped up. *D* was the person who'd had *Melinda* the past several months– this much I knew for sure. But who was *D* and how had he figured out I was the boat's owner? Whoever he was, he'd kept good care of her. She looked as good– if not better –than the last time I saw her. The old mushroom claw anchor was still here even, though it took me a moment to realize this, since what looked like a new length of rope– about 25 feet –had been tied to it and was wrapped neatly around the stem of the anchor. Stepping over the bench seat I went towards her bow, and there, also, neatly wrapped together in a compact bundle was my casting net. It looked like it'd been mended in several spots (it'd certainly needed it), and attached to it now was the same sort of braided rope that was tied to the anchor.

Already I felt like I knew something about this *D* fellow. He was neat. At least with boats. He had good eyesight, too, to detect those initials I had etched on the bench's underside. Especially for someone with only one eye.

After inspecting the net I returned it to *Melinda's* storage cubby-hole in the boat's bow and then walked back to the spot by the screen porch where Mister Johnson and Fred were still standing.

From halfway up the dock the two men did not look all that different in color, and this was not because Fred was light-skinned. A lifetime around boats and the water had turned the white man to a deepwater tan as dark as tobacco and the little bit of hair he had left under his wide straw hat was bleached white. As I approached the two men I could see Mister Johnson leaning on his cane, taking a long drag on a cigarette, and studying me hard. Walking up the dock I got the sudden, peculiar feeling that all of this was taking place under an open blue sky, the most glorious sky I'd seen in some time.

"Don't worry none 'bout leaving her right where she is for a while if you like, son. I'd be skittish too, if I'd lost my only boat."

"Thanks, Mister Johnson. I'll pay you whatever the dock fee is. I'm mowin' lawns, so... "

"Whoa, whoa. Tell you what. You come over here and mow this grass twice a month and you can leave her there whenever you like, as long as you like. You can even use my mower. Fred's got all he can say grace over what with keeping all these boats up." The thin man kicked lightly at the tall grass growing up over the edge of the dock with his good foot and stuck out a leathery brown hand as he made me the offer.

"That's a deal... that's a great deal. Thank you. Thank you, Mister Johnson." I reached out and shook the man's hand. It felt like the warm supple leather of a stiff old baseball glove that had been worked over real hard and softened some– first with saddle soap, then with a piece of coarse sandpaper.

Maybe *Melinda* hadn't found her way back like I'd always said she would. Maybe she'd had some help along the way, some much needed help, and she was brought back. It didn't matter to me a bit. She was back, safe and sound, and I was glad of it.

That's all that mattered now.

Plate Spinning

Once again, a strange dream. This one had little to do with Grayson, though. Well, maybe more than a little, but it was not *strictly* about him, put it that way.

Some of this one I knew exactly where it came from. The part where I was struggling to keep all those plates spinning on the end of those long thin wooden rods was more than a little familiar. There's this act on The Ed Sullivan Show sometimes, where a man balances large dinner plates on the end of long wooden dowels by spinning them on the rods' tips. He starts out with one plate, then adds another and then another, and before you know it he's got nine or ten plates going– all at the same time. Only problem is by the time he gets the last plate spinning the first coupla' plates are giving out of steam, wobbling uncertainly on the ends of their rods, and so the man has to frantically run down the line and give the rod a well-timed jolt or tweek to foster its' plate's continued spinning. Then, one by one, he works his way down the line of plates and jostles the rods in just the right fashion to keep them spinning. Always, midway through the act at least one of the plates begins wobbling so outrageously that you just know it will succumb* to gravity's eternal tug and come crashing down onto the table at any second. Not once, though, have I ever seen the man let a plate fall.

This scenario* (with one big difference), made up the main part of my dream. The variation, or spin (so to speak), on my dream was the fact that instead of just spinning plates, I was spinning plates with people on them. On one plate there was, of course, Grayson. On another plate was Leah. On another was my grandfather and on another was Patti. Somehow, the fact that these were real living people did not seem as strange to me as the next plate I saw. On top of this plate was the mascot for Oceanside High School– the Antebellum Southern Gentlemen bedecked in glorious purple and white. The next plate contained two people– the two rough looking characters in the little skiff who were unlawfully netting back in March. The same men my grandfather had managed to bluff. (Over the last several months I'd had more than one nightmare about these two.) I sensed there were more plates involved, but the only other one I could recall was the one with Jim, our neighbor's old Chow, on it.

Having witnessed (and admired), the real thing on TV several times I found that I was familiar with the process and I was able to get all the plates up and spinning and keep them up without too much work, at first. The problem was keeping them up, for just as I got the last plate up and going, like the man on the Sullivan show, I had to rush down the line and work on the first plate and then, of course, right after I got that first plate taken care of there was the matter of the second, and then the third and all the way down the line and by the time I was at the end it was time to go back and pay some attention to that first plate again. It was sort of like what the old man had told me about bridge painters as we crossed the long bridge over to River-ville one autumn afternoon while a crew was busy painting it.

"Helluva' job. Time ya' get done it's time to start all over again."

That's just what this plate spinning business was like. Time you got the last one going it was time to go back to the beginning of the line and start all over again.

Since Grayson was on the first plate I found it was easy to keep track of and I was able to pay special attention to it. The spokes on Grayson's wheels gleamed and caught my eye easily, and no matter where I was on the line if I noticed my brother beginning to slow too much I quickly left what I was doing and got him going again. After Grayson, I paid next special attention to Leah and my grandfather's plates. Heck, it wasn't all that hard. The guy on television did a good job, but shoot, he was probably hamming it up some, too. Just like magicians did.

Towards the end of the dream I began to lose my concentration. I felt like I was gonna' wake up any moment so I figured it would be a good idea to get all the plates down. I paid attention to Grayson first and was able to pull out the rod and catch his plate easily, and I placed it gently on the white-linen draped table. Next, I went to remove Leah's plate, but for some reason I couldn't pull out her rod. It seemed stationary, like it was attached to the table in some mechanical way. All the while, from the corner of my eye I could see my grandfather and Jim's plates were beginning to wobble some. Not much, but more than I was comfortable with. Dang, what in the world could be holding up her plate so forcefully? Finally, almost desperate, I hit the rod holding up my mother's plate as hard as I could, and it bent over where it joined the table and came sailing down towards the floor. I lunged to catch it and my effort and my posture (as I layed out to grab the plate), reminded me for a brief second of diving to catch one of Mick's perfect spirals.

From the corner of my eye I could see Jim's plate tilting severely (probably from the jolt I had given Leah's rod), and though I gave it my very best effort the dog's plate fell to the table before I was able to get a hand on it, and broke. Then, in the next instant it disappeared, just vanished like dust blown away, and as I stared for a brief second at this phenomenon I looked up quickly to notice the old man's plate which was now also wobbling very sluggishly and just as it was about to fall off of the rod's tip I lunged once again... and then I awoke, my heart beating a mile a minute like I'd just run the cross-country track in P.E..

*   *   *

"How do you think she's taking it, Pawpaw?" Darn, there I went– slipped again, calling him that baby name.

"Pretty well, bubba... so far. Whadda' you think?"

"Hard to tell. Sometimes, when I think she's doing good all of a sudden she gets unglued and it's back to the same old thing."

"I know."

"Why does she get like that, you reckon?"

"Good question, boy. If I knew the answer to that one I'd be even smarter than I am already, and that might be too darn scary, even for me."

The afternoon was going along lazily and my grandfather and I were going along with it in *Melinda*, drifting down the intracoastal past Mile Marker 11 just north of the little bridge. Here the waterway was wide and rife* with grassy islands strewn throughout. Most of the islands were made up of nothing other than marshgrass, but some nearer the shore came complete with tall palms and pine trees. Down by Mile Marker 12 there was a larger island right in the middle of the waterway that had more trees than any other island around, and besides a small grove of pines there was even an old gnarly oak that grew just along the island's skinny strip of sandy white beach. Here was where the old man and I (and others too, I guessed), stopped sometimes and pulling *Melinda* up on the little white beach, we took turns disappearing into the stand of pines to, what the old man called, *commune with nature*. My friends and I just called it taking a leak.

The sky was intermittently* clear and dark. When it was clear the islands looked yellow-brown and far away and the water appeared light-gray, but when the sky darkened (as it often did late in the afternoon during the summer), everything looked closer and the grass became green– greener, the deepest green

I'd ever seen. The very same green of the small lizards that scattered underfoot in the same summer months. The lizards turned colors, too, and you could watch them if you were very still sometimes as they turned from light brown to dark green. When I was younger, up until a coupla' years ago, I'd always try and catch one of these lizards and every once in a while, if his tail didn't brake off in my hand, I succeeded. Holding the small reptile gingerly in one hand I would lightly stroke his velvety back with the index finger of the other. Depending on how frightened the creature was, and how calm I was, sometimes I could feel the lizard's tiny heart beat in the palm of my hand. Once, when my grandfather caught me in the carport holding a captured lizard, the old man remarked on what a good bass bait the small reptile would make. This sudden proclamation startled me and as though on cue I relaxed my grasp. That was all the opening the little critter needed, and he instantly made his getaway. It was just as well, I thought, for the idea of slipping a hook into the velvety-white underside of the little lizard's soft pouchy chin did not appeal to me at all. There was a vast difference (no matter what the old man said), between a cricket and a lizard.

When the sky darkened, as it did now, and the grass was greenest, the water turned purple (that's the closest color I can think to call it), and it was then that the intracoastal was at it's most glorious and when I felt most alive out here. The colors so brilliant they put you in mind of a painting. Not something done by an amateur like the works I'd seen by members of the Beaches Art Guild whose efforts hang lifelessly in the clapboard dwelling up on Ocean Street that also housed the library, but a drawing executed by someone more expert; by a real artist with the ability to truly capture on canvas what was to be seen and felt out here when a big wind blew in across the marsh, undulating and swaying like some sorta' huge wheatfield, bringing with it that certain clean, electric smell of rain. Even when it poured, and we managed to get wet (despite the rain parkas the old man made sure we stowed), it was always worth the slight discomfort to see the sharp greenness of the tall marshgrass against the solid backdrop of a dark purple sky.

*   *   *

Three shrimp boats, like the picture I had in my mind of the *Nina, Pinta,* and *Santa Maria* glided silently in in-line, one right after the other, with not more than fifty yards between them. Each of the boats was escorted by a flock of insistent gulls who squeaked and squawked above and took turns diving down towards the boat, picking off any by-kill thrown overboard by the shrimpers. All three boats motored in nets-up. As they came nearer, the boats looked so huge this close up that it was a wonder– like magic –how they sat up on the water's surface.

As the last of the boats moved by one of the men on deck who was leaning against the boat's high gunnels and smoking a cigarette looked across the water at my grandfather and nodded. The old man returned the nod as the big boat motored past and then the shrimper cupped both of his hands up to his mouth and yelled:

"Big blow coming! Wouldn't get too far out!"

"Thanks," the old man yelled back. "Appreciate it."

The three boats continued on their way and a few minutes later, after the wakes of the boats had passed, I spoke:

"I thought you didn't care for netters."

"What gave you that idea, boy?"

"The way you talked about those men last March at the beach when......"

"They weren't netters, boy... those were poachers, plain and simple. Big difference. These men here (the old man nodded with his head towards the departing boats), are doing things right. I can tell by the shape of their boats they're being responsible. Ain't nothing wrong with shrimping, long as you do it by the rules. Good honest work. Big difference between that and what those scoundrels out at the beach were up to."

"Yes sir. I see what you mean... I guess."

"Good. Now let's turn tail and head in. Start the motor and we'll troll back, slowly. Sometimes, just before a big storm the fishing gets real good. It's like the fish can sense something's coming and they load up before the water gets stirred up bad and it gets hard to see. Least that's my theory."

"Sounds good to me," I replied. I was proud of myself. I'd almost slipped and called the old man that name I used to again, but I caught himself. I turned around on the back bench and pulled the black handled rope, starting the 9.5 horsepower motor on the first try.

"Stay near the edge here and we'll see if we can't pick us up a coupla' nice redfish."

"Yes sir. You're the boss."

"Now you're talkin'. You're getting smarter every day, boy... smarter every day." The old man spoke as he grabbed up a shrimp from the bait pail, flicked off it's tail with his thumb and securing it on his hook, sailed the new bait out towards the oysterbar flats right by Pine Island.

"Pretty as any place on Earth." the old man said, gazing south across the broad expanse of marsh that was the northern tip of Crying Child Island. It was starting to drizzle a little, spawning innumerable small concentric* circles on the water's dark surface; the circles' tiny widening walls bumping up against and blending into each other– new circles falling all the time, *blending...blending... blending.*

*   *   *

I usually trusted my grandfather's judgment (after all, hadn't he been all over the world?), and I had to agree when we were out on the water by the marsh islands and away from the little Beachtown it was pretty, almost like it was another place altogether. But *pretty as any place on Earth?* It was fine if the old man felt that way, fine, but to me it seemed like an awful lot to swallow. No offense old man, I thought to myself, but I was going to have to reserve judgment on that one. And then suddenly I remembered the dream about the plates and then I thought about the two-inch high doll the old man had sent me years ago, the one I still kept in the drawer by my and Grayson's bunkbeds (a Worry Doll it was called, from Guatemala).

I recalled vividly the dream and I realized for the first time all day why I should feel so anxious out here where I had always felt so differently, so calm, before. My worry, the one I would have to remember to take to the doll before I went to bed this night, was about the very last part of the dream. The part where Jim disappeared and my grandfather's plate was about to fall. What could that mean? What would the lady psychiatrist on TV say about the images of the plates? What did it matter what she would say? It was all a lot of baloney, this stuff about dreams, anyway. Let her say whatever she wanted.

It really was a lot of baloney, I thought, as I held the tiller of the small outboard and guided *Melinda* through a light rain past the thin beach of Crying Child Island, under the darkest sky I could ever recall out here, slowly trolling our way back home.

Love and Work

"Don't ever look down on a working man, boy. He's the way things get done in this world. Paper-pushin'-desk-monkeys always looking for some way to make something on other people's sweat so they can keep their own hands clean. But make no mistake about it. Them that's working, and the work they're doin's, what really matters. End of lecture."

"I wasn't makin' fun of him. I just thought he looked sorta' funny... "

"Didn't say you were, boy. Just something I been meaning to share with you for a while, and now was as good a time as any." After a short silence the old man spoke again. "You're right. That ol' coot did look rather humorous."

"Which one? The farmer or the mule?"

"Hee-hee. Good one boy, good one," my grandfather laughed. The eternal pipe dangled from the corner of his mouth.

What we were discussing was the scene in the large field we'd just passed. Heading south in the old man's Imperial on US 1, we were coming from Hilliard, just below the Georgia-Florida line, heading back towards the Beach. The farmer was decked out as traditionally as any Florida Cracker could ever hope to be: faded denim overalls, worn tee-shirt underneath, and a wide-brimmed tattered straw hat up top to mitigate* some of the relentless misery being generated by the intense August midday sun. Almost surrealistically*, the farmer sported a pair of red heart-shaped sunglasses.

But it wasn't the man's appearance that had gotten me to going so much as the predicament he seemed to be in: standing in front of a long-eared mule who'd stubbornly made up his mind that the middle of this field (which looked to be the only break for miles in a long stretch of piney woods), was as good a place as any to sit for a while. How long the mule had been sitting and the old farmer had been tugging on him to get up there was no way of knowing. But in my mind I would eternally place the two of them right there in the middle of that half plowed-up field of dark sandy soil, doing just what I'd seen them doing as the old man and I passed by.

"You been mighty quiet lately. Something on your mind you wanta' talk about?"

"No sir. Nothing really."

"Don't sound too convincing to me. If I had to guess, it's either got to do with money or women. Finance or romance. Am I right?"

"Sorta'."

"Sorta', shoot. I hit it dead on and you know it. Ain't about the first, I'll bet a dollar to a donut it concerns the latter. Women, that is."

"You're getting warmer."

"Thought so. Girlfriend trouble?"

"No sir. To have girlfriend trouble you gotta' have a girlfriend. Which leaves me out right from the get-go."

"What about this Patti you were all sweet on?"

"How did you know about Patti? Why Grayson, that sorry little son of a......"

"Whoa, now. That's no way to talk about somebody– even your own little brother. I've got connections, you know. How I found out don't matter. If you don't wanna' talk about it, okay. Just don't bust-a-gusset getting mad at someone else 'cause things aren't going your own way."

"Yes sir ," I replied, after a moment worth's reflection.

"It's safe to say this Patti is not your girlfriend, then?"

"Yes sir. That would be an imminently* safe statement."

"Any other prospects on the horizon?"

"No, not really"

"Hatten' been a fella' born yet that hadn't had that done to him, once or twice. Jilted, or never got started?"

"Sort of a combination. Naw... never got started, I reckon."

"Done that a few times, myself. Sometimes, when you get a gal on your mind that's all that'll take... I mean, that's all you can think about. Funny thing is, you can be slap-dabbed crazy about her and she may not even know you exist. It's like you're thinking so hard about her that you can lull yourself into expecting... or assuming... some sort of reciprRicatin' is taking place, but if you don't know for sure, thinking and guessing about it just don't get the job done. Brother, but it's getting awful smoky out there."

"Must be burning around here close by," I said.

"Naw. We'd smell the pine if it was close. My guess is it's over in the Okeefenokee somewhere. Big burn over there– been going on nearly a week, now. Heard about it last night on the radio."

"Who started it?"

"The Good Lord... meaning lightning more than likely. It's

okay... needs to burn every coupla' years... keeps the new growth going."

"Smoke can travel all the way over here from that far away?"

"If it's a big enough fire. Back to your love life. This a temporary jilt, or one of the more permanent variety?"

"I reckon it looks pretty permanent. She's headin' overseas with her family for a coupla' years. Her father's in the Army and he got stationed in London, England."

"Yeh, sounds permanent to me, 'less you're partial to the long-distance variety of romance."

"Yes sir. It sure does."

That's all I'd said. Hell, that's all I could say. It was all so incredibly incongruous*. To be headed down the road in this old car with my grandfather out here in the middle of loblolly nowhere, where the only human you were likely to pass was some funny looking old farmer and his mule, with the big swamp burning up and sending smoke– with it having no respect for state lines –all the way down here and with all that going on, the reality of my life being this scene right now, somewhere else in my brain I was thinking about Patti and where she was– if she had already gone. If she had, then she would be in another world, and it wouldn't be just a matter of distance, either. She'd be so far gone that she'd be out of my orbit altogether. I truly couldn't figure out how to tell the old man about all this. Where would I start? How in the world could I ever explain a situation like this to my grandfather?

"Through town or the ferry?" the old man asked.

"Ferry sounds good to me. Sound good to you?"

"Hell, why not? Can't dance."

*   *   *

At the last exit off Hwy. 1 before town (our final chance before we'd be committed to having to go through Riverville), my grandfather took a left turn guiding the old Imperial toward the river.

Alongside the wide rolling body of water we rode. With the car windows down the musty full smell of the river, a smell as old as life itself, instantly filled the car assaulting my nose and the back of my throat. The only other smell I could compare it to was a cross between the locker room after P.E. Class and the sharp smell which emanated* from the small glass decanter Leah kept vinegar in. Sweat and vinegar. The same solution the Roman soldiers had sponged onto Christ's forehead during his agony on the Cross.

The tide was headed out. Nearly all the way I assumed, for the current– you could tell from the road, even –was swift, like it was secretly trying to keep up with the progress of the Imperial. We rode over the smooth blacktop devoid* of any other traffic now right alongside the river, following neatly along it's bank. An old cow path, this road was.

Seated there next to my grandfather as he guided the old Imperial and thinking about it for a mile or so I decided 'that ain't right, that wasn't how it was... we could never keep up'. Like that poem we'd read in Mrs. John's class said, the river 'glideth at his own sweet will', and whether or not our car, or several cars for that matter, were riding alongside it was of no matter, no consequence. The river was flowing at it's own divine speed; a speed set eons ago when the Creator had formed the Moon and given it jurisdiction* over the comings and goings, ebb and flow, of all Earth's waters.

Maybe we could beat the tide this once. Maybe we could even go faster than the tide every day of the year, this year and for several years to come, but after a while we would slow down; we would have to. But the river would still be flowing– flowing towards the sea, like it had done since the beginning, like it did now, and like it would continue to do long past the time we had the will– or the ability –to race.

*   *   *

After fifteen minutes of shadowing the river's path we came to the ferry loading lot. The old man pulled up to the front of the lot and together we watched just as the *Buccaneer I*, the oldest of Mayport's two ferries, pulled away from it's moorings– headed the quarter mile or so across the river. From here we were within view of the river's yawning broad mouth and without saying a word the old man and I both opened the Imperial's front doors and emerged from the car to stretch and work out the drive's crampiness. I noticed there were only a few cars on the departing boat and then I saw that the usual cadre* of gulls which followed the ferry had diminished, too. Only a few hardcore birds worked this area in the middle of the week, I figured. Weekends, when the ferry was packed to capacity on every trip across, were a different story. Then the sky was full of seagulls suspended like marionette's in their herky-jerky motions above the boat's wake in pursuit of manna* from the hands of good-natured tourists.

"We can't stop ourselves," the old man said as we both leaned against the side of the Imperial in the otherwise empty lot, gazing at the river scene before us.

"What's that?"

"I said, we can't stop ourselves. We're determined to foul up everything we got here on God's green earth. It's as though we're hell-bent on foulin' up the whole damn planet."

"How do you mean?" What was this all about, I thought?

"Look at all the trash on those rocks down there." I walked with my grandfather over to the edge of the retaining wall built from upright railroad ties and looked down to a group of granite boulders along the river's edge. An assortment of tin cans, several plastic bags, dirty rags and a large bird-nested wad of abandoned fishing line were strewn among the chunks of stone.

"Helluva sight. Ain't the worst, though. Visual pollution's one thing, but what we're doing with some of these chemical fertilizers and pesticides is a downright sin. I'm as much to blame as anyone. Used fertilizers and pesticides on them orange trees 'til it was coming out my ears. Problem is that stuff ends up places we don't want it. Lake Apopka's dead as a doornail. Used to be the best big lake in the state for bass, but you could electro-shock in there now 'til the cows come home and you wouldn't get enough fish to feed the Preacher Sunday dinner."

I shook my head in agreement, though exactly what I was agreeing with I was not entirely sure. The old man was in a mood, and with years of experience under my belt I knew it was best to just act like I was agreeing with him. That way he usually wouldn't carry on terribly long. If he got his say and no one disagreed with him he would generally leave it at that. I had to admit, though, this was a new box of soap my grandfather had stepped up on. I had never heard the old man express an opinion on the ill effects of pollution before. Gotta' hand it to him, I thought. Just when you were sure you'd heard it all, all he had to say on whatever subject, he'd surprise you and throw in something new to chew on.

"What's gonna' happen then?"

"When?"

"If people don't stop using pesticides, and all?"

"They won't... can't. They all got blinders on. All they can see is what's right in front of them and if they think the stuff is helpin' 'em grow better, then damn the torpedoes, full speed ahead."

"But you know; I mean, you can tell, Pawpaw. Why can't everybody else? Can't they pass some laws or something?"

"They will, sooner or later. Only problem is later may be too damn late to do any good. Maybe, if we're lucky, enough folks'll come to their senses before things are too far gone. Time'll tell."

"Jeez. I never realized it was that bad. You make it sound so gloomy, Pawpaw."

"It is, boy, it is. What could be gloomier? There ain't but one Earth– they aren't making 'em anymore. The way we're headed though, one may not be enough. I'm sayin' the next twenty or thirty years will tell if we can stop ourselves. Then we'll see how smart 'a monkeys we really are. There's an old saying– 'God's in the details', but that's bull. Details are what lawyers specialize in and we all know they're 'bout as far from bein' godly as you can get. I'll tell you boy, when most lawyers refer to the Almighty you can bet it ain't the Lord they're talkin' about, but the almighty dollar bill."

Boy, but the old man was fired up over somethin', I thought, wondering what it was that had gotten his goat so. (Looking back on it now I can't help thinking maybe all this talk about pesticides had something to do with the fact he had two wives in a row to die from cancer. In that case you could see how someone could get riled up, thinking maybe they had something to do with poisoning a loved one or loved ones, rather. Of course I didn't put any of this together at the time.)

Looking out across the river I watched as the ferry began to unload it's few cars. Just past the boat– a mile beyond –lay the wide, horizontal vista* that was the mouth of the river. Here was the spot where the river died, I thought, and ceased being a river. The spot where it poured itself out and surrendered itself into the Great Atlantic Ocean.

For all I knew, at this very moment she could be crossing this vast body of water, headed over to her newly adopted home. For all I knew, she could already be there.

* * *

The *Buccaneer I* was halfway back across the river when the old man and I returned to the car. Attempting to avoid a large clump of sandspurs which had sprouted up out of the middle of the black-topped lot like some lone vegetative sentinel* in an otherwise flat and barren terrain, I failed to detect a second more obscure* clump which had also succeeded in overcoming the thick asphalt and which lay now directly in my detoured path. This second clump was made up of young green stickers which meant they were smaller. It also meant they were harder than the more mature brown variety, and it was several spiked balls from this less discernible* but equally tormenting group that managed to find their way through one of the holes in the sole of my right tennis shoe. Piercing into the bottom of my foot, the spurs stuck deep into my heel. It was the sorta' predicament which had elicited* howls, even tears, when I was younger. Here was one incidental* punishment of childhood Grayson never suffered, I thought. Standing in the middle of that large lot on one foot like a flamingo, I reached down and pulled the offending spikes out with several quick jerks, then resumed my trek back towards the car.

If she was already there I knew I could never catch up. Hell, I couldn't even get out of Oceanside for more than a day and here she was taking off halfway across the world to live in a foreign country. She would have such a head start on her life that she would be light-years ahead. It'd be like any ship that carried her across these waters would also be catapulting her at the same time into another world altogether– far ahead of me and the little Beachtown that lay across this river, forever. The finality of it was so mind-boggling, so... well... *final!*

Forever seemed like a long dang time when you really stopped to think about it.

With this next story there begins the result of a lot of things that had been going on over the past several months. By going on what I mean is brewing, really (if that word could be said to apply to human situations. I think it can.).

When the old man and I headed out on the creek that afternoon I had no idea how close everything was to happening. I really felt like I was that guy on TV spinning those plates. Besides wondering what in the world was up with Patti, there was the nagging question of what was going on with that muscle biopsy of Grayson's. It had been so long the scar on his left calf was just about all healed. That had started up month's ago and the fact that no one was getting anything done there was extremely exasperating to everyone concerned. It was just about driving Leah crazy, I could tell and I was truly expecting any day for her to start in again, you know, fall off the wagon. It was just a matter of time, I knew. So did the old man. I guess if there could be said that any good came out of all this it was that the two of them seemed to be getting along pretty well now, for the first time in years. Something about hard times seems to bring the two of them together in some way. I mean, I never really heard them talking about it, but it was more like there was something there unspoken that if anything had more power that if they'd tried to be nice to each other with all sorts of kind words.

The old man was there a lot (he had to head back a coupla' times that summer to oversee some business with the grove), and more times than not when there he was the one who got up first and got breakfast going. Even though it was summertime and Grayson and I could sleep late he would still be there to make sure Leah got some breakfast and coffee in her before she left for work. She was still working for Mr. Evans heating oil company which is located all the way up at the very north end of Penner and then about a block towards the ocean, on Atlantic. He has always been that way about breakfast, a real stickler about it. That's not to say he's the type who pushes food, but he certainly wants you to start off the day right, is the way he puts it.

This next story takes place during the very end of the summer. Like I was saying, I not only had Patti and Grayson and Leah on my mind but the old man, too. He didn't seem like his self most of the summer. I mean, he still got up early and all, but he didn't seem to be as energetic and he wasn't nearly as fast with the wisecracks, either. Maybe I was so intent on worrying about everybody else I didn't notice he had his own worries he was mulling over.

Which reminds me of what he told me that day earlier in the summer, the time we were coming back over on the ferry from Hilliard:

'*Boy, you can get riled up thinking you are the only one with problems. Let me tell you something, though. If you could just walk down the Hall of Life for a short while and look up at the Wall of Troubles seeing all the types of problems folks have got up there... then you'd run thru there looking for your own, and when you found 'em you'd embrace 'em like some long lost friend.*'

That may not be it word for word but is the gist, pretty much, of what he had to say that day. It gave me something to chew on for a while, too, which was what he was intending to do, I'm sure. Whenever I think things are getting overwhelming I try to remember that day and him saying that. It has got a comforting sound and way to it when you think all is lost, believe me.

Funny, how you can think you are over something and then when you have not been able (or permitted), to do it for awhile you get the hankering again. Reading over this next story, I have got a strong urge once again to get out on the water. Just being able to get out there and cruise around– even with just the oars –would be nice. Well, I reckon that I am just one of those folks who definitely does not know what he has got until it is gone. And that is just how you get to feeling in this place after awhile... that whatever you once had or enjoyed doing is gone.

I know it sounds incredible when you read it, but the big incident starting at the middle of this next story happened– and just about like I have portrayed it here, too.

Lately, I've had this strange sorta' feeling, like I've got something to be thankful for. I reckon I do have something to be thankful for and that's the fact that Chief Franklins kept me from going straight to Marianna. Which is where I was heading until he intervened. A few guys here have been in that place and from the stories compared to it this place is a picnic. That is not to sugarcoat what it is like here, but some of the stories I have heard (even allowing for some exaggeration), lets me know how rough it could have been if someone had not been on my side.

The Justice of the Peace and Chief Franklins do not care for each other and since the JP is like a judge he can make things tough for the Chief, so I know he stuck his neck out for me some there. Funny how things work out since his son Johnny, who is a year older than me and a pitcher in Little League, struck me out every time I batted against him. He's one of those guys who looked like a semi-pro player by the time he was twelve. Boy, he could fire it in there.

I don't think I ever got a foul-tip off of Johnny Franklins. Not once in two years.

P.S. – *I'm feeling pretty good today since it is my understanding now that I am to finally get out of this place in the next coupla' weeks. By Thanksgiving, at the latest. At least, Leah claims this to be the case. Also, she is going to an AA club that meets several times a week in a little house down Penner almost to Beach Road. She says she is not like the other folks in there and does not really belong, but just kind of going along. Still, I think it's doing her some good. After all that's happened the last month or so maybe she is ready to come to grips with reality.*

No trick-or-treat last night (the first time I've ever missed), but everyone got a candy bar instead.

November 1, 1963
(All Saints Day)

Creek Talk

"There's something about this creek, boy. I don't know... just the way it is with the trees and the light a certain way. I fished with this rod all over Europe– England, France, Germany... France was the place for trout... and I've gone after some pretty big fish off Australia and Mexico, but this little creek right here is as good as it gets. Seriously... there ain't no doubt in my mind about it, and it's right in your own backyard. You won't learn to appreciate this place though 'til you get out on your own and do some travelin'. Then you'll know. It's something you won't miss 'til you've left it all behind."

My grandfather was talking as he made ready to cast a popping bug over towards a tight grouping of lily pads– about twenty feet from shore. It was an afternoon in early October and the gravelly utterings of my grandfather's whispering low tones were the only sound on the creek now that I had ceased rowing and stowed the oars (still in their locks), alongside *Melinda*'s gunnels. We'd only been out for a little while; long enough for me to catch a coupla' nice looking redbreasts using crickets and a quill float. It seemed to me the old man was more in a talking mood than a fishing one. Of course, I was not about to verbalize this observation to my grandfather. He'd be terribly offended by it, but dang, when I was out on the creek what I wanted to do was fish. Hell, talking was for back at the house. The only thing anyone needed to discuss out here on the water was fish– how many and how big.

As much as I enjoyed fishing with my grandfather and as much as I respected his ability to locate and catch fish it seemed like all the old man ever wanted to do lately was talk. Used to be he would reprimand me no end for speaking anything more than the bare essentials when we were out here together, but lately he was turning into a regular chatterbox. Oh, well, maybe if I stayed quiet the old man would simmer down, too, and we could get some fishing done, I thought. One thing was for sure. I had made up my mind this time that I would watch myself. I wasn't gonna' call the old man *Pawpaw* anymore. It made me sound like a kid.

I should'a guessed my grandfather would be in this kind of mood when I saw he was bringing the flyrod along. Seems like everytime he broke out that dang rod he'd start reminiscing, talking about the past– where he'd been and what he'd done. But that wasn't the thing that was so irritating. It wasn't the stories themselves, but the way he told them sometimes, like I'd been there, too, and we were two old buddies and my grandfather was remembering for the both of us. It was a bit much to take and there'd been a coupla' times lately I wanted to scream at the old man to shush up and just fish, but I knew, in the words of my grandfather, that there was two chances of that happening: *'Slim and none... and Slim just left town.'*

At least he wasn't giving me a hard time about my hair anymore. After that first blow-up he must have gotten it all out of his system. All he'd said after that was something regarding the great and unlimited human ability to get used to just about anything– no matter how hair-brained.

"Yeah, seems like I can remember being just about your age and my Pa tellin' me I wouldn't appreciate what I had where we were 'til I got out on my own and had a good look-see. Man-oh-man, was he ever right."

The old man swept the nine foot bamboo rod back and forth above our heads, letting out more line on each forward cast while the little white popping bug (with it's rubberband legs which gave it the look of a spider), delicately touched the water on each backward parry*. Finally, on the seventh approach, the old man released all the looped line he held gathered in the curled fingers of his left hand and threw a long cast that rolled out and dropped the bug with the wispy impact of a pillow-feather right alongside the lily pads. Bingo! Talk or no talk, that was truly something to see and I found myself smiling as my grandfather, seated in the front, turned back and peered above the top of his wire-rim glasses at me.

"Beautiful, Pawpaw, beautiful." Dang, I forgot again; already.

"I know. I'm just glad to see you got enough sense to appreciate the true blend of art and science you just witnessed. Now if that cast don't bring out something we'll know we're in the Dead Sea." Having said this, the old man commenced to what can only be described as playing his line in. He was not jigging it in or even twitching it back in, but a gentle combination of the two whereupon he tapped the taut line he held in the crook of his index finger gently just once. Then he waited for the disturbance this created to settle back down before he repeated the maneuver.

In less than thirty minutes my grandfather managed to bring in one decent sized bass and six redbreast with the poppin' bug.

"They're bitin' good today, I must say," the old man remarked, as he removed yet another red-breast from the bug's single curved hook hidden just beneath it's belly.

"You're killin' 'em with that bug," I said. "Some day you're gonna' have to show me how to cast that thing."

"Anytime you're ready, bubba. Anytime you is ready," the old man said and he held the bamboo rod in one hand and the popping bug in the other, offering it to me.

"Naaa... not now. I'm doin' too good with these crickets. Maybe next time."

"I don't know, Bubba. This old thing's past old and goin' on ancient. I might have to retire her before too long. You better get a shot at it while the gettin's good."

"How long have you had her?" I asked as I took the proffered* rod from my grandfather's hands, admiring the burled lacquered finish that covered and protected the antique bamboo.

"I remember exactly the day I got that rod. It was on a Saturday afternoon in November. We'd just beat the tar out of Rutgers 48 to 6, and the reason I remember is I intercepted two passes that day and scored a touchdown on the last one... 57 yards. Only time I ever scored... no I take that back I trapped North Carolina's quarterback in the end zone once for a safety... but that interception was my only touchdown. Man what a day! Warm and clear. Sneaky Gleason gave it to me, he'd bought it at Abercrombie & Fitch just a month before up in New York, and I loved her when I first layed eye's on her. Never wanted something of somebody else's so badly in my whole life. He knew it, too. He was rich, hell his pappy owned a buncha' car lots over in South Carolina, and he just up and gave it to me after that game. Something to remember that touchdown by, he said. He was right. Next day he an' Cotton Owens and I went up to Roswell... north of Atlanta... and went fishing on the Chatta-hoochee River... one of the best trout streams in the lower 48, back then... and I got to use the rod for the first time. Beautiful spot. We all three caught trout that afternoon... and a beautiful one it was, clear as a bell, but it had turned cold... so cold you'da gone to church just to hear about Hell. Temperature'd dipped down in the low thirties, but the sun was out most of the time and we kept taking nips from the quart flask Cotton carried and I swear somehow towards the end of the day we were all so goosed up we didn't know which end was up, but we kept catchin' trout... nice Brookies... native to the river there. That was the first place I ever fished with her, but I'll tell you that rod's been some places, bubba. All over."

"Boy, I'd sure love to try freshwater trout fishin' sometime," I said. I'd never been up to the mountains, not even the relatively close ones of North Georgia and North Carolina but I'd often dreamed of trying my hand at catching the wily trout my grandfather had told me about.

"I'll tell you what. You get to where you can cast that thing decent and we'll go up there. Scout's honor."

"Really?" I asked, excitedly

"I said scout's honor, didn't I? Besides, I got some old buddies up in Atlanta I need to drop in on. You just work on making a decent cast with that rod and we'll go."

"You got a deal," I said, handing the flyrod back to my grand-father.

The old man threw the popping bug out once more by a small clump of lily pads not far from the creek's sandy shore. Just as my hand entered into the wire bug cage for another cricket I heard a loud...

"WHOOOOA!"

and looked up to see my grandfather jerk up hard on the supple rod.

"Woo-ee! Man, he's a biggun'!" the old man said, pulling on the rod which was arched severely– more than I had ever seen it bend, and struggling mightily to gain some line on the boxy reel.

"Don't you know it!" I yelled out. "Don't lose him." I could see right away my grandfather was having more than a little trouble with this fish.

"I'm not planning on it boy, but I think he's got other ideas."

The old man was having little success at regaining much line. For every six inches or so he was able to reel in, the fish was putting up even greater resistance and he tore off another coupla' feet of line in a matter of seconds .

"Lordy, I hope that knot holds. If I'd a known we was gonna' hook up with Moby Dick I'd a been more careful tyin' it."

"How come he's not jumpin'?"

"Don't know, boy. Maybe he ain't in a jumpin' mood. Either that or he ain't a bass," the old man said, still putting pressure on the rod. He'd quit trying to regain line and instead I figured he was just hoping to maintain, and keep the fish from heading towards the lily pads alongside the shoreline. "Could be a big 'ol redfish, though."

"Can I help you any?" I asked grabbing the net as though ready to land whatever it was my grandfather was hooked up to.

"Get ya' oars out and let's see if we can keep this critter from heading back into them lily pads," the old man yelled.

"Okay," I said throwing down the net and swinging both oars out over the water. "Just tell me which way to head."

"The opposite way he's heading," the old man said. "I can't seem to get in any line. Don't think he's wrapped up in them pads yet, but he'd sure like to be. See if you can pull us back a little... not too hard, but just scooch us back a little. He's getting way too close to them lily pads– he can smell 'em."

I pulled on both oars and moved *Melinda* back, and I could feel the resistance. It was like we were trying to tow a paint can full of concrete through the water.

"How's it feel, boy?" my grandfather called out, still holding onto the rod, which, if anything, was arched even more severely than a minute ago.

"You can tell we're pulling something," I said. "Should I keep going?"

"Yeh, just a bit more. If we can get him back just a little more he'll have to fight on his own, and that's all I ask," the old man said. I could tell my grandfather was truly having a struggle with this fish.

"Seems fair to me," I said, continuing to pull on the oars. Just as I completed a full pull on both oars and had them above the water to begin another cycle something happened I'd never experienced before. We were moving– but the wrong way.

"Good golly, Miss Molly!" I said. "What was that?"

"Well, unless you hooked a motor up to this boat real quick-like that fish just pulled us."

"Can't be. How in the world could he do that?"

"I don't know, but he did." And then it happened again. The fish pulled the small boat with my grandfather and I in it a scant foot or so. Not much, but enough that you could tell it.

"Unbelievable!" I said.

"That's the problem... nobody's gonna' believe it," the old man said. "Listen son, just put the oars in the water and don't pull. Just try and keep him from pullin' us. You keep the boat stationary, and I'll bring him in."

"Yes sir. You still think it's a redfish?"

"I ain't got any idea what it is. But I'd sure as hell like to get a look at him, whatever he is. Even if we can't land him... hell, I just want to see what he looks like. Keep us right here and I'll get him in... at least a little closer."

"Okay. I'm just gonna' hold her right here like you said, Paw... yes sir." Almost, but good, I'd finally caught myself.

"Good. Do that." The old man began slowly pulling the rod up now; bent as much as it possibly could stand, I thought.

"I don't know how much more of this this old rod will take," the old man said.

*   *   *

"What's the biggest fish you ever caught on it?" I asked my grandfather half an hour later. I was leaning over the large ice chest in the middle of the boat, both hands on the oars which stood straight out from the sides of the boat. Again, I'd almost said it, said Pawpaw. It was hard not to, but I'd caught myself.

"Hooked a monster trout weighed an easy twenty pounds in France, once," he said, in a sort of struggling voice. "But that was over twenty years ago. Lost him right as I was about to net him, though. Biggest fish I've ever brought in with it's a twenty-eight pound redfish off the Cape, down by the Banana River. Didn't think the rod'd take that either, but after about forty-five minutes I landed her."

The old man's breath was getting shorter, I could tell, and he was struggling something awful with whatever was on the other end of the line. Still, he was able to slowly pump the old rod up a coupla' more times as he related to me the rod's history and each time he was able to bring the rod up to where at least the butt of it was pointed at six o'clock he was able to crank in a little more line on the ancient reel.

"You're getting him," I said, not a foot now from the old man's right ear.

"For right now. If it's a redfish it might have another run left in it and if it's anything else there's no telling what the hell it'll do," the old man said.

"What else could it be? It's gotta' be a redfish!" I exclaimed.
"Either that or a huge bass."

"It ain't jumped, though. In a lifetime of fishing for bass I've never seen a largemouth that didn't jump right off, at least once."

And just as the old man spoke, exploding forth from the creek's surface forty feet in front of *Melinda's* bow burst the largest fish I had ever seen from these waters...

SPLOOSH!!!

A beautiful silver Tarpon!

The fish came all the way out of the water, beating the creek's surface unmercifully with it's broad powerful tail, and shook it's head violently in an attempt to throw the bug.

"Whooooaaa!" said my grandfather, nearly losing his balance on the bench's seat cushion. By jumping the fish released and slackened much of the pressure on the rod's line and only by grabbing the bench and catching himself at the last second did the old man avoid ending up in the bottom of the boat.

"Holy mackerel!" I said.

"No. Holy tarpon!" The old man corrected me as he regained his composure, getting both hands on the butt of the rod before he was even sitting back up straight again. "What in hell is he doing in the creek this time of year, anyway? Don't he know it's September, not December? Must'a followed some shrimp'n here."

"Good gosh, I've never seen anyone catch a tarpon before. Coach Sutter told us about 'em last year. Said they're the fiercest fighter in the water, at least in these parts. I had no idea they could jump like that!" I said. "Boy, now I see what he was talking about."

"I told you about fish hitting a topwater lure, didn't I?" the old man said, pushing his glasses back up his nose. "He's a summer tarpon to boot. They're friskier, but this one must be lost. Let's see if we can land him and point him in the right direction," the old man continued. Once again the rod was bent back to it's former acute* arch, surely strained now as far as it could bend, I thought.

"I don't know. Tarpon on a flyrod sounds pretty iffy," I exclaimed.

"Shoot, boy, they been doing it in Miami for years. And big ones too... lots bigger than this," the old man said. "You better get back there and keep holding us out of them lily pads. We could be here a while."

"Do you really think that rod can keep up with a tarpon?"

"We're fixing to find out, son. Get back in your seat and get ready to row... when and where I say." the old man barked.

"Yessir." I replied.

*   *   *

It was getting obvious my grandfather was short tempered– not to mention tired –by the situation we now found ourselves in. This fight was strictly for bragging rights. We had come into the creek looking for bass and panfish and now the old man was hooked up to forty-plus pounds of raw muscle, bone and sinew– a Silver King. According to some of the tales I'd heard Coach Sutter tell, we could be out here for hours doing battle with this primitive creature, the most ancient of all fish, the Coach had said.

That is if the old man's tackle held out. The bamboo rod which had accompanied him all over the world had never been asked to deal with so severe a piscatorial* test before and it was somewhat doubtful, given the rod's age and condition, if it was going to be up for the fight. As far as I was concerned there would be no cowardice in cutting this fish off and resuming our search for tamer, freshwater fare. Shoot, at least you could eat a bass. The only thing tarpon were good for was a thorough, bone-jarring fight, and even then, according to Coach Sutter, more times than not a silver king (especially one this big), was gonna' outlast and defeat any small tackle rig.

But it wasn't gonna' do any good telling the old man this. There was no way in hades he would abandon this fight. So I reconciled myself to that fact and sat down once again in the back of *Melinda*, both oars in hand ready to do my grandfather's bidding.

"I'm ready. Just give me the word and I'll get you where ....."
SPLOOSH!!!
The mighty Tarpon jumped again.

This time the fish came completely out of the water, it's fanned tail flapping in a great blur across the top of the creek as though it had suddenly decided the only way to get loose was to walk away. At the same time the top part of the silver streak shook it's head back and forth at least three times and we could plainly see where he was hooked– right on the side hinge of what could technically be said to be his giant lip.

The popping bug shook against the side of the fish's mouth with each violent shake of the tarpon's head, but despite the ferocity of this movement the bug stayed right where it was– lodged in the silver king's lip.

The fish reentered the water and before long the old man's rod was bent even more than a moment ago. I noticed my grandfather had come out of his sitting position and was crouched now in the front of the boat with the flyrod's butt-end stuck squarely into his belt.

"As much as I hate doin' it, I gotta' give him his head," the old man said, letting go of some line. Feeling a lengthening of the leash, the implacable* fish took advantage immediately, tearing off up the creek; headed now towards the river and open water.

"Dang. Lettin' go is the easy part. Tying to stop the sonuva-bitch what's gonna' be hard," my grandfather said. "I don't have but about thirty-five yards of line on this thing. After that it's Katie-bar-the-door, I reckon."

"Point the front of the boat out towards the river, son. Maybe we can keep up with him. That poppin' bugs in his mouth good and this is pretty new line. If this old rod'll hold up we may have a chance yet. Boy, but he's acting real peculiar."

The old man stood straight up in the front of the boat now, the long bamboo rod cradled securely against his torso and held onto about two feet up it's length with both hands. The fish was a good sixty feet in front of *Melinda* which meant my grandfather only had about ten or fifteen yards of line left on the black boxy reel pressed hard against his belly. But again, despite giving the fish some line, the rod was curved even more severly than just a few minutes ago. I knew the rod would break any second now.

"Whoo-eee, damn!" the old man said, and even though I couldn't see his face I knew my grandfather was smiling up a storm. "I gotta' give this fish some more line, still. Go ahead Mr. Silver King, go ahead. Take all you want. There ain't much more, but damned if you aren't determined to take it all."

Once more my grandfather released the drag on the old Pflugger reel and I witnessed a blur of line come zinging off the reel and through the rod at incredible speed. He put the heel of his left hand underneath the reel to try to slow it down, and was able to reduce the rate of lost line a bit, but not much. He clicked the drag down once more and the line stopped abruptly. The shock was hard on the old rod, we both knew, but what else was there to do? Still, he'd succeeded in giving the abused rod some much needed rest, and it looked like the arch on the bamboo pole was not nearly so acute now.

But that was the good news. The bad news was that there was only a scant few yards of line left on the reel, and I could glimpse– for the first time ever –part of the smooth gold anodized spool, or core of the reel. The old man couldn't afford another run like that last one, I knew. He would either have to cut the line, have a broken rod, or just throw the whole damn thing overboard and let the fish drag it back out to the river with him.

SPLOOSH!!

Again, the mighty tarpon jumped. Though nearly a hundred feet from the boat the fish still looked huge.

SPLOOSH!!!

Another jump. This time higher than any of the earlier ones, the large scales of the beautiful silver writhing streak reflecting the gold of the setting sun as he twisted and turned above the black creek.

*   *   *

Thirty minutes later my grandfather was still standing in the front of *Melinda*, but there was something different about him, the way he not only held onto the bamboo rod, but also the way his body was situated in the boat. He seemed to be rooted there like a giant oak tree now, and I sensed some change had come over the old man during this fight with this fish. Earlier on, it seemed he had played with the fish and had nearly lost him because of it, but now playtime was over and the old man was serious. I had never thought of my grandfather as a powerful or strong man; had never really thought of him in any physical terms. He was just my grandfather, an old man who smoked a pipe, drove a big old car and loved to tease my brother and I, unmercifully. But nowhere in any of these descriptions had there ever been any room for the old man as being physically powerful. Now, for the first time, I was seeing another view of him, for he was engaged in a very physical fight, tethered with light tackle to a very powerful fish. If he was gonna' be victorious and bring this fish in it would take every bit of his physical power, his being, to do so.

"You got them oars out, boy?" the old man asked.

"Yes sir." I answered.

"Good. I think after those two jumps he's tired. He's looking to rest right now, so he'll be happy for a stand-off. Now here's what I want to do. You see where my line's goin' into the water?"

"Yes sir."

"I want you to row us, slowly, right towards that spot. I'm gonna' try and regain a little line, but I don't want that wily bastard to feel even the slightest bit of slack. You got me?"

"Yes sir."

"Okay then, let's go... slowly." the old man said. "Just glide them oars ever so gentle through the water, like we're sneaking up on him. I'm gonna' keep up with your progress with the reel here and take in whatever ground you gain in line. You get what we're doing?" my grandfather asked.

"I think so, Pawpaw," I answered. Hell, I said it again.

"Well, it's real simple, really. The trick's not letting him know."

"Okay," I said, rowing *Melinda* gently through the still black water. "Yeh... okay. I think I got it."

*   *   *

If I'd been discouraged about my grandfather hooking up to this large tarpon at first, by now I had experienced a total turn-around in my thinking and was determined to help him land the fish. It had become a challenge now and for the first time in my life I was seeing what it was like to do battle with a large fighting fish. The fact that the old man had him on such light tackle only accentuated* the experience and I felt myself caught up in the exhilaration of the battle. In some way this was different, more than just fishing now, I felt. It was hard to put into words, but somehow the battle between my grandfather and this fighting fish seemed larger than just a contest between a man and a fish. Of course, the fish didn't know any better. He'd just tried to grab a little bite and all he knew now was he was being pulled, for the first time probably, in a direction he did not wish to go. For him it was strictly a physical battle, pure and simple. The fish was only doing what came naturally, and was high-tailin' it, literally as well as figuratively, away from where he was being pulled. But up here it was something else. True, it was a physical battle, but mixed in with that were some other things to consider, also. The exhilaration and tension were so acute it did something to how you thought about things, important things, like time. It made it more serious. Not more serious, that wasn't right...it was more like it put an edge on things and made them more real. That's it! I'd hit on it! Everything seemed more *real* to me now during this fight, and I found now that more than anything else in my life I didn't want it to end. All the other stuff was real too, it mattered also, (you couldn't say it didn't), but in some strange sorta' way it didn't matter. Naw, it wasn't that it didn't matter. It was more like all the other stuff would be okay and it didn't matter to *worry* about it. *That was it!* This fight, this battle between my grandfather and this fish was what was important and was all the room I had in my head now to think about. *This was what was real!* I could concentrate all my thinking on this right here and somehow that took care of, sharpened, everything else up.

It was like the fight between my grandfather and this fish had suddenly brought everything into focus, and I felt, I *knew*, for the first time that Grayson would be okay. For the first time in months I could let go of worrying about my brother. No matter what sorta' results came back from Gainesville it would still be okay, and it would be okay because of this fight between my grandfather and the fish. This was important, I thought, and I hoped I could hang onto it, this thought, or rather this way of thinking. Heck, I wasn't even thinking of Patti out here. Everything was clearer this way.

I kept rowing, keeping a steady eye now on the line leading straight from the bowed tip of my grandfather's rod to a spot about fifty feet in front of the boat and out into the blackwater. My grandfather was perfectly still, like he was some sorta' statue of a man fishing instead of a real person. The only other motion in the boat was the almost undetectable move-ment of my grandfather's right forearm and hand as he ever-so-slowly reeled in the compensatory* amount of line, picking up the slack from the boat's movement. Together, rather than reeling the big fish into us, we were reeling ourselves up to the big fish. Complete coordination between rower and reeler was necessary for this action to be successful, for one false move– either too much or too little reeling or rowing –and the tarpon would surely sense it. And though I had complete faith in my grand-father's ability now to best this fish, there was still the very apt question of whether or not the old bamboo rod was up to the fight. That was the one weak link in the whole equation, I knew. Physically, I was sure the old man was a match, but it would take more than physical prowess. It would take finesse* to land this fish. Experience, along with a certain amount of pure luck, would come in handy, too, I knew.

"You're doing good boy... doing good. Just keep rowing like you are 'til I tell you to stop." the old man whispered, not taking his eyes, even for a second, off the line.

"Yes sir." I replied. I couldn't remember ever having said *yes sir* so many times in one day in my life. Coach Sutter would be proud, I chuckled to myself. It was all the instructions, I thought. This must be what the military was like. First being told what to do, then answering '*Yes Sir*', and then doing it.

"We're gettin' closer, and he ain't made a move." the old man spoke lowly. "This may work after all."

The bend in the rod, though still sizable, was the least it had been during the entire fight and I was beginning to think that maybe the tarpon had tired, was throwing in the towel, though I resisted the temptation of saying so out loud. Sure as heck, saying anything like that was tantamount* to inviting bad luck and the fish would be miraculously reinvigorated and would tear off down the creek with us in tow, and all because I had opened my big mouth. No, I promised myself I'd keep hush unless my grandfather asked me a direct question, now.

*　　　　*　　　　*

For the first time in half an hour the old man turned his head back towards me and spoke.

"Whatta ya' think boy? Seem like your friend here's ready to throw in the towel?"

Oh, no, I thought, and no sooner had that thought took hold in my mind than all hell broke loose.

SPLOOSH!!!

It was the biggest jump yet.

Instantly, the old man turned in time to see the huge fish dance across the dark waters of the otherwise peaceful creek. The sun was nearly set, but there remained enough light to illumine and reflect off the large platinum scales of this bucket-mouthed behemoth*. The chromed creature made a tremendous leap, its giant scales– each as large as a glistening new silver dollar –suddenly come to life. A broad swath of scales, serpentine* in shape and extending from his head to his tail, reflected the setting sun and were rose colored. Others mirrored the green pines right alongside the shore, and still others reflected the ebony creek itself. All of this I was able to take in in an instant, as though I were a human camera– the scene a snapshot photo-etched in my brain.

I wasn't sure if my grandfather had noticed, but I was sure the popping bug, which had seemed to be securely lodged in the fish's mouth during the last series of jumps, now looked like it was fixing to come dislodged from the tarpon's ample lip. We were pretty close to the fish, but maybe I had seen it wrong. I thought about it for a second and decided to break my promise to myself.

"Did you see how he was hooked, Pawpaw?"

"Sure did. Damn, but he's a smart one. All that time we thought he was resting, he was really on the creek bottom trying to work that hook out. Looks like he's done a pretty good job of it, too. Prob'ly found a stump or something down there to rub up against. Boy, don't ever try to tell me fish ain't got no sense. He knew exactly what he was doing. I'll bet the only reason he came up again's 'cause he thought he could throw it, now."

Once more the fish was tugging, and once more he was tugging hard. The old man's rod readily resumed it's previous radical arch as though it had been bent so hard for so long that it knew right what to do, what position to assume, and without saying a word both the old man and I knew not to be surprised by a lost fish. It could happen any second, now.

"Hell's bell's. At the risk of sounding like a bellyacher I'd say it'd be a miracle, a plain miracle now if that hook holds. Looked like he's just barely hooked." I sensed a tinge of regret in the old man's voice. He wasn't even trying to be quiet now while he spoke.

"I'm not absolutely positive Pawpaw, but it seems like Coach Sutter said that hinge on the side of their mouth and lip is just about pure cartilage. Maybe it'll stay in there longer than we think."

"Maybe so, son. Maybe so."

Suddenly, the fish began another run, and the old man's rod was jerked sideways and he was forced to stand once again to follow the flight of the fish.

"WHOA!!! Here we go again. He's rested all right. I think he's sensing he can just pull the dang thing out, now. No more rubbin' for him. He's headin' for the river. Start rowing, boy."

I did as my grandfather said and once more we were in pursuit of the fightingest fish I had ever encountered. The old man opened the drag and once again line, every bit our teamwork had just reclaimed and more, tore out through the rod's supple* length.

"I don't think he's gonna stop now 'til he gets to Mayport." the old man shouted as he cupped the reel in the palm of his left hand in an effort to reduce the speed of lost line. During the last series of jumps he'd taken his shirt tail out of his khakis and was using the cloth now to reduce the friction on his hand. This made it more difficult to slow down the reel, but maybe he'd have some skin left on that hand when it was all over.

"Doing good, boy! Keep her steady!" the old man called back to me. "I got about twenty feet of line left now. I'm gonna' just set the drag and see what happens. Here goes nothin'."

The old man flipped the serrated knob of the drag on the reel's left side and the bamboo rod instantly and fiercely dipped back down towards the creek. I turned my head to see what was happening and was startled to hear my grandfather yell out to me:

"Don't turn around yet, boy... keep rowing!"

How had he seen me turn my head when he was looking the opposite way? I chalked it up to advanced fisherman's intuition and kept pulling on the oars. I was beginning to truly get tired now and the sensation was only enhanced when I realized how far we had come in the last hour or so. Time does fly when you're having fun– or chasing a big fish, I thought.

*   *   *

OUT OF THE CORNER OF MY EYE I saw a tall clump of cattails and I knew right then we were hard up on the first series of big bends which led the creek back into the river.

It isn't possible, was my first reaction as I looked more intently at the golden strands of tall river grass that graced both banks, certain now that this was indeed the spot I'd figured we were. Either more time had gone by than I'd realized or I'd suddenly achieved Olympian status as a rower. Either way, we weren't but a quarter-mile from the river, and this was easily the farthest I had ever rowed *Melinda*, even in the first weeks I'd gotten her when all I did with my every free moment was row the boat up and down the creek. The only other times I'd been this far was when my grandfather had brought along the Evinrude and we'd cruised along effortlessly out to the river.

"Boy, but we've come a pretty far way, wouldn't you say, Pawpaw."

"Sure have, boy. Amazing what can happen while you're havin' a little fun." the old man said. "Looks like we got us a Mexican standoff, again. I can't believe that hook's still holdin'."

"Coach Sutter knows what he's talking about, huh, Pawpaw?"

"I reckon he does, boy. You still got that river anchor I gave you in the boat?"

"Yes sir."

"Good. Stop rowin' and get ready to heave it when I say... this is far enough. Come hell or high water, we're gonna make a stand right here."

"Okay," I said, resting the oars once again on *Melinda*'s gunnels and picking up the black iron anchor that resembled a large mushroom with three wedge-shaped cuts spaced evenly around it leaving a trio of like-size triangulated blunt prongs; prongs that did a good job of grabbing hold on the creek's sandy bottom, especially when a strong current prevailed.

I held the anchor in my lap messing furiously with the white Venetian blind cord which was tied to the anchor and loosely birdnested around it's shaft. Whatever happened, I wanted to be sure and have enough loose rope to get the anchor out, and I had no idea whatsoever how deep it was here. If it was like most of the creek it probably wasn't much more than five or six feet, but occasionally you'd hit a trough out here near the river where the creek bent and the tide flowed strong and it wasn't unusual to find some places hollowed out to twelve or even fifteen feet in depth.

I knew the old man was going to shout out *heave* any second now and I struggled against a great urge to panic. Hurrying, I was able to free up about ten feet of cord quickly and just as I undid the last large knot at the rope's end the old man yelled out:

"HEAVE!"

I threw the iron weight straight out the back of the boat. As it disappeared, the creek's peacefulness was broken with a loud and splashy:

KER-PLUUSH!

Next, I let out all of the free cord there was and waiting a few seconds, pulled against the anchor; at first gently to try and get it to grab hold of something. Then, when I felt the prongs had gained purchase on the soft creek bottom, I tugged harder, and then as hard as I could with both hands until I felt I could pull the boat back against the submerged weight.

We were anchored!

"Got her, Pawpaw," I said.

"Good. Now let's see if we can wrestle in this here beast. How deep would you say it is here?"

"Around seven... maybe eight feet," I answered.

"Not bad, but I'd hoped it'd be shallower," the old man said as he tugged on the bamboo rod. "Dang it, but this fish won't quit. I don't think there's any give-up in him," he said, continuing to pull on the rod, his left leg braced against the inside wall of *Melinda*'s portside and his right leg pushed back hard against the bottom of the bench seat he'd not sat down in for the better part of an hour. My grandfather stood like this for several minutes holding the fish where we were and just as I wondered how long this stalemate could go on the old man spoke:

"Ha, ha. I felt something. He moved a little... not much, just a little."

"You really think so?" I asked.

"Think so? Think so? Gemanettydamn, boy. I've only been hooked up to this critter for half a day. I guess I oughta' know when he's moved. Hell, by now I oughta' be able to tell when he takes a pee."

I couldn't help but laugh at this little bit of theatrics on my grandfather's part. We'd been out here battling this fish longer than either of us had planned and if it was starting to get to the old man that was understandable. Even though we were engaged in an earnest effort I'd had to fight the urge to break out laughing myself on a couple of occasions during the battle, so I knew what the old man was feeling. There was something about the implacableness* of this fish, after you were through being awed by his power, that made you wanta' laugh out loud.

Maybe it had to do with the old adage* of laughing to keep from crying. I wasn't sure about that, but I did know what my grandfather was feeling. We were probably closer right now than we'd ever been in our lives. All the fishing trips, the squirrel and rabbit shoots, all the car trips, all that time we had spent together, but this was as close as I had ever felt to the old man. For the first time ever, I realized, I wasn't wondering what the old man would say or what command he was about to give. It was as though we were a single entity* out here on the creek. We were still our separate selves, but somehow we functioned as one now in this struggle against the mighty tarpon. There was nothing my grandfather could say to me right now that would catch me off-guard, unaware, or unprepared. I felt that sure about the two of us. This was important too, this feeling, and it was another thing I did not want to forget. It all felt easy, like there was no effort involved at all.

"We still anchored good, boy?"

I gave a firm tug to the cord whose end was looped several times and secured around the worn single cleat on the starboard side of the little boat, stretching straight out into the creek at a twenty degree angle.

"Feels good and firm, Pawpaw," I answered.

"Good enough. He's got the tide with him now so we'll just sit here and see how long he can stand it," my grandfather said. "He's either gotta' give up or this rod does. Either one, it better be soon. Ain't much light left in this day."

The old man craned his head slowly up at the sky and looked west towards the river for several minutes. The silence and peace of the creek at this dusky hour reminded me of the moments just before church when everyone was either seated or getting seated, and the last few folks padded in quietly, whispering hushed greetings to friends they hadn't seen for a week.

"Shoot, you can see town from here. Never would'a thought that," the old man said.

I looked in the same direction as my grandfather and was as surprised as the old man to see, sure enough, a faint outline of a coupla' tall buildings and the top arch of the Warren Fullerton Bridge evident above the west horizon from our nestled spot in the creekbend. Lord, but if that sight didn't make it seem like we were far away from home.

"Look'a yonder! There's Quarantine Island. Stand up and you can just make it out a little to the north there," the old man said, pointing towards the dusky horizon as he spoke.

"Quarantine Island?" I said as I stood on *Melinda's* back bench seat trying to catch a glimpse of this strangely named place I had never seen, or heard of, before. From the little bit I could see it looked to be solid forest. "What kinda' name is that for a place?" I slowly asked, as though I were speaking to the creek as well as my grandfather.

The old man turned to look at me and I figure because he knew the creek was not likely to answer (at least in anyway I could understand), he answered:

"That's where ships use to drop sick folks off in the old days, before coming on into town. Hell, you could get all the way across the Atlantic, but if you didn't look good... you know yellowish... when you got this far, that place was gonna' be your home. At least for a while."

"Sounds gruesome," I said.

"I reckon it was," the old man answered. "I reckon it was."

"Anyone out there now?" I asked.

"Doubt it. Too spooky for anyone in there right mind to wanta' visit. Just ruins, mostly. I've heard tell runaway slaves used to hold up there, though. Knew they were safe out there... nobody would come check on them if they got that far. Old story goes it's really a little piece of Africa that broke off and floated all the way over here... all the way across the ocean."

"Wow," I said lowly, still straining to see the island.

*   *   *

Forty-five minutes later, my Grandfather and I were anchored in the same bend in the same creek, though it was no longer possible, lacking night vision, to see the faint outline of town. The big fish had made one more attempt in that time to become free and had almost succeeded, running the old man's line out to the point where there was less than ten feet left in the reel. I was sure then my grandfather would tell me to lift anchor. But the old man, remaining true to his word, had stubbornly refused, saying we were staying put, *'come hell or high water'*. With a scant few yards of line left, the fish quieted down again and the standoff resumed.

So there we remained, in the dark of night save for the faint illumination of a three-quarter moon that was just beginning to rise over the marshgrass behind us. Thirty minutes earlier, when the creek had still been darker than the sky above, I'd witnessed the first visible flickerings of Venus in the darkening blue sky. A few minutes later I'd caught the sudden streak of a meteorite as it swept across the jurisdiction* of Orion in the southeastern heavens. Now the sky and the creek were equally black and the thousands of tiny pinpoints of starlight were evenly sprinkled across both, and I felt like we were floating now in a world made up of a zillion diamonds and liquid black velvet.

"I know your mother's probably starting to worry boy, but we don't have much of a choice here ," the old man whispered. "We can't exactly pick up and leave now, can we?"

I had a feeling my grandfather was looking for a collaborator to back him up. Although he had rested for a while back when it had first gotten dark, the old man was standing again in the front of *Melinda* and for the first time during the battle I could feel the small boat gently rocking on the top of the creek. I wondered if my grandfather was getting unsteady. After all, he'd been battling this fish off and on now for nearly four hours. Even though it'd gone by fast, that was a long time to fight any fish.

"Heck no. She'll be all right. I'm sure she knows we're still out here ," I answered my grandfather, trying as best I could to put him at ease, telling him what I knew he wanted to hear.

"I hope you're right, boy. I got my hands full right now with our friend here... I don't need her mad at me, too."

"She won't be mad... least not too mad," I lied, knowing I was saying this for the benefit of the old man and Leah would indeed be mad. Hopefully, just mad, not furious.

"Looka' yonder! Somebody's coming down the creek," I said, pointing towards a bright light approaching us at a steady pace.

While there was nothing unusual about a boat out on the creek at night, this one had an intense beam that had to be some kind of searchlight, I thought, for the tight bright shaft of illumination was sweeping back and forth across the creek's shimmering surface as though in quest of something, or someone.

"Yeah, looks like he's looking for something, too," the old man said, craning his head back over his shoulder just enough to witness the approaching vessel. "Or someone."

As the craft came closer I could make out the shadowy shape of a small skiff with an outboard motor attached to its stern. From what I could see of her lines it looked like that new fiberglass boat Mr. Johnson had lent the old man and I; the same one that he kept out on the dock now to rent. As it came closer still I was certain it was Mr. Johnson's boat. There looked to be just a single person in the skiff operating the outboard's tiller and sweeping the light across the night and finally, as the craft closed in coming less than fifty feet away, the helmsman spoke up:

"Hello, there! Marty... is that you?"

Man, but it's spooky hearing your name called out in the dark over the water by the voice of someone you can't make out.

"Who goes there?" my grandfather called back.

"Rad." The voice called back shining the light directly on the old man's back and, raising it, illuminating his face.

"Geemanetydamn, Rad... put that damn light out. You're blasting the hell out of the night with that thing."

"Ed. That's gotta' be you," Rad said, a chuckle in his voice.

"Yeah, it's me. Who'd you expect to run into out here, Harry S. Truman?" the old man barked back. "What are you doing out here?"

"Looking for you."

"Well good, you found us. Now what do you want?"

"Pawpaw hooked into a giant tarpon! He's had him on the fly rod for hours," I interjected, swiftly.

"That right?" Rad shone the light again towards the front of the boat, quickly picking out the bent rod still pointing out towards the river.

"Woo-wee! Must be a biggun'. Got any fight left in him?" Rad asked.

"Enough. You didn't answer my question. Whadda' you lookin' for us for?"

"Not me, it's Leah. She sent me out here looking for ya'll. Well... actually Bertie did. She's pretty upset, Ed."

"What's wrong, Rad?" I quickly asked.

"I'm not sure, but Bertie's been over there all day and she called me back at the house and said to get out here and find ya'll. So here I am. Something to do with Grayson, I think."

"What? Somethin' happen to Grayson?" my grandfather asked.

"No, he's fine, but..."

"Well, what? Spit it out, Rad."

"I'm not really sure. Bertie said something about Dr. Cordray, the young 'un, calling earlier this afternoon. That's all I know. But ya'll better come on. Leah's fit to be tied."

"Damn," the old man said. There was just enough moonlight for me to see my grandfather looking out towards the creek, the expression on his face like he was looking for some place to put his rod and maybe sit down for a second to think about all this.

"What are we gonna' do?" I asked.

"Not much choice. Let him go, I guess."

"We can't," I shouted back.

"Ain't got no choice, boy," the old man said.

"You can't let him go after all the work we've... you've... put in, Pawpaw."

"Work? Shoot boy, if that was work I'm ready to clock in on a regular basis. You got a rope of some sort with you, Rad?"

"Yeah, there's some rope in the bow here. Ya'll wanta' tie on?"

"I reckon so. How big's that motor?"

"It's a twenty. Should do okay."

"Yeah, that'll pull us fine. Marty, let's change places. You come on up here and make ready to tie on that rope Rad's fixin' to throw you."

"Come on, Pawpaw. Let's stay just a little longer. You just about got him licked, and..."

WHOOSH!!!

As soon as I uttered the word *licked* the tarpon made his most spectacular jump yet. There was ample moonlight to see the wonderful writhing creature as he emerged from the liquid blackness, leaping up into the night.

"Holy-moley. Good-god-amighty. Ya'll weren't kiddin' about that thing. What's he weigh, Ed? Seventy? Eighty?"

Rad and I both looked at the old man in the front of the boat, and Rad shone the large lantern at his back. You could tell right away he was holding onto the rod again for all he was worth.

"Dont' get carried away, Rad. He's about fifty, fifty-five, tops. But he's a fighter, no doubt about it. Almost pulled this dang rod right out of my hands a coupla' times."

In between phrases the old man was grunting and I could tell, even in the dark, that here was some of the fiercest fighting yet between my grandfather and the tarpon. It was like the silver king was tired of this playing around and was ready now to resume his former life of prowling the creek and river unimpeded*.

"I'll bet," Rad said. "Man, but that fish jumped. I ain't never seen one come out of the water like that. It was like he was shot out of a cannon's, all I can say."

"Told ya'," I said.

WHOOSH!!!

Again, the powerful tarpon jumped. This time as high, if not higher, than the last jump.

"Be a real shame to let that thing go," Rad said, when the water quieted. "Ya'll got a net, Marty?" he yelled.

"Yeah, but..."

"Why don't I get out there and see if I can net him, Colonel? Whadda' you say?"

"Don't think the net's big enough, but hell, get out there if you think you can do any good. Stranger things have happened."

"Worth a try," Rad said.

"All right! I knew we'd get him," I said, and as soon as I said it the fish made a third– and final –jump, for as soon as he crested above the creek, his head a good five feet above the moonlit water, we all three heard the sickening **PING!** of something taut being stressed beyond it's capacity to hold. And in the very same instant the bamboo rod which had been all over the world and which had never been intended for such abuse– having been bent in various degrees of extreme curvature for going on four hours now –was suddenly straight again.

The three of us remained silent for a long moment. There was nothing to say. It was one of those times in life when any word spoken to help a bad situation along, to make things better, would have resulted in nothing less than blasphemy. Even I knew this much. Finally, the old man spoke:

"Well, that settles that. Good night, Mr. Silver King... and good luck."

The old man snapped off a quick salute towards the river, then reeled in the remaining line, laying the tested rod down alongside *Melinda's* starboard gunnel. Looking straight up, he grabbed the back of his neck and bent back as though working out a cramp.

"Marty, get up here like I said earlier, and let's get goin'. Your mother's waitin' on us."

"Yes sir," I answered.

*   *   *

During the thirty minutes or so it took Rad to tow us back to Johnson's Fish Camp I thought over my earlier feelings. When my grandfather had first hooked the big fish and I was so excited, so expectant, mysteriously it had seemed like nothing could bring harm to any of us. For some reason I'd held Grayson foremost in my mind when I'd had this feeling.

It was more than just a feeling back then, it was a certainty, and now that certainty was gone and all the thinking in the world– all the thinking I was capable of, anyway –was failing to conjure up that certainty again.

Why?

Was it something to do with the fish, the beautiful, powerful silver-scaled Tarpon? That didn't make sense. As glorious as the battle had been, still it didn't make sense. How could a fight with a fish translate somehow into that feeling of certainty? It just plain didn't make sense! But neither had that earlier feeling, and it had been beyond question. *I was certain of it.*

Now what?

Suddenly, from the corner of my eye, I saw a shooting star streak across the night sky, this one entering the atmosphere (from a cold and lonely trip through space and time), in the southern heavens.

Flaring low across the black firmament, it flamed brilliant for an instant above the soft blurry nightlights of Oceanside and for a brief flickering moment I thought I could sense those first stirrings of certainty returning once again.

Aftermath II

I only heard the old man tell the story of the lost tarpon once.

It was at Albright's, where we'd stopped by on a drizzly afternoon for a pound of crabmeat for the patties Leah planned on frying up later that evening. The only other person there at the time had been Dr. Cordray (older). Mr. Lincoln, the ancient colored man who worked there as bait attendant was just leaving as we came in. He tipped his hat to both my grandfather and I as we passed in the doorway, smelling all the world like the backroom he worked in and the briny products he dealt in.

Walking home from school by myself I still couldn't shake them, shake these thoughts I now had about the fight that had taken place a week earlier and I knew (with a certainty akin to that I'd had during the fight), when I was older I would look back on the time the old man had fought the tarpon as the most treasured memory of my grandfather. All I would remember as the years sifted the experience was the way my grandfather had so expertly played the ancient fish on that slight whisper of a rod– and how brave he'd been at the end when he'd lost him. Once again my mind wrapped around a word I'd just recently become acquainted with, one I'd learned while we studied the Greeks in Mrs. Johns' class: Stoic.

Thinking back, I recalled how downhearted I'd been when the silver king finally snapped my grandfather's line and I could only guess at how it had affected the old man. That's because he never said a word about it, about how it felt to lose that fish, even later, when he told the story to a few others, like Albright. I thought I knew the old man pretty well, (as well as someone my age could know an older person) and I was certain I knew how much he loved to fish, especially to be engaged in battle with a strong and brave fish, but for the life of me the one thing I could not understand was how the old man could so easily shrug off the misfortune of losing the tarpon after such a prolonged battle. Where did that come from? What went on in someone, what kind of experiences did you have to go through before you could so stoically bear such a rotten bit of luck? And after coming so very close to victory.

Still less than a week after the event the experience was fresh in my mind, which meant the heartache was with me yet. But as much as I loved hearing my grandfather tell the story it didn't seem like he was relaying the same event here inside the store. Part of it, I knew, was the fact Mr. Albright wore the scantest look of scoff as though dismissing all, or some, of my grandfather's story. Later, when I said something about this the old man laughed, saying:

"Hell, that don't mean nothing. All fishermen know not to take any fish story too seriously. Even the one's that are true. Goes with the territory. Grist for the mill."

Even so, I didn't like the smile Mr. Albright wore that afternoon inside the gloomy, smelly, store and I'd rather my grandfather not tell the story at all. Or if he must tell it he could just tell it to me. It was safer this way. In fact, it was the place where the story rightly belonged– just between my grandfather and I. There might be some folks who could appreciate the relaying of the experience but Albright sure as hell wasn't one of them. And the old doctor, hell, he'd been too juiced up to even have any recollection. Outside of Rad (because he was there, if only at the end, which meant that even he couldn't truly appreciate the full measure of what had gone on that afternoon and evening), I could think of no one else to whom I cared to hear my grandfather tell the story. No, this was one fish tale that oughta' be kept just between those who'd actually been there– the old man and me.

I knew some of my seriousness about the experience had to do with what happened when we finally got back home that night. While my grandfather and I had been out on the creek, Doctor Cordray's (the younger), nurse had called Leah asking her to please come in that afternoon. The results from Grayson's biopsy were in and the doctor needed to discuss them with her– ASAP. A nervous Leah called Bertie to drive her and to bring the girls to sit with Grayson. She didn't want him with her. Not then.

I heard about all this second, actually third hand, from my grandfather. Bertie told the old man and asked him to tell me. It was how Leah wanted it. She felt I was old enough, responsible enough now, to handle it. And she knew it would come easier from my grandfather. Learning this, it went some ways in changing how I felt about her. Boy, but she was a hard person to read. Just when you thought you knew where you stood with this woman she could surprise you by treating you like this– almost like an adult. *Almost.* Under no circumstances, though, was I to tell Grayson anything. She would do that when she was good and ready.

The old man, true to his way of doing things, did not beat around the bush when relaying the bad news to me:

"Got some bad news for you, bubba. It has to do with your brother and it's not good, but I know you can handle it so I'll shoot from the hip. Grayson's got something lot's worse than just polio......"

*   *   *

At first, when my grandfather told me this awful news I went into shock. That had to be what it was, 'cause I felt numbed by this shared information. The kind of numbness that radiates throughout your whole body making you feel weak, dizzy even. After a few long seconds rattling around up there it finally settled and rested in my brain, getting me to ask questions, the kind of stupid questions nobody could answer, like *'what are we all doing here'*, and *'what's this life all about, anyway?'*.

I, along with everyone else, had gone along always assuming that Grayson had polio. A bad case maybe, but polio. I'd gone along because I had good reason to. I was young (whatever that meant... I didn't always think of myself that way), that was my excuse. Adults were supposed to know better. Especially adults who were doctors.

The last thing my grandfather had warned me of when he spoke the bad news was Leah's reaction, and I could hear him now speaking it like some time-honored maxim:

'I don't much care to see her get to worrying. When she gets to worrying, I get to worrying.'

It didn't take a whole lot of imagination to pick up on the old man's meaning here.

When it came to Grayson, Leah didn't know half of what there was to know, half of what I knew. When it came to Grayson, Leah was suffering under one big delusion*.

Sometimes, ignorance truly is bliss, I thought as I turned at the shell driveway to walk up to the house. At least it's got a way of making things seem a hell of a sight easier.

Kicking at the overgrown tufts of grass at the driveway's edge I headed for the glass-jalousied front door. But right there, before I grabbed the door's handle, I decided instead of going inside to change clothes I would do the other thing first. So, laying my books down on the redwood two-seater in the carport I headed straight for the lawn mower. Grayson's bus would be there in less that an hour and I wanted to have it done before he arrived.

For the next forty-five minutes or so I was looking forward to all the loud commotion the mower's three horsepower Briggs and Stratton motor would afford me.

Who Knows Where the Time Goes?

Later, I would have to blame myself for the fact that I didn't go inside the house first, that I'd elected to just mow the grass in my school clothes. Maybe the forty minutes or so I'd spent out there instead of coming inside first had made a difference. Maybe not. It was one more of those things I had no way of ever knowing for sure and would be better off just as soon forgetting. It was also, I knew, one of those things that I would never forget.

So, it was for this reason that I preferred to think my grandfather had suffered it earlier in the day. True, this was not much consolation for even if I thought about it that way it still didn't mean that the time I was out cutting grass was not valuable time lost. But it was the only way I could bear to think about it at all— that the old man had gone ahead and had it earlier in the day and what damage had been done had been done by the time I got home from school. I prayed, prayed incessantly*, this was the case. Funny thing about it though was all the time I was out there mowing the grass I'd been thinking about how well my grandfather and I had been getting along lately.

Something had happened during the tarpon incident that had brought us closer together. That was the only way I could say it. The time we'd spent that afternoon and into the evening out on the creek and intracoastal, nearly all the way out to the river, had done something to us, to us both. Something happened out there that I couldn't even begin to talk about, not that I didn't want to— I simply couldn't. There was no way, rather *I had no way*, of putting it into words. It was the first time in my life that I'd had this feeling— that everything was going to be... no, not everything was *going* to be, but everything *was*, okay. More than anything I wanted that notion which had sustained me out there on the water that evening to continue with me. Having had a taste, if only a brief one, I felt changed by it. It was almost like now that I knew it was possible to feel this way, possible to *be* this way, that this in itself was enough to make (or begin to make), a change in me. I even forgot— had at least become less obsessed with —my self-regulated dictate* to quit addressing the old man in the same manner I had ever since I could remember.

These were the type thoughts that wandered through my head while I ran the lawn mower over the thick early autumn fescue and crabgrass that afternoon my grandfather lay inside; half of him on the living room couch and half of him not– half of him okay, strong like always, and half of him weak and distant seeming.

*　　　*　　　*

By the time Doctor Cordray (older), got there the old man seemed already better. When I first spied him sprawled across the couch (his left arm and leg draping down off the couch– actually on the floor), my first thought was that he was trying to play some kind of practical joke on me, never knowing what he might be up to at any given time. Then, when I got closer to my grand-father I could actually see part of his tongue hanging out of the corner of his mouth, and I saw also how slack his jaw was, the same jaw that I'd always seen firmly holding a pipe in its clenches. Then, when I came closer still and saw the vacant, far-away look in the old man's eyes and how they seemed to come alive a little when I came into view, like he'd forgotten something and just then remembered it, struggling some to straighten himself up on the couch– then it was that I no longer had any doubts about what had happened.

I knew it before I even grabbed the old man's leg and arm and helped lift him onto the couch, placing the hooked braided comforter gently over his legs, saying:

"It's okay, Pawpaw. Just lay here for a second (like he was going anywhere?), and I'll call Doctor Cordray."

I knew it before I'd even called the doctor and spoke to him, telling him what had happened.

I knew it before I'd even said the word, only thought it: *Stroke.*

I'd made it, and since it was Friday I felt like I had it made.

I had survived another week of school and at home now resting on my bunk with the book in my hands. I'd forgotten (once more), to read it first thing in the morning after brushing my teeth like I usually did, so I thumbed through the little book my grandfather had given me last Christmas entitled simply: "*Lincoln's Devotional*". The book was made up of a verse or two of scripture and an accompanying poem pertaining* to the verses of scripture for each day of the year. I found the day's date on page 134, the word typed across the top center of the page.

As true throughout the book there were two days worth of passages on this page. At the top half of the page was the passage for October 10th– the day before. I glanced at the bottom half of the page and read:

Temptation to Legal Dependence

Are ye so foolish? Having begun in the
Spirit, are ye now made perfect in the flesh?
Gal. iii. 3.

Go, you that rest upon the law,
And toil and seek salvation there;
Look to the flame that Moses saw,
And shrink, and tremble, and despair.

But I'll retire beneath thy cross–
Saviour, at thy dear feet I'll lie;
And the keen sword that justice draws,
Flaming and red shall pass me by.

I'd not been as diligent as I should about reading the little text every day, meaning I'd probably skipped over a few pages (more than a few?), during the course of the year. Still, this was the first and only time I could remember seeing any notations in the book. Someone (the old man I suspect), had made a check-mark beside this passage and I wondered for a moment about what my grandfather thought about this piece, what had made it special to him. I even thought about going into his room to show him the passage when the phone suddenly rang. I jumped off my bunk and got to it before it completed a second ring.

"Crane residence."

"Motty... is 'dat you?"

"Dosha? Dosha Fay?"

"It's me, all right. Is Mista' Ed dere', Motty? I gots to talk to him... real bad."

"Where are you, Dosha?"

"I'm callin' from da' store... da' dime phone by da' Winn-Dixie. Is your grandpappy 'dere, Motty. I really gots to talk to him in a bad way. I truly do."

"He's here Dosha, but he's ..."

"Thank da' Lord ..."

"He's here Dosha, but he's not feeling too good. He just got back from bein' in the hospital for a coupla' days. Dr. Cordray says he had a stroke. Not a bad one, but...."

"Oh, Lordy! I declare... it's bad news all da' way around 'dis day. Now 'dis! Lord, I hope he's okay."

"He's gettin' better. What's the matter, Dosha? I mean, what did you need to talk to him for?"

"Derek's in trouble, real bad kinda' trouble. You knows Derek, Motty?"

"I've heard of him, but I've never met him. Hey, wasn't he the guy that got into trouble out at the golf course?"

"Dat's him! Only it wasn't him da' one who started it. 'Dat smart-aleck white boy asked for it, Motty. He asked for it, bad."

"I thought he left. I heard he was gone."

"He ain't gone. He just as gone as he wants to be, 'dats all. The Chief knows 'dat too."

"Chief? What Chief?"

"Chief Franklins, Marty... you know!"

"Yeh, I know Chief Franklins. Is he still looking for him?"

"He sho' is, and he knows where he is, too. Sez', if the Sheriff has to go out 'dere an' get him it's gonna' be bad... bad... bad."

"Whadda' ya' mean, bad?"

"Bad, Motty. Like somebody gettin' hurt, bad."

"Oh."

"Chief Franklins sez' if Dereek don't come in by hisself by tomorrow evening at six, da' Sheriff gonna' come lookin' for 'em. Da' Sheriff don't know nothing about Derek, either. He's just another little niggar boy ta' him, Motty. He don't care a lick about Derek. Chief Franklins heard some things tho'... some of da' truth about 'dat fight."

"What are you talking about? I don't follow ya'."

"I gots some friends work at da' country club heard Kingsley braggin' 'bout how he hurt Derek and how he gonna' hurt him some mo' for giving him 'dat concussion an' 'dat broke jaw. Chief Franklins' friends say Kingsley was drunk, but not dumb-drunk. He knew just what he was saying. If the Sheriff goes out 'dere lookin' for him he'll shoot him, Motty, he will. He won't be takin' no chances, dat's for sure."

"Where? Lookin' for him where, Dosha?"

"Out on the crook of da' river. On the island... in da' big part of da' river."

"Oh." Despite Dosha's descriptive efforts it was not enough to pinpoint the location in my mind.

"Kathleen's all kinda' riled up, saying she won't stand for her baby gettin' shot. She's gonna' send Redfish looking for him, but he's done gone up to Yulee, turpentine'n. Ain't nobody seen him in a week... he's so far back in da' woods a possum gotta' bring his mail. Dat's why I thought maybe Mista' Ed could help. He da' only one I know 'dat do what he say, everytime. If he could drive up dere' an' find Redfish he could get Derek to come back in. 'Dat's the only living soul who could get Derek to come back in, an' Redfish'll trust Mr. Ed. If only Redfish could talk to Chief Franklins den' everything' wud' be okay. Everything. Dey' could get him back in here without anyone gettin' shot."

"Boy, Dosha... I don't know what to say. Leah's at work and she told me not to do or say anything that'll upset him. Boy, this here is a mess and a half."

"You sure said a mouthful dere', child. You said one whole *full* mouthful, 'dere.

"Wait a second! Do you know George?" I asked.

"What George? Dere's George Freeman, da' pulpwooder... and George Roosevelt, da' shrimps man... 'Dem' two's da' only George I knows."

"No, it's not either one of them. He works up at the Colonial station. I think he changes tires and stuff up there. You know, the place Mr. Dickerson runs."

"Oh! You talkin' 'bout Big George; dat's how I knows him... Big George Tyree. He stays over dere' behind the 7 O'clock Club. Yeh, I knows him. He 'da tireman over dere' near you off a' Penner now... dat's right."

"Yeh, that's him. Maybe he could help. Does he know Derek or Redfish?"

"I don't know for sure Motty, but I gots to think he know one of 'dem somewhere down 'da line. Short'a Mister Ed, if he 'da only one we got, we better get him... give him a try," Dosha said.

"I'll go over there right now. I can get there on my bike as soon as call him," I said.

(The plain truth of the matter was that I was concerned about my reputation; about calling a colored man on the phone. That's why I'd said I could get there on my bike as soon as call. True, they probably wouldn't let George take the call anyway (even if he was there), but true also, though I was embarrassed to admit it, I was afraid someone at the station might pick up on my voice, might recognize me. It was okay to ride up there and talk to him, but there was something about calling him on the phone that just didn't sit right with me. It was a feeling I was not especially proud of, still.)

"'Dat sure is good of you, Motty. Mighty good."

"Don't worry about it. Is there someway I can call you... let you know if I talked to him?" I asked.

"I don't know. I was gonna' head back to Kathleen's. I'll come back here tho', or send Sam up here in a little while ta' listen out for your call. How would dat' be?"."

"All right. Make it about thirty minutes. I oughta' be able to get up there and back and talk to George in that amount of time, easy."

"Okay, Motty. Da' Lord bless you for doin' dis' boy."

"It's no problem. I'll be talking to you, Dosha."

"Motty, one mo' thing. When you get to Big George, tell 'em dat island Derek is on is da' big one. Da' one out on da' north crook. Da' one dey calls the Quarantine Island. He'll know."

Marty's Tale

Well, I reckon that just about does it. That was the last story. All there's left to do is to wrap it up like it needs to be. Put a bow on it, is what the old man would call it .

Since you've come this far I don't reckon it would be fair to let you go without telling what happened to the old man, Big George and I, so I will give you what I have put on that tape recorder. Having listened to it once I will admit there are a few places where I sorta' got off track, but through it all there is a connection of events. I reckon you will just have to trust me on that.

After hanging up with Dosha I did just what I told her I'd do: I headed for my bike, on my way in search of George, or Big George as she called him. Actually, I went to the back bedroom first, the room my grandfather (whom I used to call Pawpaw), built right after we moved to the Beach. Anyway, I went to his room and peeked in to see if he was asleep or what. He was. Sleeping, that is. I didn't even have to go all the way in and check, I could tell from the way he was snorin' he was sleeping and involved in a deep sleep, too. That was fine. I don't know what I would'a done if he'd been awake, I can remember thinking that very thought at that time and being relieved to find he was snorin'. Ordinarily, I'da never left that house, and not just under Leah's strict command. I would never have left the old man there by himself. But these were exceedingly extenuating* circumstances, and besides, I knew I could get over to the Colonial station, talk to Big George and get back home before my grandfather awoke. I don't know what I was plannin' at the time; actually I don't think I had a plan. I was just playing it by ear, or O.J.T. as Mick would say (standing for On the Job Training.)

Okay, so, so far I've told you about checkin' on the old man, making sure he was all right. That's when I headed for the carport and my bike. It's not the greatest in the world but it gets me where I need to go. Looking back on it, as much as I'd been wanting a new bike as it turned out I'm sorta' glad it didn't happen. Life's like that sometimes; you find that out as you get older, I reckon, that sometimes not getting what you want is really the best thing that could happen. Seems it works that way even more when its something you want real bad, like something you don't think you can possibly live without.

Already, I'm getting sidetracked. But stay with me here, I'm getting to something, I promise.

Well, I got on my bike– the green Schwinn –and I am flyin', right from the get-go, I mean not even those oyster shells that made up our driveway can slow me down. I'm goin' so fast I'm ridin' on top of 'em. Down Sunset, which is the street our house is on, down past the spot where you turn off to go to Mick's house (or the middle of the woods), down past the streetlight, which is close to Will's, all the way down to Tim's where I usually cut through his yard, glad that he wasn't outside (I didn't have time to even slow down and explain to him what I was up to, and I didn't want to appear rude). Where I was headed to cutting through Tim's was the little rutted path that runs from the back of his yard to the Pak n'Sak. Once I was at the Pak n'Sak it was a short jaunt across Penner to the Colonial Station. Not to say it wasn't dangerous. I'd have to say that traffic on Penner is about as bad as it gets at Oceanside; the closest you'd find if you were lookin' for a real traffic jam. I take that back. Ocean Blvd. can get worse, I suppose, and Beach Road, the closer you get to the beach from town in the summer with all the tourist traffic (half the cars around the Fourth of July seemingly with Georgia license tags), well, you get the idea. Let's just say Penner can get pretty busy.

After sitting at the edge of that parking lot there by the street for what seemed like forever (in truth, probably about a minute), you get kind of anxious waiting. That's exactly what happened to make me want to get off my bike and stand up. If you've ever ridden a bike you know what I mean. It gets tiresome sitting on that little seat, especially if you know you ain't gonna' be goin' anywhere anytime soon. So I was having to wait there not fifty feet from the filling station, my destination; and it is getting irksome, to say the least, having to wait for a break in the traffic to get across. It wasn't like it was bumper to bumper, but everytime I thought I could get across I would look the other way (like you're supposed to), and there would come another dang car. Finally, I had had about all I (or any sane person), could stand and I decided to inch out a little into Penner; to force my way out into the lane. And, in essence, that's just what I did.

I had seen the car coming all the way down on the left, back where Penner takes a pretty sharp curve and there's sort of a blind spot behind this humongous oak tree; believe me I knew about that spot and how cars could suddenly appear there seemingly from out of nowhere, but I figured I could make it across without any problem, or much of one, anyway. (You think getting across in a bike's a problem you oughta' try pushin' some jackass in a wheelchair across, especially in the middle of the summer when the asphalt's really cookin'.)

I went. That's the only way to say it is, I went. Probably shouldn't have, but with circumstances being what they were and the old man, my one and only grandfather, or grandparent of any description, being in the shape he was in back at the house by hisself, I went.

As luck would have it, the car that came speeding up around that corner from behind the tree, the one car that happened to be there at that spot at that particular time in history out of all the possible cars from Oceanside that it could have been (seemingly faster, once it hit the straightaway and saw me there), would have to be driven by none other than Gerald Rickenbacher. He's the guy who gave me a hard time in front of the bakery a couple of summers ago when I was washing the windows for Mrs. Arnett. I knew he saw me crossing, or trying to cross the road there, and I swear on a stack of bibles he began speeding up in that old Chevy of his, a black '51 ugly as sin and twice as loud (he needed a new muffler in a bad way and the smoke he spewed was as black as the car itself), but like I said, I had already gone and by then it was too late to turn back, I was in no man's land by then. Just as far back as it was ahead meaning I was in the middle of the road, or just about. Normally that would be okay, that would be enough, because the other lane was clear, no one was even close to coming, but you have to remember who was driving that one car that was coming. And was he coming. You could hear him downshift that old ill-tempered rattletrap (it had what you call a three-on-the-tree transmission, meaning it was a stick shift on the steering column instead of on the floor), and boy that old jalopy got down and roared when he threw her back into second. That is, after he ground off a handful of teeth with that clutch on the way to winding her back down. Once he was back into second though you could hear that mess of an engine rumble and roar after a little initial sputter like it was having to be coaxed one last time to do this thing it was being asked to do: that is get up a good head and tear off. He was coming right at me and I was stopped, frozen like a deer in his headlights, not knowing what to do. Only I wasn't a deer and it wasn't dark so he didn't have his headlights on (I doubt they worked).

Now, it's not a hard thing to run someone down if you're in a car and they're not, allowin' that you're intendin' to do so in the first place, of course, and that's exactly what Gerald Ricken-bacher looked like he was intendin' to do. When he was about half a football field away I could see from even that far there was this look in his eye that said he wasn't kidding around this time. It was a look saying he was coming straight as an arrow and I was one big bulls-eye. Who knew what he was capable of? For all I knew right then he might already have killed several people that day, people in his own family (maybe all of them), and he was so far gone by now that one more person, a fellow Oceansider, wouldn't matter too much. He was goin' to hell, or Raiford, anyway so what the heck, he might as well get the satisfaction of running up the score as high as he could on the way. I'm not trying to puff this out or anything, it's just the way I need to tell it, like Chief Franklins told me to after everything was over, after I got back from the island; to take my time and begin at the start and be sure and include everything that came into my mind, whether I thought it pertained* or not. He would decide what to leave in and what to leave out. So if you got something else or better to do then you better stop right now and go on, 'cause its gonna' take a while to get it all out.

Okay, if you're still with me I am trying to cross Penner to get to the Colonial station to find Big George and Gerald Ricken-bacher has me pinned down, about to splatter my guts (not to mention my bike), all across the road, and he is really flying; he's doing 60 mph easy and it's a 35 mph speed limit at that stretch. I'm figuring right then my ass is grass. And at the last possible second that I can move and still live to tell about it, I move. Don't ask me how, I'm not certain myself, even now. All I know is I somehow managed to get going, pulling my bike alongside when he passed and passed close.

If nothing else had happened I would have known just from the sheer force of the wind at my back that something big had just barely missed creaming us (the bike and I), but something else *had* happened. He came so close he actually hit my bike as he went by. Well, maybe not the bike itself, but the rear reflector got hit– hard enough to send it flying off down the road where it rolled for who knows how far. I guess that's not too surprising, really. Anytime you've got a collision between a fast moving car and a bicycle reflector... well, anyone can guess who's gonna' win there, it doesn't take an Einstein. Even after I got all the way across Penner and looked down it to the back of Gerald's

Chevy I could still see that reflector rolling right behind him, a close second. Before too long it was just about out of sight being the small size it was, but by then it had started veering over towards the edge of the road. Finally, it sailed off the shoulder and out into the field. It was still traveling fast when it left the road, though. My being so long-winded in telling this might have you thinking that a good bit of time had passed, but that was far from the actual case. This all happened lickety-split. Within ten seconds, I bet.

I'm certain Gerald could still see me (if he was lookin') when I shot him the bird, which was only the second time in my entire life (up to that point, of course), I had done such a thing not in jest. I had had it, plain and simple. Between all of the agony I was going through right there trying to get to Big George and the old man being layed up like he was (plus the memory of Gerald doing this before to Grayson and I), it was all I could take. I was at that point I guess everyone gets to sometime. You spend your whole life afraid of someone or something (usually someone), and then, finally, things begin to happen, events begin to conspire* one right on top of another to where you get to the point that you don't really give a damn, let the chips fall where they may. I reckon another way of puttin' it is to say you are riled up. This sort of attitude will get you through just about any situation where you are scared, as long as the one you are scared of is not of a similar mind at that same time.

Maybe Gerald saw the finger and maybe he didn't. I guess I'll never know for sure, but in my mind I sorta' think he did. Anyway, for whatever reason he did not follow up. Either he could see that I was at that certain point and he wasn't (all he'd been doing was cutting up and he hadn't killed anyone– yet), or he could see that I was headed for the Colonial station and he was reluctant to bash my brains in in front of an audience, knowing he could get me alone anyway at some other time in the future at his convenience. But not today. Come to think of it, though, not any day, anymore.

Something happened on Penner that day, unsaid maybe, but real nonetheless. He, Gerald, had had his shot, had taken it so far really that he had crossed that line of kidding around. It was like if he didn't do it then I knew he wouldn't ever, really. He'd had his chance and passed and because of that I knew now I had the upper hand in our aggravated relationship. It's how I do everything; not doing anything until it becomes a crisis. Until I am jammed in a corner. Then I can act. I am that way with school, not really studying until some big test comes up and then cramming hour after hour the night before and I am that way with girls, too. It about takes thumbscrews to get me to work up the nerve just to talk to a girl, to just say hello, and the idea of actually doing anything, of kissing one– well, as bad as I've wanted to, so far Fonda M. has been the only one, and that was only once in Tim's closet, under almost extreme duress*.

*　　*　　*

I made it to the station when all was said and done and Big George was there. It's hard to say what it was between us, but ever since that first time I saw him, when I went up to the station to see if there was anything they could do with Grayson's bent wheel and he put it in that anvil and worked on it and straightened it to where it was like new, we have been friends. I've never been around anyone, white or colored, who I felt such a kinship with so quickly. He could tell I was feeling low and the way he began talking and the things he talked about while he was working on that wheel lifted me right out of that mood. Not by trying to coax me out of it by talking about happy things, but more like letting me know there was things worth living for and being excited about regardless of how low you got– and him in the situation he was in, a grown man changing tires at a filling station (not a very nice one, to boot), but being up about things, anyway. When you stop and think about it, all we really talked about were two things: fishing for speckled trout and a new car that went by the station as we were talkin'– a red Mustang, the first one either of us had ever seen (it being the first year they were produced). Boy, that was some sight, that brand spanking new car candy-apple red rolling regally down Penner like it was Hollywood Boulevard or something. Anyway, just the sight of that car and the sight of Big George lookin' at it (and me too, I reckon; I'm sure my mouth was open just as wide as his), was enough to get any person who still had a pulse going real good. Big George and I both watched that car sail down Penner as far as we could watch it and finally he just broke out in a big grin saying something like if that wasn't the prettiest sight he'd layed eyes on in many a moon then he wasn't no better than a flattened Nassau County polecat, meaning one that'd just been run over. But back to this time and the reason I was here now.

I probably made my first mistake by going directly back to the bay where he was, but I didn't stop to think about it I was in such a hurry and I could see him, George, right there. Per usual,

Mr. Dickerson was in not too friendly a mood and as soon as he determined that I was not there on official filling station business he let me know in no uncertain terms that I was not welcome. In the minute or so I got to talk to George I managed to convey the gist of what was going on, though, and learned that he knew Derek a little but was better friends with Redfish, so by the time Mr. Dickerson ran me off from there I still felt pretty good about delivering the message, like I told Dosha I would. Even after Mr. Dickerson gave him a dirty look, right when I was leaving and heading back to the house, George called my name with my back towards him and told me he was gettin' off in twenty minutes and he'd meet me as soon as he could get there at Johnson's Fish Camp. Boy ol' Dickerson looked royally P.O.'d about that, too. He even said something about he (George), wasn't going nowhere until he (Mr. Dickerson), said so. There was plenty left to be done and he might need him to stay late and finish up. Boy, did he ever push the wrong button on George by saying that. I got a little glimpse right then of why Dosha called him Big George– he never seemed that big to me before that, pretty much he looked about average size really –but something happened when ol' Mr. Dickerson spoke so harshly like that to him and George got real big, real fast.

Thinking back on it, he never did raise his voice or anything like that, it was more like he just quit smilin' like he usually did and he got a very serious look on his face, and I mean real serious; sterner than the old man or even Coach Fordan or Coach Longer could get to lookin', and brother all I can say is I remember being so very happy, overjoyed really, that it wasn't me he was gettin' serious with. Even the little bitty crack, that little space that is left at the bottom between it and the floor when you shut the front door of the Colonial station (or any door, really), was plenty big for Mr. Dickerson to get through after George had had his say. And like I said, now that I think back on it George never did raise his voice or speak meanly. All he said was, 'I'm leavin' at 4:30 today Mr. D... personal business of an extremely urgent nature'. Something like that, that was all. And again, it wasn't that he was being mean-sounding, it was more like he was serious-sounding, and smart too; that's it, he sounded real smart, like he was in control. This once he was gonna' call the shots no matter what anyone else, Mr. Dickerson included, thought. I reckon George was feeling sorta' like I felt with Gerald only a few minutes before. Funny, we should both get that way at nearly the same time on the very same day.

*   *   *

Just like he said he'd do, George met us there at Mr. Johnson's. In fact, he pulled in there at almost the same time we did and if he'd have known about the shortcut off Penner through the woods he'd have probably beat us. I'm gettin' a little ahead of myself, though, 'cause I went home first– to call Dosha or rather Sam, her oldest boy, back at the pay phone like I said so they'd know what was happenin' and could tell Kathleen, Derek's mother, and so I could check on Pawpaw. Yeh, that's right... I called him that and after I swore I wouldn't, or at least would try not to do it, again. But that was before. I'm getting' over that, I do believe. Sometimes you do or say things just because you think it's the only way you can prove that you're more grown up than you really are. Most of the time it probably doesn't matter a lick to anyone else either, even though you think that's who you're doin' it for– everyone else. Once you figure that much out you can pretty much go back to doing (or as in this case, saying), whatever it was you thought you needed to change.

Back at the house, and I got back in just about twenty minutes, too, so I was pretty sure Leah hadn't called (boy, I sure prayed not). Pawpaw was still snorin' like a baby only he was turned over on his side some and I knew he had awakened a little, just enough to move. At first he had a catheter down there which has got to be as painful as it gets– just thinking about it gives me the heebie-jeebies –but he had gotten so much better so quickly that that was gone now and he just usually needed the duck of which we had an ample supply, Leah not being prone to throwing anything (no matter how worn or old), out. I didn't want to disturb him, no, that was the last thing on my mind, but I figured that I should at least check to see if he had taken a leak without me being there to help, you know soiled his pants, so I quietly pulled down the light blanket that was pulled over his legs up to his waist and wouldn't you know it that was all it took! *'Where have you been?'* he wanted to know. He could talk pretty well now, a little slower than he used to and sometimes he had a hard time comin' up with the right word and he'd get that look on his face, but if you'd never seen him before and didn't know him you wouldn't really think there was anything much wrong.

Well, I had a choice to make; a decision. I could either level with him and try to explain what was going on (in other words the truth), or I could make up a lie real quick which I am not proud to admit comes pretty easy to me, for the most part. If there's anyone I have trouble lying to though it is the old man. I had never even really tried to before and again I am not especially proud of it but I have to admit that for just a second I thought that it might be possible now, seeing as though he was in the shape he was in, that I could pull it off. But just then something he had said once came to me. It was when I had told him a thing that was not an actual lie– just an exaggeration –and all he had said was: *Don't kid a kidder, boy.* It was enough.

I made the right choice then and told him what was going on, about Dosha's call and how she had said that he was the only person she knew of who, when the chips were down, would do what he said he would. I watched him really carefully when I told him that to see if I could detect some kind of emotion from him, but it was hard to see his face.

He was sitting up now on the side of the bed and his head was down for the most part with both arms out from his side, his hands grabbing hold of the edge of the bed also. It did look a coupla' times like he was shaking his head ever so slightly, but it was so subtle* it was hard to read much into it. After a second he raised his head a little and looked me right in the face and said something like *God, this is one mess we do not need to get caught up in,* and I have to admit I was taken aback some. I really thought that he liked Dosha; I knew he did, in fact, so I was mystified as to why he would be so reticent* to assist her in her time of need. I have neglected to mention this before, probably because I was somewhat confused by it, but there was a relationship between Dosha Fay and Kathleen, meaning they were kin in some way, not sisters or anything as clearcut as that, but they were related and very close. When you get down to it it is one of those situations where their friendship had built up stronger than they were related. Folks, colored and white, can be that way– many are. Blood may be thicker than water but one person's regard for another can be stronger still. It is possible, related or not. So there was a reason other than her being a Christian woman and wanting to do the right thing, for wanting to help Kathleen.

Again, I was surprised he had said what he did, but he'd said it so lowly that even though he was looking right at me I wasn't certain that he knew he'd said it out loud, maybe he thought he was just thinking it. I don't know that much about strokes but he had mentioned once (I forget the occasion), that it was how his own father had succumbed. And him lying there thinking that very same thought day after day, more than likely. That has got to be a lot to deal with, knowing that what finally got your own father had got its grip on you now and there is very little you can do about it. The only thing that could be worse, I reckon, was this story Mrs. Johns read some to us once by Wm. Faulkner about an old lady who was dyin' and as she lay there on her death-bed she could hear her son or husband or some relative right outside her window sawin' wood to make a pine box for her eternal rest. Only thing is she didn't seem all that upset, if I remember that story right. Whether I was or was not surprised by the old man's reaction did not matter a hill of beans, for if anything the stroke had made him even more stubborn than he normally was, which is saying a lot, believe me. There was no way I was going to be idiot enough to try and argue with him like this now, either. I might seem slow on occasion, but I am not stupid.

It wasn't 'til I mentioned the thing about Dosha's friend who worked at the Country Club and what they'd overheard Kingsley Cormack saying that I noticed a perceptible* change in the old man's attitude regarding this situation. It may sound corny, but as soon as I said it it was like a lightbulb went off inside his head. I don't know what I was thinking– well, looking on back on it I wasn't thinking, and that was the problem. I did not have a plan but was going off half-cocked trying to think it out as I was going. Plus, I was relying on George to know what to do. It never occurred to me to get the old man involved, I can absolutely state that with a totally clear conscience because it is the total truth– no ifs, ands or buts. But once he heard that little bit about Kingsley, well, that busted it, it was all over. He, the old man, was in with George and I and the only thing I had to worry about was whether or not *Melinda* could handle three people.

*   *   *

We– the old man and I –decided the best thing to do was just leave Leah a note. We didn't have to say what we were up to or where we were headin', but she would see the Imperial was gone so there was no use lying about it. There wasn't anyway she would know we were out on the creek unless she thought to look in the utility room and saw the Evinrude was gone. But why would she do that? The only problem was I had drained the motor's lower gear unit just a few days before and she was still on the sawhorse sitting above the pail of old oil like I'd left her. All we had was half a tube of new oil and it would take a full tube and then some to fill her so I had just left her there until the next time I went over to the fish camp where Mr. Johnson kept plenty. Little did I know at the time that I would be paying Mr. Johnson and Fred a visit so soon.

Pawpaw could stand okay and he was already dressed so there would be no delay there. It was helping him walk that proved to be the hard part. He was weak. Like I said earlier, he could talk okay and if you didn't know him you wouldn't know any better, you'd just think he was some kind of frail old man, but we finally made it, him holding on to the walls of either side of the dark hallway all the way down until we got to the place where the heater was and then he had to kind of lean forward and reach out real quick to grab the doorway right there, and then he was steady again. He stood there for the better part of thirty seconds or so regaining his strength, collecting himself because then he had to go all the way across the living room floor where there weren't any walls close by to grab hold of, but he made it. It was like he was actually getting stronger right in front of my very eyes, but by the time we got to the front door he was pooped again, I could tell.

What was I thinking? Like I said earlier, I wasn't. There was no way he was gonna' make it. But I sure as heck didn't want to be the one to tell him. If anything, that would just make him even more determined and I thought right there at the front door when he was holding onto the doorframe for support that that was the best thing to do– to leave him alone and let him determine on his own that he couldn't do it. You might say I had some experience on how to handle the handicapped, especially those of the stubborn variety. If there is anyone living more stubborn than Grayson it has yet to be brought to my attention.

Please remember, as I'm sure you already know, that you cannot believe everything you read. What I am referring to here is the fact that I never intentionally tried to hurt Grayson, regardless of what you may have read in the past. The incident with the lighter– the hotbutt, it was true; but I knew what I was doing, I knew just how to make it warm for him, but not really hot. Listen, if you had to take the enormous amount of s_ _ _ that comes outa' that little butthead's mouth day in and day out and not be able to do anything about it, well I don't know of many folks who could take it on a continual basis. Let's just leave it at that. Oh yes, I never tried to push him out of his chair that morning, either. Just when Mrs. Towner pulled up in the bus I went to push him and hadn't noticed his front wheel was stuck sideways, you know like a shopping cart buggy does; it was that simple. Instead of rolling forward, though, it just sorta' tumped over and as he was going I decided right then at that very second to at least get some credit for it. Heck, he was going now regardless of what I said or did. That's why I said: *There you go*. Scout's honor. He, of course, refused to believe it, but I am certain that deep down he knew the truth of the matter, too.

To my utter astonishment the old man kept on going. I really didn't think he was gonna' make it out of the house but after he had a little rest there at the front door he seemed to gain some strength. The step down onto the carport was not a big one—about half a step, but he eased down it slowly, then reached out to grab hold of the round steel pole, one of several around the outside of the carport which held up the roof out there.

*　　*　　*

If there are any scholars who are reading this I am going to say something which will more than likely sound plagiaristic* to some so I am saying it now right here since there are no footnotes or bibliography accompanying this text. There is this writer, Stephen Crane, who lived in the late part of the 19th century, and it is not because of the same last name that I like him, though that doesn't hurt. Like much in this life, it is strictly coincidental. He was a Yankee by birth, but of course as is always the case that was no fault of his. He wrote some famous stories in his short lifetime, but probably his most famous was a book by the name of 'The Red Badge of Courage', which is basically about the hardships of the Civil War as experienced by a young boy in the Northern Army by the name of Henry. Mr. Crane allowed once that even if he himself had never been in a battle he believed that he got his ideas, the feel of it, on the football field. Like Pawpaw told me once, back then in the early days scrummage was a vicious and brutal game and it wasn't all that terribly uncommon for someone to get hurt bad or even killed playing it. What I'm getting at here is the fact that once he was outside the old man seemed to get better. It was like a cloud, say, or a fog which had previously enveloped him suddenly lifted, and I think it was because he was outside for the first time in weeks that this occurred. Something happened when he got outside that made me think of a famous line of Stephen Crane's... *that it requires sky to give a man courage*. That one line says it so well, says what it would take me, or any other ordinary soul, at least a paragraph.

From there, the front door, once we were outside it was a P.O.C. or piece of cake as my good friend Mick would say, to get to the old man's Imperial. And the change which I had seen instantly wrought upon my grandfather's visage* seemed to be lasting for his body did not seem such an encumbrance* to him now and he was able to get himself to the side of the car, having to hold onto the hood a coupla' times for balance on the way there, and into the driver's seat. It was like from the time way in the backroom when he had first stood up to now out here in the car he had shrugged off twenty years and was steadily heading back to being just the old man I had known– no longer among the infirm. If no other good came from this effort it was well worth it to see him so much better and nearly like his old self once again.

I got in the car, too, having already stowed the Evinrude in the Imperial's cave of a trunk where Pawpaw kept folded up an old furniture mover's blanket for just such occasions and I looked at the old man as he inserted the key into the car's ignition (which proved a little troublesome for him, but finally he got it in), turned it and we were off– the first time the old car had moved in nearly a month.

Backing her up, it was impossible not to notice the tall grass outline that had grown up underneath the old Imperial (like some aerial view of the car we were leaving behind in the sideyard), and it was extremely unsightly, to me at least, the way I feel about lawnmowers and keeping the grass mown and all. This bothered me no end, bugged the hell out of me really, and was the first thing I would attend to upon our return, I thought. Although at that exact moment for the first time in my life I was not entirely certain when that would be. That's when the excitement part came in, I do believe. Leaving that house with the old man and not really knowing when, or if, we would return. Not to be overly melodramatic, but I don't care what anybody says... the imagination, at least the imagination of any normal youth... boy... gets to going when you think about doing something you've never done before, and in which the police are involved or are on the fringes of becoming involved. Anyone who says different to this is either a liar or is devoid* of any sense.

I still had no plan as to what we were doing, though. We both knew where we were going– to Johnson's –and we would have to get out on Penner to do that, at least for a little ways, a half a mile or so, there being no other way to get there in a car. Even though I still had no real plan I did feel good about the fact we were headed to the fish camp, for here was a person who could talk to the old man and talk him out of going where it was he intended to go, if that became necessary: Mr. Johnson. In other words, Mr. Johnson was old enough, cantankerous enough himself (if need be), and had known Pawpaw long enough not to be afraid to tell him if he shouldn't go.

*　　　*　　　*

The way I had it figured we could get some oil from Mr. Johnson for the motor's lower unit, strap the motor on *Melinda* and be out to the big island in less than an hour. That time we had come close, close enough to see the tops of the trees on the island it had taken almost three hours but you have to take into account I was rowing then and with the motor we could cut that time in a quarter, easily. I was certain of it.

Regardless of what the old man said about *Melinda* plowing through the water, with the Evinrude strapped on her she was transformed from a simple creek skiff into a sleek and speedy motorboat. At about 3/4 throttle she could plane with the two of us in her and that's when she would move, so even with an additional person along, Big George, the way I figured it if I throttled her almost wide open we could still get up on the water and go. I may have been jumping the gun some here (having us out on the water and on our way to the big island already and we hadn't even got out on the street yet), but you have to remember my mind was going a mile a minute and not just on this thing, either. As usual, there were several things going on up there, meaning in my head: Grayson's condition, which still had everyone thrown for something of a loop and Patti, who I still had not given up on entirely, though it looked more and more like she was gone and never coming back– at least for two years, and then the condition of my good friend, Mick. Boy, but if I didn't have a bunch of irons in the fire, worry-wise.

Just the week before while Mick and Davey were horsing around one afternoon after school Mick bent over and his tee shirt shimmied up his back and something strange caught Davey's eye– that sight of Mick's backbone. It was such an odd sight, one he wasn't ready for that I think it scared him really, although he never used that word *scared* (he didn't have to, you could tell), and they both went right away to Mick's house to show his mother to make certain if it was something unusual and upon it being brought to her attention it was decided he should have it checked out and in only a coupla' more days it was settled that Mick had curvature of the spine and would need an operation to correct it. What it all boiled down to was that in less than a week Mick was in the hospital at the Naval Air Station on the other side of town to have his operation. For the next six months he was in a cast from below his waist right snug-hard up under his chin, the object being to keep his spine as straight as possible while it did its healing from the operation. I can only speak for myself, but I would be so scared to have that happen to me I'm not sure what I woulda' done. Hospitals scare the living heck out of me, Grayson having been in a number of them– down in St. Pete, over in Pensacola, and of course, Hope House. And every one of them places you would not want to spend any time at, even just to spend the night. Not that this place is any Holiday Inn. I reckon a lot of it has to do with the fact that I can't think of hospitals now as a place people go to get well, probably since they haven't done Grayson much good, but rather as a place for sick folks only, and those fixin' to die.

But the old man wasn't ready to die, not yet anyway. I swear he was gettin' stronger looking by the minute, it was like that Imperial was some kind of reverse time machine...you know, the movie they made from the H.G.Wells book. Only difference was instead of everything outside the Imperial going back in time it was him seated there in the driver's seat going back, looking younger every time I gazed over on the way to Johnson's.

Anyway, we finally pulled onto the old dirt road leading back to the fish camp which was off another paved road off Penner (which we negotiated, by the way, with no trouble– traffic having lightened up considerably), and we could see that George had not gotten there yet and again it is nothing to be proud of but for just the scantest part of a second I was thinking that maybe he has thought this thing over further and decided it is not such a good idea, what with the law being involved if only at the edges right now and right then here comes the old maroon and gray DeSoto with George behind the wheel. That car of his was old but it purred like a kitten, which I know is catering to cliche' but so be it. The old car ran well.

*   *   *

George got out of his car and came over to where we were and was polite as could be, as I had always known him to be, but it is strange when I think this is the same man who only less than an hour ago was telling a white man (one who was his boss, too), what *he* intended to do. I guess somewhere in the back of my head I might have had the notion that since I didn't really know him all that well perhaps he would try the same thing with Pawpaw which would have been a big mistake for there is no one alive who can measure up to him in pure oneryness regardless of age, size, race or whatever else. But I shouldn't have worried about it if I was thinking, because there was no reason for George to be anything less than cordial. The only reason he got huffy with Mr. Dickerson was because he had good reason to and he was in the right all the way around. It turned out even that George knew Pawpaw and remembered him well, though the old man did not recall him which was understandable seeing as though George had only been about 16 or 17 years old when they first met and that was over 20 years ago. It was the time the old man liked to talk about when Redfish hefted 80 lb. bags of gravel-mix two-at-a-time on one shoulder all day and whistlin' to boot when the rest of everybody else was struggling with just one bag at a time.

George was the one who remembered this and the two of them spent a minute or two gettin' reacquainted during which time it began to drizzle even though the sun was still shinin' and since we were all standing there on the main dock we decided it would be a good idea to go on up to the house, at least the screen porch, until it stopped. Besides, I needed to get up there anyway and find Mr. Johnson or Fred so I could get a tube of lower gear unit oil to squeeze into the Evinrude.

*   *   *

There is an age at which a boy essentially pins all his hopes on his father. It is not a conscious decision. He is a boy, his father is a man. It is that simple.

If the boy's father should be taken from him during this time... well, that pretty much tears it. He, the boy, is in trouble. Either he will look for his father in every other man he meets or he himself will become his own father. It's not like there is another one waiting in the wings to be called in when needed– a supply of second string fathers being kept somewhere.

Baseball, football, hunting, golf or just goofing around. All of these are things the boy was certain he would learn from his father, but now must rely on others or himself to pick up. Again, none of this is really something the boy thinks about before it happens, he just assumes let us say, that his father will be around to help him when the times comes that he needs the help.

I don't know what got me off onto that. Well, I am being less than totally honest. There is a reason (anyway, this guy from town who was with Chief Franklin' that afternoon when all the questions were flying told me this), that we say the things we do, whether we think so or not. In fact, he said, oftentimes that reason is hidden from ourselves (by ourselves?), and all we can think is that we misspoke or made an error somehow when we catch ourselves saying something that we thought we didn't mean to. Anyways, I reckon what I'm getting at is the fact that I was fortunate in that when something awful happened, my father dying, the old man was there to help out because lookin' back on it there was just no way in hell that I was gonna' get another father anytime soon. If you've got any idea of what Leah is like and her circumstances then this would certainly be no surprise. She is always in such control of herself and anyone else around her (like yours truly), which brings me to another observation I have made since the trip to the island (that's when all this stuff started coming together in my mind, after I got back from there). The reason she drinks is because it's the only way she can let herself go; let go and not have to be in such control all the time. I used to think that what she was trying to do was kill herself, especially when she got really gone mixing the pills with the drinking, but now I have changed my thinking about this and feel that it is the only way she can feel alive, not having to hold on so desperately for everything to work. Only problem is, unlike most folks, she doesn't know when to stop. Every one of my friends... Mick, Davey, Will, Tim... all of their parents drink, sometimes more than they should. I have been there and seen it firsthand on many occasions, but never have I seen any of their parents get like Leah. It's too bad, because even if it feels strange saying so, she is probably attractive to most men and she is certainly smart. But she does have this problem. Plus, if I'm gonna' be totally honest another thing she has that nobody in their right mind would wish to take on is two kids. One in a wheelchair, to boot.

Like the old saying goes, that and a dime will get you a cup of coffee. What it all boils down to is the fact that if it were not for the old man there would not be anyone there for us (because Grayson counts in this too), and without him there a lot of the time like he is we would really be lost. I should include Leah in this also, though she would deny it to her dying day, those two with their history of getting along so poorly, there being so much resentment on her part. I'm far afield now and apologize if I've lost you. But, like I said earlier, there's a reason this stuff comes out.

*   *   *

As soon as it started drizzlin' we all three high-tailed it up to the screen porch (Pawpaw is getting around pretty well now), and right after we got up there here comes Fred the colored man who has been helping Mr. Johnson ever since he started the fish camp and it is Fred who finds the tube of gear oil I need and he even offers to help me but it doesn't take two people to do it although it would be helpful sometimes to have three hands. I could tell also that Fred was not especially overjoyed with the idea of going back out into the rain, anyway; that he was being polite more than anything, probably because the old man was there.

There are two screws you take out at the bottom of the motor where the shaft comes down and engages the propeller... that's where all the gears are down here... and what you have to do is insert the tip of the tube of oil into the bottom screw hole and squeeze oil up into the housing until it starts coming out of the top hole, about six inches above. When you see the first bit of oil coming out of that top hole that's when you know it's full and time to put the screws back in (top one first), which is when it would be handy to have one more hand. But I have done this on a number of occasions with the old man watching me and tell Fred thanks, but no thanks, and set off to get the motor out of the trunk of the Imperial. It had been raining quite a bit lately which makes the grass grow faster even this late in the year and as I am going to the car I notice that it's getting a little high around the backyard here. It's been over a month since I last mowed it. In the summer I came over twice a month and kept it looking real good and I make a note to myself to get back here in the next coupla' of days and hold up my part of the bargain, which is to mow the grass here at the fish camp in exchange for the dock fee for *Melinda*.

I unloaded the motor and took it over towards the fish-cleaning sink where I could smell right away that someone had been utilizing the facilities recently. There were some scales and fish guts still wet on the wooden counter next to the sink where folks clean their fish and this little bit would normally dry out pretty quickly as there is a shed roof over the top of that area. Leaning the motor up against the counter, I began fillin' it with oil and I started thinking about what it might be like out on the river. The rain had let up and the only thing fallin' now really was the drops from the trees when the wind blew but you cannot use the creek as a gauge for how the river is. Still, the creek looked real calm and even though I knew that was no indication that the river would be of the same temperament I nevertheless imagined it as being calm, also. So far, neither the old man nor George had said anything about how it might be out there, but this did not concern me.

There is a type of boatsman who the only time he will talk about the weather is if he is certain he is not going out in it. Otherwise, it is bad luck. It just so happens that I would classify both Pawpaw and George as that type of boatsman. Don't get me wrong, this is not a bad way to be– only cautious, and tends to be an attribute of folks who have experienced either some terrible mishap or close call while in a small launch in rough waters. Of course, the worst place to be in such circumstances is far off shore in the open sea for not only is there the terrible and tumultuous* wrath of Neptune in all his glory and fury to deal with out here but even if under such conditions one is fortunate enough to be delivered up from the briny deep there is still the no minuscule* feat of actually beaching your craft and living to tell about it. On more than one occasion sailors and boatsmen have fought valiantly against a storm at open sea only to be defeated on the home stretch in an exhausted state by a steady succession of mighty breakers delivering the vanquished back to dry land, as if to say: *'There. There is the price to be paid for such foolhardiness. Weep if you will... but pay.'* Pawpaw and George were both the kind of boatsmen who did not wish to spawn such a scene and I... well... I had been lucky enough not to ever even had to consider such a scene other than the time Pawpaw and I went out with old Doctor Cordray, but that was just a lake and we were never that far from shore. The worst that coulda' happened out there was we woulda' had to swim a-ways. I'm not so sure the old Doctor woulda' made it though, considering the condition he was in at the time.

*   *   *

Did you ever think your life was one big puzzle and someday, somehow, you would put it all together and everything would make sense? I reckon that is how I always felt about myself and the predicament I was in, meaning, of course, the people I was most closely associated with, Leah, Grayson and my grandfather.

I remember this interview with President Kennedy back when he was running for President. It was 1960, so I guess that would have made me around eleven. Something he said then struck me as worth remembering, and even though he was talking about politics it always seemed to me like it could spill over and apply to about any situation that was serious... important, to you. What it was he said was something like *'politics was all a big mystery until your first defeat... then you understood it perfectly'*. There is something about losing at a thing that makes you understand it better. I really don't know how else... how better... to say it. It's like the winners get to win, but the losers get something, too... get something out of losing. Maybe what they get is some sort of understanding. I can see I need to think about this some more.

*   *   *

The only time I can remember not feeling puzzled by everything... by life itself... is back when I was riding on the *Silver Meteor* with my father. Back then everything seemed all right. Thinking back on it, I don't guess I knew any more on that train than when I wasn't on it, but it was like it didn't matter. I wasn't worried, or puzzled, by anything. Once that train pulled away from the station there at Riverville (with the little jolt it always has at first), everything was A-O.K. I could walk up and down through those cars real well (better than most adults who usually had to grab onto things to keep from stumbling), exploring, as long as I stayed out of the grown-ups way and didn't bother my dad. He had work to do, train-work like punching folk's tickets, making sure they were settled in their sleepers and when he wasn't doing that he was talking, making plans with the other conductors or playing cards, even. I know because I saw him playing more than once. That's not to say that he would ignore me. We talked lots, but usually he was busy.

Sometimes, we'd meet in the little passageway between cars where you can swing in the top half of the door like a Dutch door and look right out into the real open air and we would stand there together and watch wherever it was we were go by. I always liked standing in that area; the rocking and rolling of the train seemed even moreso there and sometimes you'd come upon someone close up to the train and they would wave and before you knew it you'd wave back real quick and they'd be gone. Someone likely you'd never see again your whole life but it didn't matter 'cause waving like that connected you somehow and that one time was enough; enough for a lifetime. With that person, anyway.

Out of all the times on the train, though, mornings were the best and I know why. It was because of the Dining Car. Night time was too important, folks got dressed up and all and it was quite a production in the Dining Car at suppertime so I usually just got a sandwich or something like that, but in the morning at breakfast I got to sit down in the Diner just like a paying customer. The breakfasts were great, too. Anything you wanted. Eggs, bacon, sausage, toast, juice, milk, cereal, cantaloupes...

you name it, they had it. The cereal was in those little boxes that looked like exact miniature replicas of the regular size ones. You could open them up and eat right out of them if you wanted, turning the box into its own bowl.

The first time I ever tasted a honeydew melon was on the *Silver Meteor* on the way to New York, I'll never forget. At first, I just thought it was a funny-looking cantaloupe, but then I saw it was green inside, too, and my dad squeezed a lemon on top of it and I took a bite and it was pure heaven. If you ever get to ride on the train, order it if they've got it on the menu. There just isn't anything better than a slice of honeydew melon first thing in the morning when you're riding past people's backyards in Virginia or North Carolina, watching folks get ready to go to work or kids heading to school and you're sitting down to a table with white linen and shiny, heavy, silverware... forks and spoons and knives. That first taste of the melon and knowing the cooks are getting you some scrambled eggs and sausage going, too. Boy, it's like being a king... or at least a prince.

You just can't help but feel like you are someone special when you're eating a meal in the Dining Car of a moving train.

*   *   *

BY NOW I HAD THE EVINRUDE READY TO GO, and if anything the weather was looking even better. The sun, which had been playing 'peek-a-boo most of the day, was out in full force now which always makes things seem happy and there was a type of friendly little breeze coming in from the north. It was looking pretty nice. When I came back up to the screen porch Pawpaw and George were both standing back outside now and the old man was talking with Mr. Johnson (who I noticed drive up in his pickup truck while I was messing with the motor). Like I said earlier, if there is anyone at Oceanside who can stand his ground with the old man it is Mr. Johnson. He does not raise his voice and shout like Pawpaw does, but he has got his own way of getting his point across and if it is something he feels strongly about he will, too. That pretty much sums up the scene at the dock that was going on when I came back up. The old man was speaking quite animatedly* about what he intended to do while Mr. Johnson just stood there listening, nodding his head just the least little bit to let the old man know he was paying attention, letting him have his say. Even if Mr. Johnson were the arguing type I think he is smart enough to know it would do no good to argue with the old man as he is the world's champ (Grayson coming in a close second).

Anyway, after Pawpaw told Mr. Johnson what he planned on doing Mr. Johnson just continued to shake his head, a little more strenuously now, saying something to the effect that he wasn't so sure it was a good idea to get involved in this situation, all the while assuming his usual posture of leaning on that cane with one hand and working a cigarette with the other; jabbing and pointing through the smoke with his fag to help make his point. Maybe the smart thing to do was to just let George go out there and see if he could find who it was we were looking for. Hell, he'd even lend him a boat and motor to do it with. 'No', the old man says. Redfish does not know George and besides it is he, the old man, who owes it.

At first I wasn't sure what he said at the end there, if he'd said *owns it* or *owes it,* and it took a little while before I could make sense of this. It was not because the old man was slurrin' his words either, like he had been the last several weeks, because he is now speaking the Kings' English, without a hitch. It's just that it was difficult (especially when someone is excited and the words sound so similar like these two do, anyway), to tell exactly what it was being said: *own* or *owed*. In this particular incident, though, the difference in meaning between these two words was immense. If what I'd heard was *own*, well what in the world was Pawpaw talking about here? What did he own that had anything to do with getting out to the island? Things started rushing into my mind, the kind of things you would describe as owning. There are any number of these, true, but I was also trying to narrow it down to something that would fit in with the discussion. A boat, a car, a house, an island? I couldn't make any sense of it. What would he own that would matter right then? That's when it began to dawn on me that he had to have said *owed*. And that right there changed things from *what* to *who*.

Who did he owe? Here, like the old man liked to say, was the $64,000 Question. Who did he owe that had anything to do with Derek or Redfish, or had any bearing on whether or not we got out to the island to talk with them? I was listening real good now, believe me, along with George who was still standing outside on the big dock with the rest of us, as well as Fred who was making like he was tending to the fish cleaning sink, cleaning it out and all but who I knew had to be listening with at least one ear to what was being said.

'That don't mean you owe him, Colonel' is what Mr. Johnson came back with exactly, and he was saying it serious too. Just like you'd plead with someone, even though you knew you were more than likely gonna' lose.

'All I want is to have my say and I want every man here to hear it too, so I got witnesses. Then you can go do what you want.' He looked around at all of us there when he said this. Calling us all men who most folks at Oceanside would not consider so– a boy and two negroes –well, that gave us something we didn't have until then. Just what it was is hard to put into words but it was something we needed and didn't even know we were doin' without until we got it.

*   *   *

Mr. Johnson started talking about the island itself and how there was never any good luck around it if you were looking for someone it was shielding. That's the very word he used too; I remember because it struck me as an odd choice of words– *shielding*.

Then he broke out into this story about what had happened almost fifty years ago when he was just a teenager and I noticed Fred was coming over towards everyone on the big dock now and the old man tried to stop Mr. Johnson, tried to interrupt him once saying we needed to get going if we were gonna' get out there and back before dark. But Mr. Johnson wouldn't stop and he wouldn't let the old man not listen, too.

'You're gonna' héar me out before you go', is the gist of what he said, and then he continued on about how three boats of men took off one afternoon on a calm summer's day back then for the island searching for a negro they claimed was wanted for violating and murdering this young girl who worked at the Bay Street Bank; the same place where this colored man was a porter. They knew he was out there and they intended on rowing out, getting him and bringing him back to lynch. Any trial, or even the thought of one, was superfluous*. The sad part about it is that only one boat of those men was necessary, 'cause there wasn't but one of him, but so many folks were caught up in the spirit of the moment (Mr. Johnson's own words), that when everything was said and done there were eighteen men that took off that afternoon in three boats, which meant there were seventeen men that were gonna' have real bad luck the next day.

They made it out to the island with no problem, searching the forest and old buildings out there all the rest of that day and into the evening, night and early morning, when a group of men finally caught the negro who prayed for mercy, begging that he was innocent and could prove it if they would only listen. Some of them were all for stringing him up right then and there, but there were more who demanded that they take him back so everyone in town who cared to could see him swing. So it was decided they would take him back into town.

On the way back over from the island an hellacious storm came up from seemingly nowhere. It had been clear with no trace of a cloud when they started out, but about a third of the way over it started getting real dark real quick and by the time they were halfway across it began blowing and getting real loud and from the direction of the island there suddenly came what looked like two big funnel clouds towards them, weaving back and forth across the river. The clouds got darker and denser looking every second, scurrying and bouncing across the top of the river until they were just about on them and right before they caught them they joined together into a single cloud that turned the scene into one of total mayhem and terror. Eight foot whitecaps, tornado-force winds, boats being overturned like they were made of balsawood and men everywhere treading water for their lives. Out of all those men only one made it back to shore; able to float back on a board that had formerly been a bench in the largest boat, and this man swore that as he was making his way back across he looked back and saw the negro, shackled at his wrists and ankles, swimming– using a modified sorta' dog-paddle –towards the island. After that, word started going around, and everyone agreed; the only reason the one man was spared was so that he could be a witness– to tell others about what had happened. There was much conjecture* after that on whether or not the colored man had made it back to the island, but by that time things had pretty much settled down. Though there was some scattering of talk from time to time about going back out after him again, for whatever reasons a second party never was mustered.

Later, about three months after all this happened, it was discovered by a young detective who wouldn't give up on the case that a fellow worker of the young girl's, another clerk, had committed the heinous deed. After that there was just never anymore talk at all of going back out to the island. The reason he knew this story so well, Mr. Johnson said– taking a long puff on his cigarette and standing there leaning on his cane for a moment – was that the one and only survivor of that ill-fated expedition had been none other that his very own Pa.

*   *   *

Whether it was the effect he was trying for or not we were all real silent for a coupla' moments after that. But before too long Pawpaw spoke up saying something to the effect that it was a real interesting story and he appreciated bein' allowed to hear it, but that this mission was in no way connected to the one we'd just heard about. We were headed out to the island to help *save someone* not destroy them and besides even if there was any truth to the superstition surrounding the island we would not be subject to it seeing as that we were aiming to do something positive, something for the good.

All Mr. Johnson could do was shake his head slowly which is just what he did as he threw down a cigarette butt and ground it out on the dock with the twisting toe of his good foot. He had done all he could and would no longer try and stop us. We were grown men and if we didn't know what we were doing by now any amount of persuading by him was not gonna' do much good, anyway. After that there wasn't much left to do but go.

*   *   *

Melinda has got a little stowage compartment up in her bow and in there way up in the front where it gets narrow is where I keep a battery lantern. Before we left, Pawpaw told me to go check and make sure the batteries were still good, which they were, and after that I carried the motor out almost the full length of the leftside dock and strapped her on real tight to *Melinda's* stern. She had never had three people in her before, at least since I had owned her, and I was curious to see how she would sit in the water with the additional weight. It had always been either the old man and myself or just me in her, but I was fairly certain she would do well, regardless.

Pawpaw said for George to sit up front as he weighed the most and this would help balance her out best. He, the old man, would sit in the center on the small fold-out canvas campseat Mr. Johnson told Fred to go get out of the shed, and of course, as usual I would work the tiller at the rear.

Because I was a little on the nervous side, with everyone watchin' and all, or because I had just not used the motor in quite a while I could not get her to start and this had me perplexed a good bit as the Evinrude had always kicked over no later than by the third pull, usually the second. But after about six or seven pulls the old man turned around and glancing at the motor first and then me said just one word: 'Choke.'

Well, needless to say I did feel pretty much like a complete idiot. But determined not to let it get me down on myself I pulled out the choke and the next pull she started right up. I'm not completely certain, but I thought I could detect a slight chuckle coming from the front and not the old man's little tickled laugh, but again I became determined not to let it upset me to the point that things like this used to. I let her warm up for a few moments, about half a minute or so, and then I pushed the choke back in and popped the gear lever down into forward. Since we were pointed straight out towards the creek all I had to do was give her a little gas and we were off.

She was riding well. A little lower that I was used to but it didn't seem to make much difference as I idled her away from the dock and the camp. Looking back towards the fish camp I could see Fred was standing up on the big dock; Mr. Johnson was going back inside the house, and I gave a little wave back. Fred threw up a hand in return and as if this were a signal I began turning the throttle and *Melinda* picked up speed. The big difference I noticed was that with the additional weight her nose did not come up out of the water like she did when it was just the old man and me, or especially if it was just me, but still she seemed to respond pretty well.

Sitting right in her middle, Pawpaw held out both of his arms, grabbing a gunnel with each hand to steady himself and the little bit of George I could see it looked like he was leaned forward some on the front bench, spray from the creek flying by him on either side. It wasn't cold, but it sure wasn't hot either and as far as we had to go I knew that George would probably want to stay as dry as he could, so I slowed her down a little and yelled up to him that there was a rubber poncho up in the bow he was welcomed to use if he wanted. He said thanks, he would get it later if he thought he needed it and I torqued the throttle back up to about three-quarters and we glided across the creek through the series of short curves that led out to the spot where the creek opened up wider and I could tell here, too, as we made those short turns at that speed the extra weight was making a difference. Usually, if I wanted, I could zip through here pretty quick. *Melinda* handled well through these turns staying up on top of the water and going right in the direction I pointed her even with the old man on board, zigging and zagging smoothly, but with George's additional weight she seemed to get stuck in the turns, sitting there for a while, not responding as well as she normally did. Still, it was passable, though I revised my earlier opinion figuring it might take closer to an hour to get out to the island instead of just 45 minutes. Which meant it would put us out there at close to 4:30. If they were on the island like Dosha claimed and were not hiding and it didn't take any more than 30 minutes or so to talk them into coming back it would still put us back at Johnson's by 6:00 or so, well before dark. This was what was going through my mind as I steered *Melinda* through the twists and turns of San Pablo Creek on our way out to the river.

*   *   *

The weather still looked good, but I noticed a little breeze had picked up. I could see the marshgrass ahead on either side of the creek where it gets narrow stirring like a wheatfield swaying in the wind. The light looked good on the marsh too; it was the type light that makes you feel safe. That's something I have noticed; that from down below St. Augustine to all the way up to Nassau County above Fernindina, how the light can be different. What I was seeing on the marsh was how it looked around here; it's just how the light was there at this part of the coast. If we'd gone up a ways, say thirty or forty miles, it'd be different, still. Probably, it is different every mile really, different just a little. Not enough so you can tell, but just a little. It takes 30 or 40 miles to tell the difference. If the light is different, then everything is different. The same thing... a piece of wood, bricks in a walkway, the marsh... look different in different light so it stands to reason that's part of why things feel different when you go from one place to another. That's why trains, like the *Silver Meteor*, are´so great. You can sit back and notice the difference of the places as you go up and down the coast.

You'd think that with what we were up to the only thing I could think about would be this mission the three of us had taken on, but it wasn't. For whatever reason (or reasons), I had Patti on my mind more at this time than at any other time since I'd heard she was gone. To a lesser extent I was thinking about Grayson also, and somehow I seemed to equate and put the two of them together and I thought about this as we moved farther down the creek towards the river, the spray still flying by up front just missing George and the old man, while at the rear behind us was left a wake whose waves pushed up hard against the marshgrass, really making it sway and undulate with the introduction of each new rolling swell. I had no trouble understanding why I should be thinking about Patti, nor did it mystify me that I should be thinking about my brother, either. What was mysterious was why I was linking the two of them in my mind so out here.

I haven't done a very good job of explaining it, but whenever I am out on the water (maybe other folks have this same thing happen to them too. I've never talked to anyone about it), I think differently. I'm not certain if it has to do with the water or the fact that it is possible to see so much further out here, but even when you're behind some tall marshgrass you still know that as soon as you come from behind it you will again be able to see a far-ways and this I think is the main reason I think differently, clearer, out here. Only sometimes it doesn't seem clearer at first. Sometimes it seems more jumbled, but I have noticed lately (since being on the island), that it is only at the beginning, when I am first thinking about something that I get this jumbled sensation. I think it's because sometimes these thoughts seem incongruous (one of Mrs. Johns' words), at first like they are boiling and roiling, cooking, and only after a while spent simmering do they coalesce (another one of her's), and become clear. I am guessing at this but for some reason I get the feeling that it is similar to being out in the desert, being out on the water. There isn't a whole lot out there to catch your eye and distract you just like out on the creek at it's wide spots and the river. For the most part they are both wide open spaces. Being out on the ocean, of course, must be the pinnacle* of this sensation, but I've spent fourteen years hugging the shore and think about that sorta' like experiencing the desert, even though unlike the desert I've at least seen the ocean. I just haven't ever been way out on it. Someday.

I knew from experience that there was a reason I was thinking about Patti and Grayson both out here. Just what that reason was though eluded* me at the time. As we came nearer to the spot where the creek spilled out into the river, past the tall cattails where I was so surprised to find us the time Pawpaw latched onto the tarpon, I began to get the notion, or rather the notion came to me, that there was really nothing I could do about either of these two people as is true about anyone, really. There was nothing I could do to bring Patti back, she was gone; and there was nothing I could do to make Grayson any better, to take away the fact he had the disease he had.

Of course, this was all stuff I was thinking before we ever got out to the island.

*   *   *

I have always been partial to the creek and the intracoastal waterway. For some reason these waters have been able to hold my interest longer and fiercer than either the river itself or the ocean. I certainly know that I've had better luck fishing-wise in these closer-in waters, but maybe it also has something to do with the fact that *Melinda* is far better suited to the creek and intracoastal. True, I've been out on the river plenty with her when the old man was along but never when it got to kicking up or looked like it was fixin' to. But there is something else too about these skinnier waters that appeals to me. The fact that these backwaters and estuaries are where the ocean comes in and actually spills onto land mingling with the earth, refusing to stay contained in its ocean and river boundaries, is somehow satisfying, more pleasing, to me.

Tourists get all excited about going out on some charterboat or partyboat way out twenty-five miles or so from land and hooking into a big grouper, but I just don't see where all the excitement is in that. Hell, you might as well be pulling up a bunch of cinderblocks for all that's worth. Now, sneaking up into a quiet cove on the creek or intracoastal (just cutting the motor if you got one and glidin' on in), and throwing out a gold spoon or mirrorlure and jigging it back in in an attempt to lure a gator-trout or a big red... *now that's exciting!* There is some real anticipating going on there, especially when you can see the backs of a school of reds ripplin' through that cove and you throw just ahead of them waitin' for one to strike. Like Coach Sutter says... *'If that doesn't get the juices going then you'd best check your pulse for vital signs'.*

*   *   *

It amazed me how strong the river flows especially up at this spot we were headed for, not that far from the mouth. Once you leave the protection of the creek and are headed out to the river then you get the real feeling of the power of water. Pawpaw says it's because the island puts a squeeze on the river here, dividing her up and all of a sudden forcing the same amount of water into a space that was only about 75% as big. Makes sense.

A coupla' times I have been out here with the old man when the wind and the river started picking up and unless you are anchored well under these circumstances it is amazing how quickly you can be swept along with it, the river. Put it this way. You would not want to be out there some days we have been out in a craft that was not entirely seaworthy and with a good motor like the one the old man has. 9.5 horsepower may not seem like a lot, but if you think about it in another way, that it has the pulling power of 9.5 horses, well, then you can see how that would be sufficient. On the other hand if you are use to carrying two men and add only one more that increases your cargo by 50% right there, not to mention anything extra the other man brings along. But George had just brought along himself and looking back on it it was a good thing. Good that he brought himself, and good that that was all.

Boy, did he get wet though. George, that is. Pawpaw got a little moist too, and even I, seated in the stern, saw a fair amount of spray that afternoon. But I had already offered the poncho to George and still that part of him that wasn't covered got soaked. I don't recall there being any whitecaps at that point, but there were some good-size swells. Like the old man said, *Melinda* does not exactly cut through the waves as she is more of a plower, and that is precisely what we did there for a while, plow.

*   *   *

If you have never operated a boat the size of *Melinda* under such circumstances then you might be hard pressed to understand that it is better when you are plowing through such swells to go as fast as you can. If you keep your speed down it tends to accentuate the impact instead of mitigate* it and you can get so jostled around after awhile that if you've got false teeth they might shake out and if you don't then you may need some after the ride which is a long and convoluted* way of saying it can knock hell out of you in pretty short order. If you speed up though you don't hit the waves or swells so much. It's more like you are riding the tops of them and the plowing effect is diminished, somewhat. After awhile you begin to appreciate any diminishing that comes along. Another thing that helps is not to hit the swells head on, but to try and engage them at an angle if at all possible. Of course, this all depends on where you're heading... what kind of angle you can use... and as luck would have it we were not able to use much of an angle that day we were headed out to the island. From where the creek emptied out into the river it was pretty much a straight shot out to the island, but I had that motor going pretty much wide open when we hit the river and this helped considerably in reducing the plowing effect.

Just because a northeaster is coming in doesn't mean that you can tell it right away by looking at the sky. Sometimes you can look out and see nothing but clear blue sky with maybe just a few wispy white cotton-candy looking clouds and you would swear it was going to be a wonderful day. There might be a little breeze going but a good rule of thumb concerning breezes is any wind you can detect on land should be magnified by a factor of at least three to give you a truer picture of what its like out on the water. If this seems like exaggeration then you just head out to a lake or river some fall day when you think there is only a light wind evident and see what it's like. I'll bet a dollar to a donut you'll find it a lot breezier out on that body of water than you thought it was out in the backyard. I guess that's why you hear the term *small craft warning* so much. It's a phrase you get to listening for when that's what you're operating, a small craft.

The way I figured it we had a good twenty minute ride left out to the island which would put us there at just about the time I had calculated earlier. As far as I could tell from looking at his back the old man seemed well, and I had no concerns about Big George. I felt certain he was doing well. He was so stocky and muscular that it'd take a heck of a lot more jostlin' than he was receiving at the hands of being in *Melinda's* bow to rattle him.

I have been out on the river at various spots before but never this far north where it takes a big bend to the east on the final leg of its journey to the sea. That explains why I had never seen the island before (other than the evening I saw the tops of some trees when Pawpaw was hooked to the tarpon); though I have been up this creek the old man, George and I went up that afternoon, only never this far before. From the fish camp there are really several creeks or places where the water divides heading back to the river and this particular one we took to get out to the island happens to be the most northerly, as well as the most far-flung. Put it this way. Other than for the express purpose of going out to the island, there really is no reason anyone would take this particular route to the river. There are no homes on either side of the river out here and if you were headed out to sea then you'd just go up to Mayport and put in there or take the intracoastal which is a more direct route from back at the fish camp. Even from the road, the one on the other side of the river that follows right alongside the river's banks and which will take you to the north landing of the ferry at Mayport, you cannot see the island. The trees and vegetation are so dense, so thick around there that the road is forced back almost a quarter of a mile from the river at that spot, not to mention the sudden eruption of giant sand dunes around here, too. I reckon if you were really set on spying the island from that side of the river you could pull off on the skinny shoulder of the river road and hike through the dense vegetation (you'd better have a darn sharp machete with you), then climb the tall dunes for a ways until you got to one high enough to see clear through to the river. Wouldn't be a bad idea to pack a picnic though, as all this would take a considerable amount of time, I have no doubt. As for me I prefer the route we were headed on that afternoon, at least under most and more normal circumstances. What prompts me to say these words is not a vainglorious* attempt at melodramatic effect, but the very concrete reality of the sign.

It's not that unusual to see various types of signs and markers when upon the creek or river here or any place really. Nearly everyone has a sign on their dock or stuck out on a pole in the creek pleading: •**NO WAKE**• and occasionally you will see some homemade sign advertising the fact that such and such a person is in possession of a good amount of bait or shrimp or mullet or crabs and directing you to their whereabouts. For the most part these signs are informational and pretty much to the point, but occasionally you come across one that is more philosophic, expressing a definite opinion or desire. I have even seen a sign declaring both *Impeach Earl Warren* and *Get Us Out Of The U.N.* on the creek before down in a narrow part of the creek in front of the Mathews house (or shack is more like it as it always appears unkempt looking), at least that part of it seen from the water. These are sentiments not all that uncommon and can be seen along the road in most parts of the state, I would guess. I'm certain about that around Oceanside, as I have seen both of these plenty outside of town, in the country, usually.

The most disturbing sign or marker I have ever seen on the water though is one down south not far from Pawpaw's house. Once, a couple of years ago when he and I were out on the lake in his boat, way on the other side of the lake we pulled back into a cove where there was a little Ma and Pa marina. Right in front of the place there was a marker sticking up out of the water with the following two messages, each stenciled upon a weather-beaten board:

No Trespasin
If You Are A Nigger Or A Jew
Do Not Bother Coming Any Farther!!!

We Do Not Receive Any Assistance From
The U.S. Government And Reserve The
Right To Refuse Service To Anyone We See Fit.

Someone had gone to a lot of trouble to make these two signs and I think Pawpaw was a little embarrassed by it to tell the truth, it being on his lake and all. Somehow, he had never seen it before.

Well, as neither of us were either of the type of people listed on the sign we stopped there to get some gas and while he was gassing up one of the six gallon tanks the old man got into a discussion with the owner of the place. Pawpaw is not one to stir up trouble and normally believes that every man is entitled to his own opinion, but again I think it irked, riled him some to see something like this on his lake, him taking a proprietary* view of it. His was about the first house built there, after all (of course, not counting any Indians who might have lived there in bygone centuries).

Before long the two of them were going at it pretty good and at one spot the owner of the place asked Pawpaw if he was a nigger-lover to which the old man said 'No' even though it was none of his business if he was. Then the man asked if he was a Yankee and again the old man answered in the negative. The other man said that was good too, he'd been meaning to add Yankee to that sign for a while now, but just hadn't gotten around to it yet. It's hard to explain their attitudes here... they weren't really arguing, in fact there was a good bit of chuckling going on... you know, the kind when two people are trying to egg each other on... sorta' friendly, but with an edginess, too.

Pawpaw paid the man for the gas and a coupla' cokes we got also and as we were getting back into the boat and Pawpaw was about to start her up the man came over to the edge of the dock and giving the boat a little shove off with his foot said:

'You know, the only good Yankee is one that's headin' back north with a nigger under each arm.'

I must admit that the old man and I both smiled a little bit at this one, and to be perfectly honest about it I thought it was pretty funny at the time and had to try real hard not to laugh out loud. Again, this was well before I had ever been out to the island, or even knew it existed.

The sign I am talking about that we came upon that afternoon though was not like any I had ever seen before, either on the water or on dry land. Here is what it said:

Quarantine Island
For Your Own Safety
STOP
Turn Back Now.
Do Not Attempt To Land
– Or –
You Will Be Prosecuted
To The Full Extent of The Law.

* * *

We used to know some folks who lived out by Camp Blanding who had a tin roof and once when my father was still alive we went out there one night to a party and I can remember that it started raining and how good it sounded, that rain falling on the tin roof. It must have been late because I remember laying on the bed in one of the bedrooms half asleep and half listening to the sound of the rain on the roof. A pleasing sound, it made it seem like the house was holding you safe. It is one of the best feelings there is, being in a bed in the dark when there is a gentle falling of rain on a tin roof. I remember I could hear them all laughing and the sounds of glasses clinking and the radio playing music low and my father's laugh, it being the happiest sounding. It sounded rounder, more full, full of happiness and that sound of him and the rain just above me on the roof... goin' to sleep like that was like what goin' to heaven must be like. There is nothin' else like it, even close, unless it is riding on a train at night in a pullman, falling asleep just as you're picking up the rhythm and roll of the tracks.

There is one, you know, a rhythm to the tracks. At first you think you can pick it up like the beat in music... what's called 3/4 or 4/4 time, and you listen for the pattern to repeat itself but it's not that clear cut. It is looser like and after a while you begin to sense it has it's own beat, own time that depends on the track itself and also the train, how fast it is going and if it's straight or on a curve and the engineer too comes into it even. All of these things have a say in it. The pattern is there, only it's in the whole ride, one long song. In some way a train, or at least a train ride, anyways, is like a river.

*   *   *

I'll tell you some more about that sign we saw now, the one before you get to the island that gave me the heebie-jeebies so. Little did I know at the time that what was about to happen would affect me (as well as all others concerned), even more than the time I got stuck in that window.

By the time we got to the sign we'd been traveling nearly an hour so we were already a good bit behind the schedule I had set in my mind. One of the things I had failed to take into account, (as well as everyone else, too), was the fact that the tide was coming in real strong at that time. It was what some folks call a double-tide. I've heard some call it a south moon under, meaning it was a legitimate tide, but also the moon, which was full, was in such a position as to have an even greater effect than usual on the ebb and flow of the river. Even going full-out, meaning I had the throttle turned all the way over, wide-open, we were not making nearly as good progress out here on the river as we had back in the creek, and it just seemed like everything was working against us, the tide and the wind; even the water. It seemed like even the water itself was making us sluggish.

Besides churning up like it was, there was something else. The water seemed deeper somehow and the color of it, about a yellowish-dull gray, I had never seen before; that complexion of it seemed even to make us slower. It was really not the kind of water I would care to be out in under normal circumstances. It looked like the ocean itself on a bad day, but like I said earlier I have never been out far so I reckon this is just what I imagined it might look like. The funny thing about all this though was the fact that it was so clear. There was not a cloud, or even the hint of one, in the sky.

When we got to the spot where I was certain the old man could read the sign I slowed up a little, not too much because it was so choppy it was better to keep moving, but I sorta' hung around that sign for a few seconds, looking in front of me to see what kind of effect it was having on Pawpaw, and after a few seconds, when he didn't turn around, I called out: '*Whadda' you think?*', but there was no answer. He didn't even nod or move his head in any way to acknowledge that I had said anything and that's when I knew. Something bad had happened again.

*   *   *

As I'd feared, the old man had had another stroke, right out there on the river. From the back he looked perfectly okay; both his arms were out, his hands grabbing ahold of *Melinda's* gunnels like eversince we'd left, but sometime in the last ten minutes or so, since we'd left the creek, he had slipped. I could sense this when I grabbed his shoulder and pulled it back towards me. Then his face... that's all I needed to see, was that right half of his face, and I knew.

George hadn't noticed anything, though. He had his hands full just trying to keep from drowning sitting up front like he was and getting the lion's share of spray from *Melinda's* plowing bow. When George turned around I could tell from looking at his eyes that Pawpaw was in a bad way. George motioned for me to slow down and I did and while I kept *Melinda* facing steady into the swells he took hold of the old man and holding him under his arms turned him around. Both of them were seated on the front bench, but turned around now facing the stern, and me.

I didn't have a lot of time to study exactly how he looked, I had my hands full, too, now trying to keep *Melinda* steered properly. That is, with her bow facing right into the growing swells... some of which were reaching whitecapped status... instead of having them come slapping up behind us over her stern. But even a quick glance evidenced that he didn't look too well. It is amazing how one minute you can feel pretty good about yourself like you are big and all, lifesize if you will, and then all of a sudden you can feel pretty damn small, diminutive (another word from English), as though you are nothing more than a speck or maybe some extra flotsam* for the river to wash ashore. That is a scary thought, especially if you are out there right in it when you are thinking it; feeling like at any moment with just the right little bit of bad luck things could suddenly go very wrong for you and those with you.

I reckon the main thing that saved me then was realizin' that I didn't have all that much time to dwell on this. It was more like the thought just shot through me like it was letting me know this was a possibility that I should prepare for. Of course, how do you prepare for something like that... disaster? It scares the hell out of me, even now when I think of what it must be like to drown. I've thought about it before a lot, too.

By the time we got to that sign we were not that far from the island itself which was a good thing because the way things were going I'm not too sure we could have gone much further on our own. Not the way we were then and not the way the river was getting. Like I said, the old man had suffered another stroke right out there on the water and George was holding onto him now sitting on *Melinda's* front bench. He was doing a good job 'cause so far they had not fallen out of the boat and let me tell you that was no mean feat, being able to stay inside *Melinda* with the way the river was kicking up. I would not describe it as hurricane conditions exactly, but there were some severe waves, not just swells anymore, rising up from the river's surface.

It has been my observation that folks not well acquainted with the water, either the ocean or the river, don't take it seriously when they hear that there are, say two to three foot waves about, but what you have to stop and think is that means two to three feet above the surface of whatever water you are in or on. Also, waves on the river are not coming every ten or fifteen seconds like in some Elvis Presley *Blue Hawaii* movie, but are coming constantly, one right after another; the whitecaps of one wave lapping and spitting forward leapfrog-wise, crowding into the ones in front of it like kids at school breaking in line to get to the cafeteria.

After just a very little of this it gets tiresome, and it wasn't too long before I came to understand what Stephen Crane (again no relation, though I would be proud if there were), meant in his short story called 'The Open Boat', when he says:

"... *These waves were most wrongfully and barbarously abrupt and tall and each froth-top was a problem in small-boat navigation.*"

and, also, when he says:

"... *A singular disadvantage of the sea lies in the fact that, after successfully surmounting one wave, you discover that there is another behind it, just as important and just as nervously anxious to do something effective in the way of swamping boats.*"

That, better than anything I could ever write tells what it felt like out there on the river that day on our way to the island. Even if it was just the river we were in and not the ocean itself.

If you are wondering how I came to know so much about Stephen Crane and his writings it's because he's the author I picked this year in Mrs. Johns English class, the one I chose to do my mid-year report on. I admit that the last name is what drew me to him at first, but after awhile, after I found out what he was like and the things he wrote about, I found that I truly enjoyed it. First, I read "The Red Badge of Courage", and then several short stories, but out of all of them my favorite is "The Open Boat". There is no doubt upon reading that story that it was an experience he, Steven Crane, lived through firsthand. Incredibly, it all happened right around here, not too far south of Oceanside itself. And the spot they started out from was the docks right in Riverville, New Year's Day 1897. That is what I call some real history.

There is no making up some of the stuff he wrote about; what it was like with four men in a ten-foot lifeboat trying desperately to get to shore and fighting an angry sea for a day and a night and another half-day to do so. In this story there comes one of my favorite lines:

"*Many a man ought to have a bath-tub larger than the boat which here rode upon the sea.*"

The reason I put that in is because it is exactly how I felt out there on the river with the waves jutting up and the three of us in *Melinda*, who is really a two-man boat, still a quarter of a mile or so from the island. Strange, how a quarter of a mile can seem like a short ways one second and a far, far ways the next.

That's how it was that day. Right before we got to the sign I thought we had it made and had only a short distance to go but upon reading what it had to say and then discovering that the old man was in trouble again and then the waves suddenly coming up, all that changed and it was like life was different now. There is no other place I can think of than out on the water where things can change, can go wrong, so quickly. If I didn't before, I sure know that now.

Anyway, George had a good hold of Pawpaw, I could tell that much from looking at them and that did make me feel better. I knew now that all I had to do was keep us from getting swamped or capsized and I knew, too, what that meant was that I had to get us to the island. There was a fair amount of water inside the boat, about three inches I'd say, but I didn't feel like it was urgent enough to take my attention away from steering *Melinda*, with both hands now, towards the island. I could see that George was looking down into the water swirling and sloshing all around his feet also, and I knew that if he thought it was important enough he would start bailing. There is a gallon bleach bottle, the new kind made of plastic with the top third cut off at an angle but the handle left on which makes it a good bailer, and also an old coffee can like Old Dr. Cordray kept in his boat. Both of these I keep up in the little cubbyhole in *Melinda's* bow in case it becomes necessary to get water out of her, and that was reassuring to us, George and I, right then. You'd be surprised at how many people there are, with what I would call smaller craft, who do not carry with them some sort of can or bottle or cup with which to scoop water out when it is necessary to do so. What these folks are thinking I don't know, but sooner or later there comes a time when you need to get water out of your boat and as good as two hands are under a spigot or beside a stream for cupping water to take a drink the same cannot be said for their ability to bail out a boat. Boy, if I'm not starting to sound like the old man now when he gets up on his soapbox, in one of his lecturing moods.

Like Pawpaw says, I will go ahead and give you the Reader's Digest version of it now and quit beating around the bush. What it comes down to is that if it had not been for Derek coming out to get us when he did I am not so sure that I would be around today to be beating around any bush. That is the long and the short of it, I reckon.

And to think— we were just out there on our way, we thought, to rescue him.

"The second you set off to find yourself, you are lost."

I'll bet you can guess by now... yes, here is another one of the old man's sayings. Who else? I heard him say it about a year ago and it was one of those things that sounds good at first but doesn't seem to make much sense later on. I can see now that I just didn't get it back then.

Why were we heading for the island or should I say why was the island pulling us towards it? If ever there was a *64 Thousand Dollar Question*, this was it.

*   *   *

One thing I haven't said much about so far (neglected's the word), is my friends. I don't know why, but it just isn't easy to talk about things like that, at least for me it isn't; but it hit me the other day how much I had come to rely, to depend, on my friends. Who I am talking about here mostly is Mick and Davey, and what it was I was counting on was just the fact they were there. I know. It sounds corny, but what can you say? That there would be two other people my age living in a such a strange out-of-the-way place like Oceanside and thinking about and liking the same things (for the most part), and then on top of that that we would all get along (mostly), and no one would have to move (like half the kids I've known have had to do); well, it's a miracle is about the only thing I can think. You couldn't ask for a better friend than these two. It's times like this... thinking about Mick and Davey... that it seems to me here is the best evidence that someone is *'running the show, after all'* as the old man would say... you know, that there is a God. That he exists and is looking out for us, for the most part. I mean, he can't do everything. Well, he could if he wanted I reckon, but if he did there wouldn't be anything left for us to do and since he is smart enough, he, of course, knows this ahead of time. It's sorta' like he helps us out just enough to keep us going, but not enough to make it a cake-walk. I reckon what it comes down to is if He did everything then we wouldn't be any better than robots when you got right down to it. Again, I have gotten off the subject and after promising to check myself better. I'm not gonna' even make anymore promises now. Maybe that'll get me to stick to what's important.

Like I was saying, there was Derek, a wanted man whom the Ocean County Sheriff was looking for, out in his boat and I don't think I have ever been happier to see another human being– at least not out on the water. He was doing lots better than us, too, there was no doubt about that. Where I barely had control of *Melinda* (even though I had a motor and all Derek had was two huge oars), there wasn't any question as to the fact that he was doing a vastly superior job of getting around out there. Also, like I said earlier, the fog was startin' to come in real heavy by now and with each passing moment it seemed like it was getting harder and harder to keep my bearings. Before, all I'd had to do was look over my shoulder and I could see the thinning line of mainland clear as day and looking ahead there was the island growing larger, but by now the fog had obscured my vision so much that it was no longer possible to tell which was mainland and which was island. My guess right then was that it wouldn't be too much longer before I couldn't even tell where the water was much less either piece of land. I know it sounds like I'm exagerrating but it's the truth– that fog was coming in like the kind where you can't even see your hand when you straighten out your arm and hold it all the way out in front of your face.

Anyways, Derek was doing a masterful job of handling that giant jonboat and if there was anyone else in the whole wide world at that moment as glad (or gladder), to see him rowing towards us right then it was Big George. Funny thing about it is, I don't really recall him yelling or shouting out like you'd think someone would be prone to doing in such circumstances, but I could tell anyway that he was glad we were being joined. In dire situations folks have gotta' way of getting themselves understood in all sorts of ways, I reckon, and if anyone is an expert at this it is Big George, I can assure you. I'm not gonna' beat it to death, but it was like the time earlier that very same day (as hard as that is to believe; it seemed like such a long time since then), when Big George informed Mr. Dickerson of his intentions in regards to quitting-time that afternoon. Mrs. Johns calls it *nonverbal communication*, and it's a subject she's talked about in class on more than one occasion. I reckon if Big George is an expert at anything besides mechanizing, this is it: *non-verbal communication.*

I watched him practice this talent that very day out there just a little ways from the island when Derek all of a sudden quit rowing and with hardly a word, just a quick *'Here, catch!'* grabbed up a large sisal rope from the bottom of his boat and slung it over towards us, whereupon George– without standing up which would have tipped us for sure –reached into the air above his head with one hand and made a clean snag of the rope. In no-time, lickety-split (still one-handed; he was holding Pawpaw's shoulder with the other), George tied the end of the rope off crisscross style and cinched it clean and neat on *Melinda*'s front starboard cleat. Having completed his task, all he did next was give me a little look, but in that half-second it spoke volumes, telling me we were tied off right and he had care of the old man. Right then I felt as safe as if I were back on dry land, which is saying a lot since it was only moments before that I had started figuring we might all be goners, done for.

Thinking back on it, I reckon then is when I got the first whiff of some of the strange sort of things we had to look forward to out there on Quarantine Island because when I happened to look up into the sky (the fog really, because by now it was all over us), I saw a split, a clear division in the cottony white covering right overhead through which could be seen a section of perfectly clear blue sky. That wasn't the oddest part, though, for within that narrow band of blue flew a loose and wavy line of longneck geese, which ain't all that unusual for the time of year it was– fall; only I'd swear on a stack of Bibles they were altogether heading in the wrong direction for that season of the year. That string of geese, you see, looked to be headed North.

*   *   *

Like I knew from the moment I first saw him out there, Derek had no trouble towing us safely through the fog to the island. The only thing he said was for me to '*kill it*', meaning to cut off the outboard, and then he was back on his bench pulling on the oars. Boy, but that spooked me some for a second, my heart skipping a whole beat, because all I could figure was that he was asking if we had killed the old man. That's all I could come up with until it struck me he was talking about the outboard. I don't have to tell you I was plenty relieved when it hit me, what he was truly saying.

I tried helping by paddling with the single oar we had (which seemed like a toothpick compared to the ones Derek was using), and it didn't take long to see what I was doing was far from being helpful. After that Derek didn't say anything else. But he did turn his head back once when I was trying to help row and he looked back at us like someone who was trying to figure out what it was that had suddenly impeded* his steady progress. It was when he looked back then that I first noticed something seemed different about him. But I couldn't put my finger on it right that second and it was several minutes before I finally realized what it was about him that looked different. Seeing as though there was nothing else for me to do right then (after all, we were being towed), I studied it intently and only when I was fixin' to give up (it always happens like that), it came to me. It was his eye, or rather the fact that he had one again that caught me up short.

*   *   *

They say the Sunshine State has no real change of seasons, but I have always thought different. When all there is is just a little change I think you take it more to heart, that little bit of change you do get. Somehow, I've always been able to think about those scenes of cold winter weather up North and translate them in my mind to down here. When I see a report on the news about a blizzard in some place like Buffalo and the next day it is overcast or a little on the cool side I can imagine Oceanside suffering through just as bleak a cold spell as its Northern counterpart. How you think about a thing or a place even can have a lot of bearing on how you remember it.

Reckon what I am getting around to is the fact of how I could come to think of that fall day on the river when the fog rolled in covering us up as a winter's day, for that's how I remember it now. At least at the time Derek was towing us towards the island. Before we actually got there.

*   *   *

'One thing I could teach you boy it'd be don't be scared of work... 'specially hard work. That's the only kind, truly. If you ain't workin' hard, you ain't working... that's what I say. The other thing would be if you're headin' out on the water, count on bad weather.' The old man really has got this thing about work... hard work. I reckon if there's any one thing he wishes he could impart to me... well, heck, if you read what I just said you know where I'm heading.

He doesn't hold office work in too high esteem* either, if you haven't guessed by now. Desk-Monkeys is the way I've always heard him refer to it... 'you know, folks who work inside air-conditioned offices all day, pushin' papers and making their livin' off the sweat of someone who's really workin'', he will say. He's got this other term, too. It's one I didn't get at first, but after a while it began making sense. Skimmers. It's what he calls lawyers and bankers and stock-brokers... folks like that. Everyone except Life Insurance agents, I reckon. 'At least they're giving you odds with the stuff they sell, he says. If you die someone gets something, and if you don't, well then that ain't exactly like losing then, is it?' Like I said, I didn't get it at first, but then one time he said something like '...*so and so doesn't really work, he just skims his off the top from the hard toil of other people*'; then I got it. Leah contends it's because he quit being a lawyer and later secretly regretted it is why he comes down so hard on these folks, but I'm not so sure I agree with her. One thing I do know is about the worst argument those two ever had was the time the old man called someone they both know a *skimmer,* and boy oh boy, did the fur fly that day! It didn't take a minute for that disagreement to become full-blown and personal and she even said so to his face, that the reason he was so hard on folks was they were leading a type of life he had quit and instead, because of that, he had had to work extra hard and really he was jealous. Brother, like I said they really went at it then. That was the time Grayson and I got to arguing too... over whether or not he (the old man), was coming back anytime soon. That's the funny thing about arguing, at least the kind'a arguing Leah and the old man do. Somehow, if you don't watch out, it's got a way of becoming contagious.

*   *   *

Quarantine Island, I gotta' say, was like no other place I'd ever been to before. At first, it seemed pretty much like any other island around Oceanside. It was land, surrounded by water, and it had trees– live oaks, pines and palms mostly along with the usual saw-palmettoes and scrub-pines that inhabit this neck of the woods. What I mean is it looked a lot like the rest of the world around Oceanside, but still it was different. It's hard to describe. It was the feel of the place is the best way I know of describing it.

As soon as we got closer to the shoreline, Derek towing us right along, the weather began to break, like we were entering another place or something. That's the only way to put it. I mean, I know it was the same place, or rather it was a place that was where it always had been and should be, stuck out in the river there at its widest spot, but I swear it seemed to me when we got close to the shore that for whatever reason it wasn't like the rest of Oceanside.

For beginners, the shoreline itself was different. Every other island on the river and strung along the intracoastal waterway in these parts has a sandy shore, but this place had a muddy one. Now my experience has been that there are two kinds of mud, at least around here– the dirty kind that your feet sink down into readily, and the other kind, the clean kind that is firm and holds you up. The mud along the shoreline at Quarantine

Island was the second, the clean kind, which was a good thing for us 'cause it must have been low tide when we got there seeing as though the shore was a good thirty yards or so deep, which I thought was sorta' unusual for an island. I know it doesn't sound like a big deal, but there was something about the fact that the shore was so broad that hit me funny. Looking back on it now I reckon you could say it even tipped me off sorta'– that what we were approaching was not your everyday run-of-the-mill island. No, this place was far from that I could tell when my feet first hit dry land, or mud, rather. Derek was towing us so fiercely that even when he beached first, quick-ly letting slack the tow-rope, we were still coming on hard enough for *Melinda* to glide in strong and pull up well onto shore so Big George and I didn't have to get our shoes and pants wet. All we had to do was step right out like we were royalty or something. This was with an outgoing tide occurring, too.

Right away Derek came over to us to help Big George and I with the old man. It is no easy feat, believe me, getting a grown adult who is unable to help himself out of a small launch, even if it is on shore and not on the water. We managed, though. Big George had Pawpaw under the arms and I had his feet and in this way we were able to get him out of *Melinda*. But we weren't standing there for more than a few seconds (both of us wondering what in the heck to do next), when all of a sudden Derek was there and with barely any effort at all he picked the old man up in both his arms like he was no heavier than a small child, and turning towards a clearing in the dense dark jungly foliage of the island we were up against, called out to Big George and I: *'Follow me'*.

What was said next was one of those things you hear but right away can't believe; like you think your ears are playing tricks on you... *did I hear that right?!*

It came from the old man, still groggy but seeming to be com-ing out of it some, and it sounded like it was directed at Derek.

'Son?', he murmured

*   *   *

NOW, WHERE SHOULD I BEGIN to tell of the many wondrous and fascinating events which happened there during our stay at Quarantine Island?

To say we were guests there is about the best way of putting it, I reckon. Somehow, that doesn't quite capture the way things seemed, though; the way they truly were. I reckon the thing that caught me most off-guard (after I'd gotten used to the fact that Derek knew his way around, his whereabouts, quite intimately), was the fact that there were more than just a coupla' folks on the island. This wasn't anything like what I was counting on. All I was expecting to see was Derek; maybe, Redfish, too, if he had made it like Dosha said, but by the time we'd been there less than half an hour I'd already counted a dozen people besides Derek and his brother in this big moss-draped clearing we came to after following Derek through the dense jungle path. Every one of these folks were colored, too, by the way.

This had me mystified and I felt a tremendous urge to start asking questions (of Derek, I suppose, since he was the only one there I really knew), but heck, I didn't really even know him when you got right down to it. Because of the connection between us– him being the one to find and return *Melinda* –it was natural for me to feel like I knew him some, I reckon. But the time never presented itself. He was always either talking to someone or giving directions to someone else, and not being eager to interrupt I figured I could wait a little while longer. Anyways, you can sense when someone does not want to be interrupted. Sooner or later an opportunity would present itself, I felt sure. The question I had in mind most was two-fold: where had these folks come from, and what were they all doing here?

It didn't seem possible that this many folks could be living out here without anyone... you know, anyone on the mainland... knowing about it. Sure, there'd been rumors and stories for years, (according to Pawpaw), of folks living out on the big island but no one I knew or knew of had ever seen or heard of any real people living out here. That's why I considered it like a fairy-tale and figured everyone else thought about it the same way, too. I knew there'd been a time when people really did live out here; after all, it's where ships would drop off folks who were sick or contagious with something really bad before finally docking at Riverville. I knew that much. It was an historical fact (after all, that's how the place got its name). But that there would still be people living out here with no way of getting to the mainland except by boat, and no one on the mainland knowing of their existence didn't seem real at this late date. It just didn't seem like something that would still be going on in the second half of the 20th century. It flat-out didn't seem possible. Not wanting to, as the old man says '*cater to cliche*', I have to say that our arrival at Quarantine Island seemed like nothing more than a dream and a pretty wild one at that. Only problem was I knew what a dream felt like and as strange an experience as this was, still it was no dream. I knew that much. Just what you would call it, though, I had no idea.

*   *   *

An *experience*.

That's what I finally settled on, while we were still out on the island, when me and Pawpaw and Big George were still together. It sounded good as anything else I could think of; better really than anything else I could come up with. Like I said, there was over a dozen folks and they were each and every one looking at us at like we were the strange ones. To them I'm sure we were. After all, everyone else belonged there. Let me try and describe just what it looked like:

First, after we had walked awhile along the trail Derek led us along... maybe a half a mile or so... we came to this big open area where the trees and brush and all had been cleared out for years. That's where all the people were. It looked like a big circle- a football field or so wide, but still a circle. Placed around the circle were houses, I guess you'd call them. Really, they looked more like huts of some sort. I mean, most of them weren't built like what you would think a regular house should look like, with a front door and windows and a regular roof and all. These houses were round and were built with sticks- skinny pine-logs and big pieces of bamboo seemed to be the main ingredients. The logs were standing up straight, though, instead of laying across sideways for a cabin and they were all held together with what looked like long interlacing strips of tree bark. In between some of the cracks someone had taken mud and filled them in. It must have been some special kinda' mixture because I checked on this mud in the house we (Pawpaw, Big George and I), stayed in, and it was hard- like concrete. At the top of the houses, of course, were roofs, but not like any sorta' roof I'd ever seen before. From all sides of the round house the roof went straight up like a teepee and was made entirely of palm fronds. What it reminded me of mostly was those little Chinese bamboo hats that are painted different colors and put into tropical drinks. All these roofs though were not painted, but remained the same natural color of palm fronds– green. There was one big opening on each of these huts, or houses, which, of course, was the front door. You could tell, because folks were going in and out of them. Some were just openings with nothing to go across them and others had large blankets or pieces of colorful cloth hanging down to close them up. The huts, at least the one we were in, had hard-packed earth floors. Besides the huts there were a coupla' buildings that looked more like what you would call a log cabin. These cabins were built with pine trees with the bark stripped off. It wasn't your everyday run-of-the-mill pine they'd used either, but what is called heart-of-pine which is a very dense and sturdy wood, a little more yellow than regular pine and a heck'uva lot harder. If some bad storm ever came up out there on the island or a hurricane, say like Doreen, I would not want to be in one of the huts these folks had built, but those cabins looked like they could withstand any winds you could imagine: hurricanes, tornadoes, even twin waterspouts!

All the structures I am describing were within this large clearing so they were exposed to the full brunt of any storm or rain, but never while we were there did any of them– even the smallest hut –get wet inside. Whatever else you might want to say (or think), about how these people lived, they sure knew how to build a roof.

*   *   *

When we came to the clearing the first time it was really a sight. We were walking along through the woods (or jungle's more like it), much like the woods back along the intracoastal where Mick and Davey and Will and the rest of us used to spend a lot of time, where everything seemed close up and it was always on the dark side even on the sunniest day (the vegetation was that dense), and all of a sudden we came to this spectacular cleared area with houses and huts and all; a secret city really. Well, it's hard to describe the feeling that gives you– to see a small town in a spot where you would never in a thousand years expect there to be one!

Besides the two dozen or so houses in the clearing there was one other building and it was the largest and was in the very center. What I would call it would be a headquarters.

Like the huts, it had a palm-frond roof, but there were no sides to speak of– only big logs or poles to hold the long roof up. I'd say it was about twenty feet wide and around fifty or sixty feet long. It reminded me of a similar looking structure right in downtown St. Augustine where they used to sell slaves back before the Civil War– the Slave Market, it is called. Because it was not a house there were not house-like things inside it. Instead, there were several long benches made from the same kinda' pine as the log cabins and also there were hammocks connected to the poles. You could tell from those benches they had been there a long, long time. They were worn and the wood, though dark, was almost what you would call polished. Most of the hammocks were made of rope that looked like the same type of cotton rope the old man always seems to have nearby and likes to use– Venetian blind cord. The only difference was, this rope, though not quite as thick, seemed stronger somehow, like it had been treated with something to give it more strength. Like I said, most of the hammocks under this large roof were made of rope or string, but there were a couple that were just sheets with sticks at either end to keep them open. Oddly enough, these sheet beds, though they looked more substantial, were not as comfortable as the rope hammocks. I know because before very long I had tried out both types. The rope hammocks had more *give* or something to them and were really lots more comfortable for sleeping, or just taking a nap. The first question I asked, in fact, had to do with these rope hammocks. It was Derek I asked:

"Where'd ya'll get these hammocks?" I asked.

He just looked at me for a long second and didn't say anything, but I could tell right away it was a stupid question and I wished I could take back my words. He never did look mean– it was more like he was puzzled. Even the old man and Big George looked at me like I'd finally taken leave of my senses. Then he answered with the two words I knew even right then, only seconds after I had posed the question, that he would answer; the only words with which he could answer:

"Made 'em."

This took place that first time we all walked together through the little hut town... the village I will call it... and needless to say I didn't ask anymore questions for a while.

*   *   *

The way I had it figured we wouldn't be sticking around here for very long; just long enough for Pawpaw and Big George to talk Derek into coming back and giving himself up. Besides, I had to get back. I had a big test coming up Monday and as much as I did not look forward to studying I had resolved myself to the idea of looking at the chapters some. Again, I'm getting ahead of myself, already telling you about coming to the little village without explaining how the old man got better and the mystery surrounding that.

When Derek took hold of Pawpaw right after we got to the island, well, that was a strange time. I've already said how it sounded like the old man called Derek *son*, but I haven't mentioned anything about how he suddenly became okay again, just like that. Brother, it was a whirlwind turn of events for all of us and when you stop and think back about how it must have been for the old man, well, I can see how you might think I was making all this up. In less than a day he had gone from being bed-ridden to rising up and taking that trip to Johnson's and then the trip out to the island and then plunging back into his sickness all over again out on the river and now when we finally arrived suddenly becoming okay again. I am no doctor but I don't think even Dr. Cordray (either one), could explain (medically), what was going on with the old man. One minute he was ill and looking close to death and the next he was almost his old self again. It's the kinda' thing that when you look back on seems even more wondrous than when you are going through it. Shoot, at that time so much seemed to be happening. I reckon we just didn't have ample* time to be amazed right then.

Even though Pawpaw was feeling lots better, compared to how he was before Derek came out and rescued us, still I could tell he was tired. I mean when you stop and consider that he had had a full-blown stroke out on the river and now he was just about back to normal again it was nothing short of a miraculous recovery. Even so, I could tell he was tired now. Truth was we all three were, though we didn't know to what degree at the time with all the excitement of what was essentially the discovery of a whole little society, a civilization, right there beneath our (and lots of other unsuspecting folks), noses. I mean, even though we were right there and saw it with our own eyes it was still hard to believe what we were seeing. It put me in mind of the old man's lecture on being certain you knew what you were seeing when you were looking at something... like how when you think you're looking at something that is say, yellow, really it is *every other color but yellow* and because of that, because it is every color but yellow, yellow is the one color that is reflected back instead of absorbed and that is how you see it... see it as being yellow. I know that's not much of a job of explaining, but the old man can tell it so it makes perfect sense.

Anyway, there we were just about in the very center of the island right smack dab in the middle of their village and it didn't take long for us to realize we were tired. All three of us were sitting on one of the polished benches beneath the main long hut that I called the headquarters when Derek, who was in one of the rope hammocks, motioned for this girl to come over, which she did right away. Then he introduced her as being the daughter of the Chief who unfortunately was feeling ill just then. Otherwise, he would have been there himself to greet us. Needless to say, we were all a little amazed at this, at Derek even saying that someone was a Chief. Not to say I had never heard this term before, of course I had, but the way he said it he meant it and that's what was so unexpected. Something else was happening that was unexpected too, at that time. The girl Derek had called over looked pretty, I noticed after a short while, and this was an unusual thing for me to think because I had never thought of any colored girl as being pretty before. When I say pretty I don't mean that she looked like Patti or any other good-lookin' girl at Oceanside High. Let's just say she looked pretty in her own way, and leave it at that.

Usually I'm not bad about staring, even when there is great temptation, but this time I was having an unusually difficult time with the temptation. This time the girl I was trying so hard not to stare at was not wearing any top, of any sort!

*   *   *

It was becoming apparent (at least to me), that what was going on here was these folks somehow had come to believe they were still in Africa, had never left I suspect, and were living their lives based on this belief. The girl, about my own age I would guess, spoke to Derek in a language I first thought I'd never heard before, but it sounded familiar, somehow. Again, I was still trying hard not to stare, but I soon got the definite feeling that the girl was aware of my intermittent* gandering because before long she covered herself up, albeit in a nonchalant way. That, plus the fact that she stared right at me for what seemed like forever while she tied the scarf or whatever it was around herself. I found it was easier not to stare after that.

After thinking about it for a little while, I realized Derek and the girl were speaking a tongue I had actually heard all my life: Geechee. It is a dialect colored folks– the descendants of slaves, at least those who live out on the barrier islands of Georgia and South Carolina –have spoken for hundreds of years, since they first came over the ocean from Africa. Every once in a while you will catch snippets, little bits of it spoken around Oceanside. I reckon that's because it's so close to the islands where it is prevalent*. Never had I heard two people talk it in a conversation like a regular language, though. There must be something about being on the mainland that makes Geechee speakers not want to talk it (that's just a hunch on my part), but it was fascinating listening to Derek and the girl speak it together.

Every coupla' words sounded almost recognizable like I was just on the brink of understanding them, but I had to think about it and that is something hard to do– think, when you are listening to someone talk and trying to understand them. I could swear it was a language I was nearly familiar with, but still it escaped me. It was like a fly ball or a pass that you figure you have got a good chance of running down, but at the end you barely miss and you are mad at yourself thinking that if only you had tried a little harder, had given it just a scrunch more effort you'd have made it. That's what it was like trying to understand the girl while she was talking to Derek.

While all this was going on I could tell Pawpaw was getting antsy... that he was ready to get back down to what had brought us out here in the first place, namely to talk Derek into coming back into town and giving himself up. I reckon his antsyness was obvious to everyone else too, because Derek told Pawpaw that there would be plenty of time a little later to talk him into giving himself up to the Sheriff, but that first we should rest and get something to eat.

Derek then instructed the girl to get one of the huts ready for us and that we would be staying there at least for one night and I think she began to argue with him about this; it sure sounded like arguing to me, but finally he got his way and she left to go and do as she was told. But not before giving me one more parting stare. The only way I know all this was because Derek told us what they had said after she left. Looking back on it, that conversation was the beginning of a whole different way of looking and thinking about things for me.

*   *   *

I said before that the weather that afternoon when we first got to the island and on into the early evening looked winterish (even though it was only early fall), but by the next morning the gunmetal sky had cleared turning it into the most beautiful morning you'd ever wanta' see.

It was the kind of day that comes to Oceanside every great once in a while and that fools you into thinking for a while that you are living in a special place instead of some little town in North Florida. It was one of those days when the weather is so glorious everything you see looks perfect, no matter what it is.

I remember a day like that earlier this year, in April I believe. A school day it was, because I was just getting there a little late, and right when I pulled up on my bike about to roll my worn front tire into the bikestand alongside the others it dawned on me that here was one of those days I am talking about and suddenly everything seemed different. It was all the same, of course; nothing really had changed but it was in the weather- so clear, and it was in the air- so clean. It was such a gorgeous day that it made everything seem different, like you were seeing things right, like they truly were, for the first time. Even that long old bikestand which had sat out in front of the school for who knows how many years looked great, even if it was old; in fact, you could say that's why it looked great- because it was old. You could see it had a fresh coat of metal paint, but there was the flaky eruption of rust, still, beneath the new paint and ordinarily that wouldn't be too attractive a sight, true, but right then it was. It was beautiful, perfect, just like it was. Everything was like that that day. The tough knotty clumps of crabgrass growing up in the sand by the bikestand, the bricks (each of them that made up the school), the unlit empty hallway (lined with lockers smelling like ripe bananas and peanut butter and jelly sandwiches and pulpy paper lunch bags), that I ran down just as the bell rang... everything. Weather, an exceptionally pretty day, can be like that. It can have that kind of an effect on you. You don't have to do anything but take it all in either, and that is the best part of the whole thing.

*   *   *

That first night we were out there on the island we slept on the ground which is something until then I had never done. Before that though we had supper. The best fish I ever tasted. The fact that I was starving probably had a lot to do with this and ordinarily I don't care for fish when it is cooked in a stew like the folks on Quarantine Island served us that night but this stuff was something else. I'm not sure what all was in it, but I remember besides the big chunks of white fish meat there being rice and onions and okra and tomatoes and some kind of peppers because it was spicy. It was so spicy in fact that I thought I'd quit eating a coupla' times but the taste of it won out every time I considered doing that. They poured the stew from a big round black pot with two loop handles just like the kind you see in cartoons where cannibals are cooking somebody and we all had wooden bowls that looked to be homemade, but still nice. The spoons were wooden too, but very nice, almost fancy with a lot of carving on their handles and polished nearly smooth as stone. While we were eating under the long main hut-lodge nobody said much, which was another good clue that the food was good. I remember looking over at Pawpaw and Big George, who like me were both sweating the stew was so hot, and Big George's eyes were watering so much it looked like he was crying, but I knew it was from the spiciness of the stew. Then he said something like:

'*You know it's good when you can't stop... even when your mouth's on fire.*'

Pawpaw and Derek and a coupla' the other folks eating with us laughed at this and I remember letting out a chuckle or two, also. It was funny, not just what he said but how he said it and it was the first time any of the three of us said something that those colored folks laughed at. It was the truth, and as far as I was concerned it pretty much summed that supper up. (There is something about eating together that brings folks together. I reckon the Methodist Church had already figured this out with Wednesday Night Supper.)

* * *

After supper is when I got to go sleep on the ground. I won't say I was looking forward to it, but I reckon in a funny sorta' way I was. Like I said, I had never done this before. Believe it or not, even with all the times the old man made like he was fixin' to take us camping to some place like Ocala or Micanopy we had never gone. One weekend he was fixin' to take me, but upon inspecting the musty old green Army tent he'd brought up from downstate we discovered there was a big rip in the netting and seeing as though it was summer and the mosquitoes would surely give us fits we elected to put this trip off until such time as the screen could be repaired. Anyway, that night on Quarantine island I finally got to sleep on the ground inside the hut the Chief's daughter had fixed up for us and it was the most relaxing sleep you could ever imagine. It might sound sorta' strange, but there was something about laying right there on that thin blanket on the ground (just like folks had done before civilized times brought about things like beds), that seemed, well, romantic, sort of. I know that is a strange choice of words, that there is probably a better one for how I felt that first night, but I will always contend, no matter what, that the simple act of laying on the ground and going to sleep there for the night carried with it a happy kind of sad feeling... and here's the strangest part: I had that feeling not just for myself but I carried it for the ground, the earth, too. It was one of the few times in my life where I felt like I truly belonged right where I was; that it was okay, more than okay, for me to be there. Better than that, it was more a feeling like not only did I belong there... on the island... but that there was no other way things could be. Without me there things wouldn't be the same, everything would be different. I know– it sounds conceited, as well as corny. For some reason it made me think of this time I was feeling sorry for myself once and Leah, getting tired of it I'm sure, said to me:

'Remember, bub... *the world doesn't owe you a living.*'

*   *   *

The next morning when I woke up it was still dark. Not pitch black, but dark enough to look more like night than day. Pawpaw was asleep on a type of cot; it smelled like it was stuffed with horsehair which wasn't all that unpleasant really, not like you'd think it might be, and Big George was asleep and snorin' for all he was worth in the large hammock stretched across the hut. Before we'd gone to sleep someone came in and quietly placed a candle in the center of the hut, directly on the ground. It smelled good, sorta' like orange-peels roasting and later the old man told us it was put there to keep mosquitoes away. It did a good job because I didn't have one bite, nor do I recall a complaint from either Pawpaw or Big George. Usually I don't have much of a problem with mosquitoes, not like Grayson. We can both be sleeping in the same room and he will wake up with a ton of bites where I might have one or two at the most. His will be big welts too, as big around as a nickel when mine, if I got any, will only be little bumps. I used to think it was because he couldn't swat them very well, but Leah said it has to do with his make-up, his body chemistry. Some people just attract them more than others, she said, which seemed strange to me since if we were brothers why wouldn't we have the same *make-up*, as she called it?

When I got up Pawpaw and Big George were still sleeping so I was extra careful to be quiet. It took a moment to get acquainted with my surroundings, but in a few seconds I could see pretty well, well enough to get out of the hut without bumping into anyone or anything, and in a jiffy I was through the front door, which was nothing more than just a piece of colorful cloth. I remember being impressed with that cloth because I stopped there for a few seconds outside the hut and felt it. It was like silk, real slinky and smooth and it was beautiful. There looked to be colors in it I had never seen before; I could tell that much even in the little light there was at that hour. A lot of red and green and yellow, but there was also this purple-looking color. I consider myself something of an expert on purple (after all, it is the official color of Oceanside High School: *Purple and White... fight, fight, fight*), but this was a different purple than I'd ever seen before. It wasn't dark purple like the tee-shirts we wear in P.E., and it wasn't light purple like the football team's helmets, but it was somewhere in between. Almost a chrome purple, if there could be such a thing. Against all those other bright colors it seemed special, like royalty. It was nice to look at.

It looked like I was the only one awake so I was extra careful not to make much noise. The fire at the center of the clearing where the stew was cooked the night before was still smoldering and you could smell the odor of the wood from just the ashes. Generally, when you smell wood burning around Oceanside it is pine because bulldozers are clearing off land somewhere, but this was another fragrance altogether. It smelled lighter, not like it had turpentine in it but maybe something like licorice; just a little. Like I said, I have grown up smelling pine my whole life so that is what I am used to, but I gotta' admit this new smell was pretty nice smelling. There was something clean about it too, and I thought for a second to remember to ask the old man what it was. If anyone would know it would be him since he has been all over the world and back, and on numerous occasions.

It's funny how just a coupla' things– like the purple in that door covering and the smell made by a smoldering fire –can have such an effect on you, but the combination of those two things seemed to put a stamp on the morning for me, signaling that it was gonna' be an extra-special day. I figured that's just what we were gonna' need, too– something extra-special to get out of the mess we seemed headed towards. Besides the trouble that was likely brewin' with Derek and Redfish I had my own personal problems coming up with Leah, also; of that I was certain.

That morning was one of the most beautiful I have ever seen and I'm sure it wasn't just because of the nice weather, the colorful cloth and the good smell coming from the dying embers of the night before's fire; although none of that hurt. More than that though was the fact that Quarantine Island, at least the part where these colored folks were stationed, was the most beautiful place I have ever seen. The forest around the village was so dense that even though the cleared area was a hundred yards in diameter it still afforded something of a protective canopy around the whole village. It was the big monstrous oaks mostly, along with the fact that they were all supporting as much Spanish moss as I have ever seen a tree carry. There were many tall palms too, what are called Royal Palms which are the tallest kind and have the habit of gently swooping up with their long slightly curved trunks to peek over the tops of everything else. All trees are beautiful if you ask me, some more than others, and if I had to say which is my favorite I'm not so sure it wouldn't be the Royal Palm. The way their trunks curve ever so slightly reminds me of a giraffe's long neck gracefully gazing out over the tops of the other trees in the forest.

There are several stupendous Royal Palms on San Pablo Creek at different spots and I have always been able to tell where I am out there by locating one of these tall giants. The average person may not be able to tell the difference between any of them, but after a while you get to seeing that there is a difference between each and every one of these trees. It's the angle of the trunk I suspect, since the actual tops where all the palm's fronds are clustered do look much alike and if I can only see the very tops I generally still don't know where I am, if I didn't know to begin with. Once I can see a little of the trunk, though, I know instantly where I am and what direction I'm heading. It's sorta' like the way Tim can tell you the name of any baseball player just by seeing his hat on a baseball card. It's flabbergasting, but true. I swear, it's something he can do; a talent he has had since I've know him, that he can tell you what player it is by just seeing the hat. He's won many a quarter from the likes of Davey, Mick and yours truly, not to mention others with this little trick, too. You can cover up the rest of the card totally, but if you let him see the player's hat (from the bill up with no part of his forehead showing at all), he can tell every time who it is. Never have I seen him fail at this little trick and never, since I have had *Melinda,* have I failed at recognizing where I was when I could see a little of the trunk of a San Pablo Royal Palm. As much as I admire Tim's talent I wouldn't trade with him for a moment, though. I may not garner any extra quarters with my talent, but out on the water it comes in handy, from time to time.

*   *   *

Like I was saying... that first morning we spent out on Quarantine Island was one of the most glorious beginnings of a day you could ever imagine. I reckon the only thing lacking was the fact it didn't occur right here in Oceanside, but on the island; a shortways off, but still a place I was totally unaccustomed to. (Funny, how you can live right near a place all your life and still it can seem foreign when you do get to it.) I know, I'm the one who's always harping on getting out of this place, but having done some thinking about this the way I see it is one of the criteria for thinking a place is beautiful has gotta' be your familiarity with it. I mean, let's say you are visiting someplace you have never been before and it just so happens that that day is an extra-special beautiful one there. How would you have anyway of knowing that it was extra-special? Think about it. If it was your first time there, how would you know it isn't always like that?

Simple. You wouldn't!

So, if you are going to be fair in judging how beautiful a day it is, it has got to be in someplace that you have got some history in, for better or worse. If I contradict myself, so, I contradict myself. Truth be told, someone lots more famous than me said that first– a poet from around the Civil War, Walt Whitman was his name. Mrs. Johns is always reading little bits and pieces of his sayings, from his poems, and if I'm not mistaken that is one of his. Makes sense when you stop and think about it since no one can be right all the time (not to mention it's a darn good way of covering up when you *are* mistaken about something).

Anyways, even though I had never been to the island it was close enough to Oceanside for me to judge that it was an exceptional morning. As I walked through the clearing past all the other huts and towards the center where the long hut was that feeling was growing in me that, hey... it is really a beautiful day here! The air was still for the most part and the sun was just starting to come up to the accompaniment of what sounded like a thousand birds. All of them were singing from the same page too, as the old man would say; like they were cooperating instead of competing like birds usually sound– at least to me.

At first, I thought I'd just hang around the big hut and wait for someone else to get up but there was a restlessness in me just then that wouldn't let me sit down and wait for anyone. Anyway, I wasn't all that hungry like I usually am in the morning (the meal from the night before was still with me), so I decided to take a little walk.

All around the clearing where the forest came right up to it looked about the same to me, but I remembered when we first got there which way the big hut was pointed and so I was able to determine in which direction the trail we came in on was. I would take that narrow path back to the river, I thought. Besides, I was curious about *Melinda* and how she was doing. If I followed the path back towards the river it would lead me right to her, I reasoned.

It took a coupla' of minutes to pick up the beginning of that path back towards the river but it was, for the most part, in the spot I figured it would be. Any trouble in finding it was due to the fact that the forest was so severely overgrown just up to the edge of the clearing that it was near impossible to decide what little opening might be the beginning of a trail. Actually, I passed over it a coupla' of times in my haste to get going. It was only when I slowed down a bit and began to really hunt that I discovered the head of the trail leading the half-mile or so back down to the river.

The last and only time I had been on the trail Derek was leading so I didn't pay all that much attention to where I was going. All there was to do was follow him, and since he was carrying the old man at the time it was easy enough to do that. That's not to say he was lollygagging or anything; to the contrary he was making good time, but I have always been pretty good when it comes to running long distances (coming in third in the 8th-grade Cross Country last April), so it was no big deal to me. Big George was right behind me and as big and strong as he is I don't think running is the thing he excels at. I will say this though: once or twice while following Derek I got a stitch in my side and had to slow down a little to keep it from getting any worse. I never felt like I was about to get left behind, though... that's for sure. What I'm getting at here is the trail did not seem evident to me now that I was out on it and on my own.

It was early and there wasn't a lot of light in there, nor was there ever a whole lot even on the sunniest day, I imagined. It took some doing to stay on the trail and there were one or two times when I had to guess which way to go, but I reckon I guessed right every time because before too long I was there... at the river.

*   *   *

If what I saw around that little village earlier was considered a beautiful morning, then there are no words left for what was going on when I came to the shoreline there beside the river that morning.

The sun was just coming up and unlike the last time I had layed eyes on it, this time there was no fog over the water.

This time it was as clear as you could ever hope to see and the sun coming up over the water was a sight that was just *too beautiful for mere words......*

*   *   *   *   *

...... After a few minutes or so it was about two-thirds of the way out of the river and right at the spot where it still touched the watery horizon it looked like there was suddenly a big wide base spread out beneath it... like a fiery ball with it's own pedestal to keep it steady.

It was still diffused enough you could look right at it without it hurting your eyes, and I could see it right there before me as it emerged from the water, *just like the river itself was giving it birth.*

It looked so big you'd think you could get in a boat, row out and touch it; sure didn't seem possible it was as far away as Coach Sutter said: '*ninety-three million miles... give or take a few feet!*'

*   *   *   *   *

Something has got to be really huge to look that big and still be that far away... that's all I can say. And to think this same thing has gone on for millions, some claim billions, of years.

*   *   *   *   *

Every twenty-four hours this same sun has come up over the horizon without missing one time... *not even one time!*

*   *   *   *   *

To think all this has taken place for that long and not believe there is someone, some entity, in charge. Maybe not in control... but in charge. Like the old man says:

'*There is a difference... a big difference.*'

*   *   *   *   *

These sayin's the old man throws at me; I've always been able to figure them out except this one:

'*Bein' happy's good. Sad's better, though. It's truer.*'

*   *   *   *   *

What in the world would possess someone to say something like that? All I can figure is it's some sort of word trick, which, as Mick would say, is just S.O.P. (Standard Operating Procedure) for him.

When you have been on a trail, any trail, only once (especially a jungle trail), you are not really all that familiar with it. I don't care how good an outdoorsman you are, or think you are, it takes more than one trip down a trail to get familiar with it. And that's just the way it was that morning I took off back down towards the river. Not to say it wasn't a good trail; no I wouldn't say that, it's just that I guess because I wasn't used to it that I got lost. Exactly how long I wandered around that island I can't say for sure. Let's just say it turned out to be one of those things that happens to you that you can't appreciate at the time it is happening, but later you look back on and are glad about. You see, if I hadn't gotten lost that morning I doubt seriously if I'd have ever seen *The Town.*

Calling it a town might be something of an exaggeration, but if everything else is woods and jungle and all you think is around is a little settlement with huts, when you see real honest to goodness buildings made out of brick and mortar and several (more than several) of them at that, then you can understand how you might think of it as a town. It was surprising anyway, no matter what you'd call it. I was wandering around out there pretty sure I'd gotten off the trail because the little footpath was nowhere to be seen and it was thick, real thick, with saw palmettos and scrub oak vines that you would need a good machete to get through, but I was pretty used to that type of terrain since it was so similar to our woods behind Tanglewood and so I was able to move through it okay. There wasn't any doubt though, I was lost and getting moreso as I went on. But again, like I said... if I hadn't of gotten lost I never woulda' seen that town.

I call it a town because that's just what it looked like it'd been at one time... maybe fifty years before. If it hadn't been daylight I bet I would have missed it altogether, it was that hard to see through all the jungle. Most of the buildings were made out of the same stuff the Spaniards used to make their forts out of-coquina, which is a mixture of sand, mud and a zillion tiny little shells.

Coquina are small, the kind of little shells that are all over the beach and that you can pick up hundreds of with one scoop of your hand when the sand is just right, sorta' soupy. The shell of a coquina is so thin you can crush it just by squeezing it hard between your thumb and index finger. There's a little animal that lives in this shell and when you got a bunch of them in one place they make a pretty decent soup. All you gotta' do is cover the bottom of a pot a coupla' inches deep with these critters, add water and boil for a while. When the water gets hot the tiny shells open and that's when you start to get the flavor of the little animal. When you see sandpipers running along the beach, right where the tide is coming in, stabbing the sand with their beaks, that's what they're after– coquina. When the surf comes in it takes a little of the sand back out with it, exposing these shy little critters who immediately burrow their way back down into the wet sand. There's just a half–second or so that they're exposed and that's when you see the pipers working, sticking their long, thin beaks in the sand. Grabbing a coupla' handfuls and making a broth out of them is one thing, but nabbing them one at a time seems like a lotta' labor for just a little dinner. I have seen the beach sometimes when there was zillions upon zillions of little coquina shells piled up half a foot high that had been cracked open, and all by sandpipers, you can be certain since there is no other animal on earth that is equipped with just the right tool (that thin beak), that could open these tiny creatures. Whoever it was that first had the brilliant idea to use this available and ample* resource as a building material was pretty sharp.

There are spots on the Old Fort down in St. Augustine where cannonballs have hit the coquina walls and instead of doing any real damage they just got stuck like the walls were made out of some sort of space-age foam. Instead of cracking or crumbling, the walls would give way a little and just get compressed. After the fighting was over they'd send some guys over the top to pop out the cannonballs, drop them in the inlet below, and patch up the walls. That fort has been there for four hundred years and you can still see spots on it where cannonballs either bounced off or stuck into it. The old man took Grayson and I down there a coupla' years ago. The thing Grayson liked best about the fort was the fact there were so many ramps all throughout it, like it was especially designed for a wheelchair. It was the only place he'd ever been, he said, where he could get around easily. He could even make it all the way to the top. I remember that trip well because of two things. Naturally, the fact that we were going with Pawpaw and Leah wasn't coming was memorable, but when I look back on it the reason he took us probably was to get the two of us out of her hair for a day.

It was summertime, and the day before we'd been out on the carport after coming back from the Pak n'Sak. Grayson has always liked hot things and was bragging about how he could keep two Atomic Fireballs in his mouth at once without having to take either of them out, all the way to the end. Personally, I prefer to crush them up and eat a little bit at a time. The best way to do this is to just leave them in the wrapper and pop them with a hammer. If you don't have a hammer handy a brick will do. Believe me, there is an art to doing this correctly.

If you hit an Atomic Fireball too hard there is the very good chance that the wrapper will tear open and you'll have candy everywhere. Of course, if you don't hit it hard enough, nothing happens. The right technique can't be taught. It's more like it's one of those things you have got to do yourself a few times to get the hang of. With a hammer, you hold it about half a foot above the fireball and give it a sharp quick *bop.* It's gotta' feel like the hammer is bouncing off the candy's surface for it to be the right amount of force. Like I said, if you hit it too hard you'll tear the cellophane wrapper and little red and white pieces of candy are instantly everywhere. Too soft and nothing happens, or maybe it will split right in two. When you hit an Atomic FireBall just right it splits into several smaller chunks and dozens of tinier pieces and the wrapper stays intact. Now you can just open one end of the wrapper and you've got something you can nurse for a while. Anyway, that's the way I do it. Like I said, though, Grayson prefers to consume them whole and sometimes more than one at a time and it was on that Friday afternoon that we got into the skirmish that prompted the old man to get us away from there for a while.

After Grayson was able to stand two Atomic Fireballs without spitting either of them out, even for a second, I got the bright idea of seeing how hot he could really stand. Right next to the carport was a pepper plant Leah had put in. It wasn't a real plant that you would eat from, but rather what is called an ornamental plant which means it's alive... but just for looking at and admiring, I reckon you'd say. Anyway, Grayson was full of himself, bragging about how he could stand hot things better than I could and how Atomic Fireballs were nothing; just a nice little piece of candy, no hotter than a marshmallow when you got right down to it. He was really rubbing it in like he enjoys doing and that's when the idea of the pepper plant popped into my head.

In my own defense, I gotta' say I made the challenge without thinking, and without knowing how hot those little peppers were. Some of them were red and some were green and they were all small– only about half an inch high. Not really being of a mind to torture him too much, it was a small green pepper I dared him with. Honest Injun, it never crossed my mind for a second that the green ones were lots hotter than the red. After all, who would think that something green would be hotter than something red? I'll say this for him though; even sweating as much as he was and turning about eight shades of red– from beet to fire engine –he never gave in or spit it out, and he finally swallowed the thing. Of course, Leah found out about it later in the day and I don't think I've ever seen (or heard), her get madder, at least not at me. All the while Grayson sat there with this angelic look on his face, like he was the most innocent little boy in the world. When you get right down to it that ticked me off more than anything, even getting yelled at by her; the fact that Grayson did such a damn good job of pulling the wool over her eyes. It wasn't my fault those little green peppers were so hot, and I dang sure didn't force him to eat one.

All I'd done was double-dare him, which is about as All-American a thing as anyone can think of doing.

*   *   *

Anyways, back to those buildings out on the island... the ones made out of coquina like the Old Fort down in St. Augustine. They looked to me to be the oldest thing I'd ever seen, or at least the oldest thing man-made. I reckon I just sorta' stood there in that scrub brush for a minute or so trying to focus in on what it was I was looking at because to tell the truth I wasn't real sure at first. I mean, it's not that big a deal when you see a building that you know beforehand is historic– like a fort –made out of such an unusual material. But when what you are looking at is some buildings out in the middle of the woods, well, then that's a different story, altogether.

There was something else about those buildings, that was unusual. The only way I can express it is to say there seemed to be some presence there, even though I could not see or hear anyone around. I'm not talking about ghosts either, but I could swear that someone else was around there. The sun had been up for a little while. I could tell because it was getting lighter out, but around the time I got lost it began getting overcast bad and there was a gray slag sky threatening a downpour. If it'd stayed clear I would've been able to tell where the sun was and known my direction by that. Before too long everyone back at the main camp would be getting up (if they weren't already), and here I was lost. And on an island, too. I knew the old man would begin trying to talk Derek into giving himself up soon and if he was successful they would be looking to head out shortly. After all, it was the day of the deadline the Sheriff in Riverville had given Derek, so in essence it was now or never, so to speak. And here I was only a mile or so away but still lost, and I mean lost bigtime. I could yell, I still had that left, but I wasn't quite up to that point yet. I would give myself another fifteen or twenty minutes and see if I could figure it out. By then, perhaps, the skies would clear and I could tell where the sun was. It was worth a wait. Besides, I was sorta' interested in what those old buildings were all about. There was something about them, above and beyond the fact they were constructed from coquina, that intrigued me a lot, and I reckon if the truth be known I wasn't ready to leave that spot quite yet.

As I got closer, right up to those old buildings, I could see plainly that they were made of lots more coquina than even the Old Fort. In fact, that's about all they were was old shells since the windows, doors and roofs which had been made of wood had long since rotted. What I was looking at was the skeletal remains, albeit the main part, of that old town. Whereas the Old Fort was sort of a combination of shells and mud, these buildings looked to be just about all shell, with just enough mud to keep them up. They looked like something that would be easy to destroy, but when I sorta' punched this column–looking wall with the butt of my hand to see how tough it was, boy, was I surprised. You'da thought it was a new brick or cinderblock wall instead of that light shell.

I could still sense some sort of presence. Even moreso, now that I was right up next to the buildings, and for a second I thought I heard something stir like a possum or raccoon scurrying among the foot or so of old fallen oak leaves that made up the floor of these old buildings and then I saw something that convinced me someone or something *was* there– a quick flash like a shadow or something out of the corner of my eye! Then I caught it– just what it was. A trap door of some sort lifted up from the floor in the middle of that first building, the one I had just punched, and a figure emerged from behind it and took off for the jungle.

Man, you want to talk about getting spooked, even in the daytime. *Whew, was I ever!*

And then, right then, I heard another sound; like someone walking through a thicket of saw palmettos which was a good guess on my part because when I turned my head to the left towards that sound that's exactly what it was– a man, a big black man, wading through a large clump of saw palmettos and heading *straight for me!*

*　　*　　*

If there is one thing I know for sure about myself, healthwise, it is that I have got a pretty strong heart. If I didn't I wouldn't have survived that encounter that morning and, of course, you would not be reading this account. This next thing I am about to say is gonna' sound like I am repeating myself, because when I stop and think about it it is very similar to what I have already said once about him (that time out on the river), but so be it:

Once again, I was never so glad to see someone as I was Derek that morning. I think he was as glad to see me, too. I could tell right away because he was grinning a perfect double row of white teeth as he approached me and spoke:

"What sorta' notion got into your head to get out this early, boy? You must have a powerful explorin' bug in you, is all I gotta' say," Derek said.

"I guess maybe you're right. Man, but you scared me to death."

I said, laughing, but in a nervous sorta' way.

"Well, I ain't grinning for the heck of it. I'm glad to see you! I was plum certain there for a minute you was the Sheriff. Plum certain," Derek said.

"I'm not, thank goodness," I said.

"Amen to that. What the heck you doin' out here, though? You oughta' be back in the village with you grandpa and Big George. They gonna' be wanting to get back, shortly," Derek said.

"I know. That's why I headed out for a while... because I knew we'd be leaving today. Aren't you coming with us?" I spoke this last question trying to be as nonchalant as I could, like it didn't make any difference to me at all, all the while figuring Derek could tell what was going on. Still, I could not wait to hear his answer.

"I don't think so. I like my chances a right bit mo' out here. Me and the Sheriff are not on what you'd call the most cordial of terms."

"That's what the old man says. But he also said if you came back with us and gave yourself up no harm would be done, seeing as that you'd have some witnesses." I was still trying to act like it was no big deal to me, but I think Derek could tell that wasn't really the case.

"That sho'nuf nice of your grandpa, going out on a limb for somebody he don't know much, but I do believe it'd be better for everyone concerned if I just kinda' held back here for a bit longer. Say... you not lost out here, are you?" Derek asked.

"Not exactly," I answered. Again, I wasn't sure how much of this Derek was buying.

"Well, just in case, why don't I lead the way back. We ain't that far away, but if you don't know exactly where you are it could take a while to happen your way back," Derek said.

"Lead on," I said.

*　　　*　　　*

By the time we got back Redfish was wide awake and in the midst of making breakfast on this big two-burner kerosene stove. He had a big pot of coffee brewing over the fire, too. It smelled great in that little village, the mixing of all those aromas– the breakfast smells of eggs and bacon and grits and the smell, too, of wood burning. That's a smell you don't get very often unless you go camping or live near some part of the woods that is being cleared. Thinking about that got me to thinking about the fact that our woods were still imperiled and it looked more and more like we were gonna' lose them unless someone did something fast. As treacherous an act as it was, for some reason it seemed fair now to put that sugar in those gas tanks of all that heavy earth-moving equipment liked we'd all talked about. But right now I had all I could handle with the situation we were in the middle of here; so I put that on my brain's back burner for awhile in an attempt to keep up with present doings. It was hard to believe with all that was going on also back in Oceanside with my friends, at the same time I was out here on Quarantine Island. I don't know; it just seemed like another world... far, far away.

Right away, I spied the old man and Big George sitting at the big table there under the main hut, each of them deeply involved in eating the breakfast Redfish had fixed. Something was funny, though, different; and then it hit me. There wasn't anyone else around. All those folks we'd seen and met the day before were gone. When Derek and I walked into the village, Pawpaw didn't even miss a lick, but he just held up his fork signaling that he saw us and motioning for us to come over to him.

"Where you been, boy? Looking all over for you the last hour." Pawpaw said.

"Took a walk. Wanted to see what the rest of the island looked like," I said.

"You should'a told someone," the old man said.

"I would have, but the two of you looked like you were resting so well ... "

"Morning, Marty," Big George said, sorta' interrupting, but in a nice way.

"Mornin', George," I said back.

"Where is everyone?" Pawpaw asked Derek. "Redfish says he ain't got no idea."

"I ain't either," Derek said. "It's common knowledge we're expectin' a little visit today. My guess is everyone decided to imitate Marty. Figure it'd be a good time to do some exploring." I studied Derek's face as he said this, trying not to look too obvious, and it looked like he was telling the truth; that he didn't really know where the rest of the folks were. Either that, or he was a darn good liar.

"You thought any about what I told you last night?" the old man asked Derek.

"Yessir. I thought about it a good bit and I've made my decision," Derek replied.

"Which is... ?" the old man asked.

"Like I was telling the boy here on our walk back, the way I see it my best bet'd be to just hang right here 'til the Sheriff cools off some… " Derek was saying.

"That could take awhile," Pawpaw said.

"Could be," Derek said, sort of a thoughtful look on his face when he said it.

"Then come on back with us. I'll make sure no one takes any potshots at you, son." the old man said. I noticed he called Derek *son* again and that seemed strange to me, but no one else seemed to notice or pay much attention to it.

"We appreciate that, sir. But there ain't no colored man gonna' get a fair trial back in Riverville, not with the Sheriff and old man Cormack against him like they both allied against my brother," Redfish interjected..

"Well, ya'll gotta' do what you think is best. But for one, I think you're making a big mistake," the old man said. "When the Sheriff heads on out here it's gonna' be too late… way too late."

"That's a chance I reckon I'm gonna' have to take, then," Derek said, grabbing a biscuit from the panfull looking more like a pyramid being disassembled right in front of us than biscuits. "'Course, Redfish can go back with you if he wants……"

"Shoot, boy… what'chu talkin' 'bout. Sheriff just as soon get his hands on me as you. We go together, or we don't go at all," Redfish said, sliding a plateful of eggs and bacon and grits down the table to me.

"Well, if we can't talk either of you into coming back I reckon we oughta' head on out ourselves. Marty, hurry up and eat and then go get your stuff out of that hut and come on… and grab my jacket, too, boy. George, get Derek here to take you on down to that boat and see about that motor, soon as you get done eating." The old man said all this like he was barking out orders.

"Yes sir, I'll…" Big George started to say.

"Pawpaw, I know just about everything there is to know about that motor," I interjected

"I know boy, but you do like I said. Go get our stuff and come on. We need to get on back. I don't like the look of that sky. Derek, we appreciate the hospitality and only wish you was heading back with us, but like I said, you gotta' do what you think's best," Pawpaw said.

"I appreciate your understanding, Mr. Ed. I surely do. I'm only sorry ya'll had to come all the way out here," Derek said.

"No problem, son, no problem. I did it for Dosha as much as for ya'll. We appreciate you coming to our rescue like you did," the old man spoke, looking at Derek and then at his brother.

*   *   *

After I finished my breakfast I went back to that little hut like the old man said to get my cap and windbreaker and grabbed the old man's jacket, the sort of thin plaid one he wore lots when we were out on the water. Derek's dog, which I'd noticed the night before, was in the hut curled up in the center of the floor asleep and I swear if he wasn't the cutest looking canine I'd ever seen. He was mostly cream-colored with a white mask and interesting little black spots like someone had flung an ink pen or a paintbrush at him and left all those markings. And his tail, when he was standing, stayed curled up on top of his back and to one side. The best way to describe his eyes was to say they were sort of triangle-shaped and slanted up some like he was Japanese or Oriental. I found myself hoping that Derek and Redfish would be alert out here as much for this dog's sake as their very own. I knew it wasn't right from a moral standpoint, but I couldn't help it. That was the way I felt about him.

Just as I was coming out of the hut, trying to be real quiet not to wake up the pup, there stood Derek, right in the doorway. I admit I was surprised some to see him there, since the way I heard it he was gonna' take Big George down to the spot we left the boat so he could check out the Evinrude before we set out. I was certain the motor was okay, it had just gotten swamped was all and woulda' started right back up after a minute or two, but I reckoned if anyone could detect any possible mechanical problems it would be Big George. But there was Derek right in front of me.

"Hey, there," I said "Whatcha' up to?" I asked him.

"Looking for you, Marty," he said.

"You got me. I thought you were gonna' show Big George where the boat was," I said.

"He still eatin' biscuits. I told him I'd be along directly. I wanted to talk to you first, seeing as though I might not get the chance to again... leastwise for a while," Derek said.

"I was just getting our stuff together. Say, that's quite a dog you got there. Noticed him when we first got here," I said.

"Yeh, he's somethin' else, that's for sure," Derek said.

"What kind is he? I don't think I've ever seen one quite like him," I said.

"He's got a little bitta' Chow in him, but he's mostly Akita. I call him Pepper," Derek said.

"I can see why. I know a little about Chows... there's one in our neighborhood... but not that other. What'd you call it?" I asked.

"Akita. It's a Japanese breed. Real loyal and dedicated... smart, too," Derek said.

"He's neat looking," I replied.

"Yeh, they good looking dogs," Derek said. "Listen, I been wantin' to tell you face to face I didn't have nothin' to do with your boat missing back last spring," Derek continued.

"Shoot, I knew that. Dang, you went to all that trouble to get her back to me and all," I answered.

"I was hoping you'd recognize that," Derek said.

"Man, you'd have to be pretty dense not to," I replied. "I found that note and all, and I knew it was the truth right from the get-go. Besides, she looked better when I got her back than before I lost her. I was just glad to see her again. Lots of folks wouldn't have gone to half the trouble you must have to get her back to her rightful owner," I said.

"Well, I'm glad you saw it that way. I appreciate the use of her. She came in real handy back then. Besides Pepper, that boat was the only other friend I had in the world back then... least it sho' 'nuf seemed that way at the time," Derek said.

"Answer me one question," I said. "How in the world did you ever figure out who she belonged to ?"

"Oh, it wasn't so hard. Oceanside ain't all that big a place, when you get right down to it. Fact, I bet everyone just about knows everyone else... even if they don't know it," Derek said, laughing. "Like I said in my note, I saw your initials carved under the bench in the back there, and then that day out on the water when I was crabbin' and you and your grandpa was fishin' I noticed how you was studying that skiff. I could see it in your eyes, even with only the one good eye I had at the time. I asked Redfish later... he knew your grandpa and knew a little about you. Dosha filled in the rest. I made up my mind right away to get her back to you as soon as I could... without getting myself in any compromising situation," Derek grinned.

"One more thing. Not to be too personal, but how in the world did you ever get your eye back together?" I asked.

"Naw. You said just one question ," Derek smiled. "We ain't got time for that now. Your grandpa don't seem like he's in any patient mood this morning. You'll have to save that one for another time."

"All right," I said. "You're right. We'd best be getting."

"Before you take off I got one more quick thing to say to you," Derek said. He was looking sorta' serious now. Not gruff-like, but not smiling either.

"If they's one thing true about this life it's a natural born fact that sometime or other you gonna' find you gotta' serve somebody. Don't worry... I ain't gettin' religious on you, but it's a fact and I reckon you gonna' find it out for yerself, soon enough. It don't matter if you're colored or white, it's just the way things is. I'll be honest wid' ya' though, they's even been some white folks I didn't mind serving, all that much... the ones treated me fairly and was truthful with me as I could expect. Can't say that about all of 'em, but some was. If I thought the Sheriff was a fair man I'd go back wid' ya'll lickety-split, but some white folks, when they look at a black face too many times, it's like it's reminding 'dem of somethin' they'd jest as soon forget." Derek paused for a second, and I wasn't sure if he was waitin' to hear if I had something to say to all this or what. But after another moment or so he started talking again.

"Ain't nobody'd choose to be a slave all they life, but when you stop to think about it I reckon in a strange sorta' way dat' just part of the price some of us had to pay to get over here. Wasn't like a bunch of colored African folks was fixin' to head out on they own, back then." Again, Derek paused for a second and began petting Pepper, who had come out of the hut and sidled up next to him, waggin' his tail.

"What I'm gettin' at is, when you get older, try to keep that in mind. You gonna' think you down sometimes, and you gonna' think you up other times, but if you stay even-headed 'bout it all, and keep the faith and bein' fair, you be okay."

I didn't know what to say after hearing all this. I managed to mumble something like *I'll try*, and shook my head some, but that was about it. Out of all the adults I had ever come into contact with, Derek was the first one I felt never tried talking down to me. It was almost like it was too much to take in, but the way he spoke (one minute he sounded real colored, the next like he was a graduate of some Ivy League College), it seemed like the simplest thing in the world. I just wish I could remember it all exactly like he said it, his inflections* and all, 'cause it was as near listening to poetry as I've ever heard anyone speak in everyday conversation.

*　　*　　*

In a little while we were all down on that big muddy shore fixin' to head back to the mainland. I don't know if we took the same path down or what, but it seemed lots shorter this time. Sometimes it's like that though– the first time you go down a trail you've never been down before seems the longest. By all, I mean the five of us: Pawpaw, Big George, Redfish, Derek, and myself, not to mention Pepper who was having a great ol' time chasing sand crabs along the shore, barking at 'em and digging 'em up. Once he found one though all he'd do is toss it up into the air with his muzzle, sending it sailing, to then go scurrying off. It was all a game to him. It was like he thought they were put there expressly for his amusement.

The Evinrude strapped to the back of *Melinda* was started and idling sweetly, just purring as evenly as could be. It was a strange sorta' feeling standing on that shoreline, all of us together. It felt like some of us were returning to the everyday world while others would be staying behind for who knew what. I reckon it might not make a whole lotta' sense, but for whatever reason it reminded me of the feeling you get right before an astronaut blasts off into space. It's exciting, but it's scary too. Anything could happen, no matter how well you had it planned out. Only this time it was the ones who were staying behind that were takin' the chances.

"I wish I could get you two to reconsider," the old man said to Derek and Redfish as he got ready to step into the launch. "Or at least one of you."

"Oh yeah, I can bet which one, too," Derek said, sorta' smiling.

"Well, yeah... you probably could, and you'd probably be right," the old man replied. "Let me just say this son so I can say I told you so later... and hopefully there's gonna' be a later so I *can* tell you so. If you and your brother were to follow us across the river and on back in to town, I promise I'll do everything I can to prove your innocence."

"How can you do that Mr. Ed when ... " Derek tried interrupting for a second, not knowing here was a nearly impossible feat where the old man was concerned.

"I already know the whole story... from Dosha and Kathleen both... and I'm certain we can prove beyond any reasonable doubt that your actions were strictly in self-defense. There were two other men out there that morning and..."

"Yeah, but they was Kingsley's friends, and... " once again, Derek tried in vain to interject.

"I know that. Whadda' ya' think...I was born with grits for

brains? But the second you start to put just the least little bit of a crack in Kingsley's story, they both gonna' jump ship like scalded rats... you watch. I been down this road before, son. I've done this very thing before... I'm tellin' you. If I've seen it played out once, I've seen it a hundred times. Once you get a little crack goin' in their story, they're gonna' start himmin' and hawwin' like you wouldn't believe, scrambling all over each other to get to some safe spot, and the fix they gonna' be in then there ain't gonna' be but one safe spot for any of 'em... the truth. And that's all you gotta' do son, is get them there... straight to the truth. If you hang in there it'll out, believe me. Just gotta' give it a chance, son. You'd be surprised what can happen when you start pushin' a little... especially when folks ain't expectin' it."

After Pawpaw said this, and it was a mouthful believe me– I don't remember him ever being so earnest in what he was saying –well, we all just sat there on the shore for a moment and it got real quiet. Even Pepper quit playing with those crabs. I reckon he could sense something important was going on. You could just look at him and tell that, the way his ears sorta' stood up and the way he cocked his head and all, looking at the five of us. It got so quiet that the Evinrude sounded loud now. But it was still idling perfectly, purring like a contented little kitten.

Anyways, after almost a whole minute with no one saying anything, all of us just looking at Derek, he finally spoke. By the amount of studying that was on his face for that long minute we were all real anxious to hear what he had to say.

"Well, it sure 'nuf would be a great load off to get this thing behind me," Derek said, like he was trying some to convince his ownself.

"Whoa, now, brother... what about our plan? Don't tell me you gonna' fall back that easy," Redfish said to his brother. "Mr. Ed a good man and all, but it ain't like we'd be going in front of the Supreme Court or nuthin' like that. If you was to go to trial in town you wouldn't have a soul on your side in that whole courtroom, not to mention the whole building."

"That ain't entirely right, Redfish," the old man said.

"How's that, Mister Ed ?" Redfish asked.

"I said, that ain't right. He'd have one friend."

"And who do you figure that'd be?" Redfish asked, the question all over his face and his mouth formed into a giant O like even it, too, was looking for an answer.

"Yours, truly," Pawpaw said.

"Say, what!?" Redfish said sharply, his face almost grimacing.

I had never heard anyone say this before and it struck me as both a funny– as well as the most perfect –thing to say.

"You heard me the first time. I said I'd be there for him," the old man said.

I wish I could explain the exact look on Redfish's face right then, but I don't think I can. Derek pretty much looked the same as he always did, but Redfish was another matter altogether. It was amazement mixed with disbelief, but not the sort of disbelief like he thought the old man was lying but the sort that thought it was just something that couldn't possibly be true. Once again, there was this silence which it seemed was becoming the usual state of things out there, more and more. This time it was not a comfortable silence, but one that was searching for anyone of us to mercifully break it. The old man was the one to do it. And none too soon, either.

"Derek, it seems to me like it's your decision. I know Redfish is your older brother and I'm sure he's a good one, but he can't live your life for you... you gotta' live it the way you see fit."

"I 'preciate that Mr. Ed, I truly do. But things has gotten so far along now that I can't see how we gonna' get any justice in this town. It's just too sewed up, if you know what I mean."

"I know what you're saying. Like I said, you gotta' do what you think's best." With that the old man, looking a little tired for the first time that morning, offered a hand to the two men in turn and they all shook hands. Maybe it was just me, but I sensed a definite reluctance on the part of Redfish. But he did shake, though.

"I wish ya'll well," the old man said as he shook each of the brother's hands.

"We'll be fine," Derek said.

"It's just that this island might be big, but it's still an island and they'll be bringing dogs with 'em; you can bet on that. They gonna' be all over this place like a duck on a Junebug," Pawpaw said.

"I know. But they ain't gonna' come close to finding us where we gonna' be," Derek said.

"I hope ya'll knows what you're doing," Big George said.

"We knows," Redfish replied. "Trust me, brother. They ain't a chance they gonna' find *anyone* out here. It's gonna' be like one big ghost town when 'dat Sheriff steps foot on 'dis island."

Everyone laughed when Redfish spoke this, which was good 'cause it sounded like something we needed right then to break some of the overly serious mood permeating* that shoreline.

In the next two minutes the three of us that were going were in *Melinda* just like we'd been less than twenty-four hours before, me at the tiller once again. Big George and the old man were where they'd been before, too. As much as I'd miss Derek, and to a lesser extent Redfish, I couldn't help thinking also about that little dog as I opened up the throttle of the Evinrude.

Waving, we left Quarantine island that morning under breaking skies and an incoming tide.

*   *   *

EVERYTHING WAS GOING SMOOTH for the first coupla' minutes of our trip back til we saw that boat. Actually, it was just about a ship. At least it looked big enough to qualify for one by the time it came up alongside us. It happened so fast I wasn't sure what the heck was goin' on at first. I mean, there I was holdin' onto the tiller still looking to the rear towards the island where Derek and Redfish (and Derek's little dog), had just disappeared back up the trail into the woods and all of a sudden I heard the old man begin to moaning like he did that afternoon on the beach when those poaching netters showed up. But it wasn't til we were halfway across the river that I became convinced who we were seeing and who we were afraid of seeing was one and the same party.

That's right, it was the Sheriff.

The Sheriff hissself was in that big Ocean County boat, the one that looks like a Coast Guard cruiser. As soon as he could make out who it was he started yelling out through this big bullhorn for us to halt and to stay idle while they approached. It was not an action I was looking forward to performing, but the fact that they were in a much faster vessel, plus there were several officers with their firearms at the ready and pointed directly at us quickly dispelled* me of any notion I might'a had to make a run for it. Besides, it was not the sorta' thing the old man would'a taken kindly to, and that in itself was reason enough for me to obey. Until then I reckon Pawpaw still believed in the essential correctness of the Sheriff and what he was up to. Whatever anybody thought, there wasn't any doubt to the fact that the Sheriff and his men were serious... real serious.

I slipped the motor into neutral and Big George, per instructions of one of the patrolmen, put out the anchor. Lucky for us it was pretty calm. Like I said, the tide was coming in which worked well for us 'cause we could use that some to get back to the creek mouth– our entrance to the backwaters of Mr. Johnson's place. The skipper of that cruiser was adept at maneuvering his vessel, for in less than a minute he'd closed up neat to our port side nicely without any hint whatsoever of swamping us. The Sheriff put down his bullhorn, and for the first time you could make out how pock-marked his face was. But he was dressed real neat, with a tie on even. Then he signaled to his skipper to cut their engine and addressed us:

"Gentlemen, I'm afraid I'm going to have to ask you to abandon your vessel and board with us," he said, first. "I have got it on good authority that you have been actively engaged in aiding and abetting a known fugitive from the Ocean County Sheriff's Department, and that being the case I have no choice but to place you all under arrest. We are proceeding to Quarantine Island in pursuit of our fugitive, but I will tell you that any cooperation on your part involving the successful apprehension of said fugitive will speak well before the magistrate back in Riverville." This was a whole mouthful, but unless I am mistaken that is pretty much what he said, and how he said it.

It didn't take the old man long to chime in, though:

"What in hell are you talking about Sheriff? All we're doing is a little bird-watching out on the island. Last time I checked that wasn't no arrestable offense."

"Mr. Bartram, I understand you to be a good and reasonable man, but I don't appreciate your aiding and abetting an individual we are in pursuit of," the Sheriff said. Unless I was sorely mistaken he did not seem as cool-tempered as when he first addressed us, and it was fixin' to get worse I thought, knowing the old man's knack for pushing folks if he felt he was being worked into a corner.

"Sheriff, I'll say it again. We are not aiding and abetting anyone. We just came out this morning to take a look at some of the aviarian specimens afforded by the aforementioned island." The old man threw in some legalistic terms either to confuse the matter or to make the Sheriff madder. Whichever his intent, it seemed to take pretty well in both regards.

"Mr. Bartram, I don't know you and you don't know me, but like I said I hear tell you are a good man with a good reputation. That's why I'm trying to remain patient with you. But my patience only goes so far." It was just about now that I noticed the Sheriff looked to be sweating a good bit and was red in the face, also. He was overweight some, but not all that much. He was wearing a short-sleeve shirt, too, so it was hard to imagine he was hot, it being a very mild day.

"I'll make a deal with you, sir," the Sheriff said to Pawpaw. "You show me where that sorry black bastard is and I will permit you to be released on your own recognizance. Also, I will see to it personally that no charges are brought against you and the boy." Man, oh man, but did that Sheriff ever make a mistake then. There was just about no way that we were gonna' help them to begin with, but that sealed it there. Plus, I could readily sense Big George stiffen and his anger come up when the Sheriff used such ugly words to describe Derek. I knew Big George to be

a sensible man but I couldn't help but think this was the sorta'
thing he would take real personally.

"How about this man here?" Pawpaw put his hand on Big
George's shoulder. "Would you afford this man, our bird-watching partner, the same consideration?" he asked.

"I didn't say nothin' about him, sir. He will have to go in front
of the magistrate, but I feel sure we can work something out.
And you are admitting now that you have conspired to aid our
fugitive?" the Sheriff asked.

"I'm not admitting nothing, Sheriff. I was simply askin' a
theoretical question," Pawpaw answered.

If he was red before, the Sheriff was downright purple now.

"Let's quit playing games, Mr. Bartram. We have official police
business to conduct and you are being of no assistance to that
end. I strongly suggest that you capitulate* and begin to aid us
rather than that nigra'. He has seriously injured one of Coastal
county's most upstanding citizens and I am not going to rest
until he has been tried and the proper punishment meted out. If
it is your intention to go down with him, so be it. There's room
for the two of you in the county jail and I'm sure they've got a
bunk for the boy over at the detention center. Your decision."
The Sheriff shouted over at Pawpaw.

For a minute everyone was quiet, like a standoff. It reminded
me some of the standoff we had out there on the beach with
those poachers back in March. The Sheriff had made his
position clear as he could and the old man was thinking, I could
tell. That's why it was surprising to hear the next words coming
from Big George:

"Lord a'mercy... looka' there, would ya'!" was what he said, or
something close. He pointed back to the island as he spoke and
what he was pointing to was plain for all to see.

From the center of Quarantine Island rose the thickest, darkest column of furious black smoke I have ever seen in my life, at
least up to that point.

*   *   *

ALL THAT DAY AND ON INTO THE EVENING Quarantine Island burned, and I do mean burned. Sitting out there in the middle of the river that morning with the Sheriff pulled up tight next to us we could see the orange flames through the dense dark woods of the island, they were that intense. Later on, I heard Big George describe it, saying something like... *'Man, that fire was so strong and so widespread it lit up that dark jungle, just like you'd dropped a big 'ol chunk of the sun in there'*. And sitting there watching it happen nobody needed to say anything. We all knew what was going on and we all had a good sneakin' suspicion of who had got it going on, too. The Sheriff was none too happy, as you could well expect. I'll never forget his words:

'Damnation... leave it to a stinking nigger to spoil his own den.'

Once again, I could feel Big George wince, stiffen-up, but those officers still had their guns and he was smart enough to know this was not the time for something foolish. I'm not saying it in his defense or anything, but I do believe the Sheriff was so shocked, the wind so suddenly knocked out of his sails, that he forgot there was a colored person within hearing. Maybe not the first time he said it, but this time I do believe that to be the case.

Well, there was no way we all (or anyone, for that matter), were going over to the island right then. Maybe the next day or the day after, but not then. Of course, that put the Sheriff in a little bit of a quandary now, and we all knew it. He'd already said he was gonna' put us under arrest if we wouldn't agree to board his boat and go to the island with him and here Derek had managed to call his bluff, to stymie him, and without even being seen. It was one of those times when everyone is thinking the same thing but no one wants to say it out loud and I just knew it was a long embarrassing coupla' moments for the Sheriff. Finally, the old man broke the quiet.

"If you don't have any further need of us right now we'd like to proceed on, Sheriff. Contrary to popular opinion, this bird-watchin' business is tiring stuff," Pawpaw said.

Boy, oh boy, I thought. We're not out of the woods yet and here he is goading the man on. It took him a second or so to say anything, all he did was stand there on that boat deck looking down on us and for just the briefest, scant part of a second I thought he might draw his revolver and unload on us. You could tell he was that mad. But to his credit he just looked real mad and left it at that.

"Be downtown at my office at seven-thirty tomorrow morning, Mr. Bartram. And bring the boy and the nigra' with you. We'll figure out what we're gonna' do about the three of you at that time. Until then you are freed on your own recognizance."

"Thank you kindly, Sheriff. We'll be looking forward to seeing ya' then," Pawpaw said, tipping his hat. Cordialities out of the way, he motioned me with a nod of his head, which I knew meant to start the Evinrude.

*　　　*　　　*

We pulled away from the larger craft slowly and after a minute Big George let out this huge and glorious laugh, and softly putting his big black ham of a hand on Pawpaw's shoulder, he said:

"You somethin' else, Mister Ed. You somethin' else, altogether."

"Can't help myself sometimes, Big George," Pawpaw replied.

Leaving the middle of the river and heading for the far shore I kept the Evinrude's throttle at a little less than midway, just so I could look back every once in awhile to the island.

From the corner of my eye something in the river forty feet or so ahead of us caught my attention and as we got closer to it I spied my green cap, the one with the big **'D'** emblazoned on its front; the very same hat that had flown off my head right along this same stretch of the river less than 24 hours before (it sure seemed longer). And now, here it was floating on top of the water, just like it'd been waiting for me to come back and pick it up. Reaching down with my free hand I motored over and scooped up the cap, and with a single motion, seeing that it was still dry I put it on, pulling the bill down low to help block out the brilliant rays of the late summer's mid-morning sun, golden beams dancing atop the silver jewel of a river.

When I sat up again I noticed the old man and George were both looking back at me. I'd gotten us a little off course when I bent over *Melinda's* gunnel to retrieve my cap, but no harm done. It was N.B.D., or No Big Deal, as Mick would say. Quick to remedy the situation, I straightened out the Evinrude's tiller, heading us back towards the creek and Mr. Johnson's.

It was strange, this sorta' sensation, but for the first time ever I didn't feel funny about wearing that green cap anymore. And for the first time in I don't know how long I could sense we weren't in any big hurry, now.

Anyways, I had this one certain feeling... that the incoming tide, as well as the river, was still with us.

– The End

Dear Grayson,

Hope this epistle finds you doing well and in as good spirits, under the circumstances, as possible. So, how are things over there in good ol'Pensacola? Is the Crip House there any better than the one here? I know it's been awhile since I've written, but you have not done such a great job on that front yourself either bubba, so don't even think about giving me a hard time.

Like I said the last time I wrote, that place sure was no Holiday Inn! What I couldn't tell you in that letter was all the things that went on there. I wouldn't put it past some of those folks to open soneone else's letters so I never could be sure what was safe. I don't want to get into it right now— there will be plenty of time next month.

Like I told you on the phone Sunday night, I am sending along the article about Pawpaw. Also, I am sending a copy of another article I clipped and have held onto for a while. It has got to do with that time we went out to the Island. I'll tell you more about that later, too.

Man, a lot sure has happened since last Thanksgiving; it's hard to believe that was only a year ago. Mick is getting better, I reckon. I went over to visit him Saturday, the day after I got out, and he was laying down in his mom's bed since it is the biggest in their house. With that cast he needs lots of room so he has moved into her room and she is sleeping out in the Florida room— you know, the room that use to be their carport. Mr. Baker is still in the Merchant Marines until sometime next year but they seem to be doing allright. Mick said to tell you hello and wants to know if you wnat him to mail you some cigs? You nicotime fiends are all alike.

The Fightin' Rebel's game was cancelled last week like I'm sure most games all over the country were. So far they are 7-0-1 and are getting lots of recognition. Even Piombello is starting to pick them, although I doubt if he will pick them over Jeff Davis. For the first time ever I think we have got a chance against them. Time will tell. Want to bet? Good. If I dont' hear from you before the game next Friday I'll consider it a bet.

Leah seems to be doing pretty good. She is still going to the meetings at that Clubhouse on Penner I told you about every Monday and Thursday nights and so far she has stayed on the straight and narrow. I tell you what... I have to admit being surprised some because if the things that have gone on around here during the last couple of months didn't drive you to drink... well, you get what I'm saying.

I can't really think of anything else to report from around here. Davey and Will are allright; going to school and still playing football a little afterwards and on the weekend some, like everyone else. Because of Mick being in that cast though it isn't the same, they say. I would agree with that.

If I could rip a day off from the calendar it would be, of course, November 22nd. What other two people in the world would have the bad luck to have their grandfather go into a bad coma on the very same day the President of the United States is killed? It still does not seem real. Rev. Timmons has been over a couple of times and it seems to be doing Leah some good (yeh, I know you hate it when I call her that instead of mom, but it's a habit I have gotten into for awhile now). Aunt Bertie spent the night Friday and Saturday but has gone back home now.

Tired of typing so will stop now and end tomorrow. See you later, alligator.

- -

Thursday Nite
November 28, 1963

Finally, there is some good news!

As of early this morning yours truly is the proud owner of a new dog; at least he's new to me. At around 5:30 a.m. I could swear I could hear this dog whining and since Jim passed on while I was still serving time in the wonderful OCJDC I knew it wasn't him– although for a second before remembering I thought it was him. Anyways, when I got up to see what in the hell was going on there he was– the neatest looking little curly-tailed critter you ever layed eyes on with his leash tied to the carport pole right outside the front door. His name is Pepper and I am pretty certain I know who left him there. If they come back looking for him it will be hard to give him up. In spite of how lousy everyone is feeling these days he is a cool dog and has got a way of making you happy, even if nobody is in the mood for that now. When we come over to pick you up for Christmas I'll fill you in a little more (and who it was that left him here). Til then, take care and don't do anything I wouldn't do. Ha, Ha!

P.S. – I'm serious about that bet. You better write and tell me if you are too scared to make it. I could use the $1.50. Also, I'll send you a picture of Pepper as soon as I can get up to Pic N'Save to get them developed.

Your older, smarter,
& better-looking brother,

Marty

Oldtime Fla. Native Suffers Stroke; Remains in Coma

(UPI) **Mr. Edward Bartram**, a long-time Florida resident remained in critical condition at Saint John's Hospital this morning after suffering a stroke Friday afternoon. Bartram, a resident of Lake Juliana in the central portion of the state was in Oceanside at the time visiting relatives.

An attorney for twenty years, Mr. Bartram was also a veteran of World War II where he rose to the rank of Colonel. Bartram served in the U.S. Army in London, Italy and North Africa. Immediately following the war he spent a year as Goodwill Emissary for the United Nations touring the world and touting the newly formed organization. Upon his return to Florida he devoted his attention full-time to the citrus industry. He served two terms as Director of the Florida Citrus Commission between 1952-1958 and is currently on the Board of Trustees of the Florida Crippled Childrens Homes in St. Petersburg and Pensacola.

Mr. Bartram is a graduate of the Georgia Institue of Technology in Atlanta, Ga. where he played on the 1917 National Championship Football Team under Coach John Heisman. Fellow players at the time claim Bartram was instrumental in assisting Coach Heisman develop the forward pass, a play illegal until then.

Mr. Bartram has a daughter and two grandsons in the Oceanside area who, along with doctors, remain guardedly optimistic about his condition.

Huge Blaze Covers Island; Arson Suspected

(UPI) Large plumes of heavy black smoke blanketed most of Mayport and East Riverville yesterday morning and late afternoon thanks to the largest fire to hit Northeast Florida in several years. Quarantine Island, steeped in history and situated just south of the San Juan River, continued to burn into the early evening. Due to its remote location no attempts to contain the blaze were made. The exact cause of the fire is still under investigation, but County Sheriff Richard Francis acknowledged a local man is the prime suspect.

"As soon as it's safe we'll be going in there to ascertain the whereabouts and any chances of survival of our prime suspect." Sheriff Francis stated. "I doubt though that anyone could have survived that inferno and we're certain at this time that no attempts to escape the island were made. We patrolled that area of the river from just before the time the fire was started until late in the afternoon. I'm certain we'd have seen anyone coming out of there."

The individual under investigation is said to be Derek Hammonds, a resident of Oceanside and a suspect in the brutal attack last spring of Kingsley Cormack, also of Oceanside. Sheriff Francis is requesting local residents to be on the lookout for Hammonds, a negro approximately twenty-four yrs. old, 5'11" tall and 185 pounds. Hammonds should be considered armed and dangerous and no attempt at apprehension should be made. Instead, suspicious parties should contact the Sheriff's office in Riverville.